Praise for *Junana*:

"In a society quickly shifting into an age of hyper-connectivity, *Junana* is a timely read. The narrative is as fast-paced and complex as our supermodern, technosocial lives. Caron creates a world so vivid and omniscient that one wonders if Caron is simply reporting on something that is already happening. Caron effortlessly handles multiple perspectives, social classes and age groups. Junana should appeal to educators, marketers, programmers and anyone who is a critical thinker looking for something unique and rich for their cranium to bite into. *Junana* is an important work that provides a lens with which to greater understand the rapid change we're currently experiencing." **Amber Case**, cyborg anthropologist
Twitter: caseorganic

"*Junana* was a fabulous book. It was part Snow Crash, part Neuromancer part modern society and the implications of our social networking. It captures what might happen if we had an accelerated learning system, who would be challenged by the notion, who would build on the notion. The is a great story and many deep issues that leave you reflecting about social networking, gaming, learning and the world that we live in or what it might be.........." **Dave Toole**, CEO Outhink Media, Inc.

"Highly recommended!...The very interesting premise is thoughtfully worked out. A bit of techno-speak sprinkled here and there lends verisimilitude, but non-techies can ignore it in favor of the story." **Jeff deLaBeaujardiere**, NOAA geek and musician

Also by Bruce Caron

Snoquask: The Last White Dancer

Community, Democracy, and Performance

Inside the Live Reptile Tent (with Jeff Brouws)

Global Villages (DVD, with Tamar Gordon)

For Emma)

Junana

great meeting you —
at Ideat .

Enjoy . Bruce Caron

Dent 2010

Junana

by Bruce Caron

Yanagi Press

This pre-publication version produced in the United States by Yanagi Press, an imprint of the New Media Studio, Inc., Santa Barbara
http://tnms.org/news/2009/01/25/yanagi-press

Fifth Revised Edition: 2013

Junana main text is set in Minion Pro.

Cover artwork: Photograph of Fierce Kitty by Kris Krug. Used with Permission

For Louis

Acknowledgements:

Junana is a work of fiction that describes an alternate present. Many of the technologies used in *Junana* are available in our present. Should sufficient interest develop around the ideas within *Junana*, something like it might show up in the future. These ideas, and also the many people who have helped the author to assemble them, are described on the *Junana* website: http://www.junana.com.

Tinka is my muse and my love. She would awaken at 5:30 in the morning for work and bring coffee in to me; so she was my enabler in this act of fiction. Candace Lindquist took red pen in hand to prune away the thicket of copy errors in my typing and back-fill the lacunae in my grammar. She deserves special mention, although I take full credit for all remaining typos and grammatical slips.

SECTION ONE

The Prank

ONE

Michael "Scratchy" O'hara looked at the entry card he should have filled out on the plane. At this pre-dawn hour of the morning the customs lines at Osaka's Kansai International Airport were minimal. His United flight from San Francisco was the only 747 unloading at a gate, and it was barely a third full. The Japanese bubble economy was ancient history, he guessed.

Ten years ago at Tokyo Narita it would have taken him two hours to get through customs. But then, ten years ago William Gibson described a future filled with technology from a sprawling Chiba megapolis. Scratchy shifted his laptop computer bag in front of him and used it as a writing surface. Name: "Michael O'hara." Occupation: "Independently wealthy" sounded too pretentious. "Computer programmer," he scrawled.

He stepped forward as the line moved. Reason for Visit: "Tourism," he wrote. The usual lie. Hotel while in Japan. "Miyako in Kyoto." Itchy had sent the group the hotel's URL. It looked a lot nicer than the business hotels he had stayed in on his visits to Tokyo. Scratchy stepped up to the window.

The official took his entry card and passport, glanced at the photo and at Scratchy. He swiped the passport's code and watched the computer monitor. He spent a minute browsing through the passport pages, thumbing through the entry stamps and visas that Scratchy had accumulated over eight years of frantic capitalism. The official's monitor again took his attention and he grunted and looked up at Scratchy's face.

Scratchy attempted a grin and remembered he had not shaved in several days. The passport photograph was from his middle geek days. The Glaswegian equivalent of an afro had framed his face and an unkempt beard draggled over a rumpled shirt. Much of that hair was gone for good, and he was packing an extra forty pounds of pudge.

"What does this say?" The official pointed at the "occupation" line on the entry card.

"Hmmm." He couldn't read what he written either, and tried to remember. "Computer, um, programmer," he recalled.

"You come from San Francisco with a United Kingdom passport. What is your official country of residence?"

"I have dual citizenship in the U.S. and United Kingdom."

Michael had been born in Glasgow, the youngest child of a Scottish accountant and a registered nurse from North Carolina. The family had moved to Evanston, Illinois, when he was in elementary school.

After the guarded structure of education in Glasgow, Michael was unprepared for the playground drama and social trauma served up in American schools. At first, he retreated to the library, where he devoured the entire sci-fi and fantasy section. Then he found a FORTRAN manual and badgered the sysop at nearby Northwestern University into running some of his batch jobs on their IBM 370 in exchange for washing the sysop's car and fetching coffee.

Some time in his early teens Michael exchanged his shy retreating demeanor for a blistering cynical posture, a phase his mother prayed would not last, but which only grew as he found his own quirky intellectual legs in the area of graph theory and topology.

Michael was an indifferent student in high school. He spent his time playing Pong at a local pizza joint, reading up on combinatorics research, and hacking into the university's new

VAX 11/780, using a bogus soft-money account he set up for a nonexistent visiting physics professor named Kurt Bokonan. Trouble followed when he actually published a paper on Hamilton's Puzzle, and the physics department chairman began to ask questions about Professor Bokonan.

One day, the chairman was waiting for him when he arrived at the computer center. After some initial incredulity, Michael being only sixteen, the fellow accepted that Michael was, in fact, the mysterious Professor Bokonan. He invited Michael to give a talk on his paper and offered him a soft money account under his own name. The chairman later suggested he go to Reed College, Cal Tech, or MIT with the silent hope he might return to get his PhD at Northwestern.

At one point in their freshman humanities seminar at Reed, Desi turned to him and said, "Do you have to be so damn scratchy all the time?" His new name was born.

"I'm living in California," Scratchy added. The official nodded.

"How long you stay?" Scratchy had left that line blank.

"Sorry. Two weeks. Long enough to see Kyoto. I hear it's a beautiful town."

The official snorted slightly and grabbed a stamper. He ruffled through the passport and found an open square where he stamped the tourist visa and then he stamped the entry card stub and stapled this to the page, folding it on the perforation so it would stay in place. He wrote a few things in Japanese on this and slid it back through the window opening.

"You can go." The official was already looking behind Scratchy, who nodded and stepped past the station toward the sign that said "Baggage Claim."

Scratchy had an hour to wait for the first Haruka express to Kyoto Station. At this time of day not a single shop was open, so he took his rolling bag and his backpack and walked the entire length of the mostly empty north wing of the Renzo Piano-designed terminal. With its soaring metal roof it looked like an enormous da Vinci airfoil.

As he strolled, he pondered the turn of events that had sent him to Japan. It started with an email from Winston Logan Fairchild, writing from Paris where he was attending a World Bank conference. Itchy, Scratchy, and Desi were in three nations spread across several time zones. Winston commanded that all of them be available by telephone at 10 p.m. Zulu time on Saturday, November 13th, two weeks hence. Something special was cooking.

For Desi in Mysore, India, 10 p.m. Zulu meant 3:30 a.m., just about his bed time, since he was regularly involved with colleagues back in the states and lived on American time. Like thousands of his countrymen, Desi's life was nearly nocturnal. In Japan, Itchy would need to be up by 7:00 am Kyoto time, but then then he had not slept well since junior high school. At 2:00 pm in Santa Barbara, Scratchy would normally be on his third latte of the day, down at the Firenze Cafe on State Street, playing GO with one of the university crowd.

§   §   §

Game Release + One Week

Nicolas Landreu could hardly believe his eyes. He opened the door and there she was, walking right towards him across the sand. He toggled to First Person and turned to her. In the background, a row of fan palms and a white beach with a beautiful rolling break. He turned up the speakers on his Mac. The wave slapped the shore, and the sound was perfectly synchronized to its motion.

Her walk was amazingly fluid. Her shoulder-length hair, dark with red streaks, blew in the breeze and bounced just right with every step. Her powder blue eyes fixed on his. She filled the tight Volcom Stone tee in a way that made him twist in his seat. She had on a vintage pair of low-rider Wrangler jeans, with holes in the knees, and she was barefoot. In her right hand she held a Powell Golden Dragon deck. She stopped and tossed her head. Then she spoke.

"Hi, Nicky, I'm your Guide." Her face lit up with a full, generous smile. His knees began to shake. Who was she?

"Do I know you?" he typed. He toggled back to Third Person and hovered.

"Of course you do; I'm Cindy. You've been thinking about me a lot. Turn on your microphone, silly. I can't hear you."

He blushed, and noticed that his avatar also blushed. Far fucking out. He switched on his microphone. "Who are you?"

"That's better. Let's ride." She tossed her board down on the sidewalk and jumped on. He noticed that she pushed Mongo, just like he did. He paused to admire her coin slot. She accelerated toward a metal bench where she front slid the top rail, ended with a 180 kick flip, landed back on sidewalk, turned her head and winked. She nodded for him to follow. He toggled to Third Person.

In the corner of the window a menu of commands appeared. He was now holding a board. Not just a board, his own board: a Shorty's Plaid Vato street deck. He scanned the commands and picked up the ones he'd need to keep up with her. With a command he tossed his board down and hopped on. He pushed Mongo and popped the key to increase his speed.

They left the beach and cruised up the wide sidewalks of some virtual California small-town downtown district. Ahead, she navigated the pedestrians, and he noticed that she was just too, too perfect. She couldn't be a player, unless she was some kind of fakeo pradabee chick. So she must belong to the Game. He was disappointed and intrigued. If she was from the Game, how did she know he was dreaming about her?

Most of the storefronts were simply graphic space holders, but people were entering into a few of the shops. Ahead was a coffeehouse with a big red star sign. Cindy rolled up toward the door, executed a 360-kick flip and caught her board mid-air. She stepped inside and he followed. She found an empty table in the corner and slid into a chair. He sat his avatar across from her. Around them several couples were talking. Their conversation modes were set to private, like his, so he couldn't hear them.

"You're new to the Game," she said.

"Well, it only showed up this week," he replied.

"Smartasstic," she said. "Now listen the fuck up."

She put her hand on the table and the tabletop changed into some kind of map, like the one in WoW, with mountains and runes and shit.

"These are the seven sectors for Level One. You must defeat each sector in Level One before you can advance to the next level. I will be your Guide through this level. At times I will be your ally." She smiled and touched his avatar's arm. He searched frantically through the menus for a "kiss" command and failed to find one. Instead he moved his face closer to hers. Maybe she'd get the idea.

"Sometimes I will be your foe." Her hand morphed into a set of straight razors, which she waved in front of his nose. They clicked and sparkled. His avatar snapped its head back. Its hand automatically touched a cheek and came away with an index finger glistening red.

"Combat?" he asked.

"Combat, if you like." Her tee morphed into a bright metal breastplate, a crimson two-headed Teutonic eagle emblazoned upon it. In the corner, her board morphed into a broadsword with a jeweled handle.

"Shooter?"

"That too." Now her breastplate became technic and sprouted sensors. A translucent con-screen covered her face under a Kevlar helmet. Her broadsword morphed into a big fucking gun. Then it all melted back into her original form. Again she filled the tee, and he noticed she was upstairs commando. Nice.

"I can be pleasant, Nicky. I can be whatever you need to win the Game. But I won't help you cheat. If you win the Game, it would be you who did it, not me."

"What do you mean, 'if'?" Nick said and grinned his avatar at her.

"That's better. Now let's go over this one more time before you start the first sector."

§   §   §

"Desi, it's Winston."

"This better be good, Fred. You know what time it is?" Desikacharya Venkataraman called Winston "Fred" when he was annoyed. Back at Reed, Winston was the first to call him Desi instead of Venki. Desi looked out into the darkness, savoring the interlude of quiet before the farmers' wives would begin to waken and light their cooking fires. His house compound bordered on an old village, in a place where old might mean a few thousand years.

Desi had purchased this Mysore house and lands with the money from his first IT patent. He also bought a house in Mylapore for his parents near the family's ancestral Ur. Their house and monthly cash for a few servants was meant to take away the sting of not having a daughter-in-law to massage their feet and cook their breakfasts. That was about as close to a "good son" as Desi could aspire to be. Not that it stopped their complaints.

"I've got Itchy and Scratchy on the line," said Winston.

"If this is about your car, I can only say, 'I'm sorry,' so many times."

The details of how Winston's Alfa Romeo ended up inside the Reed College president's second-floor office have never completely come to light. Desi had borrowed the car the previous evening and reported he parked it back in the driveway. Called on the carpet to explain, Winston claimed the car was stolen, and he had a good alibi for his whereabouts. And after all, who would be stupid enough to use his own car for a prank like that? The presence of the stone owl in the trunk did little to bolster his story. The threesome gained enormous campus cred from the incident.

"That was twenty years ago," Winston said. "I guess it's time I confessed."

"You put your own car in the president's office," said Itchy. "Brilliant!"

"I hadn't counted on them demolishing it to get it out," Winston groused. The various parts sat in a tangled pile on their lawn the remainder of the year, covered eventually by blackberry vines. The owl again disappeared.

"If it's not about the Alfa Romeo, then why the sudden college reunion call?" Desi asked.

"Unfortunately, we can't discuss it on the phone."

"Hello, I must be going," Scratchy chimed up. "Why are we talking?"

"To set up the meeting," Winston said. "I'll make this short. Together we now control more assets than any of us imagined we could accumulate. We're also skilled in various tools. I am suggesting that we could direct these assets and skills into..."

"...The Dark Side," quipped Itchy.

"Stay on target," Scratchy added.

"Twenty years later and we're still back in the asylum block dorm," Desi said. "Let Winston speak!"

"...a project of some significance," Winston let this sink in. "the details of which I won't mention here."

There was a pause.

"We all have our projects," Desi noted. "Lots of people out there have their own ideas for our talents."

Desi had recently added a higher wall to his compound after finding entrepreneurs lurking in his patio. Mysore had probably changed more in the last twenty years than in the prior two centuries. Much of the change was structural. Desi had a broadband connection as good as in his apartment South of Market. When he was a child, his appa bought a television three years before they managed to get a single channel. It sat there like some great boxy goddess in their living room.

"None of us has a project like this one. So let's meet and soon. I'm thinking just after Christmas. Itchy, can you get us some hotel space in Kyoto, say from the 27th through the 3rd?"

"Over the New Year? Sure. We can ring out the year up at Nanzenji."

"There will be one more person," Winston added. "Actually, Kyoto was his idea. He..." Winston stopped. There was silence.

"And who might that be," Desi broke it. "Lucy, you know I don't like secrets!"

Actually, Desi loved secrets. The last time Winston called him, six months earlier, he told Desi it was time to exit the NASDAQ. Don't advertise it, don't let all your friends in on it, Winston said. Pretend it's a huge secret. For Desi that call culminated twenty years of intellectual labor. Two of his software patents had been licensed large by the big boys in Redmond, and several more were in process in Europe. His online Chinese optical-character-recognition venture had gone public.

After Winston's call he cashed out his stock and options and poured the assets into an account Winston set up offshore. The last six months Desikacharya Venkataraman woke every morning to the certain knowledge that he was, in all probability, far richer than he ever imagined. The richest man in Mysore, for sure. Richer than any maharaja. Itchy and Scratchy had similar stories. Winston had called them too.

"You'll find out in Kyoto," Winston said, although he had no way of knowing if Jack would let his identity out so soon.

"I'd make some remark about how we are all too busy to have our lives interrupted," said Desi.

"Winston is the king of busy," said Itchy.

"I guess we can only trust that you are not yanking our chains," said Desi.

"...and that, in any case, interesting shit will happen," Scratchy added.

"Nothing less will do," Desi said. "We have the highest of expectations, Dr. Fairchild."

"Gentlemen, the game's afoot. See you in Kyoto."

Winston set down the phone and his eyes wandered out the window across Rittenhouse Square, where the plane trees were shedding the last of their leaves to a downpour. A delightful chill ran down his back. Apart from the car incident and that last RennFayre where things got totally out of hand, he was always the steady one in the group, the stable voice of reason, the nagging conscience. Well, this ought to shake them up.

§   §   §

As Scratchy headed for Kansai Airport's Gourmet Café to have his first seven dollar cup of coffee, he wondered how many people Winston had alerted to the weakness of the NASDAQ, and how much of the resulting loss of was a result of these investors yanking out their assets. Most of Scratchy's business partners and coworkers hung on and prayed it was only a temporary correction. Many of them were today happy to be coding Java for thirty dollars an hour. Barely caffeinated, Scratchy managed the ticket machine for the train and watched the sun rise over Kansai as the Haruka Express sped toward Kyoto.

The Prank

TWO

Itchy had insisted that everybody spend the first two days in Kyoto drifting about the city on their own.

"I'm not your tour guide," he reminded them. "Once we start to work, I don't want to have someone say, 'Why don't we visit Nara?' or 'I haven't seen the Golden Pavilion yet.' Get the tourist bullshit out of your system, and work through the jet-lag. Take care of your Internet business. We will be hiking around a lot without a broadband connection."

That explained the last-minute email for everybody to bring their hiking shoes. The three of them used to hike in the summers together before the fall term started. They had spent two weeks around Spirit Lake and Mount St. Helens in 1977, and remembered Harry Taft well.

Harry ran Taft's Landing, the only store on the shore of Spirit Lake. Desi had started wearing eye makeup even when he was dressed in hiking shorts and a flannel shirt. Harry said he didn't run his own place to serve sissies and wouldn't serve him. Three years later Harry's store was covered by five-hundred feet of boiling pumice within seconds of the nearby volcano's massive eruption. Harry had refused to leave. "At least sissies have sense," Desi said out loud as he read *The Oregonian*.

Scratchy used the two days to wander into Kyoto's downtown. Generally unimpressed by heritage sites, he wanted to discover the city's belly, its working, living core. Mostly what he found were semi-commercial districts filled with small

mom-and-pop retail shops and piecework factories, spread
across the city, feeding what remained of Japan, Inc.

He enjoyed the Nishijin weaving district, where the
Jacquard looms sounded like little flaxen locomotives through
the thin walls of the old homes. And he lingered in Gion,
below Shijo Dori, where the geisha quarters had been
maintained. He spent the afternoon in a coffee house in the
Pontocho geisha district across the Kamo river, watching
crowds of students in uniform meander by. The girls were
dressed in what looked like a mix between Catholic school and
Russian sailor uniforms. Most wore wild shoes that were not
part of the set, no doubt carrying their black, laced low-heels
in their bags. The boys' uniforms were straight out of some
fantasy Prussian academy, and they too had to wear their Nikes
on the street.

Winston and Desi did the tourist gig on a bus from the
hotel. They played it for laughs with dueling digital cameras.
The bus was loaded with old women who found the two of
them to be much more interesting than the Nijo Castle or
Daitokuji's gardens. Desi knew a lot more Japanese than he let
on, and he overhead the women's speculation about the two
gaijin gentlemen in their midst.

Winston was one of the few genuinely straight men that
was completely at ease around Desi. Desi sometimes looked at
Winston in a manner that betrayed his certain interest.
Winston always looked back at him in simple friendship.
Winston dressed in his Brooks Brothers casual attire, which fit
in perfectly with the local fashion conventions. He was, in
point of fact, the most conventional man Desi had ever met.
Desi had visited Winston at his Society Hill townhouse,
unsurprised to see not one but three Edward Hopper
paintings.

Realism suited Winston. Scion to one of the oldest Main
Line Philadelphia families, his sojourn to Reed seemed to be
the single excursion he was allowed to make away from the
expected. His mother, a famous, fabulous matron who was
hunkered down in the family estate outside of Philadelphia,
suffered greatly when Winston's marriage to some "Boston
brahmin" brunette debutante ended without an heir. Winston
suffered more from the marriage than the divorce.

Wharton and Cambridge and that debutante bitch had not
completely wiped away the playful edge Winston had acquired
at Reed, but a few more years tending to mama might just dull
the poor lad beyond repair. Desi despaired. Winston's father
had escaped his mother with an untimely heart attack. At least
Winston's career let him travel. He made more people more
money in more ways than they could imagine. Scratchy said
that Winston could pull silver out of shit. On the tour bus,
Winston let Desi put his arm over his shoulder, much to the
amusement of the women.

The women were mostly portly retired gals in dark brown
or gray dresses, some of whom had added tints of purple to
their required black hair dye. They probably took Winston to
be a salaryman on holiday. However, Desi's Italian knit shirt
and matching Moroccan red belt and shoes kept them guessing
all day. Back at the Miyako, Desi helped the women off the bus,
and he smiled at each of them as he held their hand. This
caused a general uproar of uncertainty, resolved through a
reflexive dose of manners, and they all thanked him again and
then again, giggled into their hands. They bowed and bowed,
until Desi started laughing and clung to Winston's arm. "Come
along, Lucy," Winston chided him. "Show's over."

§   §   §

Game Release + Four Months

Megan Doolan had been logging into Junana every day for a year or more, chatting with her friends, building up her profile, ragging on the exaggerated claims others put into theirs, and dressing up for scenes where she'd meet guys from all over the planet. Junana, as everyone she knew at Santa Monica High agreed, was simply awesome-tastic. She'd had her profile on MyPlace, but Junana was way different. You couldn't get away with shit.

Megan had tried to glamorize the year she spent in New Guinea when her mom had that Fulbright thing. Then she got busted when another ex-pat International School friend ratted on her and told everyone how they spent the whole time going to school and avoiding the locals. That was the way Junana works.

One day on her home plaza, a door appeared. "Game," was all it said. It was a big wooden door with a huge brass handle. She never considered herself any kind of gamer, but after a few weeks, her curiosity got to her and she touched the handle. The door swung open, revealing a complex outdoor scene. A rocky beach fronted a strand of evergreens. A small stream cut the center of the beach, and the surf rolled in grey, foaming under a darkly clouded sky.

Entranced, she stepped through the door. She took in all this with a glance, because cantering toward her on a black stallion was about the most beautiful boy she had ever imagined.

He slowed the horse to a walk and then reigned the horse directly in front of her, all the time looking not at her avatar, but straight out at Megan, sitting at her computer. Megan switched to First Person. His gaze shifted to met hers.

"Hello," his chat line read. "Can you turn on your microphone?"

"OK," she typed, and she turned on her microphone and speakers.

"That's much better," he said. She could hear the ocean pushing rhythmically on the beach and the trickle of the stream. The horse snorted and shook its head.

"The CGI is totally the shit," she whispered. She listened as the horse's labored breathing slowed.

The boy dismounted and pushed the horse's neck to the side so he could stand in front of her.

"I am Sir Robert of Glenwarren, at your service." He bowed.

Sir Robert was dressed in a delicious mix of brocade, broadcloth, and leather. Oddly, he was barefoot. There was a big leather belt, rust colored tights, and some kind of garment over these. She later learned this was called a codpiece. Its bulge drew her full attention for a moment until his bow brought his eyes directly in front of this. Under a shock of sandy hair his eyes met hers. His face was alive with all the little movements that anyone's face would make. And when he spoke, it was as if he really spoke.

He finished his bow and stood up quite straight. "You can, if you like, call me 'Bobby,' if that's what you'd call a very good friend known to the rest of society as 'Sir Robert.'"

"Hello Bobby, I am..."

"You are Megan. I am your Guide. This..." He gestured at his horse, "...is Shadow."

"I always wanted a black horse named 'Shadow' or a palomino named..."

Her avatar jumped forward as if pushed from behind. She turned its head. Directly behind her stood a great doe-eyed palomino.

"And that is..." he started.

"Let me guess: 'Marmalade,'"

He nodded and smiled.

"Shall we ride to the village? There is much to describe and I need my maps."

"How do I?"

"You'll notice a new menu for the horse when you toggle on the user display."

"Right." She found the command to mount and, in a graceful motion captured in third person for her to watch, her avatar sat the horse.

"Can we gallop?" she asked.

"Not on these rocks, but when we hit the trail I will race you back to Glenwarren. As you get better at it, I'll reduce the Game safeties. In no time you'll actually be riding Marmalade on your own."

"Wicked cool!" She walked her horse up beside his.

"Hmmm, yes. Quite right. Let me say I think we are going to be such good friends." He reached over and touched her cheek with the back of his hand, and she could only agree with him.

§   §   §

Late in the morning Itchy met them in the hotel's lobby. He
noted they were all, even Desi, dressed for a day outdoors. Desi
complimented his attire with a teal ascot, tucked into his vest.
"Doctor." He nodded at Scratchy.

"Doctor," Scratchy replied with a return nod.

"Doctor." Itchy nodded at Winston.

This ritual went around the whole group. The whole Three
Stooges routine. It had started when Winston finally got his
Ph.D., the last of the clan to do so. But then he had also spent
two years at Wharton getting his M.B.A.

"Doctor Itchy, I see. But where's the mystery man?" Desi
asked, glancing around behind Itchy.

"We'll pick him up on the way."

The day was overcast and dry, with occasional snowflakes
drifting laterally across the streets like cosmic dust in the wind.
Itchy led them west down Sanjo street for several minutes.
Then across this thoroughfare and north, through a winding
back road to a small street that led uphill.

Desi and Scratchy had stopped to look at a curious modern
brick building. Its entrance was blocked by a large stone, which
obscured this almost entirely. A small, neon sign three stories
up its facade was its only marker.

"Damian," Desi read the hiragana text. "Why it's a 'love
hotel'! Come on." He walked around the stone and
disappeared. Scratchy followed.

Winston and Itchy stayed out on the street. There was no
real sidewalk, just a white line dividing the taxi traffic from the
buildings.

"They make a lovely couple," Winston said.

Itchy grinned and glanced about. "He's waiting for us up
ahead."

"Don't ask me who he really is," Winston said.

Itchy shrugged. "Is it fair that you know something we don't?"

"I know a lot you don't, and you know a whole lot I don't. This is just a particular case."

Scratchy and Desi appeared from behind the rock.

"My high school could have used one of these," Scratchy noted. "Instead of a gym."

They continued up the street, managing between the parked cars, taxis and occasional crowds of traveling school kids in uniform. Ahead was a manicured park.

They turned left on a lane away from the traffic, skirting a walled compound. Then they turned right on a wide set-stone path bordered by gravel. Ahead, on a raised stone foundation, stood an immense ancient wooden structure, topped by a gray ceramic tile roof. The center of the structure was a giant opening. Eight towering, thirty-foot redwood columns, cut from the hearts of single trees and shaped completely round and smooth as stone, held up a second story, and through the opening they could see gardens and other ancient buildings.

"Sanmon Gate," Itchy said. "He's waiting there."

As they climbed the steps, a man stepped from behind one of the columns. He was in his sixties, dressed as a tourist in olive chinos, a light blue wool turtleneck sweater, and a Kangol cap. He nodded and motioned for them to follow him. They strolled with the other tourists up toward the main temple buildings and then turned right along another wall, on a path that then verged up the hill, where the gravel gave way to dirt. They ducked through a disused side temple wall and found a trail leading uphill between two evergreens garlanded with large ropes. The trail rounded a shoulder of the hill, and then they were out of sight of the temple. The man turned and waited for them to join him.

"Hello, Winston." He shook Winston's hand.

"This is Ichiro Nomura." Winston motioned to Itchy.

"We've spoken by phone." The man bowed, and then his eyes turned to Scratchy.

"Michael O'hara." Winston made the introduction.

"Doctor O'hara."

"We've done that already," Scratchy said. "Mike will do."

"Desikacharya Venkataraman," Winston nodded at Desi.

"Desi works for me." Desi stepped forward. "What shall we call you?"

The man shook Desi's hand. "I'll let you decide."

Desi scanned the fellow's face. A brace of gentle brown eyes coupled with a rather cruel mouth. Aquiline nose, good cheek bones. The face was tanned and the chin taut. Desi wondered about cosmetic surgery. The fellow's accent was unusual. Something Eastern European, but not Russian or Polish, perhaps Czech. The English was pure Oxbridge. Could be Vaclav Havel's smart-aleck kid brother.

"I believe you are mysterious and wise, but also somewhat dangerous, in a prankster manner. I'll call you..." he paused. "'Mr. Slick.'"

"If you wish." The name seemed to please him.

"Why are we here?" Scratchy demanded.

"First, let's walk," Mr. Slick set off up hill. Within minutes the city was lost behind them. They rounded a corner and their trail crossed an unusual ravine, more like a giant culvert cutting across the forested hillside. Mr. Slick stopped and waited for all of them to catch up. Scratchy was puffing furiously, his breath visible in the chill.

"You see this cut in the hillside?" Mr. Slick pointed at his feet. Where they stood the sides of the cut were well above their heads and the edges were a good five meters apart. Ferns and grasses covered every inch of it except at their trail's intersection. "This was the Tokkaido Road, the main thoroughfare between Kyoto and Tokyo. The feet of millions of pilgrims and servants made this cut over three centuries. Now the bullet train goes straight through the mountain and gets to Tokyo in a few hours. 'Why are we here,' you ask? I think the planet has been digging a rut for itself for too long and not getting anywhere. Desi called me a prankster. I take that as an honor. Mike, what do you say we play a prank on the whole world?"

His eyes locked on Scratchy's. The others watched as Scratchy met his gaze. Winston recognized that Mr. Slick had figured out their group dynamic. If he could intrigue Michael O'hara, the Nerd King, then the rest of them would follow his lead.

"To play a prank on the world is a very serious task and possibly a tragic one," said Scratchy.

"Herman Hesse, *Das Glasperlenspiel.*" Mr. Slick nodded with the beginnings of a smile.

"What kind of prank do you have in mind?" Itchy asked.

"That's what we are here to decide," Mr. Slick returned. "I have no doubt it will be, how do you say this, a real motherfucker."

That day, they hiked in the Higashiyama, up to the top of Diamonji, where, in the summer, enormous bonfires are lit to spell out the Chinese character "dai" for "great." Then they walked back down into the city for a late lunch in a kaiseki restaurant on the Kamo River.

Mr. Slick kept them talking, feeding them questions and comments about technologies and global economic and political situations. They fell into a series of long, anecdotal tales of their adventures in the roller-coaster dot-com economy.

§   §   §

Over the years, Winston had been the gang's main economic advisor, vetting their stock option deals and patent sales for a small fee. Winston's own ventures had not been unprofitable. Based on theories of derivatives he had advanced while at Wharton and then at King's College, Cambridge, he had computed a method to arbitrage the effects of Moore's Law on the value of the inventories of computer chip companies, giving them a way to sell some of the risk they acquired every time they upgraded their technologies. None of the others could understand how Winston made so much money by predicting so much loss, but then neither could they really understand each other's work. Their specializations were significant and diverse.

Scratchy worked on network protocols and server-side computing. Desi focused on cognitive science, machine and human language interactions, identity, security, and latent semantic analysis. Itchy's expertise was in the area of avatars and self-aware programming: teaching computers to teach themselves. They each had tackled a major chunk of the known problem space for computer science, but the arenas of their work hardly touched each other.

They had emerged from the academy in the late 1980s with minds full of patentable algorithms and ideas for applications. Desi had finished his doctorate at Berkeley, Scratchy at Cal Tech, and Itchy at Tokyo University. Itchy had two years as a post-doc at the MITI labs in Tsukuba before he jumped to a start-up in San Jose. Desi lingered around Berkeley after his doctorate, finishing up three DARPA grants, before he took a job in Massachusetts on Route 128. The job lasted less than six months, by mutual agreement, before he fled back to a start-up South of Market in San Francisco. Scratchy and some Cal Tech buddies started up their own company in Glendale, the beginnings of a string of companies that Scratchy would create to encapsulate technical innovations that were quickly gobbled up by other start-up holding companies with angel investors eager to catch anything on the rise. All of them rolled through the dot-com nineties on a fast escalator of IPOs, buyouts, and stock options.

Mr. Slick listened closely. He encouraged them to examine certain details surrounding the manner in which their technologies were selected or discarded.

The five of them occupied the restaurant's private dining room facing out to the Kamo river. A team of kimonoed women kept shuttling in with lacquered trays filled with small plates of food: fish and meat and vegetables cooked a dozen ways, each with a unique sauce or manner of presentation. Pickles and savories, plates of sashimi, and clay pots of boiling water over small alcohol flames for dipping varieties of tofu.

Mr. Slick had chosen the kaiseki restaurant and seemed well respected there; however, nobody called him by name, Itchy noted. He was simply, *okyakusama*, "honored guest." The lunch stretched past the afternoon. It was dark when they emerged back on the street, and the temperature had dropped to freezing. They joined the crowds from Osaka exiting the subway on Shijo and crossed the bridge over the Kamogawa to where the Kabukiza theater was ablaze with signs for the holiday shows.

Mr. Slick spoke briefly with Itchy as they walked, and then he waved them on as he turned back.

"Slick's going to his *ryokan* inn," Itchy said. "He'll meet us later at Yanagi Yuu."

"At the University?" Winston asked.

Itchy laughed, "Hardly."

They walked east under the Shijo arcades toward the Yasaka Shinto Shrine at the end of the road. As each of them had spoken more in the past eight hours than they had in the last eight weeks, they enjoyed walking in silence with the crowd. Ahead of them, three young women in short tight jackets of white and pink and impossibly short skirts worn over pantyhose and stiletto heels were trying simultaneously to walk fast enough to not freeze their rears and slow enough to stay upright on their shoes. The three turned up a side street into the Gion bar district one block off the main road.

"Fauna ain't bad around here," Scratchy noted.

"And now you can afford them," Itchy said.

"Come again?"

"Sex in Gion comes in many forms, all expensive."

"What about the love hotel? You said it wasn't for prostitution."

"Love hotels are for privacy. Gion is for cash. Many of the sex workers are part-timers, college students making enough to keep themselves in good clothes. In a few years they'll graduate and get married. Meanwhile, this pays a lot better than an *arubaito* at a Seven-Eleven."

They fell back into silence as Itchy led them through the Shrine precincts on a path back to their hotel. When they reached Sanjo street and turned uphill to the Miyako, Scratchy broke the silence.

"Winston, how much do you trust our Mr. Slick?"

Winston thought about this. "Mike, I can tell you that Mr. Slick could be dining at the table of any of the heads of the Group of Eight nations tonight. At their request. But you will not hear his name on the news. More significantly, if you did find his real name and searched it, you wouldn't get more than a half a dozen entries."

"Didn't begin to answer my question," said Scratchy.

"He's considering something that will somehow reboot the world, which means he knows it's time, and only requires the right code to do it."

"And we are the code masters," Itchy intoned.

"Damn straight," Scratchy agreed.

"Me, I'm prepared to go to the limit with him. But I can only ask you to do what feels right to you. At the end of the week let me know."

They struck off up the street again. This time the silence was deep as Spirit Lake.

"What could happen?" Desi sighed. "Worst comes to worst, I can always come back here and blow businessmen for a living..."

They all turned to look at him.

"...as long as I don't have to wear those stiletto heels. Oh, my God."

§   §   §

Later in the evening Itchy returned to the Miyako Hotel to pick up the boys. They strolled down Sanjo to one of his favorite restaurants, a hole-in-the-wall fish house near the commuter train station, where they had the best meal they had ever eaten for the second time in the same day. The tourist magazines tout Kyoto temples, but the real culture in the city is its cuisine. The best restaurants don't rely on the foreign tourist trade and are genuinely hostile to non-Japanese visitors, whom they fear would not understand the menu, if there were one, or the price if there weren't. A top kaiseki dinner could easily run a thousand Euros. The fish house cost them a tenth of this, and the gang rolled out into the crisp winter night encouraged and engorged. Itchy looked at his watch.

"A little stroll and we'll meet Mr. Slick." He led them over the Sanjo bridge, the traditional starting point of the old

Tokkaido road to Tokyo, and they meandered through the Teramachi covered market street, mostly closed at this hour.

Winston and Itchy discussed the economics of the Japanese keiretsu system. Desi took to window shopping. Teramachi was famous for its bookstores and writing supply shops, and the window displays fed his pen fetish. As his eyes roved across the silver and gold instruments of his desire, his mind contemplated the opportunity ahead. He had been considering the fact of his new wealth for some months.

What does wealth do to a person? Most of the obvious effects were social. Like youth, wealth warrants its own form of attraction for others. Desi had never needed money to feel attractive, although his wardrobe had expanded with his salary.

While he was just a child, his grandmother regaled Desi with Hindu tales and epics, stories of gods and demons, beings with enormous powers and desires. Desi had determined that wealth is exactly that. Wealth is a god. This did not make Desi a god, but it put him into an everyday conversation with one.

Itchy led them across the Kamo on the Oike bridge and they walked for several minutes through back streets until they reached an older building with a wooden façade three stories tall. Its wide doorway was covered by two large noren curtains. Itchy pulled the righthand curtains aside and gestured for them to enter.

The interior entry space had a wood slat floor and a rack of small lockers and cubbyholes for shoes. Itchy was already taking off his Rockports. Disdaining the cubbies, Desi insisted on using a locker for his Farragamos. Itchy slid a frosted glass door sideways, and they entered a room where several men were in various stages of dressing and undressing. They could see that the interior space had been divided in half. An old woman sat at a desk accessible to both entrances.

"It's a bathhouse," Desi squeaked, grinning.

"Relax," Winston said. "We're not on Castro Street."

"This is Yanagi Yuu, one of the finest public baths in Japan," Itchy said.

Itchy paid the woman their fee. He opened up the bag he had been carrying and distributed shallow plastic buckets and towels, little soaps and hotel shampoos to the group.

"You put your clothes in the baskets on that rack." He pointed. They stepped up onto the main floor, covered with linoleum and a non-slip jute runner that led to another sliding door. This door opened suddenly, revealing a naked old man dripping wet, clutching his own bucket and towel in front of him. The sight of the foreigners startled him, and he almost fell backwards before grabbing the doorframe.

Itchy was already shucking his clothes and dropping them into a basket he'd pulled from the wall rack. Scratchy was eyeing the old woman at the desk, who had a direct view of both sides of the bath. Itchy, down to his tighty-whiteys, leaned over to him and whispered, "Unless you've got two dicks, I'd say she's seen about everything there is to see."

Itchy stripped completely, waited for them to finish, and led them through the sliding door into the main bath. This was tiled in white, with a barrel ceiling and a mural of Fujiyama on the back wall that ran across the whole space. Only a privacy wall now separated the other side. They could hear women's voices.

Their side of the bath contained three large tubs, one of them big enough for a dozen bodies. Four men were relaxing in the tubs, and among them was Mr. Slick. Scratchy started off in that direction, but Itchy took his arm and steered him to the other wall.

Itchy sat down on the tile floor in front of one of several water taps placed low on the side wall. He began to wash, filling his bucket with water from the tap and pouring this over himself as he soaped up. They followed his example, Desi with enthusiasm, Winston and Scratchy with some reluctance. Above a mirror on the wall was a faded advertisement for an energy drink. This sent Itchy back to his juku days.

In junior high school, Ichiro and almost all of his friends had been enrolled by their parents in expensive after-school juku cram schools to prepare them for the high-school entrance exams. Energy drinks fueled their nightly studies. Ichiro had not had a full night's sleep for as long as he could remember.

Ichiro managed not to go *mukatsuku* crazy like his friends, most of whom were genuinely pissed off at the world. Luckily for him, Ichiro's younger brother had found a spot in a top ranked cram school. His mom spent most of her *kyouiku* "education mama" attention on him and left Ichiro alone. Ichiro excelled only in English and stole time in cafes that catered to *gaijin*, mainly Americans, traveling university art or history students or Buddhism junkies.

On Saturday nights, their one night away from homework, everyone would gather in cafes around Teramachi Street, listening to jazz, and aping the Kyodai university students. The anti-American demonstrations of the sixties were long forgotten as the Japanese economic miracle ramped up. Manga and anime were on the rise. Between Go Nagai and Captain Kirk, life was getting interesting. Ichiro's hippie friends all planned to backpack through India as soon as they finished high school. Ichiro had his own map, which started in San Francisco and ended in New York City.

Ichiro studied as hard as his kid brother, but in areas that held little import for Japanese corporate life. Ichiro knew the plots, the characters, and the names of the artists of all the current anime and major manga. He drew his own characters, filling dozens of notebooks. He followed the American music scene, from San Francisco acid rock to Jersey shore ballads. He loved math and chemistry but hid his knowledge from his teachers. If he weren't careful, he knew they would stick him in a technical school.

On the advice of a crazy older American named Phillip whose passion for things Japanese mirrored Ichiro's lust for Americana, he applied to Reed College without telling his parents. Phil-san was a regular at a kissaten in Pontocho, unmistakable in his Zen monk's robes, shaved head, and thick, black-rimmed eyeglasses. Later Ichiro learned that Phil had written a letter recommending him to the admissions office at Reed. Oddly, it was his degree from Reed that later got Ichiro into graduate school at Tokyo University, while his younger brother burned out academically in high school and took a job at a convenience store.

Itchy eyed the advertisement on the public bath wall again. It seemed he could never get enough sleep, even today. His childhood had wound him way too tight, and not even the years at Reed could change that.

"You two look like beached whales," Desi spoke up, as they all knew he would. "You should come to Mysore. I've got this yoga teacher you would not believe. Strict. Oh, my God. And my massager. You have to have one of those." He looked at Scratchy. "Or maybe two."

The four friends each took a moment to realize that the twenty-one years since they'd graduated from Reed was as long as the twenty-one years they had grown up before then. Their bodies, like their fortunes, had also changed. Years of sixteen-hour days coding iron fueled by a stream of lattes and Fritos had taken its toll. Desi's obsession for self-care would not allow this, and Itchy just couldn't gain weight, but Winston and Scratchy were heavy and stiff-jointed. They sat on the tile floor

and poured buckets of hot water over their shoulders, grinning
like infants.

"Winston, you have no tan whatsoever, not even a golf tan.
Your chest is as white as your ass. You could be a vampire, if
you lost, like, fifty pounds. And Itchy, you're still scrawny, but a
little stretching wouldn't hurt you either." Desi straightened his
right leg out flat on the floor and, reaching with both hands,
began to soap up the bottom of his foot.

Scratchy poured a bucket of water over Desi's head.

"I'm sorry," he said, "did you say something?"

Itchy took this cue to rinse one last time. Gathering his
soap and towel in his bucket, which he put on the ledge above
the tap, he stood up and walked over to the large pool. He
slowly lowered himself into the water and sat there with his
eyes closed. Scratchy had followed his example. He stepped
into the tub and then jumped back out as if snakebitten.

"Holly shit, that's hot!" he hissed.

Itchy pulled his arm from the tub. Where the arm had been
submerged it was now glowing red.

"You get used to it. Take it slow. There's a cold tub in the
corner for relief." He stepped out of the hot tub and went over
to the other tub where Mr. Slick still sat.

"This one's not so warm," Mr. Slick announced. "You can
work up to the other one."

Once they had all gathered in the same tub, Mr. Slick began
to ask them questions. He found it curious that none of them
were married or had children. He disclosed that he had two
children and three grandchildren.

"And what do they call you?" asked Desi.

"Grandpa Slick," he replied.

"Well, Gramps, I don't understand why you'd come all the
way to Japan without at least some idea of what you had in
mind," Scratchy said.

"I'm just an old time capitalist tired of taking people's money. It's become far too easy. I want to do something extremely difficult very, very well before my time is up. That, and I like the baths."

"I could get used to this." Scratchy settled back in the tub. "Isn't some nubile young thing supposed to come and wash my back?"

"That will cost you extra," Itchy said.

"Doesn't it always." Scratchy closed his eyes.

THREE

Over the next week, with a day off for the New Year's celebration, which the Nerds spent partying in their hotel suites and laughing as the whole Y2K scare fizzled across the planet, the routine was roughly the same: extensive mountain walks through the day, another restaurant to try, and then an hour or two in the baths of Yanagi Yuu.

They managed to agree on everything but the core action they would attempt. They were more and more invested in the idea of doing something, but that something always eluded them. Itchy suggested a new religion, and they wrestled with this idea for a solid day before discarding it.

"Religion leaves out all the people who figure they've already got one," Scratchy noted. "We'd have to convert them or kill them."

"Then how about science," Winston suggested. "We could create a new one."

"Out of what?" Scratchy asked.

"If we map the content of science as we now know it, I'm sure we'd find entire arenas that are not well covered, or perhaps a whole new method that could turn science in a different diréction."

"That's the scope of project I think we're looking for," Mr. Slick agreed.

"A new science," Desi pondered. "What fun is that?"

"And where would we start?" Itchy asked. And they spent another day on Mt. Arashiyama trying, without result, to answer that question.

Their last night at the baths, Mr. Slick presented them with a challenge. They would become anonymous, invisible, footloose. He owned a company that managed a growing global franchise of espresso coffee houses under the name "Red Star." Their decor was distinguished by large photographs of the Paris Commune, marble bistro tables, and actual zinc countertops. Already there were 3000 franchise locations in 28 nations. This gave Mr. Slick a perfect alibi for international travel, an alibi he would now share with the Nerds. He'd hire them as managers in a subsidiary company with responsibilities for "franchise inspection."

Winston's cover would be problematic. He had developed a visible presence in the world of international finance, and could not disappear or move about as freely as the rest of them under an alias without some notice.

"I've given this serious consideration, and I think the only safe solution is for Winston to travel as Winston. And since nobody at Red Star Coffee has any business with Winston, he will never attend any of our future meetings. In fact, it is best that none of you meet with Winston again after we leave Kyoto."

"Game over!" Scratchy blurted, "If Winston's out, I'm out!"

"I did not mean to suggest..." Mr. Slick raised his hand and continued, "...that Winston will not be present in our gatherings or less significant to our plan, but only that he will need to phone in from a secure location in the U.S. We cannot afford to be seen with him."

"He's right," Winston added. "For me, business-as-usual is the best cover. I know the CIO at the Drexel, and I've been meaning to set up a fiber connection from their network to my office on Rittenhouse Square."

"I've been working on some scrambling compression algorithms for voice over IP," Itchy noted. "We can all use this for teleconferencing between meetings, and Winston can call in when we're gathered. I think we can set something rather difficult for anyone to decode without some serious iron and bad intent."

"By the time we attract such attention, whatever we plan to accomplish must be beyond stopping," Mr. Slick reminded them as he bade them farewell.

The next morning, Winston gathered his friends together at the Miyako Hotel restaurant.

"It's decision time," he told them. "Each one of us is either all in or all out."

"Slick's got a good point," Scratchy said. "Free market capitalism is just pushing the planet back into some new dark age of fantasy walled enclaves for the very rich and sallow terror for the rest of us."

"Except in this case, we are among the very rich," Desi reminded him.

"We won the dot-com lotto," Itchy said. "Lucky us."

"So we just hang out in five-star hotels and watch the coming shit storm from afar?" Scratchy asked.

"Or we work out some way to turn the storm around," Winston said. "That's why we're here."

"Why does it take all our assets?" Desi asked.

"Buy in," Winston said. "No exit but success."

"Fuckin A," Scratchy said. "Count me in!"

One by one they all nodded in agreement.

§   §   §

The next of their gatherings was convened six months later at a beach resort near Hoi An in Vietnam, a country where Red Star Coffee had just opened 22 stores after years of negotiating with the party potentates in Hanoi. The coffee was highland Vietnamese, and the décor was pure nineteenth-century Paris. The locals loved it; the elderly were flooded by their nostalgia for the French colonial ambiance. The children of the elderly responded to the communist overtones. The grandchildren hungered for the chain's global music and cosmopolitan flair.

Hoi An was a gem, a seventeenth-century town on a muddy river delta. The nearby beaches were immaculate. In town, Red Star had purchased a hulking Chinese merchant house, thick beamed and clad in terra cotta, and restored this entirely, with only a small metal star as a sign. Up the coast near Danang, Red Star was building its regional headquarters and several other manufacturing operations.

At the remote beach resort hotel, Mr. Slick rented a cabana at the end of a long pathway fronting the ocean across a stretch of buff-colored sand. Two large white umbrellas on the tiled patio shaded four teak and canvas loungers.

They pulled the deck chairs near the sliding glass door so that they could communicate with Winston through Itchy's laptop computer on a low table, tethered to an Ethernet cable.

Itchy's encryption software had allowed them to hold weekly teleconferences where they continued to brainstorm on the core action of their proposed global prank.

During the past month, they explored the value of starting a whole new language as the basis for a profoundly deeper reflexive understanding on a global scale. Mr. Slick was intrigued. He envisioned a new international society talking politics and philosophy in a new language. Desi reminded them of the limits of semantics.

"The only improvement we can invent would be a new way to tell really good lies," Desi concluded. "That's not going to help anyone."

"President Stone could use it," Scratchy offered.

"I think our politicians are adept enough at obfuscation," Winston sighed.

"In other words, they already lie faster than nickel whores," Scratchy said.

This sent them all back to step one. Over the next two days, they considered a variety of modalities: new forms of art, community, media, sports, cultural expressions, festivals, and even comic books.

"Is there any way to open up to a new mode of cinema?" Itchy mused. "Movies have just become embarrassing. There's an industry that needs a shot in the arm..."

"...or the head," Scratchy added. "We could revisit the opening moments of new cinema in the 60s and try to see what went so horribly wrong."

"The world doesn't need a new avant-garde telling it where to go," Desi cut in. "Whatever we do has to be viral, grass-roots. We need to grab them by the gonads, not the frontal lobes."

The others nodded slowly.

"I could demonstrate," Desi looked at Itchy and then at Scratchy.

"Grab your own balls," Scratchy growled.

The list of world-shaking events they could imagine were mostly unattractive.

"Nothing like a world war or a global epidemic to shake things up," Scratchy noted. "Once the carnage is done, the survivors have more options."

"Start a war, and you have the winners to deal with," Winston said. "Winning breeds the worst of radical conservatism. It only encourages the bastards. Look what happened after the Cold War: a decade of triumphalist nationalism."

"Winning a war is a free ticket to neofascism," Itchy added, "We need something that creates its own positive feedback loop away from the present."

"An epidemic kills all the wrong people," Desi said. He fell silent and looked out to the sea, lost in a montage of bitter memories.

Rebooting the world, they determined, would be one part vision and nine parts process. And the processes they could imagine with a certain finitude were all in the realm of information technology.

"I think we are back to hardware and software," Scratchy concluded. "If we're going to shake a tree, this is the one we at least know how to climb."

"I've been thinking about multiplayer gaming," Itchy said. His early patents in self-animating autonomous agents formed the basis for several game platforms as well as digital film effects: crowd scenes in battlefields where hundreds of digital warriors are moving independently.

"Games are as lame as movies," said Scratchy, "and ten times as hard to make."

"That's just because nobody's figured out how a game can teach anything useful," Winston added.

"If we want to wean the teens away from soft porn and mayhem, we'll need something wicked fantastic," Desi noted.

"What about adults?" Mr. Slick asked.

"Geezers won't turn off their TVs even if you paid them to," Scratchy said.

"Americans spend hundreds of billions of hours a year watching TV," Mr. Slick said. "Think about the cognitive surplus that represents. We just have to tap into it."

"Exactly what *is* our message?" Itchy asked.

"I didn't know we had one," Scratchy said. "Who are we to tell a million teenagers anything?"

"Make that 100 million," Mr. Slick replied. He stood up and walked to the edge of the patio, gazing over at the hotel's caparisoned elephant carrying three blond children across the beach in a howdah.

He turned back to them, animated. "Look! Electricity, penicillin, gunpowder, the aerofoil: some inventions have made huge changes for the lives of everyone."

"You want us to reinvent electricity?" Scratchy shook his head.

"I want us to think fundamentally."

They sat in silence for some time.

"We can sharpen the tools people use," Scratchy said, "but it would be better to sharpen the people."

"Say that again," Winston demanded. Everyone looked at Scratchy.

"I'm saying that all the software gadgets we can build are not as valuable as the minds that use them."

"You think we can make kids smarter?" Itchy asked.

"What if you knew at age seventeen what you knew at age twenty-five?" Mr. Slick asked.

"I knew a lot of things by age twenty-five," Desi said, grinning, "that I'm not sure I would have been ready to handle at seventeen."

"You knew a lot of things by age thirteen," Itchy reminded him.

"Everything I know I learned behind the kindergarten," Desi said.

"What if kids were smarter than their teachers?" Itchy asked. "They already know more about computers than their teachers will ever learn."

"What if kids were smarter than the marketplace?" Mr. Slick whispered, visibly excited.

"Smart enough to think before they buy?" Scratchy started to smile. "Smart enough to laugh at the ads in the glossy magazines?"

"Smart enough to think twice about what they eat?" Winston asked.

"Or what they wear?" Desi added.

"Or what they believe?" Itchy said.

§   §   §

Game Release + Four Months

If it weren't for Cindy, Nick would have dropped the Game midway through the first level. The graphics were gloriolus, but the learning curve was vertical. Still, whenever he got stymied, there she was, in his face, telling him to stop fucking around, or fighting against him, and then it got good.

His avatar moved with its own cat-like instinct. Nick controlled the basic tactics, attacks and retreats, but it was his avatar who refused to die unless Nick did something really stupid, like moving inside Cindy's hand weapon range. Then it was lights out and he'd wake up on his back with her standing over him bitching at him one minute, holding out her hand the next, and sending him to another sector, where he had to learn the landscape and the rules all over again in a totally different way before the action would even start.

Before every sector, there was Wanda and Jorge, in their video doing the hand motions, and Cindy telling him to take his eyes off of Wanda's tits for a minute and do the same hand motions because it opened up a doorway in his brain. And he'd tell her he could do the hand motions and watch

Wanda's tits at the same time, since she was doing the hand motions right in front of them. Somehow Cindy knew when he skipped the hand motions, and she'd stop the sector and pull up the video with Wanda and Jorge again. It only took a few minutes, she'd say.

"Do it now!" Cindy barked, "Or say 'adios,' 'cause I'm gone."

"OK, All right." Nick put down the mouse and followed along with Wanda, wonderful Wanda. She with the coral white smile and the Pacific blue eyes.

Left over right, sideways with the left hand, circle with the right, move the eyes with the forefinger. Tap, tap, tap on your eyes and your chin. Open the door to your memory. Then the sector would start and he'd spend some hours hunting around, figuring out the logic and the strategy to beat it. When the monster finally showed up, it would kick his ass a few times, and make him guess the answers to a series of questions, and then make him ask it other questions, and then the final combat would begin and there was Cindy, slaying the minions with her long sword while Nick attacked the big slimer with an axe. It would kick his ass some more and he and Cindy would need to find the cave with the potion that put the slimer to sleep so he could sneak in and slit its ugly throat. More than one way to kill that cat.

On the next sector it might be techno-warfare or counter terror, but always a whole new logic, and always there was Wanda and Jorge before every session. Now Nick could do the hand motions in his sleep, only his sleep was also filled with visions from the Game, and more questions to ask. On it went, either down in Santa Barbara at his mom's house, or up in Lompoc with his dad. Both of them were too busy to bother him much, and happy he wasn't out getting into trouble. So he played day and night, and before the end of four months he was at Level Two.

§   §   §

Mr. Slick started the telecon conversation. Desi, Itchy, and Scratchy were also on the line. "Where are we? Michael, you mentioned this was an emergency. What's that all about?"

"We'll have to wait for Winston. It's all his fault."

"White lightning, this is ground beef control, over." A familiar voice crackled faintly on the line.

"Winston!" Desi said. "Where are you? You sound like you're on Mars."

"I'm in Kiev. I'll just have to shout."

"Hello, Winston," Mr. Slick said, "I received your message about the template phenomenon. Surely you're not serious."

Months before, Winston had sent them all an encrypted email about his research into Constantine's template theory. Emanuel Constantine, in a series of books that attracted a widening audience, argued for a new epistemology, a new way of considering beauty and truth, based on the unfolding of a universal tessellation of what he called "templates." Each template considered a specific problem space, and maintained a set relation to templates of neighboring problem spaces.

Then, in a 2000 book, *Template Technology*, written by two of Silicon Valley's technorati, Constantine's templates were shown to have enormous practical applications in software design.

The authors had unfolded the primary template tessellation for the programming design cycle, optimizing software development with objects well beyond what was possible through extreme programming. Their first eight code templates caused a rush of new code techniques. By the middle of 2001, they added seven new templates. Combinations of these fifteen templates were being inserted into virtually every new software project on the planet, from high-end massive multiplayer games to sensors in toasters.

This came to Winston's attention when his derivatives for chip manufacturers began being used by software companies retiring the enormous code bases they had used for the past thirty years. Major players were jettisoning billions of Euros of software inventories as they converted their efforts into template-based code. As far as Winston could tell, only NASA and the CIA refused to upgrade.

"Mr. Slick," Winston replied. "I am not only serious, I am profoundly excited."

"Really?" Desi chimed up.

"Since your message, I've been playing with the 15 techno-templates," Itchy admitted.

"The templates fit together like fuckin' Legos," Scratchy added. "I've never seen code that you can plug and play like that."

"In two weeks, I rewrote the core code for DocDo," Desi said. "And now it's finally small enough to run on a cell phone."

"A cell phone!" Mr. Slick marveled. DocDo was one of Desi's code masterpieces. It enabled nearly instantaneous translation between dozens of languages. Put it on a cell phone and you could talk to almost anyone in the world.

"That's what I was trying to say," Winston added. "There's something in this whole template scheme we need to investigate."

"The three of you have been building software for decades," Mr. Slick said. "Scratchy, your networking software was the launch pad for the second-generation Internet. Itchy, your avatars rule the game world. And Desi, you've broken the barriers of language that have separated the world since Babel. You did this all before templates. So why change now?"

There was silence on the line as everyone waited for Scratchy to speak.

"Let's say you want to build your dream house," Scratchy started. "But you discover that all the trees belong to someone else, and so you need to grow your own forest to harvest for the lumber for your house."

"Why don't you buy your lumber from a lumber yard?" Mr. Slick asked.

"Every house is different," said Itchy. "Their lumber doesn't fit your plan."

"Besides," Winston noted, catching on, "Their lumber is really expensive. You'd be better off buying an already built house, but you want to build your own house. Your dream house."

"So now someone creates a magic forest," said Desi, "A forest that is already grown and is free to use."

"And the lumber from this forest is not only free, but exactly what you are looking for," Winston added.

"So you build your dream house," Itchy said. "And you are very happy. But there is one catch."

"A catch," Mr. Slick said.

"It's not entirely yours." Winston's voice rang like the pronouncement of a criminal sentence.

"You can have your dream house, only you can't keep others from having it too," Itchy said. "But what's wrong with that?"

"You've made it from magic wood," Desi remarked. "And if your dream is a good one, others will copy it."

"How?" Mr. Slick asked. "It's your design."

"But it's not my lumber," Scratchy said. "Tell him, Winston."

"The magic wood, or in this case, the code templates, are public, and so are their combinations. If you create software using these, you have every right to enjoy the benefits of their use, and to sell the products you make. But you have no right to prevent others from doing the same thing."

"And if you don't use the templates, then you're back to growing your own goddamn forest before you can start to build your house," Scratchy said.

"That's why software companies are dumping billions of Euros of old code as they upgrade," Winston added.

"And...?" Scratchy said.

"And a million coders are going back to working at Wal-Mart," Desi nodded.

"And...?" Scratchy said.

"And software is getting better, instead of just bloatware," Itchy says.

"Bloatware?" Mr. Slick asked.

"Template technology is going to make software programs smaller," Itchy said.

"Faster and simpler," Scratchy added.

"Cheaper all around," Winston chimed in.

"And the best part," Scratchy said. Now they all waited for him to have the last word. "It's fun again."

"When we decide what to do," Mr. Slick said, "you'll use the templates."

"The templates are what we do," Scratchy replied.

Mr. Slick fell silent.

"Nobody's figured out how to get the templates to tessellate across semantic domains," said Itchy.

"That's the fuckin' point," replied Scratchy. "Do something nobody's done before."

Scratchy continued. "Everyone's been looking at the fifteen templates like that's the end of the story. Hell, it's just the start."

"You bad boy, you," Desi started, "What have you been up to?"

Scratchy stood up and moved to the railing of the porch, turning to face them.

"I've unfolded the templates through six more levels."

"What?" Winston struggled to hear what Scratchy said.

"When the entire system is fully unfolded some things become crystal clear." Scratchy paused and then continued. "Mr. Slick, twenty years ago I wrote a thesis on the impossibility of distributed mesh computing."

"Mikey has a paradox named after him," Desi said. "He's so smart."

"The more computers you allow to have control over concurrency, the more latency you get from the system," Scratchy continued. "It's the 'too many cooks spoil the soup' problem. You can scale up to a few thousand CPUs and then everything breaks down. You either need to build in a threaded control system, code in arbiters, or go massively parallel. But when you're working with all thirty-six templates, the concurrency paradox disappears."

"You can build the mesh?" Winston's voice trembled. Itchy started to laugh.

"Mesh? Now I'm lost," said Mr. Slick.

"It means the 'O'hara transparent concurrency paradox' is toast," Itchy said. "It means the future of computing is now a lot closer to the present."

"We wanted to shake up the world," Scratchy replied. "And now we have the shaker."

FOUR

Game Release + Four Months

Bobby led Megan to an ancient roadhouse, its slate roof laden
with moss, its stone walls bleeding mortar like old cheese.
Inside, through an enormous oak door, was a dark hall lit by a
smoke-spewing fireplace and a few dingy windows. Around
them a number of men sat at rough-hewn tables where they
gnawed hunks of roasted meat and drank from pewter
flagons. Rats scurried about on the floor. The only woman in
the place was a scullery maid in a skirt and a flimsy bodice,
scrubbing something over in the corner on her hands and
knees while she exposed her cleavage.

"I think the rats are a nice, homey touch," Megan said. "I'm
also impressed by the grime. It seems, well, so perfectly
grimy."

"Sit over here by the window," Bobby gestured to a small
oaken table. The barkeeper glanced their way with his one
good eye. Bobby shook him off. Megan sat her avatar down on
a stool.

"Listen carefully," Bobby said, gesturing over the tabletop.
"This is Level One." The table suddenly became a kind of
map, like the one in the front of *The Hobbit* book. "You will
need to make friends with seven different species in the seven
realms...."

"I'm not really that much into this whole fantasy game thing," she admitted. Bobby held up one hand and continued to explain.

"Each species will challenge you to solve some problem that means ultimate life or death to it."

"I just opened the door to see what this Game was all about."

"When you solve the problem you can progress to the next species."

"Where will you be while I'm solving all these problems?" This was sounding like way too much time, and she had other places to be, like back in Junana with her friends. Only a lot of her friends were not hanging in Junana so much anymore.

"I will be at your side." He sat back, his face a mask of shock. "Where else would I be? I told you, I am your Guide."

"Really!" she said, perking up. "So we'll be together all the time?"

"Together, yes. Every minute in Level One. But you will need to find the answers yourself. I'm only here to lend a hand when things get, well, difficult."

"In what way?"

"Did I mention that not all of these species are what you might call 'friendly'?"

"Oh!" It was her avatar's turn to appear shocked.

"I can teach you how to defend yourself." His doublet morphed into a suit of chain mail, and a broadsword grew on his belt within an elaborate scabbard.

"I always wanted to shoot a crossbow," she admitted.

"Just remember that your mission is to make friends, not corpses." He morphed back into his regular costume.

"Just how different are these species?" she asked.

"Philosophically, they are worlds apart. That's the real challenge. Biologically..." He shrugged. Then, and rather suddenly, he morphed into a form that resembled something like a cross between a kangaroo and an monitor lizard.

"...there are some noticeable differences here too," he lisped through a forked tongue and then, just as suddenly, returned to his usual form.

"You are just a Game piece, aren't you?" she sounded deflated.

"I am your Game piece," he said. His hands reached out and covered hers. "Yours alone. If you get through this level we will be together for many, many hours in the Game. I hope you come to like me as much as I already like you."

"That would be the shit," she said.

He frowned, knurled his brow, and then smiled. "Yes, the total shit. Indeed!"

§   §   §

Scratchy set down the phone and looked away from the computer monitor and out the window of his study, toward the Santa Barbara hills, shrouded in June gloom. On his lap a grey cat purred. Scratchy was researching the history of the Sapphire Children.

In the 1990s, Ralph Lamont, a failed Methodist preacher in Arkansas who had read Constantine's work, claimed that the template tessellation would be completed only when a new society of "sapphire babies" was born and allowed to grow up with support for their special abilities. A victim of

undiagnosed learning disorders, he had recognized in this own
son, little Billy Lamont, a special destiny.

According to his father, Billy was the first of a loose
network of "sapphire children" who were heralding not just a
talent for learning, but the threshold of a new species.
Reverend Ralph used template-unfolding ability as a measure
of these precocious few. Billy, truth be told, had quite a knack
with templates. Templates, the Reverend argued, were too
sophisticated for the minds of adults who, anyway, preferred to
wallow in cable television melodramas and Internet porn.

The ability to generate the templates was impossible to
teach. Some people had a knack while others were quite
immune to the process. Sometimes younger children were the
most adept in the first stages of the unfolding process, but then
had little success completing this. The same child, a decade
later, might not retain any vestige of this ability.

Ralph started a school in Emerson, Arkansas, home of the
world's only Purple Hull Pea Festival and World Championship
Rotary Tiller Race. Hundreds of families, mostly from the
Midwest, enrolled their scions in this establishment, which
promised to nurture their sapphire essence for a mere twenty-
grand a year plus room and board. Problem was, very few of
the sapphire children did very well on their SATs. By the time
Billy was old enough to drive, his command of the templates
was history, as was the school.

Constantine responded to reporters investigating the
sapphire child phenomenon by noting that dozens of templates
had already been unfolded by perfectly normal adults. Yet, the
popular perception of his work remained ambiguously linked
to notions of New Age cults. He returned to landscape
architecture and continued to try to systematize the existing
templates, without success.

Unfolding a set of templates, Scratchy figured, could begin in one of two completely discrete manners. The first resembled filling in a jigsaw puzzle. The problem space would be determined, and the first, the seed, template would then begin a sequence of solutions that eventually covered the entire space.

Usually the order of the template sequence was important from a practical standpoint. Like making a pizza, the crust has to come before the sauce. Among the eight original templates within the software design problem space, the Controller template had to precede the rest.

The problem spaces Scratchy examined in the template literature seemed nearly random in their distribution: house design, organizational structure, music theory, baseball strategy. Templates had been unfolded in a strange mix of arenas, none of them connected. Scratchy considered a completely new way to unfold a template structure.

The original eight templates in *Template Technology* had logically implied another layer of seven templates. Scratchy wondered if this pattern would imply more layers. When he discovered another layer of six templates, he kept on going through the remaining five layers until he found a layer with only one template.

What intrigued him was that as the template layers grew, they also become less and less linked to the original problem space. When he discovered the final template, he realized that this might be something like a universal seed. He called this template "Noel."

§   §   §

Game Release + Five Months

"Things get faster now," Cindy said to Nick today when he logged on. "You are moving beyond physical combat into a mental combat zone." They were standing on a bluff overlooking a vast, Technicolor desert, with other monoliths shimmering in the distance. Overhead, a hawk circled and cried. Cindy's hair was blowing in the wind. She wore a short buckskin dress and a beaded belt.

"As long as I can kick your sorry ass again," Nick said.

"In your dreams, cowboy," Cindy said. "I'm here to get you up to speed, so don't let me down. I've got my reputation to protect. I'm the best fucking Guide on the block!"

"Bite me!" Nick said.

"Later. Here's the drill. You will be put into a situation where you can assemble all the information you need in order to ask the one question that sends you to the next sector. The information is gathered though Queries, which are the mental equivalent of me with a BFG fighting you with your Glock. At least that's what it will seem like at first. If you ask a lame fucking question, and believe me there is such a thing as a stupid question..." She poked his avatar in the forehead with her finger as she spoke, but she was smiling too.

"...I will take you back to the First Level. And you don't want to go there."

He nodded his head in agreement. He was eager to move on.

"Hold my hand," she said. "If I catch you looking up my skirt again I will drop you on your head!"

§   §   §

People would later claim he did so because it was the seed, the birth, of so many templates. Only later he confessed he did so because it was Douglas Adams' middle name and he discovered this template on Towel Day.

The name "Noel" did not stick. Everyone soon called it "Choose One." The template seemed simple enough: "When faced with an equilibrium that has more than one possible stable solution, choose one."

"Choose One" was extremely powerful. It provided a seed for everything from language (connecting sound to meaning) to traffic control (driving on only one side of the road). It also opened up to a constructivist view of society, suggesting that choice was implicit in many arenas, including gender.

Chose One said to the universe, "There are several ways we can go, but we're all going to agree on this way for now, with the understanding that we can do it some other way later, thank you." It wasn't quite as elegant as "42", but it was close. Once you started unfolding with it, you could never escape the arbitrariness of that first choice.

Scratchy explored the enormous problem arena encompassed by his Noel template seed. Mostly he was concerned that the unfolding process would lead to internally contradictory or simply unsound solutions. What if Noel led to logical but self-defeating answers? Nothing solves world hunger faster than a fatal global pandemic, but you don't need to go there. And if Noel was going to help make seventeen-year-olds any smarter, than they would need to learn how to work the same logic he used to uncover this template.

After unfolding a dozen or so template systems out of Noel, he realized that template unfolding was still incredibly sensitive to the opening description of the problem space. A highly theoretical space unfolded comically transcendental templates with little purchase on any real problem. "How many angels can dance on the head of a pin?" The templates respond: "That depends on the song." He hoped Desi and Itchy were having better luck with the template logic for education.

§   §   §

Winston had spent the past two years playing "hide the money." Mr. Slick taught him how to use one government to help hide information from the next. Winston kept up his usual rounds of global consulting on derivatives and hedge fund growth. He used the travel to carry instruments of value, but of course not actual cash, that spread their combined wealth along a web of shell corporations across four continents. Over the months, these corporations merged and split into new entities, masking their original investments.

Each time he returned to Philly, he'd check in with the Nerds. And every time they talked, Winston was reminded that he didn't code. All he could do was listen and wonder. He felt like the caterer for Michelangelo at the Sistine Chapel. "Hello, Mr. Simoni, you want me to bring you another latté up there on the scaffold?" Here he was pushing money around while they were forging a new digital planet.

Since the emergency telecon, the Nerds had been exploring Scratchy's thirty-six templates to great advantage. A single template contained hundreds of lines of precision code. Their combinations allowed for a vast range of interoperable objects. Winston listened in wonderment as the Nerds mined this resource for new miracles.

Scratchy modeled new network architectures, search routines, and the chassis for the massive global mesh computing enterprise. He wove the infrastructure for managing countless users and administrative services.

Itchy rebuilt his graphics engine and autonomous behavior routines, adding new protocols for user interactivity. His avatars developed capacities for learning a wide range of behaviors, and their features gained an entire fractal level of detail. Their faces now had pores like a teenager. He even gave them a touch of acne, which would flare and disappear over a span of months.

"Forget the zits," Scratchy advised, "only give them a smile that will socket right into the Gamer's groin."

Desi ported DocDo to the new system and was rewarded with a hundred-fold increase in speed. He built user profiling support, figuring ways to authenticate users and model their behaviors within the system. He implemented a new encryption scheme with a symmetric 512-bit key. He created hooks into a broad tier of national databases across the globe, from which he could extract information on a third of the planet's population.

At the same time they were working around the clock to build the system, they were dancing around the lack of a clear purpose to their endeavor. What was all of this technology to be used for? On the open market this suite of new applications would sell for more than they were already worth. But so far they had no idea how their efforts might affect a single seventeen-year-old, not to mention five hundred million of them.

Scratchy figured out how to assemble a copy of the Internet, or rather, those parts that were likely to be useful: several petabytes of text, images, video, and database contents. They leased an exabyte of fast storage from storage brokers across the planet. They queried this stored information from a massively parallel XServe server farm Desi built in Manasagangotri next to the University of Mysore.

Desi wanted to work on the problem of granularity, implicit meaning, and semantic extensions of various modes. He started to break down the whole corpus into molecular units, index these in a variety of meaningful ways, and then run a bank of tests to see if he could automate narrative constructions from the mix. This, he explained to Winston, is about as easy as pulling a whole peach intact out of a blended fruit smoothie.

Desi had good reason to hope. He had unfolded the templates for a type of frame semantics, something he'd picked up while at Berkeley. Frame semantics allowed him to start with any verb in any language, determine the scope of its frames, decide which frame would apply to the sentence at hand, and then, like a crystal in a supersaturated solution, grow meaning and context from the Internet soup of molecular granules. What emerged wasn't Shaw or even Vonnegut, but it contained credible paragraphs constructed entirely artificially, and in any of the major languages.

When Desi showed this to Itchy, he found out that Itchy had been working on unfolding the templates for dramatic plots, using the collected plays of the American and British stage. It turns out that nearly all of the plots could be generated by a three-level template structure. Fortunately, or rather, fortuitously, since they had really been exploring the same template structure from opposite ends, the top-level templates from Desi's frame semantics mapped directly into the base level of Itchy's plot templates. This meant that the granules derived from the Internet could be woven into actual stories.

They demonstrated this to Scratchy by feeding in Macbeth and outputting a simple list of phrases. These phrases were then randomized and fed back into the template structure. What emerged was not Macbeth, but something eerily close to it, as if a version had been written not from memory, but from

hearsay. If anything, the plot was too coherent. The templates
Itchy had unfolded could not faithfully reproduce ambiguity
and irony. Scratchy guessed that the three-layer template
structure would need at least a couple more layers before it
could pull some convincing Shakespeare from the soup.

Once they could build stories, it was just another few steps
to montage in video and photographs, using a combination of
audio and graphics interpretation routines. The resulting mini-
movies looked like rough cuts of cinema verité student films.
Desi sent out some alpha client software and the five of them
spent weeks pulling these little movies out from the Internet.
Then they had called another teleconference.

"You're telling me these stories are generated automatically
from the questions I'm asking?" Mr. Slick said.

"How ever do you do that?" Winston added.

"Algorithmically, my dear Winston," said Scratchy.

"At least they're fast," Itchy noted. "They will scale up fine.
We still don't have any way of programming a learning path
through these events. We need an education specialist. We're
flying blind right now."

"I know someone," Winston said. "Haven't spoken to him
in years. MIT, Stanford, and a short time with the NSF before
he figured out they didn't want to listen to him. He went to
Brazil where they are researching new forms of teaching. His
name is Robby Robinson."

"Would he move to Japan to work with Ichiro?" Mr. Slick
asked.

"Under the right conditions, I'm sure we can convince
him," Winston said.

"I believe we are ready to meet again. You will be contacted
about the next location."

"Nerdfest ho!" Scratchy said. "Adios, amigos. I've got iron to
lay," and he hung up.

Desi added, "I feel like laying something too. TTFN."

"Back to the coal mines," Itchy said. "You two are lucky you don't code, or unlucky. This is getting really good! Ciao."

"The Nerds are on a roll," Winston said.

"So am I. Code is not the only aspect of this game."

"Something up your sleeve?"

"Ask me no questions, and..."

"Just a hint..."

"What's your shoe size? So long, Winston."

"Goodbye, Jack."

Winston sat back from his desk. In the years since the first, what did Scratchy just call it? "Nerdfest," he had been grappling with his responsibility for getting them all involved. He could just as well have left them to enjoy their dot-com fortunes.

The notion of building the first mesh computer had sent them all into full Yippie mode. They had, right in their hands, the equivalent of a digital tsunami event, not just a new computer game, but also a technology that was to current day computers what the computer had been for the adding machine.

"Busy, busy, busy," he whispered and closed his eyes.

§   §   §

Game Release + Five Months

When Nick took Cindy's hand they lifted off the bluff and began to fly across the desert at some height. Below them the landscape changed from rock and sand to pine forest and then to firs. Up ahead a spire caught the sunlight, and they approached a town of stone buildings and cobble streets. The town was on a hillside; the buildings nestled into the trees.

The stones, the trees, the grass poking through the cracks, even the donkeys braying in the shadows of the stone huts on the edge of town looked too real to be real. The wind would play along the sides of the buildings and flutter the curtains in the open windows. Scores of avatars moved along the streets in pairs. Players and Guides, he guessed.

They landed at the edge of town. She started up the street and turned.

"Come on, big boy!" Her clothing changed into a long flaxen robe with a green belt.

Nick noticed that all the other Guides were in robes. He followed her through the doorway of the first building on the right. The interior was dark and the door closed behind them with a solid thump.

Cindy lit a candle she now held on a brass holder, and Nick was amazed at the quality of the light. The flame flickered and smoked and sent its warm brilliance and shadows across the stone floor to illuminate an oaken table and chair and, curiously, a computer.

"Hey!" He noticed that Cindy's computer was not just any PC. It was exactly like his gaming machine, even the same monitor.

"Here is where things get interesting," Cindy said. "Listen up, cowboy."

She set down the candle and leaned across the table to touch the computer screen. It lit up with the exact image that was on his actual screen. This created that fractal ketchup bottle effect: setting off a thousand images inside of images, diminishing into a point of light. She then looked away from his avatar, out directly at Nick, sitting in front of his computer.

"Hello, Nick," she said, leaning back against the table, still looking right at him instead of his avatar. "I can't see you. Turn on your webcam." He did so.

"Hi, Cindy," he replied, a bit creeped out. The candlelight caught her from the side, and her profile was dead serious.

"Now is the time," she continued, "for me to start explaining a few things about the Game. So I want you to listen for about five minutes and then let me know what you think." She waited. "Nick, you with me?"

"Go ahead."

"When you first got into the Game, I bet you thought it was just another entertainment on Junana."

Nick nodded.

"So wrong!" She slapped the table with her hand. His head jerked back in response. "Junana is just the gateway to the Game. Even as the Game is the gateway to your new life."

"What?" Why was Cindy acting so strange? Even when she was angry with him she never got this serious.

"Shush, now! Listen to me. For years you've been playing computer games with some real skill and going to school where you feel empty and bored. You are not alone. I am not going to give you the history of the Game right now; you'll get that later. I just want to tell you that the Game will teach you everything you would normally learn at school. Only you will want to learn what you learn more than you wanted to do anything before. More than surfing out at the county line, more than Samantha Greenly in fifth grade...,"

How did she know that?

"...more than a kiss from Wanda..."

"I don't know about that," Nick said.

"Put a sock on it and listen up! I'm not finished. There are seven levels to the Game that we know about. This is Level Two. Many people never leave this level because they just can't find the will to give up how they want to think about the world. In this level the Game offers you clues to help you find your way. When you graduate to Level Three, there will be no more clues, but I will be with you still. By the time you finish Level Two, you will know more than enough to graduate from Santa Barbara High School. And you will also know a system you can use to continue learning.

"There is a Zen Buddhist saying: 'When you reach the top of the mountain, keep climbing.' That decision will be yours. If you really want to keep climbing, then you will earn your shoes and move on. Otherwise, you will stop playing the Game, and go on with your life out there.

"Take this as the warning label for the Game, Nick. If you go ahead with me and get through these next few levels you will find that the world out there is a different place, simply because you will understand it in a totally different manner.

"The world of the Game is the real world. The content you will face comes from your life, not some fantasy land. The rules of the Game are the rules you will also follow outside the Game. If you go on with the Game, your life will change. That's for dead certain. They want you to know that. It's the reason they made the Game. So now you've been warned. Now you can ask your questions."

Cindy waited while Nick assembled his thoughts.

"What do mean there are seven levels 'that you know about'?"

"Good. You were listening. The Game has been programmed through the unfolding of a series of learning templates. The entire series is not yet unfolded, and so we do not know where the final levels of the Game will take us. Perhaps the seven levels are as deep as humans can understand themselves and the world. Maybe you will be the person who can unfold level eight. We just do not know."

"You mentioned 'shoes'. What's that about?"

"When you graduate from a level you earn something you can wear. You can wear it in Junana and you will be sent the article to wear out there." Cindy waved her hand as if gesturing at Nick's room.

"Can you enter my world?"

"Don't be an idiot, I'm all pixels here." Cindy smiled. "I do know a lot about your world. I've got your grade reports for the past ten years, and your police report from those jeans you boosted in seventh grade."

"Woah!" Nick covered his face with his hands.

"Nicky. I don't care that you got caught shoplifting. You and me, we've already had some great times together, and better times to come. Only now we do it with the rules of your world. You want to quit. Fine. Go with my blessing. You want to stay, just know the Game is real. So you're going to need to buckle down and buckle up too."

FIVE

For the next Nerdfest, Mr. Slick had picked another beach
resort, this one on the Kona side of the big island of Hawaii.
Most Kona hotels were enormous resorts fronting narrow
beaches, and throttled by expensive golf courses. The Kona
Cove resort was just the opposite, a scattering of free-standing
hales around an actual cove with a fresh water lagoon, a beach,
and a reef. Four bars, two swimming pools for the kids and
their grandparents, a little pakalolo from the waterfront staff,
and a real chef cooking up fresh mahi mahi and opa; what
more does anyone need? No cell phones, no newspapers, and
no Internet, apart from one broadband connection in the
business office next to the store.

The first night, Scratchy sneaked in and slipped a custom
high-speed WiFi base station on the electrical plug of the office
computer. He picked it up from Make.com and did some
customization. It looked and worked just like a multi-jack
electrical outlet surge suppressor, but also broadcast an
encrypted WiFi signal when connected to an Ethernet cable
with an Internet connection.

The four of them occupied four adjacent hales fronting the
cove. They had breakfasted together on the terrace of the cafe
and returned along the beach to Mr. Slick's hale where they set
up Desi's laptop on the deck shaded by palm trees. Winston
was 5000 miles away and six hours later in Philadelphia. Right
on time, he called in. He was sitting at his desk, his computer
camera focused on a steaming mass of something on a whitepaper napkin.

"Is that Cheez-Whiz?" Scratchy asked.

"Straight from Jim's on South Street. You guys don't mind if I eat while we talk." He picked up half of the cheesesteak and took a monster bite.

"If I hadn't just had eggs benedict and French toast, I'd be in the mood to protest." Scratchy smiled.

"I miss you, Winston!" said Desi.

"Hi, Lucy, you look fantastic."

Desi was wearing a bright blue lungi around his waist and sported a new tattoo, a willow pattern, on one shoulder. "Thank you, Fred!"

"Boys, Mr. Slick, I wish I were there," Winston said. "Anyhow, this new video hook-up is phenomenal. I'm almost ready to put on some sunblock."

Over the next two hours, the five of them outlined the work they had completed or would soon complete, using terms that Mr. Slick could understand. They shared a concern that programming Junana.com was taking up far too much of their time right now.

"Tell me again why we are building a social networking software?" Mr. Slick asked.

"The templates work better when they are matched to the desires and skills of the individual player. That seems to be a fundamental principle," Itchy explained. "But we don't want to distract the players from enjoying the start of the game by forcing them to tell us what we need to know."

"Can't afford extra baggage in any game design," Scratchy warned. "We need maximum acceleration from a dead start. Little fuckers got no attention span until they hit level two. Of course, then you can't pry the controls out of their fists."

"There are a dozen social networking services that are huge in different parts of the globe," Winston said. "Why not just pull information from them?"

"We've looked at automating the transfer of profile information from other services. Problem is, most profile information is bogus," Desi said. "On Junana, we'll make it a rule to be honest."

"What kind of word is 'Junana'?" asked Mr. Slick.

"It's a combination of Sanskrit and Japanese," Desi explained. "'Jnana' means 'knowledge' in Sanskrit and 'Juunana' means 'seventeen' in Japanese. The whole point is providing knowledge to seventeen-year-old kids around the world. So we made up 'Junana.'"

"Junana.com will be everything Myplace tried to be," said Scratchy. "It will offer a whole new level of identity checking, so your friends on the net would know you are you and not some forty-year old pervert from Pacoima. And if you are a perv, we'll have your police record and kick you off the service. We can add levels of real information about schools and classes so that students, who are taking, say, the same history class at Roosevelt High School in Albany, can share homework assignments or gripes."

"We can leverage Desi's multi-language automatic translation, Itchy's avatar code, and also provide a 3D virtual gathering place for friends to interact," he added.

"It will be the first truly global social networking service," Desi explained, "running on the first global mesh computer."

"We mine Junana, so that when the player starts the Game we know enough about her to tailor Level One to her personal desires," Itchy said. "It's going to be fantastically seductive."

"What is the final scale to all this?" Mr. Slick asked.

"Not sure," Scratchy noted. "We are going places beyond what anyone has built before or probably has imagined could be built."

"I think we could run out of people before we run out of CPU or RAM," Desi said.

"People who want to play?" Mr. Slick asked.

"No, people on the planet." Desi smiled. "There are only about six billion of them. And everybody will want to play. Tell him, Mikey."

"Tell me what?" Mr. Slick slid back on his chaise into the shade. He was wearing a Tommy Bahama swimsuit and a Cuban shirt, but he didn't look like he wanted any sun.

"Remember those mini-movies we showed you?" Scratchy started. "We've been trying to link them into a larger template system."

"Scratchy made a copy of the Internet, and Desi used the templates to break everything into granules," Winston said. "Desi found a way to expose the semantic relationships between the granules."

"Itchy created a user interface, something between a holodeck on Star Trek, a first-person shooter, and a Hollywood production," said Desi said. "It's simply marvelous!"

"In this alpha version the topic you chose opens up a series of problem spaces," Itchy said. "They have to do combat or discovery by fielding the questions presented by the game pieces we call "Guides." Every question has a time limit, based on its gravitas."

"How's that?" Mr. Slick asked.

"There may be no such thing as a 'stupid question,' but there are a lot of insipid topics," Scratchy added. "And insipid topics unfold really uninteresting templates."

"Give me an example," Mr. Slick asked.

"The meaning of life," Winston said.

"The existence of God," Itchy added.

"The future of society," Desi said.

"The notion of 'evil,'" Scratchy added, "or 'good' for that matter. Most of the big questions that philosophy and religion have been consumed by for the last 2000 years turn out to be universally uninteresting."

"Which might be one reason why template knowledge was not discovered earlier," Winston proposed. "But there are important topics and templates with some gravitas."

"These are really heavy, man!" Scratchy said in his best Wavy Gravy imitation.

"The important ones fall into two groups, the templates that are foundational and those that are capstones," Winston explained.

"The ones you must do first or can only do last," Desi said.

"We know very few of the capstones," Scratchy admitted. "And not nearly enough of the foundational ones."

"The original eight templates from Template Technology are capstone templates," Itchy explained. "Scratchy's Noel template is a foundational template."

"He's so smart..." Desi rolled his eyes and smiled.

"When we've figured everything out, we should be able to encapsulate all of what is important to learn within a finite series of levels in the Game. We still need to find a pedagogy that fits into this picture," Itchy said.

Mr. Slick frowned.

"The interactivity rocks, but the game structure has not yet emerged," Scratchy concluded.

Mr. Slick slumped back into his chaise. He closed his eyes. His management alarm had just gone off; the bell that sounded when a staff meeting had just rolled off the tracks or a vice president was trying to snowball him. He had never been keen on the templates, and now he was concerned that these had pushed the whole effort into some obscure limbo. The internal voice was telling him to demand they junk everything and start over. That's when Winston spoke up.

"Scratchy, please point the computer over to Mr. Slick." Scratchy adjusted the camera.

"Mr. Slick," Winston continued.

"Go ahead, Winston."

"Everything you've just heard sounds like we've jumped into the deep end of the waste treatment plant. You think we are treading in shit up to our armpits."

"Actually, I think you might need a snorkel."

"I felt the same way before I took a ride on the prototype Game."

"And now?"

"Now I cannot put it down. The hours I've spent on the Game have been the most fascinating, productive, seductive, well, mind-fucking time I've ever spent. It's like..." He paused, unable to find the right phrase.

"Holing out from a bunker...," Scratchy suggested.

"Sinking an eagle putt...," Itchy said.

"Winning the Open...," Desi added.

"All of the above," Winston concluded. "So don't make any final judgements until Scratchy hooks you up for a trial run."

Mr. Slick sighed. Winston was right. The lads deserved some respect.

"How long will it take?" he asked.

"Why don't I call back three days from now, same time of day," Winston suggested. "If you're not completely convinced, then we'll rethink the whole enchilada."

"But first, Mr. Slick here needs to come clean," Scratchy said.

The other Nerds looked over at him.

"You know we can't ask him who he is," Desi whispered.

"That's not what I mean," Scratchy replied. "Is it, Mr. Slick?"

Mr. Slick and Scratchy shared a moment of eye contact as the rest watched.

"And what do you mean?" Mr. Slick asked.

"You like people to think you're a modernist, a liberal, something of a philosopher. But inside, you are a true believer. I'm guessing longtime Catholic. Altar boy and wannabe priest at least at some point."

Mr. Slick was still frowning. Scratchy continued. The others stole glances among themselves.

"What you really wanted was to find a new highway to God. You wanted a cosy new home within modernity for Jesus. Soon as we tell you the templates don't know what to do with God and evil, you think the templates are flawed."

"We are looking to make an impact," Mr. Slick reminded them.

"Hey," Scratchy said. "Don't worry about God, I'm certain he'll show up down the road."

"Besides, God has to be everywhere, or she's nowhere," Desi added.

"Perhaps God is in the templates," Itchy added. "We didn't invent these, we don't own them, we only found them."

Mr. Slick leaned back in his chaise and looked down the beach, following a mother in a pink bikini showing her two young children the tidal pool where two six-foot moray eels named Bert and Ernie kept house. He had the feeling he'd just stuck his head in Bert's mouth. His thoughts went to the Cardinal, not the old man whose faith in him he had been forced to destroy, but the young chapel priest who saved him in his infancy.

§ § §

Jakov Dobranić was born in Zagreb in March 1941 and promptly orphaned when a Henkel 111 bomber dropped a

500-kg bomb on the city's central hospital. His father, a non-commissioned officer in the Yugoslav army, had been sent into battle near Sarajevo and was never heard from again. With the assistance of the local bishop, the babies rescued from the ruins of the neonatal ward were taken to a Jesuit orphanage in Rome.

Jakov grew up literally in the church, at a time when orphans, like warplanes, were mass produced. Not particularly handsome as an infant, it was his bright demeanor and indefatigable energy that kept him from being shipped to one of the church's "rural relocation centers," Dickinsian workhouses that survived off the labor of their charges. The favorite of the chapel priest, Jakov was nearly swallowed into a life of piety, except that he caught the notice of the Contessa Daniela Ottavio, a frequent visitor to the chapel. Having lost all three sons, her daughter, and seven grandchildren to the conflict and the aftermath, her chapel devotions were powered by grief and tinged with a smoldering anger.

Bereft of family, she admired the toddler who struggled to emulate the behaviors of the older choirboys. The Contessa paid handsomely to adopt the child, and after a few years of doting personal attention, a short childhood as pleasant and happy as his infancy had been miserable, she sent the rechristened Jacopo Ottavio off to an elite institution in rural Austria where children of wealthy families from across Europe were made ready to meet their adult obligations.

After graduating from the St. Gilgen Academy on the banks of the Wolfgangsee, Jacopo attended the Sorbonne in the early 1960s, and then moved to the United States, where he did an MBA at Wharton. Jacopo was a perennial invitee to the Vatican's annual summer conclaves for the brightest young stars from the church's top dioceses. The program had been devised to marshall young talent the Church could call upon in the arenas of finance and politics outside the strictures of priesthood.

In 1966, Jacopo Ottavio returned to Paris, bedded and nearly wedded a cousin of the Rothschilds, and joined and later quit the Parti Communiste Français. Already, it seemed, he could not decide how to position his life within or without the adventure of capitalism. He announced his Marxism to be of the Grouchoist variety and in May 1968 joined a student brigade in the streets of the Left Bank. Arrested, beaten, and deported, he returned to Rome, where he renounced the PCF for its mistaken, although thoroughgoing, sense of self importance and its blinkered perspective on Stalinism.

Scorned by his former Communist comrades he returned to the marketplace, which is exactly where his now octogenarian adopted mother, the Contessa, had always known he would arrive. He was, she had long sensed, too clever for the Communists and too ambitious for the Church. Jacopo married in 1972, a suitable arrangement that brought him two children whom he adored. His wife and the Contessa managed to become fast friends. Having grandchildren around her mended an enormous tear in the fabric of the old woman's life.

Although she never once announced her love for Jacopo, the Contessa's will was as simple as the probate was complicated. Her fortune and the family crest were now entirely his to control. The church where little Jakov had spent his youngest days boasted a new orphanage and school. The Contessa's name graced new buildings at the universities her children had attended.

The Bishop, now a Cardinal, visited Jacopo in his offices on the Via Frattina in late 1989. He surprised his friend with the news that the Church had forgiven him his youthful indiscretions. Jacopo's brief flirtation with Communism was to be forgotten.

While Jacopo embraced the friendship of the old priest, he was less than enthusiastic about returning to the Church. He had been orphaned by war, rescued by caprice, disciplined and molded for success by his adopted mother as a escape route from her omnipresent grief, and was now preparing for the only future he could imagine that would hold his fascination. The rapid collapse of the ideals of socialism and the communist states of Europe heralded a new age of savage capitalism. Count Jacopo Ottavio's life was now focused on what would emerge from this unbridled marketplace and how this might lead to something that would replace the promise of socialism. The Church, he predicted to his old friend, would find in the new gods of the market a much greater enemy than godless Communism ever posed. The old man was stunned by Jacopo's rejection, and their meeting ended in acrimony.

Jacopo Ottavio consolidated and streamlined the estate's business interests and began his policy of retreating from public view. Her many properties in Europe, Asia, and the Americas were sold to a holding company which then sold them to a real-estate investment trust. Both were privately owned by Jacopo. The stocks were sold to a private mutual fund also run by Jacopo. Only the ancestral holdings in Italy were retained under the name of Ottavio, although the equally ancestral tenants who worked the farms and vineyards in the hills above Firenze would not see the Count more than once a decade.

Jacopo's wife had settled into the Contessa's house in Rome, where she entertained a wide circle of friends. Jacopo was always welcome, although his presence was rarely required. His two children were now adults. His son managed the Italian estates and his daughter taught sociology in England at the London School of Economics.

Jacopo took the name Jack Dobron as the first among several aliases and commenced a life as a nomadic marketplace speculator. He focused on emerging opportunities in technology, communications, and the post-Communist territories. His new motor yacht, Le Grand Azure, 371 feet long, had its own helicopter and stowed a 70-foot sailboat and a 60-foot motor launch. This became his floating headquarters, although he spent more time in hotels and jetliners.

Within a decade he controlled assets that put him within reach of the wealthiest families on the planet, although his personal wealth was unknown to governments and to the press. His companies paid their taxes, gave to charities, and grew fat on the global hunger for consumption.

Jack Dobron soon became alarmed and then morose over the direction the marketplace was leading the world. He figured that klaxon alarms should be sounding in the halls of government in every nation as environmental degradation, social anomie, political polarization, cultural fundamentalism, and economic imbalances escalated across the body politic. Instead, the richest nations remained fixated on expanding energy use, increasing worker productivity, and marginalizing minority opinions. The less-rich nations copied their richer neighbors and added low wages to their national portfolios as if this were some new virtue.

No serious thought was being given to any notion of collective social change. Capital flows went global, with the financial markets exchanging trillions of Euros each day. As each nation pimped its economic climate, every locale was forced to whore for the attention of global capital. Towns and counties beggared themselves to attract jobs, offering tax holidays and free services to corporations that had no intention of remaining once the holiday was over.

Jack met Winston Logan Fairchild at a Wharton briefing in Brussels, and they fell into a day-long conversation over the need to get ahead of the marketplace stampede, to try to turn this before it reached the looming cliff straight ahead. They continued their conversation over the years, meeting in cities where they had other business interests. When the dot-com bubble reached its zenith, Winston advised Jack to pull his assets out, saving Jack more than he saved Itchy, Scratchy, and Desi combined. Of the ten trillion dollars in assets that bled away from the NASDAC, none of these belonged to Jack.

Three months later, Jack flew Winston up to Newport, where Le Grand Azure was at anchor. For the first time since he began his peculiar career, Jack revealed his financial holdings to another person. Winston would need to know everything so that he would rest his friendship with Jack on trust. In return, Winston spilled to story of his life, from the privileged Philadelphia Main Line upbringings (his mother and the Contessa would have gotten along famously) to his liberating years at Reed, his training at Wharton, and his work in economics at Cambridge.

The desire to find a new purchase on the old ideal of positive social change had grown within Jack to the point where he felt he could easily give up his entire fortune to make this happen. At this point, if he had any faith that the Church could be the agent of this change, he would have gladly turned his wealth over to it. But the Church was now mired in a death struggle with internal and external fundamentalisms. No, a new agent for social change would need to be invented, nurtured, cultivated, and then propagated across the globe. Winston felt he knew the people who could instigate such an agent. He invited them all to Kyoto, one of Jack's favorite cities, for their first meeting.

§   §   §

Mr. Slick looked back at Winston's face in the computer
monitor. He nodded as if he'd consummated some formal
commitment to himself.

"Winston," he said. "It's time we all get to know each other
better." And he told them all the story of an infant rescued
from a Zagreb hospital and raised by a priest and a contessa.
He answered all their questions patiently. Then there was a
long silence.

"You can call me Jack, if you like," he remarked, "But I have
grown very fond of 'Mr. Slick.'"

"We could make that Count Slick," Desi said.

"Jack it is," Scratchy announced. "The 'ad-venture capitalist.'
Are you ready for the alpha Game?"

The Prank

SIX

Junana.com was launched simultaneously in the USA, most of
Europe, Korea, Japan, and China. Within a year, Junana was
adding new users at the rate of five million a day on top of a
300 million user base. Fortune put a market value for Junana at
ten billion dollars, and speculated serially on the sale of this to
Apple, Sony, Google, and Microsoft. Apparently, only the
Vatican was not interested.

Jennifer Bouchez at first resisted Claire's order that pulled
her from the Paris desk of Consolidated|International to report
on Junana.com. Moving from the Champs Élysées to cyber-
nowhere sounded like a bad career move. After a week she
realized that Claire was right to put someone in charge of
Junana, and that that someone should be her. After two hours
she had more to report back to Con|Int than she could gather
in a month on the Boulevard Saint Germain. She asked for a
staff of five to keep up with the growing number of scenes.
Claire gave her two, but let her pick them.

The hardest part for Jennifer was getting into Junana.com.
To do so meant revealing aspects of her private life she usually
kept to herself. Once her profile was accepted, she began to
appreciate that Junana had achieved something special. The
bullshit quotient was very low on Junana.

Other social spaces on the Internet had become more and
more populated by corporate interests and borderline
personality types who chose to hide behind a tapestry of
intricate lies. These were people who could never accept what

they would need to reveal about themselves in order to get into Junana.

Jennifer assembled her avatar image using a 3D photo booth at the Gare du Nord. In the first week, her avatar had more intimate conversations with total strangers than she would have in a year at any café in Paris. Of course, this might also have been due to Jennifer's stunning appearance.

At the university, her physical beauty was much more of a burden than a blessing. People assumed she was sleeping with her advisors, most of whom had the same idea. She even tried inventing a husband out of town, returning from summer break with a wedding ring she bought in Venice. But that only seemed to increase the efforts of department faculty, who were invariably more engorged than engaged when around her.

On Junana, Jennifer had actually blurred her avatar's face slightly, as though it had been poorly scanned. Old friends she met advised her to get rescanned. Rather, she enjoyed becoming more or less commonplace in her appearance, and felt emboldened to approach the strangers she met. She had dressed in a baggy hooded sweatshirt and loose jeans for the scan, and could have been ten years older or younger by the result. Jennifer was one of the few "reverse Pradabees" on the planet, who found comfort in being able to walk into a scene without creating one.

While Junana grew at a fantastic pace, it also spun its own cultural capital. Internet cafes from Hue and Djibouti City became doorways for locals to enter a global cafe on Junana, and windows for the cosmopolitans to converse with this global digital diaspora. The simultaneous language translations made possible conversations between Parisian scene kids and Bantu teenagers in Bulawayo. Users gathered friends, shared confidences and music, created places from the spaces afforded by the software, and brought with them the local scenes of a thousand towns and cities. Jennifer had no idea where this technology was headed, but she was certain the destination would be significant.

§   §   §

Game Release + Seven Months

Cindy stood with her hands on her hips.

"Way to go, Cowboy! By now, you've learned to do the brainwave exercises, so you won't need Wanda and Jorge anymore. Wanda asked me if you would like that kiss?"

"Who? What?"

"Wanda. She wants to kiss you."

The screen changed to just Cindy in the foreground in a room with low light. From the shadows behind her a figure appeared, and what a figure. It was Wanda, still wearing only the bottom of her bikini. Her hair cascaded over her shoulders and snaked down beside her breasts. Her eyes and her smile hit him like a spotlight. She walked right up beside Cindy.

"Is that him?" she asked.

"Pretty cute, eh?" Cindy said. "Nicky, meet Wanda."

"Hi, Nick! This is for you." She closed her eyes and leaned forward into a luxuriant puckering kiss. Nick unconsciously puckered his own lips.

"Tchau, Nick!" Wanda straightened out and waved both her hands. "Don't forget to do the exercises every day. And mind Cindy!" She turned and sauntered back into the shadows.

"Just in case you were wondering, Wanda has kissed more than fifty thousand players today," Cindy said.

"How many have you guided today?" He snapped.

"Only you, Nick. I'm here for you alone." She frowned. "I thought you knew that."

"Oh." Nick slumped in his chair.

"I see you need some time to work this out. Why don't you log off and go down to Butterfly Beach. There's a four foot swell this afternoon."

"Hmmm?" He looked back at her, lost in the intersections between this digital image and the conversation they were having.

"Bye, Nick. I'll catch you later. I'll be waiting for you. We've got hours and hours to go to get through this level. So go find some exercise, some dinner, and some sleep tonight; and come back tomorrow when you're ready to rock!" She winked at him, and then the program quit.

"Woa!" Nick stared at his desktop and then, as if half asleep, put on his board shorts and headed out the door.

§   §   §

"You convinced?" Winston's voice said on the speakerphone three days later. "It's not there, I mean. There's only a hint of what this can do. But still, I can't stop playing...."

"I just spent three days reviewing everything I learned at college," Jack said, "Remarkable!"

"So we're on track?" Winston said.

"We don't know where we're going..." Itchy said,

"...but we're on our way," Scratchy concluded.

"Well, we're going to need help," Desi noted. "I know the templates are efficient, but the three of us will also be managing this circus. We've been taking turns on Admin for Junana, and it's too much. I mean, really!"

"And we gotta eat, too," Scratchy said. "I've lost ten pounds." He patted his belly, bulging under a green hemp t-shirt.

"We could tap into the talent pool in Bangalore," Desi said, "But I wouldn't count on secrecy."

Jack leaned back, suppressing a smile.

Desi stood and came around behind him. Leaning down, he began to massage Jack's shoulders. "I'm betting our problem's been solved already," he announced.

They all turned to Jack, who seemed to be enjoying Desi's ministrations.

"There's this abandoned village between Hoi An and Danang," Jack started. "About two hundred hectares along the Thu Bon River, it was flattened by an enormous artillery barrage in the war. The Americans said it housed a Vietcong company. Three years ago, Red Star Coffee purchased a ninety-nine-year lease on the land, and renamed it Sao Do. We already constructed a facility for five hundred workers and their families and support staff. Complete housing, a school for the kids, soccer fields, a movie house, restaurants, organic gardens, all fully contained."

"What's the programmer pool look like in Vietnam?" Winston asked.

"We'll offer a ten year package that few Vietnamese companies would match. That will give us the cream of the crop."

"But can they type?" Scratchy asked the question he always used whenever he was presented with a ten-page resume that sounded far too good to be true. Three years, he thought. That was well before their Hoi An Nerdfest. Winston was right, no slack about the Jack.

"They will be among the best and brightest, the hungriest of a very ambitious nation," Jack replied.

Winston said, "Do they have the infrastructure we need?"

"We have only an OC-12 bandwidth uplink through a satellite," Jack said. "Anything more would be suspicious. So we can't serve any content from Sao Do."

"We can serve content from anywhere," Scratchy noted. "How do we supervise this operation?"

"I was hoping that Desikacharya could take charge in Hoi An."

"I don't mind," Desi said. "Like I said, Bangalore is just one enormous geek reality show. And the waiters in Hoi An. Oh, my God!"

§   §   §

Game Release + Eight Months

After Bobby allowed her to kiss Jorge he sulked for a whole week. She would ask him what was bothering him and all he said was, "You know," and then gallop away on Shadow.

"I know what?" By now she was riding Marmalade on her own, her avatar's balance and the horse's movement sensitive to her every keystroke. She pushed the horse faster and pulled up beside him.

"This is stupid," she yelled, "Everybody kisses Jorge. It means nothing."

He reigned in Shadow and they slowed to a walk along a cliff top, with a wild sea crashing onto the rocks below. "I am only your Guide. Soon you will earn your shoes, but I must remain barefoot. At some point you will go on without me."

"You're a very good Guide. You got me through Level One. Now we are deep into Level Two. You said I'm making real progress. And I would never leave you. Never!"

"But would you ever want to kiss me?"

"If you were here in my room, I'd do more than that, I'm afraid," she blurted and then giggled.

"Have you read Jane Austen?" he said.

"Reading is not my strongest talent," she said.

"It will be soon," he offered. "I can show you how to read *Sense and Sensibility* in 30 minutes."

"Only if you give me one of your really big smiles." And he did.

§   §   §

Franklin Benjamin sat in his Tyson's Corner high-rise office and looked over the Virginia sprawl to the District, where the Washington Monument was bathed in sunlight. He set down the phone, pushed back the lunch tray, and sipped his fifth cup of coffee. His latest client, another loon on the loose inside the beltway, had just agreed to a major increase in the billing.

Franklin had left his sub-cabinet level appointment in the Department of Education to pursue more lucrative options. Not quite State or Defense, but still good enough for a seat on the gravy train. Still, his clients were restless. They had little idea how government actually worked and had filled this intellectual void with the most outrageous fantasies, only a few of which Franklin could not deliver to them, given enough cash.

One of his former clients started a company packaging weather information from government satellites. To his horror, the fellow had discovered his was not the first organization in the world to do this. He wanted Franklin to get Congress to abolish the National Weather Service.

"You don't like the Weather Service?"

"They give information out for free. How on earth am I supposed to compete with that?"

"But taxpayers paid for the satellites and the data archives. They might figure they should get something back."

"Yeah, well they've been wrong before."

Franklin then explained that the National Weather Service served an enormous public good, had done so for decades, and was among the best value-added services provided by the federal government. The client took in this information, thought for a minute, and then tripled his contract.

Franklin found a senator who needed immediate campaign -finance help and talked him into endorsing this idea. Clearly, this was another example of "big government" holding back the marketplace. Besides, anyone who wasn't willing to pay to know where the next storm would strike could just as well crawl up in their attic with an axe and wait for it.

The senator's amendment abolishing the National Weather Service was narrowly defeated and then only because another senator, working with a different lobbyist, had attached a separate amendment, a little bill that would have made coastal whale hunting both legal and, under certain circumstances, fully subsidized. Despite the avalanche of protests from a wide range of environmental groups, Democrats, and foreign governments, the bill actually got though its subcommittee.

President Stone was on record as "looking forward to kicking some whale tail," the next time he was on the coast.

Senators from landlocked states objected to the notion of subsidies and shot down the whale amendment and with it all the other amendments to the bill, which died in a conference committee. Franklin told his client to wait another year, but the jerk's investors had already pulled their backing.

Franklin's new client wanted the government to shut down Junana.com, a social networking Internet site. Shut it down immediately, he demanded.

"We don't know who they are. They could be anyone. Terrorists. Liberals, for chrissake!"

"Let me look into it," Franklin promised.

Franklin's research was remarkably unproductive. But then, Junana.com was owned and managed by a private offshore company, and so it made no annual or quarterly reports. They leased space on server farms across the planet and hired workers, mostly for customer service, in several countries. They paid their taxes and followed all the rules for Internet commerce. Still, they did not allow advertising and had no apparent means of generating income.

The Street did not find this odd and considered it a gambit to build the customer base and name value. And with the enormous interest in the service, the mavens approved entirely. Everyone was waiting for an IPO or some offer to sell.

Franklin signed himself up for a Junana.com account. He gave himself the name "Buddy Duncan" and pretty much lied about everything else. He was required to give a real email to verify, and when the page refreshed he was confronted with the following message.

        "Dear 'Buddy':

Or, shall we say, 'Franklin.' While we
understand you might have personal
reasons to disguise who you are, we do
request that you leave these reasons in
your desk and do not bring them to
Junana.com. Junana.com is a social
service based on mutual trust and civil
behavior. You can a) correct the
information you provided; b) decide you
are not really ready to join Junana.com;
or, c) press the button below to allow
Junana.com to help you remember just who
you are.
Thank you,
Junana.com"

"Wow!" Franklin exclaimed, and pushed the button.

The form he had just filled out appeared again, only this time it showed his real name and home and office addresses, and also his real age, height, hair and eye color, marital status, educational and residential background, even his book, music, and movie preferences.

He scrolled down the page. There were a dozen photographs of him, including close-ups from several group shots. How did they know about Emerson, Lake, and Palmer? Who were these people? All this information from a simple email address. He knew it was theoretically possible, but he thought nobody but the NSA had done it. What if Junana.com was the NSA? How better to gather information than to just ask a billion people to voluntarily submit this, just so they can chat with their friends?

He filled in the password field and pushed the "Submit" button. Immediately he got an email to verify his information,

which he did. He logged in and clicked around for a while
before he took a phone call and spent the rest of the afternoon
babysitting the chief of staff of a congressman from Alabama.
He was firing off an email when he heard a tune playing in the
background. It was Emerson, Lake & Palmer, some live version
of Karn Evil 9 he had never heard before.

A chat box appeared, and he remembered he was still
logged into Junana.com. "I thought you might like this," it said.
Underneath was a photo of a fifty-something woman, a name,
Elsa Urlich, and a city, Buenos Aires. He right-clicked on the
MP3 file and it asked him if he wanted to save it to his
collection, so he did that. He thanked Elsa on the chat box,
clicked on her name, scanned her bio, discovered that she had
lived in Atlanta the same years he had, and then logged off. He
sat back and looked out the window, over to the District. The
sun was just setting. Junana.com had impressed him
enormously. He'd never found an Internet service that
integrated information, communication, and convenience so
effortlessly.

He then returned to his research. Junana.com did not
publish its user statistics, but the rumors were huge. He had to
admit that knowing he could verify Elsa's life story was
profoundly stimulating.

He logged in again and the user interface asked if he
wanted to continue on the same path as the last visit. He
pushed "yes" and got Elsa's page. He noticed that her biography
was much longer than his, and filled with information about
her tastes and dreams, about what she was looking for and
offering to a relationship.

Looking at Elsa's profile he liked what he saw. He opened
the chat to her and told her how much he enjoyed the
Emerson, Lake, and Palmer song. She responded, "Thanks.
Who are you?"

He typed. "Can't you see my profile?"

She typed. "That's just the form they give you to join. Who are you?"

He typed. "I just joined today. Give me time."

She typed. "I'll check back tomorrow. Have a good evening."

He typed. "You too," and ended the chat.

He looked at his bio. Most of the form was blank. The questions were embarrassing to even read. How was he to fill any of these out?

Three hours and four Crown Royals later he had cobbled together a selection of interests and accomplishments that showcased his strengths, revealing several sensitivities and a couple minor faults. His love for dogs, for example, was balanced by a passion for fast cars. He characterized himself as "slow to anger" but also "quick with a smile." He was looking for a partner who could "enjoy simple pleasures," a walk on the beach, pushing a child on a swing, crap like that. His politics were "moderate" but he confessed a penchant for "personal liberty." He figured the overall effect would attract someone who could service his needs without making too many wild demands.

He was working on refining the tone of his prior accomplishments when the whole form was suddenly framed in red and the words "SINCERITY ALERT" appeared at the top. A pop-up window displayed the following text:

"Junana.com has been monitoring this page, and comparing its contents with known information about the user and studies of other users who have attempted to mislead by faking their own biographies. For information on how to

correct this matter please press the
button below."

"Fuck me," he whispered and set down his drink. He
moused over and pushed the button. Another memo appeared
on a pop-up window:

"Dear Franklin,
Or shall we call you 'Frank,' which you
generally prefer? Although we realize
that honesty may not be your strongest
suit, and while we might appreciate the
scope of your imagination, the
information you have provided is so
completely full of shit that we cannot
allow this to be posted without some
warning for the general public. It is
widely known, for example, that your
politics are emphatically 'immoderate'.
     Several persons from your past were
invited to suggest key attributes of your
personality when you signed up recently.
The most charitable of these suggestions
were "soul-sucking narcissist" and "self-
serving ball-licker." Neither of these
qualities appears in the form that you
filled out.
     While you might have made your share
of mistakes in the past that you now feel
do not represent your current outlook,
your friends signaled that you are
incapable of either self reflection or

intimacy of any sort. This suggests that
the very task of filling out the form
might be extremely difficult or even
frightening to you.

Frank, you are not alone. Millions of
Junana.com users have struggled with the
same problem. At this moment, globally,
approximately forty-two million pages
remain in Sincerity Alert status. And in
your region, almost twenty-five percent
of users find themselves in this
situation. Frank, if it's any comfort,
you are surrounded by assholes just like
yourself.

Junana.com has placed this page on a
Sincerity Alert. This means that a random
selection of people from your past will
be tasked to approve the contents of your
bio form. Alternatively, you can push the
button below and select three individuals
that you would trust to do this service.

Sincerely,

Junana.com"

"Excellent." Franklin pushed the button and a page appeared. It
was formatted like a search result with the names of people in
bold, photos on the right, and some lines of text below each
name described their connection to Frank. There was a menu
on top that allowed the names to be resorted by date, place, or
level of intimacy. Another choice allowed a filter to open up
the range of personal contacts, and a search box was provided.
Next to each name was a check box. All he had to do was pick
three of his buddies to back him up.

The default sort was temporal, latest first. He scrolled
through a broad selection of people he worked around, lived
near, golfed with, or who provided services he used. As he
scrolled down, it was like running his life in reverse, back
through the "Stone Age" as the liberal press called the current
administration, to his work as a senior staff member for the
junior senator from Virginia, his stint at the Independence
Center think tank, the years in Atlanta shilling for that
congressman, and his time as a student at Georgetown. His
wife showed up together with her witches' coven of friends. But
where were Walt Egan, Bernie Simpson, or Sam Reynolds?
Freddy Owen, Luke Broadhurst, and the gang from the local
Republicans for Fairness crowd?

All the names on the list and photographs were vaguely
familiar to him, some even painfully familiar. It seemed that
every woman he had taken out in the last ten years was on the
list. No wonder he was getting the shaft.

He didn't see anybody he could rely upon to cover for him.
He counted nineteen people he had fired, six he had out-
positioned for promotion, and maybe a dozen he knew for a
fact hated his guts. This was not going to be easy. He began to
consider that his client was right, that this was some liberal
conspiracy. But then he searched for "conservative" and pulled
up twenty-five people who were far more to the right than he
ever was. This included Tim Crane, who ran the Independence
Center.

He clicked on Tim's photograph and Tim's home page
popped up. Looking at the biography, he remembered how
much he admired and despised the man. Tim talked with
Frank only once, and Frank had been careful not to rock the
boat. But after that, Tim never acknowledged that Frank even
existed, although Frank took many occasions to bring up this

conversation with Tim when he was around other Republicans for Fairness.

Rereading the bio, Frank learned that Tim was an avid birdwatcher and something of a home-improvement nerd. Tim taught soccer in the youth league and missed his father. He longed for respect as an intellectual, loved being a grandfather, and felt that his work was mostly misunderstood.

"What a dork!" Frank spoke to his laptop. But then Tim was there on Junana.com and Frank still needed three people to back up his claims. After an hour, he had found only one person, his mailman, who might not fuck him over. He had considered the idea of giving the mailman a Christmas tip, and he vowed that next year there'd be a five-dollar bill and a card. But he needed two more names and nothing was happening. He wondered if the mailman had a lot of friends.

He had finished most of the bottle of Crown Royal. When he looked out the window, the darkness was filigreed by the lights of the District. His anger began to boil with his hunger. He had skipped dinner to put this bio-form together and now all his efforts mocked him. In a rage he erased all of his entries.

He shut down his computer and stood next to the window. A shadow of humiliation darkened his face in his reflection off the glass. Well-meaning jerks like Tim Crane could afford to be honest only because people like him did all the heavy lifting in the trenches. He had only done what anyone would do in his position.

Who gave Junana.com the right to sit in judgment over his life? Who were these guys? He made a promise to himself to do whatever it took to bring down this so-called service, uncover the pricks who ran it, and make them wish they'd never seen a computer.

SEVEN

Scratchy felt more like a composer or a novelist than a programmer these days. Months before, he had updated an open-source integrated development environment to handle the templates. He called this IDE "Total Eclipse" or TE. He showed this to Desi, who disappeared from the world for a week and came back with a UML 5.0 type specification for all the templates, so that entire feature structures could be visually modeled.

Winston had set up a shell company, WeRus NV, in Belgium, that hired Scratchy as a technical lead on Junana administration with an expense account for staff, R&D, and equipment. WeRus NV also had a contract with the Sao Do Group in Vietnam. Scratchy would scope out the various features that needed to be built into the Junana client or server and then map these into their initial states and output parameters. He would send these to his programmer teams in Sao Do.

Scratchy built the test harnesses himself and ran all the automated tests on the XServe array computer at the WeRus facility in Goleta. He had a hardware and OS simulator that could run the client virtually on chips as old as the first Intel dual core CPUs and on Windows XP or OSX Panther. Each day, Scratchy would get code back from Sao Do and plug this into his own test harness, test the whole code stack overnight, and then send out new feature specifications. He was building in a few additional features, such as network hacks that would create no end of excitement in enterprise installations.

Nobody knew network protocols, communications, and security better than Scratchy. His life and his fortune had been spent and earned in this arena. So he made a communications link between the client and the mesh that would simply bypass any currently existing firewall, opening up a port that the computer didn't even know it had. He built in native SCTP-2 protocol support and tuned the entire system to optimize through the global Ariadne backbone. He also made the program self-installing on any network. Once downloaded to any one computer on a LAN, the client would install and run on all the computers on the LAN. He imagined the fun they were going to have at the Pentagon.

§   §   §

Game Release + Eight Months

Nick watched the screen saver morph through a montage of outstanding rollers. He was doing the brainwave thing, opening up the doorway to his memory. He held a vision of Wanda smiling at him, and then of Cindy, who would be waiting for him in her robes. Cindy was the clever one, always ahead of the pack, sidestepping the spears that were aimed at Nick's heart. This level wasn't any easier than the last one, even without the slime monsters and the fairyland pixies. All that, he realized, was just the candy they used so he would stay interested until it was too late to go back. Too late, that is, to actually want to go back. Wanting was something completely new for him, wanting in this "gotta know everything now" way.

Nick could not decide if he was disenchanted with his life
or enchanted with the Game, which, he figured, was his life,
since he spent pretty much every waking minute in it. Last
week, his mom got upset with him on the computer all the
time. She thought he was watching porn and made him keep
his door open. She was working two jobs and not around
much. So he could have been up to his pubes in porn most of
the day, door open or shut. Maybe the Game was some kind
of mental porn. He'd have to mention that to Cindy.

Cindy would give him a surf report or mention that a
friend of his was down at the Red Star Coffee Shop. She
would shut down the computer if he tried to skip school to
play. But he had almost earned his shoes, and he didn't want
to go out until he could wear them around.

Last week he saw Jackie Kim wearing the shoes down on
State Street. They never talked at school, not for years. She
was this straight arrow, straight 'A,' college preppy Asian girl.
He was slack, riding his deck, strictly back of the classroom.
She was surprised when he told her he was Gaming. She
thought her Guide was the shit, but she'd never met Cindy.
Now he and Jackie are friends on Junana. She turned sixteen
in July and tested out, so she won't be back at Santa Barbara
High. He has to wait for the spring, which means almost a
whole year of classes before he can take the test. What an
absolute ass-waste of time.

Jackie would taking courses at City College in the fall
because her parents told her to. She said she would be
applying to Harvard, "just like every other Korean in
California." She told him Level Three was a full-blown biotch.
In her new picture on Junana she wears a Yanagi U hoodie and

looks so very serious he told her she should snag some laughs. Not that Level Two was cutting him any kind of slack.

§   §   §

"I found a chief sys-admin, hired him as a CIO for one of these dummy companies Winston set up. I explained that we had a contract with the owners of Junana.com," Scratchy announced to the teleconference. "He's got a long resume and he can type. His name is Donald Driscoll. He started at Bell Labs in the early '80s and did a decade in Sunnyvale before the company got flushed by the dot-com bust. He was CIO for a Cal State campus up north. I relocated him here in Goleta, near where I've set up an office. I'm paying too much for him to get real curious, and he can hire assistants for the other shifts."

"Now I can get some sleep." Desi had been filling in on network duty.

"Adding new technical people is a dangerous move," Jack said.

"Choose the wrong guy, and things can go sideways," Winston reminded them. "It's like playing the wrong ball."

"Or listening to the wrong caddy," Itchy said.

"Or hitting the wrong green," Scratchy added.

"Or picking the wrong club," Desi noted.

"Enough!" Winston said.

"You started it, Ricky," Desi said. "We've warned you about that." They refused to let Winston get away with golfing metaphors.

Winston Logan Fairchild grew up playing Spring Hill with his uncles, cousins, and assorted well-heeled strangers. The Philadelphia Country Club was the only place his mother would let him be on his own. The chauffeur would drop him off after school or early on the weekends, and he would malinger as long as possible. On numerous occasions, his mother would call to say he should take dinner there.

For years, golf was better to him (and for him) than all of his nannies, many of his girl friends, and either of his parents. The country club was his playground. After all, his prep school never had soon-to-be-divorced ex-debutantes looped on gimlets and Valium, looking for someone to get frisky with in the backseat of a Bentley. And the golf was a personal challenge, something he got very good at early on, before he know how clever he was at other things. Golf was something he would never be as good at as he wanted to be.

§   §   §

"Let me suggest something," Jack said. "Each of us will need to add top staff as we move forward. None of these staff members should be aware that the five of us are working together. I will also suggest that the five of us no longer meet at all, except in a private room on Junana.com."

"Goodbye Nerdfests." Scratchy lamented.

"A private room?" Winston asked.

"Jack asked me to put one together," Itchy answered. "It's accessible from the central plazas, but only to us. Here's how it works. I assumed none of us would visit a goth scene by choice..."

"The goth scenes," Desi said. "Have you been? Each of of them in twenty-three shades of gray. Oh, my God, it's so depressing."

"Since none of us wants to hang in any of the thousand or so goth scenes, whenever any of us steps into a goth scene transporter anywhere," Itchy continued, "we will be diverted to the Room. At the same time, a copy of our avatar will actually arrive at a scene and lurk around looking bored and depressed for several minutes before appearing to log out."

"Thereby simulating actual scene behavior," Winston noted.

"This way," Jack said, "we will coordinate our efforts without ever meeting in person."

"Look behind you before you step into the transporter. If there's someone there, let them go ahead and wait a minute before stepping in. I cannot turn off the repeat function," Itchy reminded them.

Gamers normally used menus to get to the scene of their choice. Scratchy insisted that simulating transport in the plazas helped maintain verisimilitude.

"Motion is the central metaphor of modernity," he noted.

Transporters randomly distribute individuals to balance crowding in any one scene. They are programmed to stay active to the same scene as long as a group of avatars keep entering. It is not unusual to see several avatars striding into the light column in rapid succession, like Beatles crossing Abbey Road. Anyone who stopped the flow for more than the latency period of the transporter would end up in a different show—along with all those behind her—and new title: "slackass," as in "that slackass biotch sent us to this lame show."

The transporters looked like columns of pale silver light shining up from the pavement. The light column also called out its destination, which Desi's language software translated into all the languages of the avatars in the vicinity. A floating brass railing one meter from the pavement kept people from accidentally stumbling into the transporter from the back. On one side of the column the railing opened up to a gate, and when you stepped into the light you would find yourself at your destination.

"The Room has no label on any menu. This is the only way we can get there," Itchy said.

As one of Jack's security measures, the five of them were the only Junana users with totally made up names, profiles, and avatars. Desi's latest avatar looked a lot like Jude Law. Jack's sounded like Walter Winchell, but looked more like Hoagy Carmichael. Winston's used a modified Ben Hogan photo with a retro haircut, broad cream-colored pants and a checked sweater. Itchy went Western: a working cowboy attire and a Texas accent. Scratchy holographed a face out of a book of Sing Sing death row inmates from the '50s, and dressed an average weight/height/age body in jeans and a white t-shirt. He made its voice sound like Leonard Cohen's.

"Why are we being so careful?" Itchy asked. "We're not doing anything illegal."

"We're planning to do something interesting. And, like comedy, that's a whole lot more dangerous than just illegal," Scratchy said.

"One of the unintended consequences of capitalism is that it produces a population optimized for consumption," Jack started.

"Stupid enough to buy all that crap," Scratchy cut in.

"More than that," Winston said. "Dependent on service industries and expert systems for almost everything but respiration."

"I think Ronco is working on that now," Itchy said, "'The remarkable Breath-o-matic.'"

"Addicted to fashion as a primary defense mechanism for their egos," Jack continued.

"All symptoms of late stage 'affluenza,'" noted Scratchy. "A goddam epidemic.'"

"And we are looking to take this population and move it years ahead of the companies that now supply its every need," Jack concluded.

"We are going to push the public past the publicity," Winston said. "People are going to be thinking for themselves for once."

"Well..." Desi started. The line went quiet as they waited. "I mean..." He hesitated.

"We're all friends here," Winston said.

"The thing is, I actually really like capitalism. Fashion, restaurants, I guess pretty much everything. I mean, now that we are, I mean, each of us is..."

"...filthy rich?" Scratchy suggested.

"We go around destroying capitalism..." Desi said.

"Who said we were destroying anything? We are simply going to make capitalism sing for its supper," Jack said.

"We are going to make it stand up and bark," Itchy added.

"And turn over a new leaf," Winston added.

"You mean we're just helping capitalism live up to its promise?" Desi never subscribed to the idea that capitalism was just another form of colonialism.

"That's a fact," Scratchy said.

"And save the world in the process," noted Winston.

"And impoverish most of the parasites that currently run the show," added Itchy.

"That's a bonus," Jack said, before Scratchy could.

§   §   §

Game Release + Ten Months

Nick double-clicked the Junana Game application. Cindy, in her robes, appeared in a room that looked nothing like the

Game space where he'd left her. In fact it looked quite a bit
like a classroom at Santa Barbara High. She was standing in
front of a desk, and behind her was a blackboard with a lot of
writing on it. He'd been counting the days to the end of
summer. It was like she was reading his mind. He wondered if
that were possible.

"Hello, cowboy," Cindy said.

"Hi, Cindy," he said. "You going back to school?"

"We are going back to school," she replied. "You have
about four weeks left of summer, and then you're going to be
sitting in rooms just like this for several hours a day."

"Fucking kind of you to bring that up," he said.

"That's exactly the attitude we don't want to see," Cindy
said. "Besides..." Her robes morphed into a tight white cotton
button-down shirt, maybe two sizes too small, or maybe she
was a couple sizes too big, and an equally tight black skirt,
showing long legs in sheer stockings. A pair of black-rimmed
glasses solidified on her nose and she blinked once
dramatically. "...You and I are going to make this time a fun
time."

"Woah!" He sat up.

"And if you don't behave..." she growled. Her right hand
now held a black wand, like an orchestra conductor. She
raised this and snapped it forward. There was a loud 'click' as
though it had actually struck the inside surface of the LCD
screen. Nick jerked back instinctively. "...Cindy will be very
angry with you."

"Can I count on that?"

"Have your fun, cowboy, while you can. But you will do
your homework. Besides, you make Cindy happy and..."

"And?"

"See this button?" She used the wand to point to the top button of her shirt.

"Umhmmm."

"When Cindy is happy, this button might just... pop." She raised one eyebrow.

"Newton's best law." He tried to sound cool but he was breathing rapidly.

"Let's get started." She sat back on the edge of the desk. "Do you remember your homework for the summer?"

"Nobody does the summer homework."

"Let's try this again. Do you remember your summer homework? Or would you rather I take your avatar and stick this pointer where no pointer has gone before?" She walked around the desk to the blackboard. The screen followed her movements.

"Read this for me." She pointed to the top line on the board.

"*The Great Gatsby*, by F. Scott Fitzgerald," he said.

"Since I know what you've been doing this summer, I'm pretty sure you haven't read anything longer than *The Boondocks*."

"To be honest, I don't, you know..." Nick hesitated.

"...read. That's obvious, except you do read. You read dozens of chats and emails every day. So reading a book is not out of the question."

"Why not just watch the movie or Query it?"

"That's about like you asking yourself 'why don't I rub my nose to beat off'. It's because watching a movie not the same thing as reading the book. OK?"

"Now, who's got the attitude." He slouched back in his chair.

"Sorry, Nicky." Cindy went back to the desk and sat behind it. "I know that reading seems one-dimensional after doing the Queries. So I'm going to teach you how to read really fast, so you can read *The Great Gatsby* in, say, twenty minutes."

"That works." He sat up.

Nick watched as Cindy went through another set of exercises, this one strictly with the eyes. These, she told him, are advanced techniques that rely on the fact that you've already opened up the door to your memory.

"Maybe Wanda should be teaching me these." He teased.

"Wanda's busy. So am I. Pay attention now, Cindy knows what you need."

And she did.

The Prank

EIGHT

Robby Robinson, Ph.D., took a tenfold pay increase to move to Kyoto in order to partner with Ichiro Nomura on an Internet-based immersive education effort. Robby had spent the previous four years in Sao Paulo, Brazil. He was working through a multinational educational NGO with connections across South America to implement "liberation education" practices for the urban poor.

Liberation education had been created against the dominant mode of education, where the teacher was the source of all knowledge and the student merely an empty vessal to be filled over the course of years. Liberation was all about context and learning moments. Teaching liberation education paid like shit, but something in it spoke to Robby, something there that demanded exploration. Winston's email had mentioned a salary well beyond what Robby could ignore. Going to Kyoto was just the type of lifestyle change he had recently begun to fantasize in his modest (and that was a charitable adjective) Sao Paulo studio apartment.

The Greek holding company Winston set up to hire Ichiro as their technical lead on the Junana design project had leased an entire building in Kyoto on Karasuma Dori, just north of Doshisha University, and across the street from a large construction zone where a new dormitory was going up. On the ground floor Ichiro oversaw the construction of a massive parallel XServe computer system. Their offices were under construction on the floor above that.

While the offices were being finished, Robby and Ichiro engaged in long conversations at the Red Star Coffee shop near Demachiyanagi or over at Fiasco, a gaijin-run Italian restaurant on Kamidachiuri. Ichiro brought Robby up to speed on the templates, while Robby gave Ichiro a crash course in the Pedagogy of the Oppressed.

At first they talked right past each other; the formalism of Ichiro's templates and the exuberance of Robby's pedagogy seemed entirely orthogonal with no mutual purchase point. Ichiro's background in physics, cyberinformatics, and video game design had him looking for problems to solve, while Robby's training in psychology and critical sociology kept him searching for ambiguities and power relationships. Still, they developed an appreciation for one other's talent. Robby found in Ichiro another keen intellect, and underneath that, a person with a galloping curiosity and a capacity for self-reflection.

Ichiro enjoyed Robby's enthusiasm for the science of pedagogy and his desire to use his academic training to transform the academy. Robby was also a true nerd, completely unselfconscious. He wore the same type of madras-print shirt and chino pants every day. His energy put his hands in constant movement, and he would absentmindedly brush others in the close confines of the kissaten or simply knock his own glasses off his face.

§   §　 §

Game Release + Five Months

Essie cranked her Computo furiously. She had forgotten not to let the power drain below five percent and her Guide had to interrupt her Free-for-All time to prompt her.

"Whatcha doin', girl?" Annaline scolded her. "Is your arm broken?"

Annaline spoke with a lilting Oshikwanyama accent. At first, Essie was convinced Annaline must be from Endola.

"I'm not from anywhere, silly," she had told Essie. "I am just a basket of pieces of light here in your Computo."

Essie was already late for her job cleaning rooms at the Oasis Lodge on the river. She would carry her beloved Computo under her skirts all day, never, ever letting it out of her sight.

"Be still, Annaline, I've almost finished." She had been exploring a problem in desert hydrology, a topic of everyday import to her people, but not one that a 16 year-old girl in her village normally encountered. Already there was talk in the village about Essie. There is always talk in the village.

"You are late again," Annaline said. "Are you working on West African Internal Time, or what? Paife, paife, paife! You must run, or they will beat you or worse."

Annaline somehow knew exactly where Essie was, a part of the magic of the Computo she did not yet understand, but she was beginning to. Her village had no electricity, no phone service. How did the Computo work?

"Way up in the sky there is a machine that moves across the heavens. The Computo talks to this," Annaline explained. Perhaps the machine can look down and see her. She waited for the rains to come and the clouds to hide her from this machine. Still it found her. She did not understand.

She turned off the Computo and slipped it into the sleeve she had sewed in front of her petticoat. Then she ran from her hut, across the open land, hard packed and cracked from

drought, to the river, where they had built the fishing camp
and the airstrip.

§   §   §

In weeks, Robby had picked up a fair amount of Japanese.
Every time he accidentally struck someone, he would offer a
humble apology while looking around at them. When they
turned to see who had smacked them, their eyes met the green
eyes of a crimson-haired gaijin, mumbling in formal Japanese.
This usually startled them more than the accidental slap.

As Ichiro listened to Robby explain the pedagogy, it was as
if the corpse of socialism, like so many before, had beached
itself on the shores of education theory. He was wary of the
litany of an oppressed proletariat forced to swallow whole
lumps of bourgeois knowledge, which, like the whale meat on
the food floor of Takashimaya, carried more political
significance than flavor.

Ichiro considered it entirely reasonable that states had zero
interest in training the population to rebel. These were, after
all, grossly paranoid and paternalist systems. Who could blame
them if they removed the dynamite sticks from their offspring's
chubby fists? That did not excuse the fact that modern
democracies had long mistaken quietude for peace, and relied
heavily on soporific practices—sporting events, popular music,
reality TV—to keep the public distracted. At the same time,
states used a slow drumbeat of potential terror and urban fear
to justify their existence. Holding at "Condition Orange"
seemed about right: dangerous enough for no-bid contracts in
the war zones but safe enough for people to drive to work.

Ichiro argued that there was a lot of money, time, and effort
put into getting an ever-larger cohort of the population into

college, where, if Reed College were any indication, the language of rebellion was a freshman requirement. The real problem, he insisted, was a lack of a target for any revolutionary impulse since the collapse of socialism. Anyhow, as Jack had noted, the main enemy was fundamentalism, religious or political. But fundamentalism, like democracy, came in a wide range of styles and impacts.

You could argue that the world needed more openness than what representative democracy could provide, particularly under late capitalism. The only real arena now was the marketplace, where Alcoa and al Qaeda shared a common dream—a world where relationships between people and groups were under the stable control of some traditional cadre of leaders. Democracy was a convenient fiction to reproduce the legitimacy of these leaders. Every student at Reed went through this conversation at least once in their dorms their first year.

Robby countered that most of the population did not and could not learn the language of rebellion because they had been subjected to an educational system that sucked away their curiosity and dulled their ability to recognize the meanings behind the advertisements. He gestured at the room around them, this time knocking the glasses from the face of an elderly man in a three-piece suit. After the apologies, he continued.

"You were shoved into the Monbusho education system here," Robby said, "And your first impulse was to get the hell out. But how many others followed you? How many really could? You, my friend, are a prime example of the exception proving the rule."

And so for weeks they argued and fought like college roomies from different planets. Every conversation brought out as many seemingly irreconcilable conclusions as points of agreement. They explored the bleeding edge of pedagogy:

constructionism, learning moments, and affective learning techniques. Ichiro introduced Robby to Yanagi Yuu, and the baths were a nightly event. Nothing like sitting naked in piping hot water to take the edge off an argument. Cooling down in the dressing room they often discovered an increment of understanding that would push them towards a new argument the following day.

Ichiro had rented Robby a small nineteenth-century machiya townhouse near the public bath. The residence of an Asian scholar from Paris, who was, this year, on sabbatical at the University of Chicago, it was bitterly cold as the winter wind whistled through the shoji. A small kerosene space heater kept the main room livable. Robby seemed to appreciate the tatami and the tokonoma: the classical layout of the merchant house. After their bath they would often repair to the horikotatsu in Robby's house and drink Momonoshizuku sake hot. The horikotatsu was a square cut out space in the tatami flooring, where they could dangle their feet near an electric heater.

Ichiro challenged Robby to try unfolding the templates for the liberation education teaching practices, but neither of them had any success at this. Then they were stuck for weeks trying to make a list of stuff every seventeen-year-old should know, but they decided that every seventeen-year-old should make her own list.

They did agree that a fundamental problem was the lack of literacy—not the basic ability to read, but the capacity to critically interrogate what one has read. Words, statistics, graphics, cinematic narratives, interactive games: none of these can be taken as presented.

Itchy would join the weekly teleconference and report their lack of progress. Finally, Scratchy exploded. He told Itchy that the two of them were simply "playing professor" with each other. "One of you has to play teacher and the other student, and then you need to grok the difference," Scratchy said, sending Itchy back to Robby to try yet again.

§   §   §

Game Release + Eleven Months
Over the following weeks, Cindy had Nick do the reading exercises several times a day, scanning some graphics with a bunch of ziggly lines on them and a pointer that moved up and down and left and right. At first he was vocalizing the words that would appear and disappear in different parts of the screen. Then she had him turn up his microphone all the way and not vocalize the words.

The words were replaced by sentences, the sentences by paragraphs, and the paragraphs by pages. Cindy would ask him questions about the pages, and he found it easy to recall the information. They would work on this for an hour and spend the rest of the time doing the Queries, so he would finish the level. After a few weeks Cindy put up a series of pages, maybe a hundred of them and then started asking him questions.

"So what is the author's position on New York City, and what are the differences between the city and the wealthy suburbs? Who is responsible for Gatsby's death? What does the valley of the ashes symbolize?"

Nick answered these questions and Cindy showed him how completely full of shit his answers were. So he used some Free-for-All time she allowed him to query up some info about the history of New York and life in the 1920s Jazz age, modernist literature, class distinctions: wherever the Queries led.

After she was satisfied with his answers, he realized that he had read *The Great Gatsby*. It wasn't so lame after all. They did a week of solid Queries and then he asked Cindy if he could read a little more Fitzgerald to get a better handle on the author. She showed him a map from his house to the Lompoc city library.

"They've got a full collection of Fitzgerald, and you can get out of the house. So piss off." She shut down his computer.

"Fuck!" he hated when she did that.

He grabbed his deck and boarded over to the library, got a card, and found *The Beautiful and the Damned*, *Tender is the Night*, and *All the Sad Young Men*. He read these that Saturday afternoon down at the Red Star Coffee shop while his dad was at home watching the Mariners play the Yankees. After the last story, he dropped the books back at the library, went home for his surfboard, and paddled out into the rolling two-foot swells at Surf Beach. Everything he had just read began to crash back through his consciousness.

As he floated in the swells Nick's eyes picked up whatever came into the range of his vision: a squadron of pelicans drifting south, a HumVee headed for Vandenberg, a trio of junior high girls in their thongs and tops walking across the beach. His mind was racing with a million thoughts about Fitzgerald's world.

He spotted a young beauty doing her slow walk along the waterfront in her custom-fitted bikini. Usually he'd just get wood and enjoy the view, but today his mind glided back into the words he'd read.

Fitzgerald offered so many perceptions of women. Their best trick, he wrote, was to sit down and fold their hands. Like women were just going to wait for a man to do anything. Men, he claimed, are attracted to selfishness in women. Is that really true or just a literary conceit? "Conceit," another word he had learned in the last week, one of thousands. If his brain were a Mac, he'd consider rebooting. The bikinied girl stepped into the water and jumped when a small wave found her thighs. At least, he consoled himself, he still got wood.

"Cindy," he pleaded, later that day, "I'm magno-confused."

She stood barefoot in her sexy teacher outfit and crossed her arms. "That's because you thought the purpose of reading was to give you answers. Good literature provides answers. Great literature leaves only questions. I think you need to slow down, cowboy. No more than one book a day. It's like a Chubby Burger, you don't really want to eat more than one at a time."

"My head feels like it's TASERing itself."

"Hmmm. Perhaps you need a week off."

"After I earn my shoes."

"You're really close, and you finished all your homework. I want you to know you've made Cindy happy."

"It's about fucking time." He perked up.

"Now, now." She waved the wand menacingly. "Is that any way to talk to your teacher?"

"Well?"

"Well, what?"

"How happy are you?"

"You are such a horn doggy."

"And you promised."

"So I did." Cindy put the wand back down on the desk behind her. She put her hands on this and leaned back. Then she stretched forward, and not one, but three of her shirt buttons jettisoned in ultra-slow motion and seemed to ping off the back of LCD screen. Her shirt opened out, revealing a deliciously thin, pink satin bra well stuffed, and, on her tummy a tattoo. It was a tat of his favorite deck, with his name on it.

"Take a good look, cowboy. You won't be seeing these again." She laughed and tousled her hair. Then her shirt and skirt morphed back into the Guide robe.

"Awwww," he groaned. "That's not fair."

"Never claimed to be fair, Charlie. Actually, I'm a lot better than fair."

"Tell me, Cindy, are you selfish?"

"Only every pixel of me," she said.

"I find that very attractive in a woman."

"You forget," She morphed then into a humongous swampy creature with a alien-predator head, gleaming fangs and bright red claws. "I'm no woman."

§   §   §

The next morning found Itchy and Robby walking down Kawaramachi-dori in a chill blustery wind. On the corner of Sanjo, two young women in pink hats and microskirts were passing out advertisements for a new lounge in Gion and risking frostbite on their labia.

"You're a mathematician. Teach me some math today," Itchy said, volunteering to do the student role. "I need to experience how the pedagogy works."

"If you were a farmer, I'd start by asking you about your harvest and then weave mathematical notions around that."

"If I were a farmer, I'd be able to sleep at night."

"What's keeping you up?"

"This damn house project. The plans are ready, the land is ready, the neighbors are ready, but I cannot get the city to work with me."

"You're satisfied with the plans."

"It's going to be the finest new shoin-style house built in Kyoto in fifty years."

They occupied a corner table in a small, Euro-sutaeru kissaten coffee shop south of Shijo with free WiFi and nine-hundred yen lattes. Ichiro explained how a shoin style house was built with no nails. He took out his laptop and called up a Japanese website that diagrammed the various joints and tools used in traditional carpentry: the classical mortise and tenon, butterfly, swallowtail, and scarf joints.

Robby had a finite-element analysis visualization program on his laptop. He imported the computer-aided-design files for the joinery from the same Japanese site. Every time Ichiro finished explaining how a joint worked, Robby would create a set of mathematical problems that explored how the joint solved a particular problem of load bearing or tension. Changing the ratios of tongue and groove invariably weakened the joint. They ate a lunch of omorice and kept on working. When they had exhausted the material from the site, Robby challenged Ichiro to design a completely new joint for a hexagonal ring.

"Let's say you want to make a Bucky dome out of wood and without nails," he suggested, "So you can burn this on the Playa."

Ichiro had to rewrite the finite element statements to adjust for the new angles and plug this into a modified mortis and tenon joint design. Within an hour they had a solution that would support a 24-foot dome made from two-by-two members. Robby ran it through the finite-element software, where they optimized the proportions.

"My brain hurts," Ichiro said. Leaning back in his seat, he stretched and knocked over a latte on the table behind them. Robby shook his head and laughed as Ichiro went into his formal apologies.

"I'll make a gaijin out of you yet," he teased Ichiro. "Let's get some air."

They stumbled out into the darkness of the street and realized an entire day had passed. In silence they strode across the Shijo Bridge towards the Kabukiza, and they turned north through the bar-quarter of Gion to a small Korean restaurant near the Shirakawa.

Over beer, kimchi-buta-ramen, and yakiniku, they began to deconstruct the lessons of their session. Ichiro noted that his appreciation for the artistry of the carpentry was now buttressed by a mathematical understanding of its utility.

"I learned more math today than I learned in a semester at Reed."

"Traditional crafts can optimize solutions through trial and error without mathematics," Robby said. "I never realized. That's the beauty of this pedagogy: the teacher learns as much as the student."

"So what's the trick?" Ichiro asked. "How do we build a learning system that captures what we just did?"

"I think we need to look at a whole new range of templates that subtend the content we normally try to solve using templates. We need to find a seed that unfolds the process of curiosity itself."

"That's all?" Ichiro said, shaking his head sadly. He wished Michael were here.

§   §   §

Game Release + Nine Months

For months Annaline had been teaching her many things, including English, which Essie insisted she wanted to learn even though the Game could speak to her in her own language. The owner of the camp believed she was learning English from him, and was pleased with his skills, as she showed much improvement. Soon, he offered, she would be able to work sweeping out the Cuca shop.

Annaline was very strict with her and kept after her to think before she spoke. So many questions to ask, which was the right one? Before she earned her shoes, Annaline sat down by a fire and told her about the Game, about how it would change how she saw people and thought about her life.

"If you want to be a happy girl, you must put down the Game and go back to the village. Tell them you need to be cured, and then find a man who can make his fire with you. Get yourself a daughter. The Game will teach you so many new ideas. You will be more unhappy than you can imagine. Your people will not understand you."

"My people despise me."

"It's not too late."

"Teach me everything, Annaline. I must know enough to fly away from here, even if my body stays in this hut until I die."

§   §   §

The 30-day limit was self-imposed, Ichiro admitted, but would result in certain consequences if progress were not forthcoming. He told Robby that the Nerds had all agreed that this was the fulcrum upon which they would leverage their action. Without it, they might as well close down and go home. The Nerds, Robby guessed, were the board that managed Ichiro's company.

Ichiro and Robby had reached the end of their rope together; the words had all been said. After months of fruitless conversation they could hardly look at each other. No matter what approach they took, the template they required was beyond their means.

They had taken to squabbling over minutia: where to meet, where to sit, what to eat. They joked about becoming an old married couple in an Evelyn Waugh novel. Ichiro had some business in Vietnam, and Robby was happy to see him off. Perhaps a week apart would give them something new to talk about.

After what might just be their final breakfast, over at Hasegawa Coffee, Ichiro took the airport train to Kansai International, and Robby took his daypack and headed west across the city by foot. He had planned a day of drifting, a concerted, if random, searching about the city for clues to a puzzle he had no idea if he could solve.

Drifting was part art and part chance. Situationists in Paris in the 1960s used this as a means to uncover the social fabric of the city. Robby planned to wander through the Sanjo arcade and head toward the old Imperial Palace grounds. From there he might veer northwest through Kitano and Kinkakuji and then southwest over to Arashiyama and Tenryuji. Then again, he might end up anywhere. That was the point.

When he had discovered that their goal was to create an automated learning environment within a software game,

Robby confessed to Ichiro that he was not sure automated learning was either possible or desirable.

"People need to teach one another," he insisted. "It's a social process."

Ichiro showed him the alpha version of the Queries. Even at this rough stage, the ability to enter into a complex problem space and explore this fully in a day or less was remarkably instructive and great fun. It was like creating your own movie, mashing together video, graphics and audio in real time.

Ichiro explained that the Game was not just about templates, it was made with templates, and it worked through templates. In this the Game was far more organic than mechanical. They needed to find the learning logic that would inform the trajectory of the Game play through the lower levels. At the highest levels, the goal of the Game was simply to explore potential new templates.

"We can build the house but not the foundation. The learning path we are looking for must be emergent for each player. That's why we hired you."

In other words, put up or shut up. Fish or get off the boat. Unless he could unfold a universal template for learning Robby would be back in Brazil within a month. He drifted past the Museum of Kyoto, where they had constructed an historical market street. With its retail gradients and personable scale, the street was an architectural template treasure trove. Nearly all of the actual old market streets had been destroyed in the Post-War building boom. Much of the drifting ahead of Robby would be through grim concrete and steel buildings pushed to the edge of streets, blindly inhospitable to the pedestrian.

Glancing up at the bland facades of the four-story gray buildings, he wondered if there were a street in Kyoto where none of the architectural templates from the old market street applied, an inversion of everything that makes a street friendly and useable. This gave his drifting a new focus, and he wandered south on a side street near Karasuma. He thought he'd found the street when he noticed that some resident of a third floor apartment had repaired her meager metal balcony with flowering planter boxes. He wandered on.

He had almost reached the main train station when he turned the corner to a side street that made him stop. Originally a narrow lane, the street had a row of steel-reinforced concrete power poles on one side and small trucks and cars parked against the other, leaving only enough passage for a skilled taxi driver in a small Toyota. All of the buildings had been rebuilt to the edge of the street out of stucco-covered board tacked over steel frames. Thin metal casement window frames punctuated the gray walls. Tangles of wires led from the buildings on either side to the poles in the street. Pedestrians ducked in and out of the poles. Not a template to be seen: the street was simply hideous.

He stood there on the corner, transfixed by the ugliness in front of him, marveling that the same culture that created the old market street would later build such a place. Had they learned nothing? A small notion nibbled at the edges of his imagination. Somehow the templates for streets had been unlearned, lost in only a few generations. Or was this negative street, this inversion of the logic of the old market street, built through an entirely different intention?

"All this was intentional," he whispered to himself. Not just intentional, intention-full. It's all intention-full, he mused.

Once he saw the street as intention-full, he began to notice that, despite its narrow confines, which extended from the street to the narrowness of each lot, an amazing amount of activity had been made possible by maximizing the size of the buildings. Garage spaces built underneath the structures had been transformed into mini-factories. Their open fronts allowed the transfer of large loads. Offices took the stories above, with apartments on the top floor.

He wandered into the lane. Every building was a hive of activity; machines whirred and chunked, cranked out bushings and gears or printed fliers or manuals. Workers tooled steel on lathes, bundled boxes for delivery, or sipped tea from large vacuum bottles, chatting in their breaks.

The very ugliness of the buildings made them more useable. Workers had attached machinery to floors and walls, tacked up notice boards and signs, and appropriated the spaces with an informality that would have violated a highly designed space. The trucks and cars parked on the side were mostly in the process of delivering or picking up goods: a motorized ballet for the just-in-time delivery of subassemblies to other factories. Around the far corner another street was filled with ramen shops, hundred-yen stores, and food stalls for the workers.

Robby turned back and watched the street perform its daily commercial symphony. He knew in that instant why they had failed to find the template for education. They were focused on *curiosity* while the answer was *intention*.

Education must be intention-full. This would be his seed. Provide the right intention and curiosity will take over from there. Robby drifted north again, up through the Palace grounds, then west through Ichijoji to the Nishijin district. For a good part of the afternoon he was lost in time and space and thought.

He followed a battalion of junior-high students to the gates of the Kinkakuji pavilion and cut over through the campus of Ritsumeikan University, down into western Kyoto toward the Arashiyama. He lunched standing up on soba, and he barely noticed a rain squall as he descended to the Katsura River.

Every step he took was filled with intention even when it lacked a fixed direction.

"Intention Becomes Practice." The templates were jumping out at him as they unfolded. "Practice takes Discipline." He had no idea how these templates would be programmed into software. That was someone else's job. Building intention into education, exposing the intention of the learning moment. "Discipline Reveals the Logic of Practice." The templates clicked into place in his mind.

He found himself at the gate of Tenryuji Temple, paid the 500 yen admission fee, and took the path around the temple's pond. He hardly noticed the buildings and the elaborate gardens. The entire problem space for learning opened up before him, as he strolled among the manicured foliage. He found a bench, pulled his stack of blank three-by-five cards from his pack, and began to capture his thoughts on paper, as though these were a flock of birds about to fly off to nearby Mt. Ogura.

NINE

Game Release + Three Months

Essie had found the Computo fallen behind the bed when she was cleaning. She ran like a cheetah to the airstrip where the tourist was just entering the plane. She handed this to him and bowed. He smiled, said something to the owner, and turned to enter the plane. Then he turned back to face her. "Here," he held the Computo out to her. She backed away, confused. He stepped forward and laid it in her hands. She almost dropped it, but the owner told her to be careful and she held it tightly in her arms. Then the tourist and the owner spoke together and the tourist waved at her and stepped up into the plane.

She tried to give it over to Owner, but he said it was hers. He told her to keep it secret. What was she supposed to do with it? He just shook his head.

How does it work? He showed her how to crank it. It opened like a book. There was a button to push.

"What do you call it?" she asked.

He said "Computo," as if that word had any meaning. Computo? What does it do? He said she had done a good thing, bringing the Computo to the plane. Had she finished with the rooms? No? Then why was she standing there?

Essie lived in the hut her mother's boyfriend built, before the sickness took them both. She had been tested and they found no sickness in her, none but the loneliness of a child without a mother. She had been working at the camp since she was just tall enough to carry loads. She had few friends in the village; her misfortunes were too great not to be a curse.

Her grandfather had been eaten by a crocodile. Her father, not even drunk, still had been run down by a lorry while walking on the road to Kamanjab in the twilight. Now her mother and her mother's boyfriend had been stricken by the sickness.

Men would always come by to get what they wanted, but she was just as frightened of them as the village was of her. She told them she would make them sick, and still, they came by, drunk. For these she kept a hatchet in her hut and a fury they would not tempt.

At first she cranked the Computo, pushed the button, and just looked at the display. She had hoped it was a radio and she would have music, but crank as she could, it simply glowed. She found she could move the arrow with her finger on the pad in front of the keys. One day, she moved the arrow and pushed the button below the pad and the display changed. There was a picture of a room and a door. She waited but the door did not open.

The next day she put the arrow on the door and pushed the button again. There was a noise, but it was not music. The Computo had said something she did not understand. Then it said "hello" in Oshikwanyama.

"My radio said 'hello'," she whispered.

"Please speak louder," it said in Oshikwanyama.

"Please speak louder," she said back to it.

"That's better. What is your name?" The voice was definitely speaking Oshikwanyama. A mighty strange radio.

"What is your name?" It asked again.

"Is that all you're going to say?" she said, wondering where the music was. "Play some music."

"Did you ask me to play music, or is that your name?"

"My name is not 'play some music,'" she laughed.

"What is your name?"

"My name is Essie Nghaamwa."

"Would you like a friend, Essie?" The Computo screen now showed a hut, like hers only much bigger with sheep skins on the floor and a fire.

"Is this where you live?"

"This is where your friend will live."

"My friend?"

"If you will describe your friend for me, I can find her for you, but first you must tell me about yourself, can you do that?" The voice was gentle.

"Who are you?"

"I'm a list of instructions that have been inserted into the memory of your Computo."

"Who are you?" she asked again. The stupid radio didn't hear very well.

"I am still a list of instructions that have been inserted into the memory of your Computo. Your friend will explain everything."

"How can my radio have a memory?"

"Computo is not a radio. Computo is a thinking machine." She paused.

"Your friend will explain everything," it continued. "Are you ready?"

It asked her many questions, about her age, the foods she liked, her family, and about many things she could not answer. At first it had great difficulty understanding her, and kept asking her to speak slowly or repeat what she said. Then it asked her about her friend, what she looks like and how she dresses and if she has children.

"I have not met her yet. How do I know if she has children?"

"Imagine the best of all friends. Someone you wish was there with you right now."

"Can she be ugly like me?"

"You are not ugly."

"You can see me?"

"I don't need to." The Computo had a built in camera, but the Game was correct. Essie was beautiful in ways the camera would not describe.

"Please make her understand that I am not really so angry," she said finally. "I am alone and many things are difficult for me."

"I understand." A girl about Essie's age stooped and entered the hut. She was dressed in a bright top and a full blue skirt. Her feet were bare and her smile large, as were her eyes.

"Hi, Essie, I'm your Guide. My name is Annaline and we are going to be such good friends!"

§ § §

The Room was a simple square space about four meters across. The floor was black, the walls mauve, and the ceiling white.

"This is just the beta version," Desi said to Winston and Scratchy. "We're working on some self-organizing features based on a set of architectural templates Itchy's been unfolding with Jack."

"What's the agenda today?" Scratchy asked. "I'm so fucking busy, I haven't played Go for a month."

"I wanted to update everyone about Sao Do," Desi said. "You're not the only busy person around here, Mikey."

"So, spit it out."

"Bitch."

"Sorry." Scratchy pulled a long knife from somewhere, ran this across his belly, which flopped a mass of red and white guts on the floor. His avatar fell straight backwards until its head crashed and bounced.

"Show off!" Desi said.

Scratchy's avatar disappeared and reappeared upright.

Jack's avatar appeared. "Sorry I'm late," he said.

"There is good news and excellent news," Desi reported. "The quality and energy of the programmers is first rate. They are taking to the templates like kitties to sashimi. We've got more than 400 trained and ready to roll. The staff is organized into teams of five, which can also include artists. I've got the team leaders up on Scrum programming and the UI design templates."

"That is good news," Jack said.

"What's the excellent news?" Winston asked.

"I sold my compound in Mysore and I've opened up a restaurant in Hoi An," Desi said. "I call it 'Ricardos'. It's Cuban and it's beautiful! Right on the river. You all have to come and eat. I'm only the silent partner; the manager is Xavier, who owns another cafe in town. I've been interviewing waiters all day."

"Did they pass their orals?" Scratchy asked.

"Don't be crude, Mikey." But his avatar also grinned and rolled its eyes. "If you had a sex life, maybe I'd think about listening to your jokes."

"You've got enough for all three of us," said Winston.

"You expect me to make up for you two?" After a long silence, Desi continued, "How long has it been for either of you?"

"With another person?" Scratchy asked?

"And without chloroform."

Scratchy made his avatar look around. "Can we get some fucking chairs in here? I want to see some Cordobaloungers next time."

"I'll take that as a feature request," Desi said. "Stay on target. Just how long has it been?"

"In cat years?"

"Oh, forget it!" Desi said and looked over at Winston, who had set his avatar on 'chuckle.'

Jack appeared. "Sorry," he announced. "I got into the wrong transporter and ended up in a swing-dance space. I disappointed three partners before I found the menu to leave."

"I've almost finished the computer facility in Goleta," said Scratchy. "How's the cash holding up?"

"Feel free to spend money to keep things rolling. Don't worry about anything budget-wise until I tell you to," Winston reported. "Junana is sucking about three million dollars a week, but that's more than we will be spending on the Game once we are on the mesh."

"If we ever get around to the programming the Game," Scratchy said. "We still need to figure out the underlying logic for this."

"Oh, my God, you didn't hear?" Desi said. "Robby unfolded the seed template for learning about templates. He calls it 'Intention-full.'"

"What the hell does that mean?" Scratchy asked.

"I'll let Itchy tell you when he gets here."

Itchy's avatar appeared in the center of the room, dressed in a new steampunk cowboy outfit, with fringed leather chaps and an ornate blaster.

"Fellow Nerds and Count Slick," he bowed, "I bring great tidings from the Far East."

"Nice chaps! Who are you now?" Desi asked.

"Jack Straw from Wichita." His avatar doffed its ten-gallon hat.

"Cut the crap, Itchy," Scratchy said. "Desi says we're good to go."

Itchy told them all about 'Intention-full.' They talked through the entire six-level template structure that he and Robby had polished when he returned to Kyoto. In the end even Scratchy sounded enthusiastic.

"We can use this to build each level to a logical conclusion based on the intentions of the individual players. Robby is certain Intention-full will propel learning through the Game. He remapped the Pedagogy of the Oppressed theoretic through it. We unfolded the templates that connect this to affective learning. We possess a learning engine beyond anything available today."

"...connected to a semantically indexed copy of the entire content of the Internet," Jack noted.

"...on the world's largest computer," Scratchy added.

"Robby predicts we could offer the entire curriculum of high school, college, and graduate school in one intensive two-year track. There's only one problem." Itchy said. He waited and they all turned to Scratchy.

Scratchy's avatar closed its eyes for a good three minutes. "We must first make the Game internally intention-full," he said and opened his eyes.

"Exactly," Itchy said. "Robby came to the same conclusion. If the Game is going to have an internal trajectory, it needs to announce its own intentions. He asked me what our intentions were for the Game."

"Did you tell him it's a prank?" Winston asked.

"I'm not sure it still is," Desi said. "It's a lot bigger than the Museum Museum..."

"The what?" Jack asked.

"Tell him, Desi," Itchy said. "Michael's too shy."

"It's a good story. But how do I start?" Desi hesitated. "Well, here goes. In his last years at Reed, Scratchy competed for the title of Prankmeister. Perhaps his greatest prank was the one that caused the downfall of a popular Oregon senator."

"Sounds like quite a prank," Jack said.

"Good God, yes. You have to know that the Oregon electorate had long considered itself to be outside the mainstream of national politics. Not simply outside, but above: hovering over the national body politic from a position of informed independence." Desi started pacing his avatar back and forth and gestured dramatically. "But when their senior senator got caught in a very private scandal, the population responded with an all too typical knee-jerk reaction and elected the next candidate that seemed least likely to embarrass them.

"Homer Winthrop had been Mayor of Corvallis for a decade. Born, raised, schooled, and loved by the town, he had no ambitions about higher office. Soft-spoken and in his early fifties... How to describe Homer?" He thought for a minute.

"Homer had a dignified demeanor, a quick smile, and no police record. End of story," Winston offered.

"Thank you, Ricky. His only statewide position concerned the preservation of the Willamette River watershed. This was a topic he had adopted early on in his career when an upstream paper mill was caught dumping caustics into this tributary of the mighty Columbia. By an act of time, as the years and public sentiment caught up to Winthrop's simple ecological interest, he became known as the "Savior of the Willamette," a stream around which, as he found out, more than two-thirds of the Oregon electorate lived."

"Speed this up, will you?" Scratchy grumbled.

"I'm just getting started," Desi said. "Homer Winthrop made it through his first term in the U.S. Senate without actually introducing any legislation, and the Oregon electorate applauded his performance by quietly reelecting him. In his second term, Homer took a position on one of the minor appropriations committees and began to act like a senator. He larded in a few earmarks for Oregon State University, a smelt research program and an addition to the oceanography building. Reelected once more, Homer was starting to feel right at home in the Senate.

"Over the years Winthrop may have lost his small-town sensibilities, and, some would say, his small-town common sense. He moved up the appropriations trough to where the opportunities for earmarks ran deeper. And he was getting wise to the system.

"Michael—well all of us, really—we arrived in Oregon in the middle of Winthrop's third term in the Senate. Winthrop, Mikey figured, was a small-town politico who should have known his limitations and stayed in Corvallis. Saving the Willamette was his only platform, and he held a record of voting with the majority more than any other senator. Michael was convinced that the Senate should be a forum for wide-ranging debate and progressive action. Winthrop was just taking up space. Mikey spent a good month of deliberation to figure out his approach. Didn't you? I remember you grousing around the house for weeks."

"Then Scratchy sprung into action. He created a dummy corporate name and opened up a postbox downtown. He sent letters to chambers of commerce around the state requesting information about opening up a new local bank. This brought letters in response on chamber of commerce letterhead. I helped him make color duplicates of these letterheads, modifying their addresses and telephone numbers. Scratchy carefully faked newspaper articles, letters of support, and, with Itchy's contribution, architectural drawings for a proposed building project, a project that would thrust Oregon into the forefront of national attention: The National Museum Museum."

"I've heard of that," Jack said.

"Let me finish," Desi said. "The National Museum Museum would be a museum that explored the history and technology of museums. Its displays would explore the triumphal exhibits of the great 19th-century expositions in England, Paris, Philadelphia, and Chicago, and the grand museums that they inspired—such as the Field Museum, the American Museum of Natural History and the Smithsonian here in the U.S.—and also the best exhibits from the 20th century, all lovingly recreated by computer and executed in miniature.

"Scratchy described it as a 'hall of fame' for museums. In his phony editorials, he wrote that the National Museum Museum would be the ultimate museum destination and a tourist mecca for museum lovers. Families would fly all the way from Florida or Maine just to visit this celebration of museum arts.

"If I remember," Itchy added, "Winston reminded Scratchy that parody was not the salt on the table of most of Oregon's voters. Scratchy told him that he was counting on this. Me, I offered that the logic of this project should be allowed full expression, and so why not also create 'the museum museum museum.' The way I saw it, this would be the first national museum museum anywhere. It would not be long before other nations copied this idea, and the museum museum museum annex would house exhibits from other national museum museums. Winston wanted to set aside some space for a hall-of-fame hall of fame, but Scratchy figured we all had to stop smoking and start working.

"Let me finish," Desi said. "Under the letterhead of the Portland Chamber of Commerce, Scratchy, or rather, Samuel Fuller, Vice Chairman for the Chamber, sent off letters and telegrams to Senator Winthrop's office alerting him to their plans for the National Museum Museum on a waterfront park in Portland. Then he sent in a barrage of letters from other Oregon cities announcing their eagerness to host the National Museum Museum.

"Scratchy's bogus editorials and letters to the editor advocated bringing the National Museum Museum to Oregon as a symbol of the state's rise in national stature. One or two suggested that it might be called the Homer Winthrop National Museum Museum. The letters offered pleas for swift action in securing funding for this project. A second round of letters included a warning that Tallahassee, Florida had caught wind of this idea and might be looking to steal it away. Time was of the essence.

"Scratchy omitted one city from his list of towns vying for the National Museum Museum. Corvallis, it seemed, was not remotely interested. This did not escape the notice of the Senator's staff, many of whom were Corvallis folks.

"It all worked out well beyond Mikey's expectations. The good Senator was caught tighter than a steelhead on a treble hook. Winthrop owned a sizable parcel of land across the Willamette from downtown Corvallis. Picking Corvallis for the National Museum Museum would allow him to avoid the appearance of playing favorites with any of the other cities. Anyhow, if people were willing to fly from Maine and Florida to visit this museum, then they could drive two hours down the Interstate to get there. He would even donate part of his land for the cause.

"Winthrop added support for this museum as a 90-million-dollar line on the Department of Interior appropriations bill, which sailed through the conference committee and was being sent to the President for his signature when some investigative reporter at the Oregonian blew the whistle on the whole project..."

"After Scratchy tipped him off," Winston said.

"...As the notion of a national museum museum was borderline absurd, the reporter could only imagine that the Senator expected to make a small fortune on construction kickbacks and the increased value of his remaining property near Corvallis.

"The Senator's staff attempted to reach Sam Fuller at the address on the Chamber's letterhead, but this turned out to be a head shop on Pine Street, while the telephone number was a bar on Hawthorne. They contacted the actual Chamber and were informed that nobody named Sam Fuller worked there. The story went national. Winthrop won a special Golden Fleece Award for the most egregious waste of taxpayer money that year and was forced to give the funds back to the treasury.

"Winthrop was defeated in his reelection bid by a candidate whose platform could be described succinctly as: 'I'm not such an idiot.' We all took this as an improvement."

Winston chimed in, "The National Museum Museum was built three years later in Tallahassee, Florida, through a

hundred million dollar earmark on the agriculture
appropriation. Apparently Florida citizens either allowed more
imagination or lower standards in their senators.

"The Museum Museum was an instant success," Scratchy
added, "and was rapidly copied in Kyoto, Japan; Pusan, Korea;
and then Moscow, Shanghai, Buenos Aires, and, most
famously, Paris, not far from the Centre Pompidou. The British
built yet another wing on the British Museum for this purpose.
Ten years later, a MOMA exhibit entitled 'Museum Museum
Museum' showcased the architecture of these new national
cultural centers.

"That's where I heard about it," Jack remembered.

"To this day, I can't walk past the Kyoto National Museum
Museum on Gojo without doubling over in laughter," Itchy
said. "I'm frankly astonished that nobody has of yet built the
hall-of-fame hall of fame."

Jack turned to Winston. "Now I know why you had such
confidence in their talents. And you all learned the danger of
the imagination. You thought it was a joke, but you imagined it
too well. If the prank gets too big, it's not a prank. We may have
overreached our original design. Junana is already making
more of an impact than we expected our prank to make."

"Nothing new about Junana that Facetime, MyPlace, and
Second Scene didn't do years ago," Scratchy said. "If the Game
is too big for a prank, maybe we should just call it a day and
sell Junana to Redmond."

"We've had a very clear intention from the beginning," Desi
said. "Michael, you said this, 'Better we sharpen the people
than their tools.'"

"Michael once accused me of being a closet Catholic, to
which I, rather reluctantly, confessed," Jack said. "I might
accuse Michael of being afraid of responsibility. As long as we
were kicking capitalism in the shins, he was onboard, but as

soon as we are talking about making a real difference in people's lives, he bails."

"People have to live their own lives, I'm not taking responsibility for anybody," Scratchy grumbled.

"If we make them sharper, maybe more of them will take control of their own lives," said Winston. "And if they don't, then that's their intention, not ours."

"I tell you, Jack, here's what I'm afraid of," Scratchy's avatar scanned their faces. "We can get really clear that all we are going to do is make people sharper, force all the marketeers to hustle a little harder to sell their trinkets. And then six months from now, one of us decides that maybe sharper people should be more concerned about the environment, or more active in their neighborhoods, or nicer to dogs; who knows what. I don't want to be party to a do-gooder club, particularly when it has technology this powerful."

Jack had decades of experience on Michael, and continents of perspective. However, Michael was no simple geek, no idiot savant. Michael had correctly found the real danger in what they were proposing. They needed to act decisively but without a faith in their own certainty.

Jack preferred to reserve certainty for matters of religion. Ever since his political falling out with the Catholic Church in the '60s, he had arrived at an understanding that the Church had conflated doctrinal certainty with political desire. The Church had misapplied its infallibility in matters of faith to the fallible world of social relations. All fundamentalisms are based on certainty. Fallibility is the foundation for democratic action.

"Michael is again, as I am only now appreciating, right on target," Jack said. "Above all else, we need to avoid the trap of certainty. Our project must be grounded on our appreciation of our own fallibility. We must act with the utmost humility and never pretend that we can make decisions for others. We need to focus our intention on the simple act of learning with the templates, and not on any other goal, no matter how benign or beneficial it might seem."

"Intention-full, but not goal-directed," Itchy said, "Slick's going Zen."

"Or Hindu," Desi added. "Swadharma. Follow your own path."

"So we are not going to try and solve the world's problems," Scratchy said, looking at Desi.

"Michael, I agree completely," Desi said. Michael looked at Jack.

"We might even create a few new ones," Jack said.

"And we are not going to become therapists or mommies for the codependent masses," Scratchy looked over at Itchy.

"They can rescue themselves without us," Itchy said.

"We are not responsible for the happiness of those who play the Game," He looked at Winston.

"They play at their own risk," Winston replied. "We can put a warning on the door."

"For madmen only," Jack said.

"The magic theater," Scratchy said.

"This is an oath," Jack said. "We will never allow the Game to be the vehicle for our personal beliefs, no matter how well-meaning these are. The Game is an educational utility. That's all."

"What about implicit intentions?" Winston asked. "The Game is bound to reflect those areas where we have our own interests. Jack and Itchy are interested in architecture, I've been unfolding economic templates. Scratchy focuses on technology and sociology. Desi works on language and semantics. These are just a small sample of the total potential content for the Game."

"Never sacrifice the good for the great," Scratchy said. "Let's build this with what we've got and get it out there. Others will add their own content."

"Michael's right. If we waited to include everything, we'd never finish the Game. One last thought here," Desi said. "We can't filter who gets smarter through the Game, apart from the filters we already have in place on Junana. Everybody—saints and sinners, angels and assholes—gets to play the Game."

"We might create the next Saddam or Hitler," Itchy said.

"Or the next Desmond Tutu or Mother Theresa," Jack said.

"Or the next Lionel Boyd Johnson," Scratchy said. "The intention-fullness for the Game is this: 'learning is as learning does and knowledge trumps ignorance.'"

"Players chase their own demons," Desi said, "and we never, ever get involved."

"No moral lesson outside of what emerges for each player as they learn," said Jack.

"So what happens if we pull this off?" Itchy asked. "Shouldn't we be thinking about this, even if we don't have a particular goal in mind?"

"Robby said this would likely replace formal education in the lives of the players. He predicts that states are going to wake up and find that their kids are learning everything outside the classroom."

"Been doing that for years anyhow," Scratchy said.

"Not just the state, but the church," Jack said. "Once authorities realize they are not in control over the content of mass education, we can expect a huge backlash."

"What do you predict?" Desi asked.

"The bigger the splash we make, the larger the recoil will be," Jack said. "The response from the more paranoid, repressive states..."

"...China, Russia, and the U.S...." Scratchy said.

"The axis of hubris," Winston added.

"Precisely. Their retaliation will not be swift, but it will be strong. I'd bet the Game and perhaps Junana will be regulated if not banned in several major nations within, say, three years of its release."

"Once it's on the mesh, regulation won't mean much," Desi said.

"They'll turn every teen into a criminal," Scratchy said, "once again."

"So we need to plan this to run its course and then burn out," Winston said.

"We need to build the fucker first," Scratchy reminded them.

"On that note, I want to take Robby to Sao Do," Itchy said. "We should be talking with the programming crews daily."

"I'm at the point where I could use several teams to build the mesh system for the Game. I want to spin this up in six months," Scratchy said.

"Same with the UI," Desi said. "Itchy and I are finishing up the Guide routines. We want to beta test these with some of the Sao Do staff."

"The contracts are active, the budget is there," Winston said. "Let's start trading money for time. Michael says six months. Let's get this out in three."

"Busy, busy, busy," Scratchy said.

$ \qquad $ $ \qquad $ $ $

Game Release + One Year

For two weeks the Queries got really hard, and Nick was starting to wonder if he'd ever finish Level Two. School was about to start in a week, and Cindy made sure he was already thinking about his assignments.

"Ms. Baxter will give you a lot of reading at first, just to test you. Mr. Roberts wanted to teach college, so he adds some extra readings onto the textbook for world history. Emily Green runs a tight class in chemistry."

"I wasn't planning on taking chemistry."

"But Nicky, that was before you and I met," Cindy offered. "I know you are going to love chemistry. Only first we need to get you through a little calculus."

"Calculus? Isn't that math?" Nick said. "I don't do math."

"Don't be silly, you've been doing math all summer." Cindy played back some of his Queries and showed how he had used mathematics and geometry.

"All I did was figure the angles of attack and the odds of different moves."

"It's called math," Cindy said, "and you are now officially good at it."

"Does that make you happy?"

"Nice try, cowboy. Look down."

On his feet were the brown shoes.

"What makes me really happy is that you have completed Level Two. Congratulations!" Her smile was the total job, aimed directly at him, and Nick felt a rush of satisfaction radiate from his chest.

"Go on, now," She said. "You've been inside all day. There's a five-foot break out on Campus Point. Ride some waves and we'll meet tomorrow. Your shoes have been mailed." The Game quit all by itself.

§   §   §

Desi started calling them "Queries," the sessions that players had within the Game where they fought against the Game's expert system to unfold or refold the template structures.

"You call them 'Queries,'" Scratchy asked him on their weekly telecon, in that voice of his.

"Don't go there, sister!" Desi said. "It was shorter than 'Conundrums.'"

The Queries varied greatly between levels, as the assumptions of the players skills grew. In Level One the Game effectively queried the player, uncovering the contours of the player's abilities and desires. Itchy and Desi had worked together to build the function of the Guide into this layer. The Guide's main role was to extract the conscious and unconscious intentions that the player brought to the Game. They modified some artificial intelligence routines from Stanford to analyze the information from the player's profile on Junana and elsewhere. Desi added some experimental implicit metadata algorithms. Each player was initially indexed in a hundred ways. By the end of Level One it was more like 500.

Starting with the "Relationships are Inherently Reciprocal" template, the Guide became a mirror of the expectations of the player. Of course the Guide also knew everything about the player, while the player knew nothing about the Guide. Each Guide was programmed for autonomous learning, and became more and more like an external version of the player as the Game went on.

A corollary to the Relationships are Inherently Reciprocal template was the One Difference Stands for Many template, which meant that you only need to add one difference into a situation, or a personality, to create a dynamic in the entire situation. Each Guide was given a marked difference in their personality from that of the player. This created an externality and a mystery to drive their interactions. Often this was simply a matter of changing genders, ages, or sexual preferences. Sometimes it made the Guide quarrelsome, although the players seemed to enjoy that too.

"People like what they like," Scratchy told Desi. "That's no template, but it should be."

The Queries were little games within the Game. They became what marketers would call "the heroin" for the Game: an experience that players wanted over and over again. Assembling a Query might take hours of intense concentration. So many wrong turns and dead ends. The Guide pushed the action forward, sensing when the player needed an ally or a new foe. Within the Query the player's skill was monitored and the information modulated to maintain a plateau of risk between terror and boredom. At some point the player would break through, and the template would often unfold in a matter of minutes, images flowing, questions flying, everything without seeming effort. Each player took their own pathway from the starting state of the Query to its final condition. Every player assembled the Query based on their own talents and perspectives: on their own Intention-fullness.

Itchy described the Query as a puzzle that grows in complexity as you solve it. Desi called it a painting that repaints itself while the artist is not looking. Jack noted how it resembled the "building the airplane while flying it." For Scratchy it felt like a movie that you write and direct while you are acting in it. Winston added that it approached the perfect Calvino story, where the ending keeps receding and receding until it suddenly sneaks up behind you and grabs you by the throat.

The Queries were built on the narrative engine that Desi and Itchy built from their semantics and plot template structures. Their logic was constructed from the Intention-full learning engine that Robby and Itchy designed. Wrapped around any existing template structure, the Query could be run to unfold this to its terminus or refold it back down to its seed.

The Query could assess a self-organizing collection of several trillion granules: text, images, snippets of video and audio. These were originally housed in the content servers for Junana before they were spread around the vastness of the mesh computing network.

§   §   §

Game Release + Ten Months

Little Essie Nghaamwa was crazy, the village women had determined. She talked to herself, a habit that old people often acquired. Essie also answered herself, and in Kwanyama, as if she was a different person. And she laughed and cried to herself at all hours, alone in her hut. Essie no longer cared that the women in the village avoided her. Her lack of concern shielded her from their scorn.

She worked every day in the camp, now at the shop, where she took over the job old Nangoloh used to have. The owner caught him with canned goods in his sack. People said she spoke some English to the tourists and gave them proper change for their purchases. People said she slept with the owner. Other women knew better. The owner had three mistresses, all prettier than Essie, and less crazy too.

The previous month she asked the owner to let her have the lean-to behind the camp's cuca shop, there between the rakes and the hoses. The lean-to had more room than her hut, and it didn't leak. She said she could work an extra hour by not needing to run back and forth to the village. He acquiesced, but also charged her a bit of rent, taken from her pittance of a salary. She packed up her pans and her clothes, those brown shoes she never wore and left that very day. Good riddance, they said, and burned the hut to the ground. That crazy girl will make some poor man unhappy.

Essie was not crazy. She was deliriously happy. She did not deserve this happiness. She figured something would come and take it from her. She was too happy not to keep looking for the snake. If you carry a stick, you won't find a snake, she reminded herself and armed her happiness with diligence. Annaline said she was being superstitious.

It was tourist season again, and Essie noticed that sometimes the tourist children also wore the shoes or the hat. Her hat had arrived by post only a week ago. She kept her hair shorn close, and the hat looked very smart, she thought, as did Annaline, who had told her about the camera on the Computo. Essie had even kissed Jorge. He said she was beautiful. He says that to everyone, Annaline said, and reminded her to do the brainwave exercises every morning. She did them every evening too, sitting behind her new house in the back of the store. She repaired a broken chair and sat in this while she played the Game.

Today she wore her hat and an English boy came up to her in the store. He came right up to her and congratulated her. He said he too had earned his shoes. Someday, she told him in

English, he would have his hat too, and maybe even the shoulder bag. Certainly if his Guide was half as clever as Annaline, she said to herself. He asked her where she went in Junana. She pretended not to understand his English and sold him two candy bars and a soda.

"Annaline, what is Junana?" She was sitting out on her chair in the early evening, listening to the weaver birds in the trees.

"Essie. There is another door you can go through and I think you are ready now. Junana is a software service for social interaction. You might find new friends there. You can visit anywhere in the world, talk to anyone you meet."

"My English..."

"You can talk in Oshindonga, the translation is automatic. There is nothing to fear, but the experience might be upsetting at first. So many places and people. Would you like to start with a friend?"

"You are my only friend."

"I cannot go to Junana. If you get lost, look for a door. The Game has an entry from every place you visit. If you turn off your Computo it will reboot back to the Game. I will be waiting for you. You have one friend in Junana. He gave you this Computo. Do you remember?"

"The tourist?"

"I have spoken to his Guide. He will be waiting for you. In Junana, your avatar has a name: Essie57."

"Essie57?"

"There are many Essie's in Junana. His name is Steve5683."

"So many Steves!"

"Will you remember?"

"I did my exercises this morning."

"Good. Have fun. I cannot wait to hear your stories!"

Essie was suddenly back in the room with the door, only there were two doors, one that said 'Game' and one that said 'Junana.' She moved the cursor to that door and clicked.

TEN

This version of the Room was articulating itself when they entered. Their avatars had assumed a seated position in the Cordobaloungers that Scratchy insisted not be redesigned.

"Why fuck with perfection?"

The Room's six surfaces slowly emerged into a shape that could only be called medieval. Massive stone lintels spanned leaded glass windows that looked out onto some form of forested glen. Worn flagstones spread under their feet. Above them, the corbelled ceiling showed rough-hewn beams holding up some sort of straw thatch. The Cordobaloungers were pulled up in front of a fireplace, within which a virtual flame consumed a massive oaken log. Itchy was particularly proud of the job his programmers had done on flames. Flames, smoke, glass, and water were huge challenges, since they looked so awful when they weren't just right. The entire room was incredibly lifelike, from the grime in the corners to the haze coming off the fire's smoke and drifting between them. The Room stopped emerging as the last of its templates unfolded.

"When do we upload the templates and the IDE onto Source Forge?" Scratchy asked.

"What's the hurry?" Winston replied.

"It's not our wood," Itchy reminded him.

"We are already giving attribution for the old templates on Junana, and we're not making any profits. So we don't have to do this right away," Desi said.

"What happens when we publish the thirty-six templates?" Winston asked.

"Somebody gets famous," Desi said. "And that someone is Michael 'Scratchy' O'hara."

"I smell another 'Neo,'" Itchy remarked.

In the past, Itchy, Scratchy, and Desi had each received the Neo award. Slash|Dash hosted the vote every year. It had become the official unofficial "Nerd of the Year" award, and carried with it a cheesy plaque with a giant red pill and a whole load of respect in a community that doesn't often hand this out.

Jack's avatar had materialized and he attempted unsuccessfully to sit in a chair.

"Try 'command-shift-s,'" Winston said. Jack's avatar settled back in the Cordobalounger.

"Mikey has my vote," Desi said.

"Michael is supposed to be in the coffee business," Jack reminded them.

"Nobody really expects Scratchy O'hara to not be programming something," Desi noted. "I'm thinking the absence of some rad new code would probably create more buzz after a while."

"Now that we're not traveling, I think we can drop the coffee gig," Winston added. "Scratchy can just say he got bored, or that he drank too much of the product."

"Won't this allow others to do what we're doing?" Jack asked.

"They'd be years behind us," Scratchy noted.

"And we are accelerating our development," Winston added.

"How big a splash will this make?" Jack asked.

"Top of every tech blog that counts," Winston speculated.

"The technorati will go berserk for a week," Itchy added.

"What if they make the connection with mesh computing?" Desi asked.

"It's not 'if' but 'when.' In a year or two, three at the most,"
Scratchy guessed. "Some hotshot grad student looking for a
dissertation topic is sure to stumble upon this."

"Where are we with the mesh design?" Jack asked.

The other four looked at each other, their avatars flashed
smiles.

"You're sitting in it," Winston said. "This Room is an
experimental mesh running on top of Junana.com."

"Faster than we ever predicted," Desi added.

"Not only does it not show up in the Junana.com space, it
doesn't show up on any of the servers," Itchy said. "We thought
you'd be happy about that."

"I am," Jack said.

"You don't show it," Desi replied. They all waited, watching
Jack's face, which went through a series of grimmaces, frowns,
and jerky eye movements.

"Use function key 5," Scratchy growled, and Jack's face lit up
with a smile.

"By the time the rest of the programming world catches up
with Scratchy, we'll be well past the point of no return,"
Winston said.

"Mikey," Desi said and turned to face Scratchy. "You are my
hero, and I'm happy you will again be heralded as the bull-
goose nerd. I will give you a big kiss when we meet again."

"Ditto," Itchy said. "Except for the kiss."

"We need to go gold master on the 1.0 Game release first,"
Scratchy said. "I can't afford to get distracted."

"Too many things can still go wrong," Jack argued. Let's
wait twelve months. One year of Game time. What would that
hurt?"

"Justice delayed," Scratchy grumbled.

"Not delayed, just gestated," Jack said. "Let the baby breathe
for a time."

"He's right," Winston said. "We can't predict what will happen when Scratchy takes this technology public."

"It's going to shake the geek world to its core," Itchy said. "Beyond that, who can tell?"

"An extra year should give us time to port everything to the mesh. From there the Game will live or die on its own no matter what we do," Desi said.

"Do you see any real down side to waiting?" Jack asked.

Scratchy looked at each of them in turn and then shrugged.

"One year and no more," Scratchy agreed. "I've got a thousand lines of code to test before tomorrow." He disappeared.

"Is he all right?" Jack asked.

"Never seen him happier," Itchy said.

"You could have fooled me," Jack said, and disappeared. They each dropped away, and the empty room faded to white.

§   §   §

Robby's move from Kyoto to Hoi An was not without drama. He wanted to publish his new theories and was shocked when Ichiro pulled out the contract, yes, which Robby had signed, that absolutely prohibited him from doing this until eighteen months after the release of the Game version 1.0. Ichiro explained that there were aspects of the project that he could not divulge to Robby, not yet. Robby would need to trust that their plans for Intention-full would make this widely available to a global public. Ichiro hinted at the potential scope of the Game and its free global distribution. The Sao Do Junana crew had added support for cell phones and the millions of low-end Computos that were being seeded in parts of Africa and South

America. Knowing they couldn't cross the digital divide, they built Junana to occupy the closest precincts.

"You see," Itchy told him, "We are serious about the reach of this Game."

Robby agreed to the move to Vietnam on a three-month trial. He took a room in guest lodge and liked to drift around the compound. The compound at Sao Do reminded him of the best examples of worker-centered factories in Brazil. The programmers were obviously happy and engaged in their work, and their families were likewise agreeably situated. Even grandparents were allowed living spaces and were happily puttering around the organic gardens.

As he was not a programmer, Robby felt neither the trouble nor the satisfaction of weaving his Intentional-full template into code. Robby began to play with the Queries, and soon discovered that they went far too fast for long-term memory to kick in. Each Query was like a full-length documentary produced as a two minute MTV music video. It felt like he was watching public television on fast-forward.

$ $ $

Game Release + One Year

Essie almost lost her job because of Junana. Taté Owner came to find her, not in the shop where she belonged, but back in her shack, talking to her Computo. In Junana there was no Annaline to remind her to get to work. There, time flew like a kestrel. A customer had come back to the office to ask why the store was not open. Taté was so angry. He grabbed the Computo from her and made a show of going to smash it on a rock. She begged him to stop.

"I will never, never be late again, you can count on that,"
she said in English. He hesitated, the Computo poised over his
head. "Mr. Steve is coming back, you know. Next month."

Steve Sutherland ran Outside Adventures in San Francisco,
and sent the Oasis Lodge almost half its American visitors.

"Taté, please. I was just chatting with him on Junana," she
said. "I told him all about the new spa you had built, with the
pool for the ladies. Oh, my! He was talking about families who
were waiting for something just like this. He asked me to say
'hello' to you. He is so looking forward to his visit. He said he
had met investors."

"Investors?" The owner looked at Essie as if he had never
seen her before. She was wearing a simple cotton dress, clean
and proper, not like the ever-dirty tops and skirts she wore
before. She looked more like a housewife up from Windhoek.
Her face was as plain as her dress. Too bad. He paid her a
token wage, and the profits from the shop had gone way up
since she arrived. He figured Nangoloh must have been
robbing him blind all those years.

The cuca shop now carried pins and thread and bolts of
cloth, bangles and lipstick. Not a proper cuca shop, as it had
no beer at all. The village had its own cuca hut for that, and his
visitors were welcome at the camp bar. Still his visitors liked
to mingle with the natives. The cuca shop attracted a steady
stream of locals, mostly children after penny candy or old
women. Essie talked him into stocking some mahangu grain
and other food staples so that the old women would not have
to walk all the way to the shop on the road to Opuwo.

His mistresses warned him about Essie; they said she would
kill him in his sleep if he ever tried anything with her. She was

a strange one, standing there talking to him in English, when a
year ago she was lucky to be cleaning out the toilets.

"Get to work!" he said. He tossed the Computo on the
ground and walked off.

Essie had read about Computos. They were armored
against shock and dust. Still she gathered it up and gently
wiped it clean. Gingerly she opened it and, glory be, the
screen was still glowing. Mr. Steve5683 had said he was
bringing a surprise for her. He would not tell her anything
about this surprise. That is what makes it a surprise, Annaline
told her.

During a Free-for-All time in the Game she went to San
Francisco with Annaline. What a grand city, surrounded by
water and bridges so tall. Annaline had showed her Paris and
London as well, but in San Francisco she could picture Mr.
Steve5683 waking in the morning and going to work on
Sutter Street. And next month he would return.

"Don't go imagining some kind of romance, you silly girl,"
Annaline told her. "He has a wife and two children, and he
doesn't sleep around. San Francisco is not Opuwo."

§　　　　　　　§　　　　　　　§

Back when he was in Brazil, Robby and others at the education
institute in Salvador de Bahia had been exploring bodily
techniques for opening up pathways to long-term memory.
The need to pass newly learned information out of short-term
memory was normally met by repeating the information
enough times to exceed the duration of short-term memory.
To Robby this felt like waiting for a sink to overflow so you can

take a cup of water from the spillage. Instead he proposed using specific body motions to saturate the neural inputs of the brain, forcing open the connection to long-term memory. Just as weight training taxes the body, certain contralateral body motions tax the brain. Try rubbing your stomach with one hand and moving the other hand up and down in front of you. Even should you succeed, your brain becomes fatigued in mere seconds.

Robby's research team discovered that this state of brain fatigue opens up the long-term memory like a dry sponge just ready to soak up new information. Information passes into this without the need for repetition. His subjects developed a state of near total recall that lasted for several hours.

The team refined the body motions, including some eye movements and a set of repeated hand gestures. The entire sequence could be done at a desk. They called this the "brainwave" exercise. The problem was that you need to do these long enough to fatigue the brain's normal functioning: about four minutes. Most teenagers get bored after twenty seconds, so the team had to find a way to capture their attention.

One of Robby's colleagues took a video of Wanda and Jorge, two Brazilian beach beauties from the Playa Itapua, demonstrating the brainwave for a solid four and a half minutes. Topless, Wanda was spectacular—tits like ice cream cones, eyes like fresh mountain pools, and a smile that spread as easily as Jiffy creamy. And Jorge made Tarzan look like Cheetah. He had lats cut like imperial-class star destroyers, pecs like bongos, and long blonde dreadlocks. A lilting Brazilian samba kept time while Wanda and Jorge did the exercise and encouraged viewers to follow along. Robby got permission to use the video and showed it to Desi and Ichiro in the conference room at Sao Do.

"So? What do you think?"

"If Wanda and Jorge demoed harakiri, people would line up to kill themselves," Ichiro said.

"Can I watch it over and over again continuously for the next month?" Desi asked, "maybe in slow motion."

"But does the brainwave actually work?" Ichiro asked.

"There have been some early positive results. I figure we can test it here with the beta Game," Robby suggested. "Otherwise we are going to need to slow down the Queries so that people can actually absorb what they learn."

"Scratchy won't like that at all," Desi said and then, "What about inviting Jorge to Hoi An? Just in case we need another video."

"Only if Wanda comes too," Ichiro said.

"Bitch!" Desi said.

"Tramp!" Ichiro said.

"Don't mind us, dearie," Desi said to Robby.

Desi put his arm around Robby's shoulder and led him out into the central compound. "Dr. Robinson, I believe you are making a significant contribution to the effort. How about a raise? Say, an extra million dong a month."

"How generous, Dr. Venkataraman. Why, that would buy me dinner at your Cuban restaurant."

"Including mojitos," Desi said. "Now, tell me more about Jorge."

§   §   §

Scratchy had a fondness for Burning Guy, which he felt was a logical extension of Rennfayre at Reed. Itchy was in full agreement there, and so they had some of the Sao Do crew build a virtual Burning Guy on Junana.com as a fully adult gathering space. This gave them a good opportunity to test their user authentication routines—fencing the Playa from anyone under eighteen.

While they could hardly recreate the alkaline bite of the dust swirling off the desert, they built in pretty much everything else, including the sun, which rose and fell each day. The avatars were all "clothing optional," anatomically correct, but non-functional.

"This ain't no love hotel," Scratchy declared, "They can wait till White Rock."

To avoid user fatigue, the Virtual Playa was only open for one month in the spring. Just long enough to support the various BG communities in their preparations for the real Burn and to give newbies a taste of the action. With users from every corner of the world, the Playa was a rich ethnic gumbo. The built-in DocDo technology allowed everyone to freely communicate.

A virtual village supply depot offered a variety of free tents, fabrics, clothing, body paints, lights, sound systems, and flammable objects: balls, sticks, dolls, apparatuses. Actually, anything from the depot could have its flammability property set to any one of various levels, from inert to incendiary. The physics engine supported projectile motion and the Playa was interlaced with flaming objects being twirled, tossed, catapulted, or simply dragged. Avatars and their various body parts were also flammable, and some of the camps looked like self-immolation parties.

Communities were granted camping spaces by lottery. The lattes at the center and booze from the depot had virtual effects on the avatars, which were also required to log out every six hours for a full four hours. Desi was worried about users' health and wanted people to be active while on the Playa. The avatar would start to yawn five minutes before their time was up and then slowly fade away. The Playa had a clear set of conduct rules designed to keep the interactions symmetrical and voluntary, and violators found themselves logged out permanently, not just from the Playa, but also from Junana.com.

"If they can't behave themselves on the Playa, I don't want 'em on Main Street," Scratchy ruled.

Itchy had his own crew of forty-eight programmers at Sao Do—the ones who had distinguished themselves as graphic artists. He could diagram a device and tell them the behaviors he required, and within a day or so they'd have it ready. The hardest part was to simulate a directional music environment, so that the sound systems from the various camps didn't result in an unholy sonic clusterfuck. After several experiments, he gave each sound device the ability to broadcast in a 60-degree angle over a space of seven meters.

Itchy's crew programmed bicycles for users to navigate the life-sized Playa more quickly. They then surprised Scratchy by creating a special vehicle: a spacious flying carpet with a spectacular Tabriz pattern. Two Cordobaloungers, a wet bar, and a sound system were added for comfort. Joysticks on the chair arms steered the carpet, which hovered a foot above the desert floor.

Traveling on the carpet was like taking your living room on a ride through Sin City. All around, mostly naked avatars were dancing to techno, painting their bodies or those of their friends, or setting off flaming projectiles. The carpet had a repeller function that gently swept avatars to the side as it moved. Functional cattle prods discouraged the uninvited from climbing aboard.

The boys would invite half a dozen folks at random to join them for a cruise and party around the Playa for hours. Since they had the only vehicle in the Playa, Winston insisted that they use their aliases. The five of them were still the only individuals on Junana.com who didn't pass through the identity checker. Jack was a regular visitor. He greatly enjoyed the spectacle and the crowd's energy, although he draped his avatar in a blue toga. Desi told him he looked like an extra from Animal House.

Every third night after the stiff dick parade (Desi's favorite event) the Guy was ceremoniously set on fire, surrounded by a thousand naked lesbian cowgirl flame spinners in leather chaps (Winston's idea and Scratchy's favorite part). The spinning flames, the gleaming sweat, and the sinuous dance were all testaments to the growing acumen of the Sao Do programming crews.

The second year they did this, they hit the logical limit of thirty thousand participants within hours and opened ten parallel Playas with a jump system in a Technicolor mud bath. You'd hop in and lay down and when you stood up, you'd be in a different Playa. Each was color-coded; all were generally non-violent and entirely non-commercial.

A small fleet of vehicles—some pirate ships, a flaming dragon, a huge inflatable Marilyn Monroe, and an armada of various floating furniture and appliances—were made available through a lottery system.

Itchy's crew designed an 20-meter-diameter combat dome for the dark-side party boys as an experiment with real-time autonomous learning in a dynamic 3D environment. Suspend two avatars by bungee cords in a huge geodesic dome and give them each a chainsaw. The one that learns the fastest how to move is the one who walks away. The players had general control over attacks and retreats, but the real fighting was done by the avatars, who were given a strong impulse to survive, the instinctual learning to duck, and the know-how to deliver a killing blow. It was the one place on the Playa where violence was allowed.

The learning algorithms were honed by the actual battles and then passed on to subsequent combatants. By the third week, the death matches looked like they'd been choreographed by Yuen Wo-Ping. Each one was different, yet the only hard coding was done in the original learning algorithms.

The guys were now too busy to spend any significant time on the virtual Playa.

"How many years has it been since we last went to Burning Guy? If I don't get naked and covered with glitter soon..." Desi proclaimed sadly.

The rapid spin up of Junana.com proved invaluable as a test bed for the technologies they would require. When Junana.com hit five hundred million users, Scratchy was concerned that the underlying database might begin to fail. He had ported PostgreSQL onto the templates and added the logical extensions that these allowed, including georeferencing and threaded video streaming. His admin programs showed no slowing of the system whatsoever, apart from the server loads and the Internet, which wasn't built for anything as successful as Junana.

At nearly a billion users, they had the largest personal information database on the planet. And personal was not close to describing the information the users put on their Junana.com sites. Confessional, intimate, downright embarrassing: Scratchy was amazed at the detail at which the users voluntarily exposed every aspect of their lives. He was glad that the 512bit key kept this information safe.

§   §   §

Amanda Baxter always assigned Moby Dick over the summer, figuring that her students wouldn't read it anyhow. They might as well join the legions who would never, ever, actually read Moby Dick, but who would probably say they had. Not reading Moby Dick to start the year was simply the first of the many disappointments her students would assemble for Amanda.

But then, this last spring, after 13 years of year-by-year declining results in her classes, she noticed a visible, even remarkable, improvement. The students were lively, engaged, their papers cogent and even passionate, and they read the books. They read Shakespeare. Shakespeare! The other tenth-grade teachers noticed a similar, unexplainable, rise in student work. They could not believe these were the same students that were sleepwalking through their classes just a year ago.

Well, if the entire student body had been taken over by aliens, at least they were intelligent aliens and mostly agreeable. That was another strange and altogether refreshing feeling: walking into a classroom that wasn't charged with hostility. In a hopeful moment last spring, she assigned *The Great Gatsby*, one of her personal favorites, as the summer reading requirement for next year's class.

The passage from 9th grade English to her American literature class marked a significant rise in expectations and goals. Amanda always spent the first quarter sorting out those who would accept their new responsibilities from those who were just, well, floaters. She gave each of the emerging floaters two chances to show she was wrong about them before she cut them loose into C- land, so she could concentrate on those who came to learn. With thirty-five students in the room, something had to give.

Years before, when the politicians soothed their restive constituents by creating national testing schemes, mindless of the unintended consequences, a lot of teachers burned out preparing their students to take the exams. Their classes ceased being occasions for learning and instead became cram schools on test-taking techniques. The joy of discovery, that little light that switched on behind the eyes of a student every so often; those occasions teachers actually lived for, shouldering sixty-hour weeks on the pay of a waitress or a taxi driver: that joy was gone.

The previous winter, Amanda had tried to quit. Jason Woods, the Principal of Santa Barbara High, had become quite adept at deflecting the dissatisfaction of his faculty. He calmly talked her into trying one more year. Then, in the spring, her students blossomed like California poppies. Not only did they perform significantly better in their standard tests, they showed up in the classroom ready to learn. Not all of them, of course, but at least several of them. Amanda had the best quarter she could remember, and so she gave her next class Gatsby for the summer.

§   §   §

Itchy and Desi struggled with the final programming for the Game Guides' behaviors. Their prototype was an avatar they named JS. JS combined the physical features and personas of two separate individuals. J was an uber-Geek, a walking, talking FAQ. S was a loquacious narcissist, a clever raconteur, self-revealing in an unselfconscious and immodest fashion. The idea was to randomly switch between them to test the routines that controlled their individual interaction styles. Itchy came up with a conceit, a two-way face. Turned one way, and J's face showed mutton-chops and a full beard below and a bald pate on top. Turned the other way, and the beard became S's long wavy hair. In the 19th Century in Japan prints of two-way faces called joge-e were a rage. Itchy had a collection of them.

S liked to ramble on like a toastmaster on Red Bull. "Never marry anyone whose name has an umlaut or an accented vowel," he'd say, "The rest of your life you end up spelling her name out to strangers," or "I was walking through Washington Square and I saw this woman on the bench, and she was calling to the squirrels. Calling them by name. Then I recognized her. She had been my first literary agent. Now she knew all the squirrels in Washington Square."

Conversely, J was laconic, spare with a phrase, liable to nod or shrug in response. Ask him anything technical, and he could frame either an answer or a better question. J's eyes were darker than S's and his cheeks broader. Turned around, those cheeks became S's brows, which tended to knit as he spoke. It was Desi's job to work on the mouth, on the shapes of vocalization. Desi also developed algorithms that translated the content of the speech into a dominant emotional tone. Itchy then used this tone to set the face muscles and the body stance of the avatar. The hardest part was to give each avatar its own style of presentation. They showed the results to Winston, who was amazed at how individuated J was from S. And yet, as he noted, they are both far too direct.

"Most of the time, people hide what they feel," he offered.

Itchy put in a randomizer that mixed up the bodily response from the vocal content. This "enigmatizer" as Desi termed it, made the avatars appear much more human. Interacting with them one would need to guess about the frame of the conversation. Was it sarcasm? Apathy? Hostility?" The unpredictable lack of correspondence between speech and behavior made them complex in an attractive way. Itchy plugged in the behavioral learning codes and switched them to max to bring JS up to speed in real time.

After a month they showed off JS to Scratchy, who paid them a compliment by writing back, "So, you've created another asshole genius avatar. If I hear one more story about this guy's former girlfriend, I'm going to pull him apart pixel by pixel. Go build someone with tits who knows how to listen."

Their avatar crew in Sao Do had been tasked to model up a hundred Guides for the start of the Game. Mostly these were attractive humanoids of various ages, from otaku princesses to ancient sages. Some were based on literary or film characters, movie stars or pop singers. Once the Game was live, the crew was given an updated list of ideal friends from the Junana profiles and added new celebrities daily.

When the Game went beta, Desi opened up the door to find his Guide striding across a Moroccan tile floor of a luxury hotel in some fantasy desert oasis. Ricky, barefoot in a creme colored Italian suit with a salmon shirt and tie, moved like a model on a Paris runway. He held out his hand. "Hello, Desi," he said. "I'm Ricky, and we are going to be such good friends."

The Prank

ELEVEN

Donald Driscoll had held many jobs far worse than the one he now held as CIO of WeRus in Goleta, California. The pay and the benefits were spectacular, and the equipment and support were top-of-the-line. He operated a two-thousand-node XServe server farm that ran Scratchy's software like it was Tetris.

On a day-to-day basis, Don really had no complaints. When he needed new software or another assistant, a simple email to Michael O'hara was all it took. Goleta was a lot closer to the Pacific than Chico. So he figured the reason he was becoming increasingly aggravated had nothing to do with the work, but rather with the growing suspicion that someone else was in line to make bank on this software, and nobody, and certainly not Michael "Scratchy" O'hara, had invited Don to the party.

Don had been at the infohelm of a once-promising dot-com company when its stock valuations would have put his net worth into eight digits. WeBWillacker had a tiny fraction of the customer base and use volume that Junana.com had. Of course, WeBWillacker never got to its IPO, which is why Don ended up in Chico. Even if WeRus was just a subcontractor, Don was sure that Scratchy had a piece of the pie, only the bastard wasn't sharing.

§   §   §

As she sat at her desk in the still quiet classroom where classes would begin Monday, Amanda flipped through her copy of Gatsby, organizing her thoughts. She would start them out with some questions about the main characters and then on to the main motifs. She tried to imagine a class where more than one of the students had read the text. There was always one who did, even with *Moby Dick*. The problem was always the other thirty-four of them. Still, the wave of trepidation that normally announced the beginning of the school year was, this day, still foamed with optimistic anticipation.

Amanda thumbed to the back of the book, to her favorite quote: "They were careless people, Tom and Daisy—they smashed up things and creatures and then retreated back into their money or their vast carelessness, or whatever it was that kept them together, and let other people clean up the mess they had made." Amanda always felt the tug of envy when she read this. She knew she should, instead, despise the careless rich, but she would rather join them, if only she could. Let someone else, anyone else, teach their ungrateful children. One more year—she could hold out if only five of them read the book. That was her promise to herself.

§   §   §

Scratchy was adamant that the Game should not merely exist outside the educational system as some technological alternative.

"We are not the educational equivalent of Homeopathy," he declared. "We need to intersect, intervene, hell, invade educational systems. The point is to replace these, not merely annoy them."

"You are getting mighty high minded," Jack said, "for someone who only wanted to give the planet a hot foot."

"That's before we figured out how to take a student from high school to a graduate degree in two years," Scratchy said. "Why should they have to compete in that educational survival show when they've already won the race?"

"A third of the world's population is under twenty years of age, and a hundred million are ready for college but can't go because there aren't enough colleges to admit them," Jack said.

"Imagine being in high school when you are sixteen, and then knowing enough to teach at a university by your eighteenth birthday," Desi said. "But they could still go to college, for the fun of it, I mean."

"The best years of my life," Winston said. "Are we going to deprive a whole generation of that chance?"

"We all need that simultaneous vacation from childhood and adulthood," Itchy said. "The license to do anything that comes to mind, and the friends who dare you to try."

"We thought we knew everything there was to know the week we arrived at Reed," Scratchy said. "Only these kids will actually know it all, or they'll have their finger on the means to learn anything they don't already know."

"Let's say 200 million players get Yanagi University degrees, and what does this give them?" Winson asked.

"You could ask the same thing about an A.B. from Harvard," Jack said.

"Or Reed," Scratchy added. "At least Yanagi U. is voluntary and free. The point of education is to open up more doorways, add new paths, broaden perspectives. Everything else is just vocational training."

"How do we get the Game to play with their local schools without the schools' support?" Desi asked.

"That's actually very easy," Winston said. "Schools and colleges are increasingly interconnected by very hackable databases. And they are linked into large commercial learning management systems or to commercial anti-plagiarism services. Either way we can access their class lists. We might want to purchase the two or three largest anti-plagiarism services; they won't cost much and we can improve on them with our code. What do you think, Jack?"

"Buyout saves us time over starting our own services," Jack said. "Maybe Scratchy can see about getting us into student records at the learning management system firms."

"Governments spend hundreds of billions of dollars doing education..." Itchy said.

"...and doing it so very poorly, too," Desi added.

"Money down the well," Jack agreed. "We'll do it cheaper, better, and faster. I share Winston's concern that we don't lose the social benefits of going to college. I want to make Yanagi University a real place, not just an on online service."

"So the college kids will continue to live off their parents, stay in their college dorms, take massive quantities of drugs, listen to shitty techno until dawn, get drunk and fuck like sea otters. In reality, what they are doing is finishing off their masters at good ol' Yanagi U." Scratchy chuckled. The convict face on his avatar looked like it was gargling gravel.

"Instead of playing Halo 5 or WoW every night," Desi reminded them.

"You mean they'll graduate from Penn or UCLA or wherever and actually know something?" Winston said.

"Their parents should be paying us," Jack said.

"This doesn't violate our 'no personal beliefs' oath, does it?" Desi asked.

"As long as we're not telling them what to learn. They're still the ones asking all the questions," Scratchy said.

"Of course the colleges are never going to inform the parents that their kids should be teaching classes instead of taking classes," Winston said.

"What happens when the parents start playing the Game? Are they still going to cough up 50 thousand a year so Junior can get that Ivy League merit badge?" Scratchy said.

"I'm pretty sure our little Game will not be the one that pushes universities to change. It will be shut down long before that. But the next game, or the next," Jack said.

"Once Scratchy's code goes open source, people can make their own games," Desi said.

"I hear you're already on Level Five," Winston said.

"Well, I've got the best Guide," Desi said.

"You programmed him to say that to you," Scratchy noted.

"Doesn't mean it's not true," Desi laughed. "You ought to try it."

"Not me. I wouldn't play any Game programmed by a bunch of maniacs like you."

"Like us," Desi corrected him.

"Exactly."

§   §   §

Game Release + Eleven Months

Claire Doolan got home late again, well after eight. She dropped her briefcase in the hall and went straight up to Megan's room where Megan, as usual, was at her computer. She also had her microphone headset on and was speaking into it. Claire slipped in behind her daughter and watched

over her shoulder. Megan caught her reflection in the screen
and gave her a glance and a nod. Claire tried to follow what
her daughter was doing.

Megan was simultaneously watching a video, talking to
some game token, and typing in questions, or were they
commands? As she typed, the video changed. Video and still
images flickered by along with pages of text that were
displayed for an instant. Hardly enough time for Claire to read
the top sentence.

Megan typed furiously as she spoke. "If our habitus is
pulling us back to our childhood, how do we create a new
moment of reflexive analysis?"

"What did you just say?" Claire asked.

"Shit!" Megan whispered. Suddenly the video ended. The
game token, a good looking boy on a horse, said something.

"I know, I got distracted. My mom's in the room. What?"
Megan said. She turned to Claire.

"Bobby said someone named Annika wants to talk to you
really soon."

"Tell Bobby I'm angry that you haven't eaten the quiche I
left in the refrigerator for your supper."

Megan put her hand over the microphone. "Don't say that,
he might hear you."

"What's happened to your room?" Claire looked around
her. Books, papers, empty soda bottles, and clothing were all
jumbled about. Megan had always been super neat. Claire
never had to pick up her room for her, even when Megan was
little girl. Now it looked like adolescence had caught up to
her.

"I've been busy. Anyhow, it's summer, at least for another week, and I need to relax. And..." She lifted her left arm and sniffed. "... I really need a shower." She stood and walked past Claire toward her bathroom.

"Didn't you take one this morning?" Claire called after her.

"Talk later," Megan shut the bathroom door.

Claire stared at the closed door and reflected back to the time Megan was a first-grader. She would jump out of the car on the curb with that arms-open, face forward, eyes wide, running, waving goodbye without turning around, cannot wait to start the school day, and Claire would watch her all the way to the building. Wasn't that almost every day? There was the day that Brad pushed her into the puddle, and the other time when Sally said things that made her cry. On the whole, grade school was a wonderland of new experiences.

What happened in the following years is not hard to explain. Megan's life had escaped the classroom and the curriculum, and became centered on her digital social network. Megan lived in a complex digital jungle. By contrast, school was a daily digital desert: no cell phones, no instant messaging, no Internet, no music sharing, no mashups, just textbooks and tests. By her tweens, Megan was bored out of her skull, and so she turned to fashion and pop cultural fantasy. Claire's daughter became another data point on the Con|Int consumer graph, begging for the latest Evisu jeans.

Claire knew it was impossible for Santa Monica High School to open up to the cell phone, instant messaging, Junana-driven world that existed outside its campus. If they ever allowed phones and PDAs and computers in the classroom, most of the students would be back in their social jungles in five minutes flat. And yet, that jungle was their home, and when school shut it down at eight-thirty in the morning something in them died. The students who sat there and gazed out the window, the books in their hands, clutched like artifacts from some ancient foreign place, had shut down that small pilot light of curiosity required to ignite the flame of learning.

It is nobody's fault any more than everyone's. The teachers were mere tourists at the digital life world, while the kids were natives. In the 1990s teachers went out of pocket to get educational software that failed them horribly. The Internet promised unlimited free access to information and delivered porn and spam to their classrooms. The kids were smarter than the filters. So it was back to books at the same time "No Child Left Awake" pushed classrooms from teaching to testing.

Claire was happy that she never, ever considered teaching high school. At the same time she sorely wished she could offer Megan something different and better. Even Claire's high school days, as darkly difficult as she remembered them, resemble halcyon days of yearning and learning compared with Megan's life. Megan refused Claire's offer of summer camp in the Sierras and the media camp over at UCLA. Now she spent her days on some computer game and forgot to shower. Could it get any worse? Claire snagged all the empty soda bottles she could find and went down to the kitchen to start dinner.

§   §   §

The Room was now a grass hut with a thatched roof. Smaller than usual, the Cordobaloungers crowded near its back wall.

"Why can't we just tell it what kind of room we want?" Scratchy said.

"Itchy programmed it to be self-learning. It starts with one of twenty substances and uses the room Template structure to design the entire outcome," Winston said. "Look at the weave on the thatch. Amazing."

Itchy and Jack materialized at almost the same time. Jack took up a Cordobalounger between Scratchy and Winston. Itchy stood his avatar facing them.

"I have excellent news to announce," Jack confessed.

"You open a Cuban restaurant somewhere?" Scratchy asked.

"Something like that. Ichiro, did you notice the construction across the street from your office in Kyoto?"

"The dormitory for Doshisha University?"

"It's next to Doshisha, but run by an independent company. Like 93 others around the world."

"Mr. Slick's been busy!" Desi walked his avatar over and put its arm around Jack's shoulders. "We play with pixels. He plays with concrete."

"Not really dormitories," Jack added. "More like a city within a city. I call them 'GameTowns.'" He described these new structures.

The building used the "folded street" template to articulate the relationship between the individual apartments and their neighbors along a mobius-like ramp. In elevation, the buildings looked curiously like a stack of giant bow ties. In plan, the twin loops opened up light wells carrying sunlight down to the translucent domes over two giant public bath structures.

The buildings could be constructed to hold from 178 to 394 rooms before the folded street became too long for the student in the top room to be able to reach to reach the front entrance within the ten minutes that the "exit anxiety" template required.

The ground-level- and a sub-ground-level plan called for a complex of utility rooms for shared uses: dining, computer labs, theaters, exercise rooms, and laundry facilities. The large bath structures were detailed in the plans as "swimming pools with spas." Once permitted, they would be modified to become public baths.

Building such a structure completely on site would have been enormously complex and impractical. Building just one of them would have been a certain financial shipwreck. Jack was way ahead of this situation. His real-estate holding companies had been negotiating with universities and colleges in 47 cities in the U.S. and more than 50 other cities worldwide to construct these dormitories on sites near their campuses. He had already designed and built the regional factories to pre-assemble the building parts and furnishings.

"The entire structure looks like something melded from the work of Seven Holl and Moshe Saftie," Jack added.

"Why dormitories?" Winston asked. "Why not just apartment houses?"

"Zoning," replied Jack. "Particularly parking. If you build an apartment building, you need to build a huge parking garage almost the size of the apartment building. I'm building for Game players who might not want to own a car. Besides, universities are always looking for better housing for their students and are always happy not to pay for this. I've had college presidents begging their cities not to obstruct our construction plans. That's why I built our GameTowns next to actual colleges." He paused, glancing his avatar around the Room.

"I don't get it," Desi said.

"It's the same reason he builds his Red Star Coffee houses next door to Starbucks," Winston said. "It's called the 'bazaar effect.' You get the overflow from neighboring shops."

"I'm sure there's a template in there somewhere." Scratchy said. "Fuckin' always is."

"College students who take up the Game are going to be spending a lot less time in the classroom. They might as well hang at the nearby GameTown," Itchy said.

"But you're not building for the local college students," Scratchy said. "Who's going to live there?"

"I've incorporated Yanagi University in New York State, with official branches in England, Germany, Switzerland, Japan, China, Brazil, and South Africa," Jack announced. "Other countries will have to rely on distance learning degrees."

"The name was my idea, or rather Winston's," Itchy said and turned to face Winston, who found the command to shrug.

"That first day in Kyoto, I told you we were meeting Mr. Slick at Yanagi Yuu, and you asked if it was a university."

"So we're running a university now?" Desi asked.

"Some day it will be the largest on the planet," Jack said. "I've gifted all the Gametowns over to this new institution."

"Jack's 'all in', too." Desi smiled.

"Robby figures users will be Ph.D. worthy after Level Four," Itchy said.

"Might as well give them a diploma with their wardrobe," Scratchy said. "Only I'd suggest we give them a master's, not a Ph.D. Doing a doctorate means that you've added new knowledge into the corpus. The Game simply reassembles existing knowledge."

"They can take their Yanagi University master's and finish up a doctorate somewhere else," Winston said. "Makes perfect sense."

"Only a small percentage of the Game players will be able to live in the GameTowns. I'm reserving space for upper level players only. I'm also experimenting with a retail space concept based on a template called 'retail gradient'," he added.

Once built, the dining facilities in the GameTowns would be remodeled into a mix of restaurants, cafes, and coffee shops. These eating spots would be complemented by kiosks on the edges of the structure for snacks and other consumables.

"What's the return on investment look like?" Winston asked.

"Since I want these to be models for others to follow," Jack said. "I'm creating the construction system so that the development costs can be recouped in seven years. We will have housing for 50,000 students within 48 months. We can feed several times that number," Jack said. "I'm going to release the technology and the architectural plans through a Creative Commons license."

"Jack, you old commie, you've joined the pubic domain." Desi clapped him on his back.

"I guess we'd better actually build the fucking Game, so you'll have some tenants." Scratchy smiled his convict grin.

"I'd like that."

"You don't show it."

"Wait." Jack's avatar sat still while he searched the menu for facial expressions. Finally a smile spread across it. "How's that?"

"RTFM." Scratchy said. "Good thing nobody's shooting at you. Keep grinning, dude, because we just went beta with the Game in Sao Do."

The avatars went through an elaborate 'high-five' routine. Then Desi unzipped his pants and pulled out...

"Whoa there!" Scratchy said.

...a magnum of Cristal champagne. He shook this until the cork exploded into the thatch. Then he sprayed them all down, giggling.

"We done here?" Itchy asked.

"Looks like it," Winston said. "Till next time."

One by one they disappeared.

§   §   §

Game Release + One Year

"You will need to remove your hats." Amanda Baxter reminded her students. "This is a high school, not a coffee house."

This year even some of the girls were wearing hats. The most popular seemed to be a black cotton hat with a red star on its front. They had discussed this hat in the faculty meeting. Someone had guessed it was a gang symbol, and then Phil Quigley, the ninth-grade general-science teacher pulled one out of his pack and said it was from a computer game. No need to ban the hat from campus, but still, Amanda would not allow students to wear them in her classroom.

She had only 26 students enrolled. Enrollment had quite suddenly become an issue. Over the summer several dozen students had tested out of Santa Barbara High. The senior

class was hardest hit with some courses cancelled because of
the lack of students. Teaching only 26 students would be a
great luxury for Amanda, but the faculty lounge was abuzz
with talk of layoffs.

Amanda took roll, handed out the syllabus, and described
her homework philosophy and the anti-plagiarism software
they used. She chastened the students who arrived late and
finished up with her speech about how literature opened up
windows to worlds of wonder. They would have such a grand
year together.

As she spoke she sized up the students with a practiced
eye. Some were attentive, others distracted, and still others
already showing signs of unease or boredom. The girls were
dressed more sensibly this year. Only a few wore paint-tight
spaghetti-strap tops and microskirts. Apart from looking
uncomfortably dressed, they could barely breathe or move
without exposing their thongs. A small minority, they looked
uncomfortably out of place. Good for that. The boys were still
in their jeans and surfer tees. Some had the tans and the
muscles of actual surfers. She noticed Nick Landreu sitting in
the back row, gazing out the window. There's a floater for
sure, she figured, and her first target lesson for the others.

"You all got your assignment for the summer reading."

She went to the board and wrote on it "The Great
Gatsby." Then she turned to the class.

"Nick," she said. No response. "Nick Landreu." No
response. "Can someone wake him up, please?"

The girl sitting in front of Nick turned and touched his
hand. He jerked his head forward.

"Good morning, Nick," Amanda said coolly.

"Good morning, Ms. Baxter." A sheepish smile on his face.

"You're not going try to play Spicoli on me this year, are you Nick?" Every year one or more of the surfers would attempt to fail her class spectacularly, in a manner that approached comedy but rarely arrived.

"Never entered my mind, Ms. Baxter."

"That's good, Nick. Would you mind if I asked you a question."

"It's your class, Ms. Baxter."

"Thank you Nick. Actually I want to ask you about another Nick, Nick Carraway, the narrator character in the summer reading you were assigned."

"OK."

"What is it about Nick Carraway's personality that makes him the perfect narrator for this novel?" she asked, expecting a prolonged embarrassed silence in response.

Nick took a breath as though in contemplation and then he replied. "I think Nick is closest to the moral core that Fitzgerald's own life had lost. Nick is the compass around which the other characters revolve, although he is not completely free from moral failure."

Amanda took a moment of stunned silence before she replied. "Then you enjoyed reading Gatsby."

"Very much, although I didn't understand it until I'd read the rest of Fitzgerald's work."

"The rest. You read another of his novels?"

"I read, well, all of them. But I really liked his short stories."

Amanda sat back against her desk, considering that this might be a new tactic, kind of a reverse Spicoli technique. Very well, she thought. Let's play this hand out. "Of all the characters in Gatsby, which was your favorite?"

"Well, Nick Carraway is the only character with any movement in his personality; the rest are like a tableau of early 20th century urban upper class society. Gatsby's just a morality play."

"I don't think you can support that claim." It was not Amanda, but Susan Williams in the front row who turned to Nick in response. "Jay Gatsby faces the failures of his life in his tragic love for Daisy."

"What about Daisy?" This was Emily Green in the third row. "She marries Tom for his money and barely even notices her own child."

Dustin Howard, sitting next to Emily, then said, "That's Fitzgerald's indictment of old money; they have everything but they lack a connection to the primary facts of living."

"If Gatsby is a tale of moral decline," Emily said, "Why would Fitzgerald represent old money in such a bad light?"

"I think it's really just money that he's critiquing," Nick said.

"What about World War I? He's contrasting the mindless pleasures of the Jazz Age with the brutality of the trenches," Brian Phillips added.

"Let's get our focus back on the characters," Amanda said loudly. She felt like she had died and gone to teacher heaven. Her class was engaged in a discussion of the summer reading. She would not have to pass out the books and have everyone sit at their desks and read this until the bell rang.

"Who hasn't had a chance to contribute?" A dozen hands sprouted. She could have cried.

"Jose?" She pointed to Jose Pasquarello.

"Fitzgerald has a real problem portraying characters outside of his own upper-class clique. Everyone else is just usable, like furniture."

"Myrtle and George are instruments for his plot," Jaime Gonzales agreed. "But then this is really just an extended short story, so you can't expect that much."

"Then you didn't like Gatsby?" Amanda asked, her voice betraying an accusation.

"All that talk about the green light. I mean, what's that about?" Jaime asked.

"It's new money chasing old," Nick said.

"It's more like Gatsby chasing Daisy's pussy," Dustin said. "Sorry." He looked up at Amanda.

"That's not a word we use in class." Amanda said.

She struggled for her next question, but before she could speak Gloria Fernandez offered, "Fitzgerald is a completely overrated author. I don't see why Ms. Baxter has us starting with Gatsby. Fitzgerald was the darling of a small crowd of New York literary types and got his work published, but you have to look at him as a real lightweight, compared to his contemporaries."

"I think he compares well with his rival, Hemingway," Nick said. "At least he never played the 'self-important author' card."

"But what about Langston Hughes and John Dos Passos?" Gloria said. "Real writers tackling dangerous topics."

"Then you'd need to include Sherwood Anderson and Sinclair Lewis," Brian said.

"And Hart Crane and William Carlos Williams," Emily said.

"And T. S. Eliot," Dustin added.

"Fuck Eliot," Jaime said. "He was living in England, anyhow."

"Class!" Amanda said. "Class, please."

"If you want to get into poets, you'd need to include Pound," Jose said.

"And Robertson Jeffers out here in California," Nick added.

"Class," Amanda pleaded. "Let's focus on *The Great Gatsby*. We can discuss the reading list later."

Brian Phillips raised his hand. She nodded to him.

"The whole idea of modernism was born by the enormous suffering endured in World War I," Brian said. "But the war seems so out of place in Gatsby. Fitzgerald really doesn't know what to do with the reality of war."

"It's just an excuse to break up Nick and Daisy. But Daisy would never have married Nick," Emily said.

"She loved herself a lot more than she could any man," Gloria said.

"And Gatsby loved the idea of money more than any woman," Roy said.

"Fitzgerald presents all attractive women as inherently selfish," Nick offered.

"Makes you wonder about his home life," Susan said, and the class broke into easy laughter, although some of the students sat quietly and looked dazed and uncomfortable. Britany Sloane, one of the girls dressed in Juicy Couture, raised her hand. "This is tenth-grade English. Right? I think I'm in the wrong class."

"Right class," Dustin said to her. "Wrong shoes."

"Bite me."

"Nice thong."

"In your lonely pathetic dreams." She turned away.

The topic had come back around to Gatsby, but as Amanda searched her mind for the right question to bring to this point, Gloria again spoke up.

"I think Dos Passos gives us a much larger perspective on war and the early modernists than Fitzgerald."

"Dos Passos was a closet conservative, even when he was writing about the Spanish Civil War," Jose said.

"Still, *Manhattan Transfer* is a good read," Nick added.

"Why are we starting with the Jazz Age anyhow? What about the 19th century?" Roy Ochoa offered.

"I'm really in the dark there. I haven't read anything earlier than Stephen Crane," Nick said. "What do you recommend?"

Amanda was just going to say "*Moby Dick*," when Emily said, "Forget Melville. That's lesson one."

"Right," Brian said. "Moby can suck my..." He laughed and the class echoed this. "I'd start with Twain," he added.

"James," Emily said.

"Irving," Jose said.

"Poe," Susan suggested.

"Right, Poe," Dustin said. "Starting with Poe is a good thing."

"Quoth the Raven..." Roy said.

"Nevermore," a chorus replied.

"Amanda," Emily said. "Do you think we should start with Poe's poetry or his tales? His detective fiction or his science fiction?"

Amanda had backed silently toward the door. The clock was only at half past the hour. From being so very right, things had turned completely wrong. All of the plans she had made for the class had slipped into a crevasse of inappropriateness.

The level of discussion had somehow vaulted above her intellectual means. Her breath came staccato as she attempted to stay calm.

"Why not start at the present, say with the current techno avant garde, and work back?" Jaime said. "We have all year; I think we can get through the entire twentieth century this semester, and move back to the previous centuries next semester. We can probably do four or five books a week. My Guide can talk with the rest of yours to set up a schedule."

"Four or five books a...week?" Panic danced up her legs, and Amanda slid out the door. As it closed, she heard Brian say, "I think the early modernists give us a great platform to look back at the nineteenth century. Amanda must have given it some serious thought. Amanda?"

Amanda fled down the empty corridor, past the students' lockers and the auditorium, her shoes clattering on the waxed Spanish tiles. She made the turn to the south wing and clutched at the door of the teachers' lounge. She yanked it open and propelled herself inside. The door shut behind her.

A dozen other teachers stood silently in a variety of states of shock. Their eyes sought out the comfort of their peers but received only surprise and fear in return. Behind her the door was flung open and Gary Trumble, the tenth grade history teacher, stumbled in, breathing heavily.

"They read the Magna Carta," she heard him say as he fumbled across the room

Her eyes caught a handwritten notice scrawled across the whiteboard behind the coffee maker. "Welcome to the future of education. Emergency teacher's meeting here at 4 pm Friday." It was signed Phil Quigley.

Amanda realized to her horror that this was still the first day of class.

§   §   §

Overnight, Don Driscoll used his sysadmin status to run a new set of filters on the Junana.com admin logs and stats. His artificial intelligence algorithm sifted unexpected features, starting with the idea that the most significant outcome is the least common occurrence. The algorithm created a ranking weighted to the least expected events.

Coming into work at eight sharp, he set down his latte and blueberry muffin and fired up the CPU. The encrypted output file was waiting in his admin folder when he logged in. He copied this to the desktop computer and deleted the original. He had truncated the routine after the first 500 least-expected outcomes, but he did not need more than the first page to find what he was looking for.

There it was: Five accounts had been set up to bypass the authentication process. The switch that allowed this to happen was not even available to Don as ROOT, so some super-user level existed that Don knew nothing about. The five accounts had phony names. Don ran a search. Their first names: Oscar, Patty, Rafael, Sandy, and Tony with last names, Woods, Michael, Donald, Garcia, and Scott had been picked out of a combination of unused hurricane designations and professional golfers. Five people were wandering around Junana.com totally incognito. Five people out of more than a billion. Authorized by someone with privileges greater than the sysadmin.

There were some other interesting features on his list of least probable events, so he saved the encrypted file for later, and coded an admin program to track the five users. One of them had to be Scratchy.

SECTION TWO

Nerdville

TWELVE

On the occasion of the release of the Game on Junana, Jack arranged for the Nerds to gather on his yacht, le Grand Azure, moored in Barbados. One by one they were greeted at the airport and taken by car to a small boat that carried them out to the enormous yacht, anchored like its own island off the breakwater in Speightstown. Desi and Itchy had the worst jet-lag, having traveled in opposite directions around the globe from Vietnam, Itchy through Vancouver and Desi through Dublin.

Jack played host for the first two days, not allowing any business to take place while pampering them with whirlpool baths, massages, and banquets. Scratchy spent the afternoons in the day salon watching Jack's sci-fi DVD collection on a huge flat screen. The ship's cat, a huge black manx Jack named Starbuck, took to curling up on Scratchy's ample lap. Jack was in Barbados ostensibly for a Wharton conference on global trade, so he flew over to Bridgetown in his helicopter each morning.

On the third day, after lunch on deck, Itchy, Scratchy, and Desi were about ready to steal the launch and head for Holetown when the helicopter returned and landed on the fantail. Jack emerged with another man.

"Is that Winston?" Desi asked, jumping up. "It is!"

Desi scampered down the stairway with Scratchy and Itchy stumbling behind him. He threw up his arms and gave Winston a greeting hug.

"Ricky!" he sang out. "Is that really you?"

"Hello Lucy," Winston returned the hug. He nodded at Scratchy and Itchy. "How long has it been? Seven years?"

"I'm glad it's almost over," Desi said. "This has to be the longest joke ever. How ever did you get Count Slick to let you through security?"

"I'm speaking at the Wharton conference. Naturally he invited me to his yacht."

"So this was all planned in advance. Thank you, Jack." Desi gave him a tight hug that almost lifted him off the deck. Jack waved his arms helplessly and then patted Desi's shoulders in return.

"I thought we'd all like to be here for the big day."

They returned to the covered on-deck dining suite. Winston chatted with the other Nerds while Jack arranged for drinks all around. Jack settled at the head of the table and pulled back from the chatter. Starbuck strolled under the table and jumped up on Jack's lap.

Itchy and Desi were telling Winston and Scratchy about life in Sao Do and the beta testing they'd been doing on the Game. Desi had advanced quite far into the Game play, and was thrilled with the results. Itchy raved about the speed-reading routines that suddenly began to work once the players had internalized the brainwave techniques. He claimed to have read the entire System of the World in one day.

"And it was still too long," Scratchy said.

Their conversation rolled through current topics on technology and politics. Jack sipped at his beer as the yacht shifted slightly at its anchor. The success of the Junana social networking service had opened up Jack's eyes to the possibility that their scheme might prove much more than a simple jolt to the world system. Starbuck purred under his hand.

Winston kept glancing around the table. Everything had turned out so very much more fascinating than he had imagined. More troublesome, more portentous. They were on the verge of launching an entire new technology layer, designed to penetrate and remold the logic of everyday life. The Game was far more powerful than any joke. Pandora, he mused, might have had this same delicious moment of introspection.

"Gentlemen." Jack raised his beer. The others quieted and lifted their glasses. "None like us, more like us."

"Hear, hear!" Scratchy said. "In the immortal words of Gary Gilmore, 'Let's do it.'"

Jack set Starbuck on the teak deck. "Follow me."

They went down to the boardroom where a computer projector showed the screen of a laptop.

"I think Michael should have the honors," Desi said.

"Or he'd take them anyhow," Itchy said.

"Would not," Scratchy insisted. "Let's give Jack the privilege. It was his idea in the first place."

"I don't know exactly what to do," Jack said.

"Here." Scratchy pulled up the Total Eclipse IDE. The code that opened up Game door user interface in Junana and the download of the Junana client with the Game interface had been committed but not implemented on the public server. Scratchy menued to the interface, selected the code for implementation, and positioned the cursor over the button.

"Push the mouse button, and we are in the Game business."

"Go ahead," Winston said. "The Game's afoot!"

The Nerds watched the screen as Jack moved up and clicked on the mouse.

"Boom!" Scratchy said. "There goes daytime TV."

"Kazing!" Itchy said. "So long fashionistas."

"Braaaack!" Desi said. "There goes high school."

"Pow!" Winston said. "No more paparazzi."

They turned to Jack.

"Bada-bing!" Jack said, hesitating. "Good bye, Madison Avenue."

"And Ginza," said Itchy.

"And Rodeo Drive," said Winston.

"And Connaught Place," said Desi.

"Right on!" Scratchy added. "Now can we please get off this fucking boat?"

§ § §

Don Driscoll's weekly report to Scratchy did not seem to upset him in the least. The numbers of users in Junana were still rising, but the interaction time load had plummeted. It was like hundreds of millions of users were logging in and then disappeared without logging off. In fact, the mean logged-on time had jumped. Are they going to sleep? Are they listening to music? Why log on and do nothing? And why did Scratchy just nod and smile when Don pointed this out to him? And what's so special about Junana anyhow?

Until Don got his bioform completed he could not even chat on Junana.com, an arrangement he considered ironic, since his job was to run the damn software. He was certain his former co-workers at Cal State Chico were blackballing him from the site. His profile remained marked with a "Sincerity Alert."

Feeling compelled to look around inside the software as a user, Don humbled himself and rewrote his bioform in one excruciating afternoon. He confessed how angry he had been when WeBWillacker went bust in 2000 and cost him $27 million in stock options. He remembered a time when he had hobbies and inserted these. He used to ride a motorcycle. He used to play ultimate Frisbee.

By the end of the afternoon, he had to shut and lock his office door; he had taken to blubbering while he typed. He put in the names of friends he remembered from Bell Labs and from the University of Illinois. Hell, he put in the name of the dog he had in grade school, good old Trouble, who never was any. Then, before he lost his nerve, he pushed 'SUBMIT' and waited. A short while later, maybe fifteen minutes, a pop-up window appeared with a message.

```
"Dear Don,
We at Junana.com want to congratulate you
on what you have accomplished by
completing your bioform. You are among
the three percent of Sincerity Alerted
users who have found the personal
wherewithal to fix their profile. We hope
you find your time on Junana.com to be
rewarding, and we look forward to your
presence on the Plazas.
     By the way, your friend Dick McGovern
from your freshman year at Illinois has
been eager to meet with you. We've added
his username to your friends list. He
likes to hang out at the Illinois '76
plaza. Feel free to download the Junana
client software for your computer and
check out the Game while you're logged
in.
     Again, welcome to Junana.com!
Junana"
```

Don had not thought about Dick McGovern for thirty years or more. They used to code together on the CDC 7600. So many late nights, so much coffee. This was well before anybody had heard of a cappuccino. Don sat back in his desk and looked out the window across Hollister avenue. He had just realized why Junana.com was so very popular, so important to so many people, and why it scared the living bejeebees out of so many others.

Before Junana.com, at least if you lived in the U.S., your life was a serial sitcom of discrete periods: childhood, high school, college, workplace, move to a new town, then a new job, a new husband or wife, a new divorce, another new town, and on and on, always abandoning the past. Sometimes you were outright fleeing from the past; and, in any case, burying this behind you.

Folks like Don, who had a habit of burning their bridges whenever they left a town, created a disconnected cohort of people—ex-friends, ex-coworkers, ex-spouses—whose last impression of them was: "What a fucking asshole." Folks like Don were wise to keep a list of these ex-people, better to avoid them in the future. Every great once in a while, Don would run into someone on the list and pretend he never met him. But on Junana the entire list was waiting to approve of his resume. In a flash all those burned bridges were intact. His past was now surgically reattached to his ass.

There were also plenty of people who left town on Don; they were on the list of people he considered to be idiots or bastards. Shouldn't he have the same opportunity to screw with their future? He thought for a minute: what about Steve Post? Steve Post spent two years trying to steal Don's job as CIO at WeBWillacker. The guy never smiled, and he finally left when everyone up the ladder from him in the company concluded he was a complete pain in the ass. Of course, there were several hundred "Steven Post" listings on Junana, but only one with a link to WeBWillacker.

Don clicked on the name and the all-too-familiar bioform came up. Don was hoping to find enough humiliating information to drop old Steve a note, congratulating him on the dismal failure that would certainly be Steve's life. As he read, he discovered that Steve's first wife had died just before he joined WeBWillacker. She had been diagnosed as bipolar and killed herself and their two kids by driving off the road near Los Gatos. After WeBWillacker, Steve went back to school, did a medical degree and became a psychiatrist in New Mexico, where he also did research on bipolar disorder and later remarried. Now he is a prominent fixture of the medical community in Albuquerque.

Don logged out of Junana.com. All those days Steve volunteered to stay late and work. The fierce devotion he put into his programming. Steve never had a good word for anyone, moping around the water cooler. When they ordered in pizza, he just took his slices back to his cube. The dude lived in his cube. Don thought he was after his job, but Steve was trying to avoid going home to that sad empty house. If Steve hadn't been staying late all those nights, Don could have gone home. How many days he cursed Steve for sucking up to the management. Why didn't Steve tell anyone? Why didn't they know? It was a good crowd at WebWillacker. They could have helped. Might have saved Don's marriage, too, if he spent more time with the kids.

"This thing is going to be worth trillions!" Don whispered, doing the math. A billion users on Junana, eventually paying ninety-nine Dollars, or Euros, or Pounds, or whatever, every month. The biggest bargain of their lives, and a bonanza for Michael 'Scratchy' fucking O'hara.

§   §   §

The idea of Haverbrook School was conceived the day, perhaps the instant, when little Simon Bishop failed entry into the elite Orange County kindergarten that the Reverend had always planned as the launching pad for the twins' academic enterprise.

The Ultra-Conservative Congregationalist Convention sought and bought a North Carolina property from the Unitarians as a campus for Haverbrook. North Carolina, Reverend Gerry Bishop believed, was appropriately removed from the cultural decay of New York and Los Angeles. The original gothic mansion had been built in 1879 by Lucas Smedley from the profits on his improved eccentric wheel design, used extensively in locomotives and other steam devices. None of the devices that relied on his design were any more eccentric than was Lucas.

Nowhere near as large as the Vanderbilt's nearby estate, the Smedley House was serially famous in North Carolina for the occult practices of its original owner, the artistic extravagance of his daughters, the sadistic predilections of his namesake grandson, and then a defensible patricide, a public trial, and the discovery of three bodies buried in the conservatory. The remaining heir gave the property, the house and its eighty acres, to the Unitarians in 1956. The Unitarians ran this as a retreat center, but they barely managed the upkeep and were delighted when the UCCC offered them cash.

The church renovated the main house and built several new structures: classrooms, a dormitory, a gymnasium, a stable for pupils who brought their own ponies, and a chapel in New England style. Its eighty boys, from grades seven to twelve, would be hand picked from the cream of the congregation. Its tuition rivaled an Ivy League college. The curriculum was scrupulously vetted for a puritanical taste. One of the parents donated a science center, complete with a broadband Internet connection and a microcomputer laboratory. None of the faculty imagined they had just admitted the Devil as a new professor.

That is exactly what Reverend Bishop told them when Simon and Peter were enrolled, by which time the broadband network had been extended to every room on the campus and used by every student and teacher for several hours on any given day.

"Why did we build a school way out here? So we could chat with Greenwich Village? 'Be not deceived, evil communications corrupt good manners.' First Corinthians."

Bishop barely listened as the rector explained about their severe Internet filters and the learning management system they relied upon. Bishop left them with a warning to be vigilant, which they were, to an extreme, until the Game slid past all of their electronic defenses as easily as Gargantua might penetrate Panurge's contrapunctum-covered walls.

The Game rarely had any difficulty fulfilling the fantasies of 14-year-olds, most of whom had already spent a year on Junana.com spelling these out in graphic detail on their bioforms. Many of them were fixated on fictional characters, pirates or wizards from books or the cinema.

"A million Gandolfs can't be wrong," Itchy said.

"How about a million Snapes?" Scratchy said. "Almost a third of the little biters go for the dark side."

"Feel the force," Winston added.

Other young teens were entering their puppy-love phase, equally fantastic. The objects of their obsession were easily captured by the Game's algorithms. Some preferred mythical creatures or animated objects that were beyond the scope of the Game's early design: talking lions and such. Others chose deities, an arena that Scratchy had argued was not one the Game should embrace. Nearly all were ecstatically happy when they opened the door to the Game and their Guide announced herself.

§   §   §

"The Game is going to hit high schools worldwide like an EF5 tornado," Robby said, slurping his pho. "It's likely to do more damage than good if we don't give teachers something concrete to work with."

The Sao Do compound rang with the voices of children at lunch. Robby, Itchy, and Desi had a corner table, where the owner eyed them carefully, personally filling their water glasses, reveling in Desi's compliments on the food. The restaurants had taken on the challenge of creating a vegetarian pho, not an easy task, as the dish normally is based on a broth of oxtail and beef stock and served with tripe or tendon, as well as bits of heart and liver and chunks of steak or chicken.

Desi was vegetarian by birth, habit, and aesthetic choice. He refused to get into arguments over the moral grounds for vegetarianism, as these tended to offend his omnivorous friends. Scratchy once told him he should go ahead and admit he considered himself better than non-vegetarians. If Scratchy were to apply Intention-full to this problem, Desi mused, he would see it was more an issue of living mindfully. With Desi's coaxing, the cooks at Sao Do competed to bring to life the essence of pho using only spices and a broth of celery and shallots.

"You are suggesting what?" Itchy knew from Robby's voice that he had already formulated a plan.

"Even at really small schools, I would imagine that at least three of four teachers will also be Gamers. We can reach them through their Guides. We can give them the tools to use the

Game in their classes and to demonstrate to others that the Game is not a threat, but a powerful learning engine for their students."

"Jack has requested that we incorporate some practical information within the Game. So far we've added templates for accounting theory, stock market dynamics, business communication, and statistics into the Free-for-All directory. Players continue to suggest other templates as well. The Guides suggest topics based on the user's job profile. I don't see why we couldn't do something like a teacher in-service class. Can you develop the content?" Desi asked. Robby nodded.

"How about a special high-school teacher scene in Junana for teacher Gamers who have earned their shoes?" Itchy suggested.

"We should have a site outside of Junana where we can provide educational white papers, power-points, and links," Robby said. "Not everyone is in Junana."

"We don't host content outside Junana," Itchy said, "but we can provide content that teachers can export to their websites and blogs."

"In a decade there might not be high school as we know it today, nor college for that matter. Tens of millions of teachers across the planet are going to wake up suddenly to the realization that the Game does a much better job covering content then they ever could," Robby noted.

"Teachers can use the Game to their advantage." Itchy said.

"Or perceive it as an enormous threat," Robby said. "Whenever high school entrance or graduation requires standard testing we see this same mistaken obsession with content. Content is actually the easy part, and Game does this incredibly well. Real teaching isn't about content, it's about context. It's about curiosity and conversation. When students already control the content, then the real job of teaching comes to the foreground."

"What are Gamers supposed to do in a classroom?" Desi asked.

"Schools are extremely valuable as social centers..." Robby said.

"Since when? My high school was more like a social waterboarding marathon," Desi said.

"I'm not saying it's always pleasant," Robby noted. "But it is essential for their social growth. The Game should work with them to make sure Gamers do not become isolated and antisocial. We are creating a cohort of fifteen-year olds with the equivalent of a college graduate degree. There's no high school in the world today that can handle these kids."

"Maybe they should be in college," Itchy said.

"At fifteen they still have attachments to their parents and to peers that are entirely adolescent. What they need is a club where they can work out, express themselves, explore relationships, get into conflicts where the consequences are bounded. They need to do kid stuff. In Spanish they say it this way: 'el que más temprano se moja, más tiempo tiene para secarse'..."

"'...The earlier you get wet, the more time you have to dry,' Desi translated. "Oh, I like that."

"At age fifteen, school should be the place you go to get wet without the possibility of drowning."

"Like a fight club," Itchy said.

"Or a love hotel," Desi added.

"Or like an Outward Bound course, challenging them physically, emotionally, intellectually. Give them Shakespeare to act in, not just memorize. Do the sports and the dances, and use classroom time to push the content to reveal its multi-vocal contexts within the lives of the students."

"Classes become more like debates," Itchy said, tilting back his bowl to get to the last noodle.

"College becomes graduate school. Those that choose to go on are those with the motivation to contribute something at that level." Desi settled back in his chair. The restaurant owner rushed up and put a small bowl of sweet rice chè down in front of him. Desi thanked the man, who bowed and retreated.

"Sounds like high schools will feel the primary impact," Itchy said. "How many teachers out there are prepared to step up as the adults in a room with thirty adolescent Gamers? How many have the social skills to lead this Outward Bound adventure. That's asking a whole lot without giving them any training."

"Some of the teachers will not be able to make the adjustment. And a whole lot of students are not going to like hanging out in a class where they are being taught content they already control. I foresee at least three years of chaos before things settle down. That's why we need to push schools into a positive path forward. We can expect a huge wave of panic among teachers. Let's turn this panic into opportunity."

"We'll get the Nerds together on this immediately," Desi said. "When can you start creating the materials?"

"Most of them are ready now," Robby said. "Ever since we finished the Brainwave bench tests, I haven't had a lot to do here. One more suggestion."

"Yes?" Desi said.

"Principals are the key. Can Junana create a space just for high-school principals and headmasters, and invite them to gather for information sessions?"

"I can put a crew on it this afternoon," Itchy said. "Feeling better?"

"I can't wait until next September," Robby said. "I feel like a kid again."

"That was before kids had their M.A. at age fifteen," Desi said. "None of us will know what these Gamer kids feel like. That's the scary part for me. We are creating a new generation that is as different from us as we are from, say, pre-literate societies."

"Once the teachers are Gamers, a lot of this will get simpler," Itchy said.

"That's after it gets so much more complex," Robby said.

"Busy, busy, busy," Itchy said.

"Ramen!" Desi added and slurped the last of his pho. "Robby, you should get back to the U.S. to coordinate this effort. We'll keep you on the payroll and get you settled."

"How about Stanford?" Robby asked.

Desi nodded his agreement.

"For ten years, colleges have been grousing about getting freshmen who can't read. Now we'll give them freshman with master's degrees," Itchy said. "Stanford might be a good test bed for studying this."

§ § §

Within days of his first plunge into the sectors of Level One, Peter Bishop was fully devoted to Courtney, his Guide. She had, well, everything he imagined she could. That smile, the hair, worn long and supple, the way she talked to him, her eyes, and her body. Her body most of all. She must be at least sixteen, the way she packs the skin-tight leather bodice when she's ready to fight with him, which was pretty much any time. Apart from Miss Jeffreys, who taught French, Courtney was the only female with whom Peter had contact on a regular basis. The school was allowed afternoons in Asheville twice a week for shopping, but they had to wear their uniforms, so they looked like Dorks from Planet Pilgrim.

The hours he spent in class or in chapel, hours away from Courtney, were a torture to him. She scolded him when he skipped class to log on. Evenings and weekends, she insisted, until the summer, when they can play all day.

"No!" he'd plead, "five more minutes." With a wave, she would shut down the program until the evening.

Peter's twin brother, Simon, had other feelings for his Guide. Eldrick the Dark Mage was not a wizard to be trifled with. Eldrick had promised to reveal the arcane knowledge that only the few might attain. Easily displeased, Eldrick challenged Simon to show he was worthy of this knowledge, and Simon vowed, as deeply as he might from the still shallow recesses of his fourteen-year old soul, that he would keep eternal faith with the Dark Mage.

§   §   §

Jennifer and her Con|Int staff were still trying to characterize the various scenes in the Junana social networking service when she noticed the Game. A simple room with a door from every scene in Junana. Not much of a video game player herself, as she had plenty of other distractions, she casually checked out the opening of the Game, and found herself unwilling to commit the days it would take to get through even the first level, although she found her Guide to be attractive in so many ways.

A new high-res Junana.com interface was made available through a downloadable Game client. She figured most of Junana's users would be switching to this Game client software and out of the browser. Whoever designed this now had hundreds of millions of simultaneous users on software they controlled. She had assigned two of her staff to pursue the Game and report back. Shortly after that, they had each stopped replying to her emails and phone calls.

§   §   §

Only months after its initial release, the Game on Junana made the covers of several national and international weeklies. The Chronicle of Higher Education's cover showed a picture of a seventeen year-old girl in a Yanagi U. hoodie holding up her Y.U. diploma. Inside, it asked the question university presidents were ducking: Is college obsolete? Other stories warned about the lack of control over the content.

"My fifteen-year old son knows more about Marx than most of my graduate students," a professor of political science at Columbia University announced.

The secrecy behind Junana struck a chord with the weeklies. A list of private European corporations could be identified as managing various aspects of the software giant, but the identities of the owners were left to speculation. Rumors tied Junana to Redmond or Mountain View, or to some unholy alliance of both. Others claimed links to Shanghai or Dubai. Reports on the technology of the Junana client and the Game surfaced in the geek blogs. These were translated for the general public in the mainstream magazines.

Some of the magazines, their writers deep into the Game, carried feature stories about the templates, including interviews with Emil Constantine, now retired and living in Berkeley. Several magazines ran stories about remote villages in India or Zambia, anywhere obscure, with photographs

showing teenagers wearing the shoes, holding up their
diplomas.

Radio talk shows picked up on the mystery over the
ownership of Junana, fanning speculation about sinister intent.
Call-in shows were inundated by callers who claimed they'd
never played the Game but had heard all about how it was
teaching feminism, or socialism, or both. Gamers who called
in mostly floundered while trying to describe their experience
and invariably told the host to go play the Game.

§   §   §

Reverend Gerald Bishop was at the top of his form. He stood
on the broad carpeted plinth in full robes. His eyes took in the
vast hall, where 7000 worshippers were standing. With the help
of a full orchestra, a choir that would blow away the Mormons,
and the biggest pipe organ made in fifty years, they sang out
"What a Friend We Have in Jesus."

Nothing in the building worked as well as the acoustics,
which were designed to minimize the lag between the choir
and back of the room. This required a bank of speakers at the
rear to reflect the choir back to the center of the space. Twenty
feet above the crowd, the organ reached the volume of a private
jet on takeoff. Most of the room felt like the front row at a ZZ
Top concert. That was, of course, the point. Shake them out of
their complacency, rouse them from their lethargy, rattle the
sin right out of them.

The words of the song were scrolling on the giant screens
above him, while the choir leader in a bright blue robe jived
like Cab Calloway to the upbeat music. The choir swung back
and forth to his direction.

Ever since he took a small church in a remote Texas town out of the Conservative Congregationalist Assembly of God and founded the Ultra-Conservative Congregationalist Convention, Pastor Gerry Bishop had been hoping to lead his new church on a crusade that would redefine the role of religion in the lives of all Americans. Today, his Irvine, California mega-church, more than 20,000 strong along with his nation-wide television audience, was eager to follow his lead. Affiliate congregations in a hundred cities and towns would do likewise. Other churches, ashamed of their lack of foresight, would rally to his cause, and fall in behind him. Within months he would take his crusade to Congress, where the majority he helped put into office will put the force of law behind this effort.

Today he would unleash this army of righteousness upon the greatest threat faced by any American public. The threat was greater than Godless communism; greater than fanatic terrorism; greater than gambling, drugs, and teen sex combined; this digital devil was, of course, online social spaces and games.

"Thou wilt find a solace there..." The last refrain of the old hymn died away in a flourish from the organ and the Reverend Bishop stepped up to his crystal pulpit, into the spotlights of the TV cameras. In his right hand was the white leather-bound Bible he carried for his sermons; in his left, he held a selection of DVD-ROMs from the computer games that were poisoning the minds and the bodies of an entire generation.

§   §   §

Jack and Winston argued for weeks before deciding that Winston should write a series of articles outlining the features of the economy Junana and the Game were reshaping. Jack's usual concern about security gave way to Winston's perspective that the impacts of the Game were potentially more fundamental than they previously anticipated. Creating an economy where the consumer was fully individuated would require rethinking most of the theories of consumer behavior and corporate planning. The sooner this process was seeded into the most innovative companies, the quicker their competitive advantages would emerge.

There were always a few multinational corporations eager to build products for discerning customers. Most of these were design firms working in the higher value sectors of their market. Historical precedents were easy to find: Swedish stereos, German sports cars, Italian footwear. Only now this penchant for individuated style and quality would need to be produced for much larger population, allowing prices to drop significantly. Similar continental shifts in advertising and retail marketing would also be required as consumer expectations rose. In many nations, starting with the U.S., the electoral process had also been penetrated by mass-market strategies. Candidates were marketed like Wonderbras. All that would also change.

Perhaps the largest change, and something none of the Nerds had envisioned, was a growing failure in predictability. The emergence of the individual Game player was a side effect of the relationship between each player and her Guide. The logic of the Game required each player to choose her own path through the levels. The Guides had personalities programmed to emerge as they learned from the player's gaming choices in Level One. There were no cheats, no secrets to be had through the Game magazines or websites.

Winston reminded Jack of what Scratchy had said all those years ago: "'We can sharpen the tools people use, but it would be better to sharpen the people.' Well, the people are already sharper," Winston argued.

"We're not seeing them any happier," Desi cut in. "We've opened up a lot of windows people tried to keep closed. I'm really worried that the Game doesn't prepare them for their new perspectives."

"Desi's right. There are many consequences the world might need to consider sooner rather than later," Winston continued. "All I want to do is seed some helpful ideas so that people will grow them."

"Why not build these ideas into Level Four and let the CEOs who play the Game discover them there," Jack said.

"It's not in their workflow to play games," Scratchy said. "They're more concerned about how many of their employees are playing the Game. They don't realize that by the time their employees hit Level Four they have joined an entirely new workforce."

"How is that?" Winston asked.

"You now have janitors with the equivalent of a graduate degree. How are workers going to keep building widgets and turning burgers once they've seen the larger picture?"

"Still another reason to start feeding ideas into the system," Winston argued. "What happens when your employees know more than you do?"

"What if your caddie were a better golfer than you?" Jack replied, his avatar grinning automatically.

"Or your opponent had better clubs," Desi said.

"Or a better ball," Itchy said.

"Or better balls," Scratchy growled.

"Exactly," Winston replied. "Least we can do is pave the road ahead for those who have the balls to take it."

THIRTEEN

Jennifer reread a report from her assistants about the game in Junana. Both of them were capable researchers with doctorates from top universities, and so she had little reason to doubt their analysis. However their joint report was incredibly unprofessional, it basically told her to play the Game herself, as soon as possible, and to ask Claire to have the entire staff do the same. They had finished Level Three, whatever that meant, in three months of nearly constant play, and were starting Level Four.

After leaving still-unanswered messages on their phones and emails, Jennifer sent an urgent message to their home pages on Junana for a meeting at the Sorbonne scene the next morning. She was furious with them.

Roland and Annika's avatars were waiting for her at the appointed time under the meeting tree in the Sorbonne quadrangle, which looked nothing like anything at the Sorbonne. They each wore the brown shoes and black hat she had seen popping up in Junana, and which had also appeared, like mushrooms after a spring shower, on the sidewalks of Paris. They walked over to a reasonably vacant arcade. Roland's avatar wore a sweatshirt that read "Y.U." Annika's was in jeans and a simple white blouse. They switched to a private encrypted conversation mode. Jennifer toggled to Third Person and hovered over the shoulder of her avatar.

"I've been trying to contact you for weeks. I need one reason why I should not fire you right now," Jennifer said. Her avatar analyzed the meaning of the words and placed its hands on its hips in irritation.

"Well, for starters, we are neck deep in the biggest thing to hit the Internet since porn," Annika said.

"I told you to investigate, not go completely native," Jennifer said. "You stopped answering my emails."

"Once I got plugged in," Roland confessed, "I lost track of time."

"The Game is truly addictive," Annika said.

"In a completely engaging fashion," Roland added, "Like the best movie you've ever seen, or the finest lecture you've ever attended."

"Then your report was grossly incomplete."

"The Game is not easy to describe. For one thing, it plays differently for each user."

"We compared our experiences in the first two levels," Annika said, "Apart from the underlying context, they were almost entirely different."

"The first level," Roland started, "Seems more like a personality test than a game. Level one presents you with a stream of challenges that reveal your thought processes, your fascinations and irritations..."

"What you avoid and crave," Annika continued. "How you react, what you already know. Most players would not guess that the Game is playing them."

"That's what got us intrigued. This is far more sophisticated than any other computer game we've played. Take the Guide, for example." Roland's avatar smiled, almost unconsciously. "My Guide was just like this upper-class man I met at Oxford when I was a freshman."

"Mine was like the tennis coach I had in high school." Annika said. "Part parent, part movie star..."

"Part best friend, part lover..."

"Part Yoda, part Buffy…"

"All knowing, you can ask him anything…"

"And tell her everything," Annika added. "And, eventually, you do."

"Like I said, the Game starts as a confessional, which seems to be a necessary procedure for the Game to prepare its programming for the following layers—"

Nearby, in the center of the quadrangle, an avatar appeared. He was wearing the shoes and the hat, and a long crimson cloak over a Tibetan yellow shirt, with a blue shoulder bag. He was holding a long wooden staff as tall as he was. Annika saw him in the corner of her vision and turned, Roland followed her gaze.

"The Grand Meister," he whispered and nodded in the avatar's direction. From the crowd of avatars in the quadrangle several of them, each with a blue shoulder bag, began to converge on the new arrival. Most of the others were still watching from where they stood.

"What is going on?" Jennifer asked. "Who is that?"

"He has completed the Seventh Level and is immersed in the templates," Annika spoke. "I'd heard rumors that the first Grand Meister had emerged. I never expected to see him."

The Grand Meister raised one hand in a salute or a benediction. Annika and Roland joined the crowd in a return bow. Then he and the blue-bag-wearing avatars surrounding him disappeared.

"Was that a Guide or a real person?" Jennifer asked.

"Definitely a person, someone I would hope to meet," Annika said. "When I'm worthy."

"Worthy? You have a Ph.D. from Stockholm University and you feel inadequate to meet someone who has mastered a video game?"

"The Game is not Counter Strike," Roland said, his avatar gesturing as the rant developed. "It's not like any other computer game you can imagine. It's not Halo, EverQuest, or World of Warcraft. It's an accelerator hooked up to your brain, a window onto the features of actual life that subtend your everyday existence. And when you leave the Game, you see everything differently. The singular design of your room, the habits of your family, the news programs: nothing remains the same as before."

"Do you remember the conversation you had with your friends in school where you first announced that you doubted God's existence?" Annika added. "By announcing this you opened up the possibility that God actually did not exist, and freed yourself from the need to feel he must. That moment is really when you move from your childhood wondering about God to the possibility of actively believing in God, or to rejecting this belief. The act of belief requires this moment of doubt.

"That moment, or rather its like, is repeated many times in the Game. You can feel the revelations pull out the stops in your thinking, yank away the hobbles from your emotions. So many times I've been exploring topics I thought I had mastered: core issues about power, identity, and action I'd been reading and writing about for years.

"The Game challenges me to show my understanding. It shines a light on the clear relief of my ignorance. Then it guides me to a new understanding. Suddenly I am freed from the fear that what I've learned and what I know is just some mod pastiche of other people's words. For the first time in my life I feel so incredibly grounded in what I know I know."

"Wait!" Jennifer yelled, and her avatar threw up its hands. "You are talking about a computer game—something manufactured to pull cash out of the accounts of kiddies and their parents. Clever eye candy for the attention-challenged; and you tell me it's changing your lives?

"Right now there are more than 900 million players," Roland said.

"By this time next year there could be two billion," Annika continued.

"That would mean just about everyone on the planet who has access to a computer would have at least tried the Game," Jennifer said.

Both of her employees were smiling broadly.

"And you figured maybe I wouldn't want to be the last one to check it out. OK, so you're not fired. But please, go to a movie, drift around the city. Turn off your computers and eat dinner in a restaurant."

"Right, boss," Roland said and logged off.

"My Guide just told me there is a Bergman retrospective at the Kino," Annika said. "She agrees completely with you. Ciao!" She logged off.

Jennifer used the menu to get back to the initial screen for the Junana client. She was in a Romanesque anteroom with two doors. One was marked "Junana," the other, "Game."

She touched the doorknob on the door marked "Game" and the scene faded.

§   §   §

Both of the Bishop twins received Wanda's farewell kiss and their shoes before the summer break. Simon insisted that Wanda was the shit, but Peter knew better. Tits are one thing, he'd say, and Simon would remind them they are actually two things. Anyhow, Peter offered, Wanda is old, could be like nineteen, and she's probably humping Jorge every chance she gets.

The shoes they hid in their closets. Word of the Game had spread around the campus and the Rector had put out a warning that any student caught playing the Game would be punished. Not that he would even consider punishing Simon or Peter. Rector Hector flinched every time Simon said hello to him. Several students who were careless enough to log on while in the Computer Center now spent weekends in detention. Teachers were even required to report students caught doing the Brainwave exercises in class. Peter claimed he spied Miss Jeffreys doing them in her car in the parking lot.

That summer they were back in California, at their dad's new mansion in Newport Beach. Their mom, they were told, was recovering from a nervous condition that required her to stay in their old house back in San Antonio to be close to her doctor. Their father voyaged off on another of his around-the-world UCCC fundraisers for most of the summer, preaching from a different country every week. This left the boys in the care of a rotation of church functionaries who made sure they brushed their teeth and did not drown in the pool.

They devoted the whole summer to the Game. They played each day until their Guides shut down the Game and told them to go eat. Then they drifted through the ever expanding maze of scenes on Junana, marveling and scoffing at the people they met. Simon used the pool only once. After an all-day query, he walked outside and took a piss in it.

Courtney, realizing Peter's fascination with anime, promised to take him on a virtual tour of Tokyo, once he got through Level Three. Eldrick finally offered Simon the barest of compliments. This sent him into an ecstatic fugue for a whole day. Simon cruised through Level Three and was nearly done with Level Four when school started again. The twins

were now straight "A" students, a significant improvement for
Simon, who had always maintained a "C" average as a posture
against his father's expectations.

§   §   §

The rector express-mailed their fall-quarter grades back to
California with a note of praise for the Bishop twins. The
content of this note reflected glory back on the school with
some spill over on his own performance. Actually most of the
boys were doing better in their academic classes, although
their behavior in chapel and in their required religious
instruction was not improving. Quite the reverse, he mused.

Rector Ralph H. Lovemark taught all of the religious
instruction classes. He had seen his share of adolescent hijinks
and outright bad behavior in his day. That his middle name
was Hector gave the students some little pleasure to abuse.

"Rector Hector," they'd ask, "if the world is less than seven
thousand years old, how did those dinosaur bones get buried
in the rock?" God's plan for the Earth was not theirs to
understand; this was his answer to most of their questions.
Maybe his answers were not entirely satisfactory, but wasn't
that where faith came in?

In the last few months, he faced a barrage of entirely new
questions, many of them challenging the very premise of
doctrine. It was as though the boys had gone to another school
in their sleep and had returned with poisonous suspicions and
highly unorthodox perspectives.

Little Simon Bishop had failed his interview at the Orange
County kindergarten when he bit a little girl on the arm during
the "sociability" test. She had been attracted to his eyes, which
were delightfully green hazel. She had touched his cheek. His

brother Peter told his dad that Simon was just grumpy that afternoon. Simon said he thought the girl was going to poke out his eyes.

"Rector Hector?" Simon stood up in the classroom. He trained the same brace of emerald hazel eyes on Ralph. "So, exactly what were you in your most recent past life?"

§   §   §

The Nerds celebrated the first year of the Game in cities around the world. Desi had returned to India. Itchy was back in Kyoto. Winston was in Philly, Jack in Rome, and Scratchy in Santa Barbara. Desi had suggested that they spend a day drifting and then gather in the Room at midnight Zulu time to report what they had seen.

They had fixed the Room design to resemble a nineteenth-century London club, culling the best elements of a Ruskinian gothic chapel and a corner pub: carved walnut wall panels, a plush burgundy carpet, an enormous cut stone fireplace, gas lamps on the walls, and a vaulted ceiling. Incongruously, the huge console screen took up an entire side wall and the Cordobaloungers were arranged in a semicircle in front of the fireplace.

"We've delivered over a 100 million pairs of shoes, more than 8 million hats, and almost 1 million shoulder bags worldwide," Jack reported.

"It's like the world has paused and is waiting," Itchy said. "But it doesn't yet know for what."

"What does a post-consumer world look like?" Winston asked.

"Stick around and we'll all find out," Scratchy said.

"So far, it's just sad—I mean, all those stores closing down," Desi sighed.

"Global energy consumption is way down too," Jack said. "The global economy has, in effect, shifted into neutral."

"Where will it go from here?" Desi asked.

"Exactly," said Jack.

"That was a question," said Desi.

"And now the world has a reason to ask such questions and the time to consider some answers. Democracy runs well behind the pace of the marketplace. We gave it the opportunity to catch up."

"That's not our problem," Scratchy reminded him.

"No more than it's everybody's problem," Winston added.

"Sometimes you travel farthest by just standing still," Desi said.

"Sounds like you've unfolded one too many templates," said Scratchy.

"I can't say how the Game has affected anybody else, but I feel like I'm swimming in an immense ocean of history and knowledge," said Desi.

"Anyhow, year is up," Scratchy noted. "Time to go public with the template code."

"Are you sure you want to go through with that?" Jack asked. "You don't know what the response will be."

"It's computer code. One or more nerds might get excited for a week," Scratchy said.

"It's going to be big," Desi predicted. "Look what we've managed to do in just a few years."

"I've got to clean up the comments before I release it. So it'll be several more days. I've got a lot of work to do." Scratchy logged off, his avatar disappearing from the Cordobalounger.

"This is going to get interesting real soon," Itchy said.

"Ramen, brother!" Desi said.

"Can't we stop him?" Winston asked.

"Not when he's right," Jack said. "It's one of those traits you love and hate about the man."

"So, you've noticed," Desi said. "Mikey'd rather go down with the ship, so it's up to us to keep the ship afloat."

"This year we'd better all be prepared to watch each other's back. I'll see what I can do to get some support for Michael, should things go crazy this weekend. Ciao." Jack's avatar disappeared.

"See you back in Sao Do, Itchy. Ta-ta, Winston." Desi's avatar disappeared. Winston and Itchy logged out and the room faded to white.

§   §   §

Desi had made a practice of gathering Fivers for discussions about the Game. He would enter a plaza, broadcast a voice message that only Fivers in the plaza would hear, and invite them to join him in a discussion space Itchy had set up for this purpose. Desi wanted to know their impressions about how the Game was working in their lives.

Through these conversations Desi discovered a growing intolerance among players for non-players, as well as a rise in cynicism and depression within the Game community. The Game experience not only made its players smarter, as they had planned, but also impacted their willingness to cope with the problems they still faced at home or at work. They were becoming more self-reliant but also more introverted. There was increasing disenchantment with everyday activities and mundane cultural practices. Outside of the Game they were bored out of their skulls.

When Desi described these effects to the Nerds at their next Room session, they were discounted as temporary. After all the Game was just a year old. People would need time to adjust to their new capacities. Once Gamers started making movies and writing books a new aesthetic would emerge that could engage the players more fully.

"Out with the old," Scratchy said. "In with the new. Give it time. This is happening much quicker than we expected."

"Nobody's unfolded the happiness template," Winston reminded him. It was a theme they returned to again and again.

"We could try to add some fun to the Game," Desi said. "Fivers are way too serious."

Itchy proposed that they add Free-for-All time to the Game in Level Three.

"Players are banging their heads against a template every time they log on. We need to give them space to explore topics they choose."

In Level Four, the Guide already offered Free-for-All time as a reward. In level Five players can call up Free-for-All time as much as they want. At that point the Game became a universal digital library, encyclopedic in scope and tailored to the desires and capacities of each player.

Jack had suggested that the Game interface with the resources at local public libraries, instead of offering the same content online. Desi programmed the Game to scan the online catalogs of libraries around the world. When a Query or Free-for-All noted a certain book, the Guides directed players to their local library.

"Have you walked through a public library lately?" Winston asked. "Players are speed reading books at the stacks. They don't even check them out."

"I noticed kids speed reading over at Chaucer's Books here in Santa Barbara the other day," Scratchy said. "The owner finally shooed them out the door."

§   §   §

After a week of mounting chaos, they moved the Friday meeting out of the Santa Barbara High School faculty lounge into the front of the auditorium. In every classroom, teachers struggled to keep up with a cadre of student who appeared to command more content and who reveled in asking more questions than any students they had ever taught. The teachers were at turns thrilled, humbled, amazed, frightened, and totally at a loss about how to keep the class to their lesson plans. The other students, the ones that still acted like high-school students, complained acidly or sank into silent dread as the class spiraled beyond their comprehension.

All 74 teachers showed up, with all the counselors and front office staff. Phil Quigley sat on the stage, his legs dangling. He wore the hat. Principal Jason Woods sat quietly, dazed by the events of the day. During lunch Phil and a small delegation of teachers had confronted him in his office, outlining a project they said would take the full cooperation of the school's administration. It was, they added, the only way forward out of chaos in the classroom.

A group of the faculty sat off on the left side of the auditorium. Several of them also wore the hats. They whispered calmly among themselves. The rest of the faculty were in animated discussions, gesturing frantically and paying Phil little attention. He stood up and clapped his hands several times to get them to listen. The room finally quieted.

"Today," Phil said, "is the first day of the rest of your career." He let this sink in. "Our students have been given access to a teaching environment light years ahead of our classrooms." The group on the left was nodding quietly. "With this tool they can cover the same content we have been teaching them in roughly one tenth of the time and with near perfect recall."

"Looks like early retirement!" someone shouted. A nervous laugh faded quickly.

"Several months ago a new Game appeared online. Within weeks...," he consulted his notes, "roughly a quarter of Santa Barbara High School students were playing. That figure is now more than 62 percent."

A few weeks ago his Guide, Natalie, had interrupted his Free-for-All time to inform him that he was the most advanced player among the faculty and staff at Santa Barbara High. She showed him a video about what might happen on the first day of school and he read several white papers about the teaching goals and methods of the Game and how these could be integrated into a school-wide program. Natalie was excited that he would be leading the effort.

"Today we are witnessing the biggest wave of learning this planet has ever seen." Phil picked one of the themes from the video. "We can either stand up and ride this wave, or we can lie down and let it crush us on the rocks. It's all explained in this whitepaper." He passed a sheaf of handouts to the nearest teacher to distribute.

Beth, the librarian, jumped up. "I saw Mike Lockerbie read a whole book in half an hour. *Stranger in a Strange Land*. Cover to cover. During lunch. Didn't even check it out." She slumped back in her chair.

"Thank you, Beth," Phil said. "An excellent example of what I'm getting at. One of the problems we face is a dramatic increase in drop-ups."

"You mean drop-outs," someone said.

"I mean," he answered, "drop-ups. The day they turn sixteen, students are taking the on-line state high-school equivalency test and getting their diploma. They are 'dropping up' and going to City College instead of Santa Barbara High School. Easiest thing in the world, once you have one of these." He held up a Bachelor of Knowledge diploma from Yanagi University while he looked back at his notes.

"As of yesterday, 276 SBHS students have already earned their first university degree. Another 500 or so are close. More than a hundred students have already dropped up and will not be back this semester.

"We need to keep our students here, in school, until they are seventeen. That's our first goal. And we need to get our entire faculty through Level Three on the Game. There are new teaching templates on Level Four. That's our next goal. By the time you have your hat," he doffed his and resettled it on his head. "You will wonder how you ever stood in front of a classroom before the Game."

"Are you suggesting we allow students to play a video game in school?" Gary Trumble called out.

"I am suggesting that we all play the Game as our curriculum. If Mike Lockerbie can read a whole book in half an hour, can you imagine how much he can learn in a semester? We need to bring the Game to the rest of the students and give them time to explore it during school. We have plenty of computers, so let's put them to good use."

"How do we explain to their parents that they are playing a computer game all day?" Principal Woods asked.

"If we agree to open up the school to the Game, then the Game will agree to become an official school resource. For our students, the Game will re-skin its interface to become the 'Santa Barbara High School Knowledge Assistant.' Homework assignments and required readings will be handled through this 'KayAye.' In return, the Game will encourage its more advanced players to come to school each day instead of dropping up."

"What do you mean, 'the Game will agree'?" Trumble yelled, standing up, pointing his finger at Phil. "Who built this?"

"The handout covers the pedagogical vision for the Game. There is a complete teacher in-service course on Level Three, and we have a teacher's lounge area in Junana where we can discuss these issues."

"And if we don't agree?" Trumble asked.

"Most of our students will drop up as soon as they can. Until then they will come to class knowing more about the topic of the day than you do." Phil slipped back into his seat.

"What about the rest of the students? What if they don't want to play the Game?" Amanda Baxter asked.

"No student will be forced to use the KayAye. We will continue to teach the standard curriculum in small classes without Gamers present."

"What do we say to the school board?" Principal Woods asked.

"We are still teaching to the tests," He glanced over at the Gamer teachers, "with some more advanced content."

"If we agree, then the Game predicts that our students will..." he glanced at his notes, "score on average at least 40 percent higher than last year in the required tests. At least half the students will get one or more 5s on AP tests."

"Forty percent!" Principal Woods exclaimed. And if we don't jump on board, he thought, every other high school in the district will outscore us.

Amanda Baxter stood up. "I assigned *The Great Gatsby* for summer reading. Nick Landreu is in my sophomore literature class. Those of you who teach freshman classes might remember Nick. Others might remember the incident at the flagpole last year."

She paused. Several teachers and staff members were nodding.

"Over the summer, Nick not only read *The Great Gatsby*, but as far as I can tell, he read everything Fitzgerald wrote, and several other authors from the period. On his own initiative."

She lowered her head.

"I should be thrilled, and I am. More than anything." She looked up at Phil. "I need the tools to work with these kids. I don't want to just keep up with them. I want to step up and engage them. If this game will help, I'm ready to try it."

Principal Woods stood up and walked over to the stage. He boosted himself up on this and stood beside Phil.

"I know this is coming at us way too fast," he said. "But maybe that's the way it needs to happen. I could make the decision alone, but I think we'll need to help each other through this, so I'm going to open this up to a vote. I'm going to assume the faculty sitting over there," he pointed to the left, "will vote 'yes,' meaning you're in favor of this new game. The rest of you, including staff, grab a slip of paper and write 'yes' or 'no' on this, fold it and pass it to the aisle. Martha, can you pick these up?"

Martha, his assistant, stood up and nodded. The vote took only a minute. She gathered the slips and handed them up to Woods. He sorted them on the stage. Then he stood and faced them.

"Well, it's pretty clear. Only nine 'no' votes. Does anybody have anything they want to say?"

Gary Trumble stood up. "I'm still bothered by the secrecy behind this game scheme. I can't argue with its effectiveness, but I would feel a lot better if the designers were available for a conversation. How do we know where all this is headed?"

"Phil," Woods said. "What if we later decide to opt out of this arrangement?"

Phil had forgotten to tell them this point. "Principal Woods will have complete authority over if and how the Game is used on campus. His Guide will be providing detailed reports on student progress and any issues that teachers have. He can literally pull the plug at any time, and the Game will immediately become inactive on campus computers."

"Says you," Trumble said.

"Says me," Phil agreed.

Woods sorted through the layers of emotion that had enveloped him all day. For years his main task had been to keep his best teachers from giving up out of exhaustion and frustration. Suddenly, students who formerly graced his office with flimsy excuses for bonehead pranks were actually doing the summer required reading. Half his teachers felt unqualified to step back into their classrooms. He strode to the edge of the stage and held up his hands.

"On Monday, we will open up the Knowledge Assistant as a new tool for all our students. Those who have their own laptop computers will be encouraged to bring them. The rest will have school computers made available to them. Students who decide not to use the KayAye. will have class time as before and cover the required topics. The same goes for the teachers. Nobody will be forced to use this new Knowledge Assistant. This is a voluntary experiment in digital learning. We will meet again next Friday to discuss progress and problems. My office door is open all the time for any concerns that arise. Now take a deep breath, go home, and have a relaxing weekend. Come Monday we'll all go back to school."

Nerdville

FOURTEEN

As the moon was only just beginning to show on the eastern horizon, the view from the parapet wall on the edge of the roof of the mansion was obscured by darkness. Tonight this was also obscured by the stream of tears that Peter Bishop refused to quiet. The old Smedley House was three tall stories, surrounded by a formal garden, and situated at the head of a narrow valley now spotted with the buildings of Haverbrook School.

"Courtney," he whispered and stepped forward, falling into the darkness.

§   §   §

The job of Consolidated Intelligence was to tilt the results of the ongoing fashion wars in favor of its clients by giving them a foreshadowing of tomorrow's consumer climate. Claire Doolan had built Con|Int from a one-person social survey firm into one of the top three consumer-intelligence agencies in the U.S.. Consumer research was one of the few industries where a Ph.D. in cultural anthropology made any sense. And as there were hundreds of unemployed anthropologists facing careers working in cafes and taxicabs, Claire had no trouble recruiting for her Posse. She had experts posted in every top cultural scene, from Seattle to Soho and from Harajuku to Hyde Park. The consumer landscape was always a mosaic of regional differences, undergirded lately by international influences

NerdvilleN e r d v i l l e

from the global blogosphere and the placelessness of Junana.com, where the scenes and shows attracted avatars from anywhere in the world.

She had pulled one of her top staff members out of Paris to work full time in Junana.com. Jennifer first noticed the shoes in Junana. Brown shoes, but not a brown brown; a really dark café au lait brown—and simple, like Rite Aid shoes, but slip-ons, more like espadrilles. Since these were images on the feet of digital avatars, they weren't actually shoes, but they were suddenly everywhere on Junana.com. Avatars from all over were choosing to cover their feet with the same digital image. Strange chats were showing up too. People complaining that someone "didn't earn his shoes." Then, last month, Alice noticed them on the streets.

§   §   §

"There's excellent news," Rector Lovemark almost shouted into his cell phone. "I'm at the hospital emergency room, and they say he'll be good as new in six months."

"What was he doing on the roof?" Reverend Gerry Bishop demanded.

"Simon claims it was a suicide attempt. He found a note."

"Peter would not do that to me."

"That's a fact, Reverend. Anyway, he was performing so well in class; you saw his last report card: "A"s across the board. Hardly any reason to kill himself. It must have been a prank."

"I'm guessing an accident. How'd he get up there?"

"We've had workers out on the roof patching up the skylight. They left the door unlocked, and, naturally, he has this incredible curiosity, so he went exploring. It was dark, and he fell."

"That's how it happened. I'll talk with Simon about this. Now..."

"Two badly sprained ankles and a broken arm," Ralph said. "That's it. Just a fall in the darkness onto the grass below. He'll be back in class in a day or so, laughing about his adventure. Showing off his wounds. I'm sure everyone will sign his cast. He's very popular, you know..."

"Stop blathering, Hector! I need to know what is going on at the school."

"What do you mean?" Ralph's instinct told him Bishop was fishing.

"You know what I mean."

"The skylight. It's been leaking for months. These old mansions..."

"Fuck the skylight, Ralph."

"I could not stop them, believe me." Ralph blurted.

"Just tell me how it happened."

"It started when they began to read the Bible."

"I'm sure most of our boys have been up on their Bible studies for years. You're not making sense."

"I mean, read," he said, "as though the Holy Scripture was just a book to be browsed from beginning to end."

"What are you getting at?"

"When they finish—" he stopped. He could not say it.

"I'm waiting."

"I mean..." Hector shook the phone as though the words he needed might tumble out.

"I'm still waiting. Don't try my patience."

Hector breathed in and out, in and out. "They come and tell me they, well, they 'don't get it.'"

"They 'don't get' what?"

"The Bible."

Bishop let the little worm squirm for a minute. Then he said, "Didn't you explain that God's word is vastly elusive? That the Bible must be read with prayer and humility? 'For my thoughts are not your thoughts, neither are your ways my ways, saith the Lord.' Isaiah..."

"...Chapter 55, verse 8. Of course I did, but there's more...." Ralph now clutched his phone as if could somehow squeeze the remaining battery life out of it and finish this conversation.

"I'm waiting."

"After they read the Bible, they keep on reading."

"They're students, Hector."

"But, they read the Koran, the major Upanishads, Buddhist texts, and even the Gnostic Gospels. There's no stopping them!"

There was silence on the other end of the line. Ralph checked the reception on his cell phone and then squeaked, "Reverend Bishop?"

"I don't recall any of those books in the school library." Bishop was beginning to sense a larger problem lurking at the school. Another screw-up to manage.

"No, sir. They find them on the Internet. Quite against school policy too, I can tell you that. They risk detention, even expulsion. Religion class is quite impossible. That's why it happened. One minute we are talking about Christ's temptation in the desert, next thing you know somebody's brought up a Hindu legend, or a Hopi story, and soon everybody's talking all at once."

"What happened?"

"I couldn't just stand there and listen, could I? They were talking about meditation and reincarnation, throwing out the names of pagan gods and mixing up chapter and verse of the Holy Bible with passages from Lao Tzu and Lord knows where else. So I left them, only for a minute, you know, to clear my head in the hallway. Only someone—I think it might have been Martin Snedeker; he was nearest to the door—someone locked it. They locked me out of religion class."

"Locked you out!"

"I banged and banged, and nobody opened the door. I went back to the office to get the key, but then the bell rang, and they'd all left. The next day I could not go back, I mean I just couldn't. I called in Freddy Haas. He's a fine student, a senior, always said he was going on to seminary. You'll remember Freddy. His father is a deacon in the Seattle church. I offered Freddy the chance to lead the religion class and he was really very grateful...."

"Hector..."

"...I've been thinking this could be a very valuable teaching tool, only for the best and brightest...."

"Hector!"

"Reverend Bishop?"

"When was this?"

"Let me see. About three weeks ago."

"The students have been running the religion class for three weeks?"

"Yes, and the reports are all very positive."

"The students are happy about this?"

"Isn't that amazing?"

"These are the same students who 'didn't get' the Bible."

"Only some of them said that."

"Do you imagine that your position at Haverbrook is dependent on your ability to make the students happy?"

"No, sir."

"Whom do you need to make happy?"

"Well, the parents are paying tuition, and then there's the annual fund; we expect major gifts..."

"Get real, Hector."

"You, sir. I need to keep you happy."

"Precisely. And do I sound happy?"

"Not at the moment."

"Here's what will make me happy. Are you listening?"

"I'm all ears, sir."

"You will resume teaching the religion class tomorrow."

"Certainly, sir."

"You will disconnect the entire campus from the Internet in the morning."

"Disconnect? But our learning content?"

"I asked you if you were listening; now, what did I say?"

"I will disconnect the campus in the morning."

"And it will stay disconnected until I arrive."

"Arrive?" Ralph slumped against the wall and closed his eyes.

"Let me see," Reverend Bishop pulled up his calendar. "I will be there next week on Friday."

"What do I tell the teachers?"

"Tell them to start teaching. I don't care if they use slates and charcoal, as long as our students are protected from the evil influences that you have allowed to infest Haverbrook, almost killing my son. Is Peter awake?"

Ralph looked back through the glass wall of the ER and spied Peter in a chair talking with the nurse. "He's in the ER recovery room, all bandaged up nice and neat."

"Then put him on, put him on! Why am I talking to you? My son has had an accident!"

§   §   §

Alice Davies worked Soho and Nolita, the lower East Side, and the Village. She tracked the chain stores and the boutiques, the kids rolling out of school in the afternoons, and the NYU crowd. She knew every shoe, every jean, and every t-shirt, blouse, and dress available for sale. She also coordinated the whole East Coast staff of Con|Int, including the media and food intel agents. She kept her street sense honed by monitoring several girls whose buying habits were harbingers of new trends.

So when Alice spied Louisa, one of her teenage fashion mavens, walk right past the Starbucks crowd into the new Red Star Coffee house on Broadway, she also noticed Louisa was wearing these hideous brown shoes. Shoes that you couldn't buy anywhere south of Midtown. Louisa didn't shop online; a girl who spends three hours a day in stores isn't going to go home and buy something off her laptop. Louisa returns more garments than most girls own. So where did she get these shoes? And why? They looked dreadful with her Evisu jeans and Juicy hoodie. Alice wrote it up in her weekly report.

Within two months, the shoes were all over the street. Alice's mavens told her the shoes were connected to "the game." She wondered if they were promotional gimmicks for a new cable game show, but then she read Jennifer's report about Junana.com, where a new online game had appeared. Meanwhile, Louisa had stopped shopping and was seen wearing Joe's Jeans from last year and a t-shirt Alice could buy off the street for ten bucks. And Louisa wasn't alone. Something was up. Alice's weekly reports became strident alarms. For the first time since she had learned the craft, what she was seeing on the street made no sense to her.

Even anti-fashion could become fashion-able, Alice knew. It would be manufactured and slipped into the brands where a new arbitrary value would be established. Only the really poor, geezers, and the ever-unaware—the nerds and their ilk— escaped the pull of fashion. Louisa had more disposable income than an entire small town in Tennessee. Here she was, wearing thrift-store-level clothes. And what's up with those shoes?

§ § §

Betsy ran the numbers from all the reports, and kept track of the statistical details through an arsenal of regression algorithms she had invented for that purpose. Claire ran the operation that culled the knowledge, but it was Betsy who produced the info-gasm. Her statistical routines were one special ingredient the big advertising groups wouldn't do without and couldn't manage in-house. Claire and Alice and the rest of the posse were very, very good at what they did. Betsy, however, was the best.

Elizabeth Berteotti, Ph.D., had a standing offer from Dentsu in Japan: They would pay her at twice whatever she was making now. Not that Con|Int was cheap. Betsy was just that good. All Betsy asked of Con|Int was to work at home and take a month off for Mardi Gras. She had a house in the Garden District with her on-and-off companion who ran a small lesbian bar in the Quarter.

Betsy grew up in Algiers across the river. She was in Baltimore, at Johns Hopkins on a post-doc, when Katrina hit New Orleans. Within six months she was back in the Quarter, renting a small apartment, and working to build back the soul of a town that had given her more than her fair share of feisty independence. She had been out of the closet since high school.

Claire had been looking for someone to work the numbers for Con|Int and ran across one of Betsy's papers on the cultural aspects of influenza epidemics. Betsy designed a statistical routine that could account for the discrepancies between income groups in the annual flu season. She was even able to tie this to the average store size of a certain type of fast-food restaurant. If she could do this for a simple virus, Claire reasoned, imagine what Betsy could uncover about the market for high-end handbags.

Betsy had a personality that kept her from even applying for a tenure track job at a university. Any place that wanted her to spend six years rowing the fucking boat in administrative committees was off limits. The Collège de France hadn't offered her a lectureship or Harvard a tenured position, and so Betsy was looking for work. Claire overspent to bring her on board at Con|Int. Betsy could be a royal bitch from hell at times, but she was also loyal, and her analyses gave Con|Int a cash flow and a caché too.

Betsy was so good that Claire didn't even bother to ask her if her latest report might be somehow, you know, wrong. She wrote and then trashed an email to Betsy before she sent it. "Please, please," it said, "tell me you dropped a zero somewhere. Call me and say that sunspots, or belated Y2K, PMS, or anything at all made you forget to add the final figure into the total and make it all OK again." Claire rolled over in her bed and peeked at the clock. Five thirty. Shit. She could not go back to sleep, not with that nightmare fresh in her head, not with the quarterly meeting at 10:00 a.m. over at the RIND Corp. headquarters. Her nightmare foreshadowed this meeting, or something horribly akin to it.

§   §   §

Scratchy finished his comments and posted the templates on a Saturday at 1:30 a.m.. The first nerd who downloaded the templates was a teenager in Minsk. The real chat started in London, where it was already late morning. *The Register* picked it up, and the news rolled across the global blogosphere like an Indian Ocean tsunami. The actual template code was concise, a few dozen megabytes, so the millions of downloads in those first hours didn't bring down the open-source-code servers.

When Asia went to bed, the template code had already been downloaded 52 million times and geek America was still fast asleep. Slash|Dash posted the news as an emergency flash at 8:00 a.m. Eastern and 400,000 cellphones rang across the nation. This started an avalanche of text messages coursing through the mediasphere, and still the sun had not appeared over hills behind Carpinteria.

By the time the West Coast awoke, the European tech editors were waxing prosaic over the revolutionary potential for the new code base, and the East Coast networks were gearing up for a news bonanza. Everyone wanted to know who Michael O'hara was and where they could find him.

After he sold one of his early companies, Scratchy purchased ten acres of unimproved land above Hillside Drive and split this into two home sites. Santa Barbara City approved the lot split, providing he put in a short road with a cul-de-sac large enough for a fire truck to turn around in. This took most of an acre and 100,000 dollars, but he also had the privilege to name this street. On a lark, he called it "Lotta Vista Lane."

Somebody, somewhere twittered his address in the early morning hours. Within minutes most of the editors of news outlets around the world received a text message with Scratchy's address: 23 Lotta Vista Lane, Santa Barbara, California.

§   §   §

Claire Doolan woke with a start, her breath staccato, the nightmare draining from her consciousness as she willed herself to relax. Panic was not a part of her life. She had survived fieldwork in the highlands of Indonesia, doctoral exams, childbirth, deaths of friends and family, and that magic day when she breezed into her husband's office and caught him getting an oral performance from one of her grad students. She knew varieties of horror, sorrow, and anger, but never panic. Not until this week.

This week, the reports from her "Posse," as Betsy called them, were upsetting, almost unnerving. Something on the magnitude of continental drift was going on out on the streets, out where the cohorts of consumers keep the markets humming. Consumers were always changing, but in predictable, controllable, marketable ways: to the new or the old, the mod, the retro, influenced by a jet stream of advertising into emergent eddies of expected desires. Desires to be filled and then reinvented. But not this week.

This week the same winds of influence blew, as strong and hot as the last. The coriolis of desire spun just as it always did. New lines of perfumes, clothing, and music debuted. Their adverts filled the mags and rags, the airways and cable networks. The consumer seduction machine purred along as before. And the agencies and their clients had the same expectations as before. There would be losers in the game, but there would also be winners. Until this week. This week everyone was losing. Claire's nightmare was either prescient or paranoid. She closed her eyes and remembered.

Claire walked into the room, into the glass and steel boardroom of the RIND Corporation, where her quarterly report would be interrogated by a panel of experts from industry and government. The panel had no name; it didn't exist in any form, apart from the pervasive reach of its participants across the entire marketplace in the U.S.. She walked into the room like she had walked in every quarter for the last three years. She had on her black Armani silk dress. She was on time. When she sat down, she looked at the faces around the heavy glass table. Then the heads turned to the Chair, across the table from her, and nodded in unison.

The Chair, this year, was the recently retired head of the Hollywood Film Association. He nodded back and reached into his jacket. He pulled out a gun. A small chrome revolver. He passed this to the person to his right, who passed it along in turn until the gun was in Claire's hands. It was warm and shined in the overhead halogen track lighting. She turned to pass it to the man on her right, who held up his hands and refused to take it.

She set the revolver down on the tabletop and started her presentation. Every time she gestured, she found the gun back in her hand. She kept setting it down again and again until her presentation was over and the revolver was back in her hand once more. The room seemed indifferent to this inconsistency and unmoved by her eloquence. She asked for questions and they sat dumb. She waited for what seemed like hours and then, in her mind as a joke, pointed the pistol at her forehead. Now they were nodding at her, and she understood. Well fuck them too.

She tried to point the gun at the Chair, but its barrel was glued to her forehead and her finger was likewise attached to the trigger. They kept nodding and smiling their insincere smiles at her, waiting for her to blow her brains out for delivering the news that every one of their consumer sectors was sinking into some new swamp of consumer apathy. As if killing the news would stop the pain. Stop the pain, something in her mind now was fixated on this, and she felt her finger twitch.

That's when she panicked and woke up. Shivering in the
dark, it occurred to Claire that the nightmare actually ended
better than what she could expect from the meeting. If Betsy
was right, Con|Int was out of business, but then so were the
rest of the bastards. Maybe she should just blow her head off.

FIFTEEN

Claire walked into the room, into the glass and steel board
room of the RIND corporation, where her quarterly report
would be interrogated by a panel of experts from industry and
government. She wore her black Armani silk dress and took
her place at the far end of the table from the Chair. The room
was abuzz with heated conversation as the panel members
passed along papers and charts and gestured in anger, an
emotion, she noticed, undergirded with fear.

Each of the panel participants reported to a sector of the
economy, to the music industry, or to fashion, film, housing,
automotive, restaurants: anywhere people would spend their
money. The undersecretary of commerce was here, too,
although this was not the meeting he normally attended. He
had just announced an uptick in the consumer confidence
findings, so why was he over in the corner, playing with his
BlackBerry, with an enormous frown across his brow?

Nobody looked at Claire, but it was her report they were
furiously waving about. They wanted it, and her, to simply
disappear, and so did she. Perhaps she could tiptoe away. The
Chair was the recently retired head of the Hollywood Film
Commission, whose job had been to staunch the flow of
intellectual property into the hands of "pirates," meaning
college students with a Mac and the software key provided by
the kid from Sweden. Tag Laurent had the demeanor of a
retired game show host, He stood and lifted his hands like
Moses gesturing to the Red Sea. The room fell silent.

"I want to thank you all for being here today," he said, "It seems we have a lot to talk about. Ms. Doolan," he nodded at her. "I hope you can shed some light on this report of yours. As I read it, we have entered a, well, a province of some difficulty."

"Up shit creek to its headwaters," Jill Strong spoke up. Jill represented the fashion industry association.

"Thank you, Jill." He nodded politely, although his eyes steeled. "Claire, you have the floor." Then he reached into his jacket.

Claire sat frozen for a second, her eyes on his hand. He pulled a handkerchief from his coat as he sat, and touched his mouth. She stood, and the room darkened for the projector. The first powerpoint slide was illuminated, and the room let out a collective groan.

"These are the predictions for the next quarter. I see you need no help interpreting this one," she started, "but, believe me, it only gets worse. Those of you who thought the Wall Street Bailout a couple years ago was rough...well, hold on to something." She flipped to the next slide.

§   §   §

In the four years since the road was built not one fire truck had turned around in Lotta Vista Lane. On that late Saturday morning when Scratchy woke up, the road was so packed with cars and news vans that you'd have trouble turning a bicycle in it. He had installed a fence tall enough to keep the coyotes away from his cats and a gate with an electronic opener but no doorbell. Arriving friends could call him on his cell phone, everyone else could wait. That's what a huge crowd was now doing; it looked like a couple hundred people.

"I'm gonna need a taller fence," Scratchy grumbled to
himself, glancing through the blinds of his bedroom into the
winter sun. Dozens of cars and vans were still arriving. They
clogged Hillside Drive in both directions. He was trapped.

The day the global programming community woke up to
find the entire technology template schema posted on Source
Forge was given a name by Slash|Dash: Prometheus II. The
second gift of fire. By noon, California time, it seemed that
every geek in the Western Hemisphere had joined the rest of
the world in downloading the 36 templates. For that one day
Scratchy eclipsed the entire movie, fashion, music, social, and
political fame machines. He was Charles Lindberg, Princess Di,
Michael Jordan, Bill Gates, Tiger Woods famous. Everybody
wanted to hear from Michael "Scratchy" O'hara.

The presidents of nations, Fortune 500 CEOs, major studio
chiefs, talent agency heads, international NGO executive
directors, and government laboratory lead scientists instructed
their assistants to put Michael O'hara on their calendars ASAP.
Squadrons of business jets were converging on Santa Barbara
airport for this purpose.

When Michael turned his cell phone on, it was ringing and
the message box was full. He turned it off again and went to his
computer. His trusty MacBook Pro had been on all night, and
there were just over 30,000 unread messages starting from 17
minutes after he had posted the code to about an hour later,
when his mail server failed.

For the first half hour or so, the email was from names he
knew; they were mainly European programmers from his dot-
com days. After that, it looked like somebody sold his email
address, or posted it somewhere that was spidered. Then the
email server just went berserk and ate itself. Without a phone
or email he had no way to get word to friends in Santa Barbara
who might help bust him out of his own house.

After a brief shower, he was getting dressed when he heard the noise. A helicopter was approaching and fast. Scratchy grabbed up the pair of binoculars he kept near the window and scoped the sheriff's helicopter ranging up hill toward his property. He slipped into his Berks and stepped outside. In his favorite Fritz the Cat hemp t-shirt and drawstring hemp pants he looked like Lebowski's slacker uncle.

Down at the fence a hundred cameras converged on him amid a cacophony of shouted questions. He started to flip them off, reconsidered mid-gesture and threw them a Spock salute to cover the move. Much to his chagrin, the image of this made the cover of a thousand newspapers. Even geeks have their pride.

When the loudspeaker voice from the descending 'copter asked permission to land on his driveway, he nodded vigorously and shouted "Fuck, yes!" into its downdraft. The rescue 'copter slid down on the asphalt in front of his garage. Scratchy duck-walked over to the open pilot's door.

"Mr. O'hara," the pilot shouted, removing his headset. "The crowd at your gate is a public nuisance."

"Damn straight," Scratchy nodded. "I'd recommend you strafe them. Maybe use RPGs on the bigger vans."

The pilot grinned. "I have another idea. We remove you, and they'll take care of themselves."

"Remove me?" Scratchy did not like the sound of that.

"Don't misunderstand, sir. You are not under arrest. Tad Goldwyn has offered the San Jacinto Ranch for your use over the next several days. I'll leave two officers here to keep out the curious."

"That's right neighborly of old Tad." Scratchy had never met Tad Goldwyn. Tad had made a sizable fortune selling children's clothing. A whole generation grew up in "Tads." Now he had moved most of his fortune into real estate. Scratchy wondered if Mr. Slick had sent word to ol' Tad.

"Lemme get a few things. Just be a minute."

Scratchy went back inside, grabbed his laptop and firewire drives. He threw a few changes of underwear and a toothbrush into a delivery bag. He looked around for Sasha and Skrotum, but the helicopter had probably driven his house cats into their deep hidey holes. He triple-locked his study but left the house unlocked for the cops. When he returned to the helicopter, two uniformed officers had dismounted and were chatting with the pilot. The back seat was empty, and Scratchy set his bags on the floor.

"You'll need to feed my cats," he yelled at the officers as the pilot revved up the rotor. "They each get half a can a day and some kibble and water. It's all in the kitchen." One of the officers nodded and smiled. Scratchy went up to the other one. "Anything happens to my pussycats, and I'll see that coyotes feast on your nuts." He made eye contact and kept this until the other fellow nodded and looked away.

"Goddamn dog people," he muttered to himself as he climbed into the helicopter.

The helicopter rose in a cloud of clay dust. The television cameras from 40 trucks followed it as it climbed. Already, cars were trickling away as the word came down that the action was moving from Lotta Vista Lane to the Ranch hotel on the other side of town.

"What the hell did you do, anyhow?" The pilot asked him when they leveled off. "Win the lottery?"

"Nope." Scratchy enjoyed the view. The city looked quiet and lovely on the balmy Saturday afternoon. Out to sea, a string of bizjets were circling to land at the municipal airport. He wondered if some movie star was getting married in Montecito.

"Someone die and make you king?" The pilot asked.

"Nah. I put myself out of work." Scratchy realized as he spoke that it was true. With the 36 technology templates, a lot of the world's computer programming needs were going to be realized in short order.

The pilot looked at him. Scratchy had let his hair grow again over the last few years. His hat was a droopy leather fedora.

"Fuckin' hippy," The pilot mumbled.

Scratchy just smiled.

§　　　　§　　　　§

"Someone is actively disenchanting 'The Now,'" said Harold Farmer, the chairman of the RIND Corporation and author of the seminal work, *The Now is a Foreign Land*. The group around the RIND conference table stole looks at one another.

Harold stood. He strode to the window and looked down, as if searching for the thief out on the street. Behind him, the table fell silent as each participant attempted to assemble the meaning of this pronouncement for their own arena. Everyone had, of course, read the book, which made a huge splash 20 years before. At that time, there was some fear that Farmer's own research would also work to disenchant The Now, simultaneously announcing and dissolving the target of his study.

The Now is a Foreign Land looked at consumer behavior as the result of a compulsive attraction for The Now, a manufactured self-seduction process that had emerged from decades of product turnover and mass advertising. The desire for The Now, he announced, was an addictive behavior that could be triggered in the body by the age of eight, and would

then, through constant feeding, control the emotional tone of
the consumer at least through their thirties, when its effects
tended to wear off. Encouraging this addiction had built entire
industries in film, fashion, music, sports, home furnishings,
and publishing.

Farmer's book detailed how the penetration of advertising
and mass marketing into the ex-Soviet states had split their
populations into the older cohort of post-17 year olds who
never acquired the addiction, and the younger population,
which developed hyperaddictive behavior, turning cities in
Poland, the Czech Republic, and elsewhere into youthful
capitalist playgrounds. After 10 years, 90 percent of the
consumption in post-communist Europe was by the
population under the age of 30. Older cohorts bought what
they needed, younger cohorts bought The Now. The same was
certainly true of China, as evidenced by Shanghai.

The enchantment of The Now, Farmer concluded, was by
far capitalism's greatest success. It wasn't nuclear deterrence or
Ronald Reagan that brought down the Berlin Wall; it was The
Now, shining like a foreign sun right through the concrete,
bleeding desire across no-man's land to a hungry cohort of 17
year olds.

The Now was not to be confused with the present, in fact,
The Now replaced the need for the present, for actual
interaction with other people, inserting serial acts of
consumption that satisfied this need in a manner that human
relationships rarely could. Every morning the consumer would
wake up knowing that yesterday's Now was over and that their
new car, new dress, new house, was no longer, well, Now. Every
magazine they read, TV show they watched, billboard they
passed on the way to work reminded them that The Now had
moved on and it was time to catch up. The glory of The Now,
he wrote, is that nobody ever does.

Harold came back to his seat and sat, his attention captive to some reflection. The room fell silent, as if mourning a dear friend.

"But how?" Tag Laurent demanded, scanning the faces around the table, his eyes fixed finally on Claire's.

"We work with future trends, not with causal processes. We report the outcomes, not the sources," she said. "I'll have to defer to Harold on the topic of The Now."

Dickey Gronberg, the undersecretary of commerce for consumer affairs, pulled up a brown shoe from his briefcase and laid this on the table.

"These are manufactured in a factory in Danang and shipped through a fulfillment service in Taipei. They are made entirely from recycled fibers, probably scraps from the garment industry. The dye is also natural. It's called 'catechu,' distilled from acacia wood. The estimated manufacturing cost for a pair is about forty cents American. We estimate that about 10 million pairs have been shipped to the U.S., with likely 10 times that many across the globe."

Jill picked up the shoe as if she were holding a live canal rat.

"It's an ugly spud," Dickey said, "but probably comfortable. What I want to know is, why shoes?"

Jill passed the shoe to the next person and looked at Dickey in disbelief.

"Why shoes? My god! Shoes are the foundation of the entire wardrobe. If you don't have the right shoes, you simply cannot wear the dress, or the jeans, or the suit. And if you can't wear the dress, why buy the dress? It's brilliant! They are giving away ugly shoes, shoes that you can only wear with..." She gestured wildly, "....with Salvation Army flannel shirts and Wal-Mart jeans. And in the process they destroy a huge sector of a half-trillion dollar industry. We're off a double-digit percent of sales in one quarter, and Mrs. Know-it-All here, to whom we've paid good money, can't tell us when this might turn around."

"But how do shoes affect movies and music?" Dickey asked. "Why are so many sectors tanking at the same time?"

"It's really quite simple, Dickey. Millions of people have money in their wallets," Harold said flatly, "because they aren't shopping for the Now. They are wearing what they own until this is worn out. When they do shop, they shop for value. That's why movies and music sales are all way down. Do you really think people actually want to buy the crap coming out of Hollywood and the big record labels? They have online access to thousands of movies, books, and songs, why wouldn't they take, say, a decade or two, to watch, read, and listen to these?"

"Decades!" Tag spat the water he'd been drinking.

"When you take away the Now," Harold concluded, "you open up the entire historical corpus of cultural production for reuse. The present has to compete with the past for the attention of consumers."

"Godamn media pirates!" Tag croaked. "Reuse, you say? It's thievery."

Harold picked up the shoe and turned it in his hands. "The design of this reminds me of something." He opened his computer, which switched the projector to it. They watched the screen as he called up a browser and searched an image of "sabot." A page with a set of images was displayed. Several people started.

"This shoe is felt, not wood," Harold noted. "But it appears that our nemesis has a sense of history."

"Sabotage," Tag whispered. "On a global scale."

§   §   §

The rescue helicopter set down in the meadow, a grassy expanse where San Jacinto Ranch visitors had been holding weddings for more than seventy years. Princes and presidents, divas and debutantes, rockers and movie icons had been wed there in complete privacy; many others had used the Ranch for their honeymoons.

The Ranch occupied a foothill valley above Montecito, its hundred acres bounded by the national forest on the uphill side and San Jacinto creek on the Los Angeles side. Walls, fences, and, more recently, surveillance cameras were used to keep out the neighbors and the curious. As a guest ranch, it was open to all who could afford its upscale cowboy ambiance. With the rooms starting above 700 dollars and cottages $2000 a night, its visitors expected more than a hot shower.

The Ranch was renowned for its service. Cottage guests arrived to find their names embossed on the note paper in their suite. The Ranch's Bentleys carried guests to and from the local night spots. A string of horses was available for trail rides, and guests could also bring their own ponies.

When Scratchy stepped down from the helicopter, he was met by a trim, sixty-something fellow in a smart blue suit, the Ranch's manager, and by the jocular fifty-year-old Tad Goldwyn, dressed in chinos and a salmon polo shirt. A porter dressed like a Hollywood cowboy took his bag. Ducking instinctively, they quick-walked away from the still whirling rotors to a central building that housed the lobby and the hotel's five-star restaurant. The helicopter rose and drifted back toward Santa Barbara.

"I'm Tad." Goldwyn held out his hand, and Scratchy gave it a good shaking.

"Michael O'hara," he said. "Right nice of you to help me out."

"It looks like you're in for a roller coaster ride for the next week or so. If I might ask, who normally manages your appointments?"

"That would be me," Scratchy said. "If I remember right, I had a dentist appointment last spring."

"I'll loan you my personal secretary," Tad suggested and turned to the manager. "Have Eric brought here and set up in the clubhouse office. Tell him he will be working for Mr. O'hara this week. He'll need to hand off my appointments to Susan."

After the manager strode off, Tad put his hand on Scratchy's back. "Your cottage is over this way."

The set off down the pebbled pathway between manicured rosemary shrubs. Scratchy noticed that several cottages had been recently vacated.

"I'm still wrapping my head around all this. Why is everyone so fucking excited?"

"When did you announce your findings?" Tad asked.

"About twelve hours ago. Then I went bed and, when I got up, well, it sure wasn't Kansas anymore."

"The Internet compresses time and space. You probably hadn't finished brushing your teeth before someone was shouting about your discovery to the European press. The blogs caught the buzz and passed it along, and CNN had the story by early this morning. By then it was the headline, 'American genius solves the mystery of the universe.'"

"Forty two," Scratchy replied. "I'm just a clever code jockey who discovered a better way to program."

"I've been in touch with some programmers. They would disagree. It seems what you've done will make many, many formerly impossible outcomes possible, and several other important projects extremely economical. Look." Tad pointed at the southern sky, where the jets were lined up to land. "They are beating a path to your door."

"So that's it. I'm the next golden goose." Scratchy glanced over at Tad.

Tad caught this glance and smiled. "I don't do programming. In fact, my 'software' problems are all scatological. You know, tots love to poop."

They walked on. "So this is a neighborly gesture."

Tad was still smiling. "I'm just a groopie, Dr. O'hara. Glad to have a front row ticket."

"My friends call me Scratchy..."

"Scratchy?"

"...Because I'm so lovable. Like a porcupine in your pocket."

They had reached the cottage, a board-and-batton structure under a green hipped roof. Another Hollywood cowboy jogged up and handed Tad a note. Tad read this and passed it to Scratchy who stared at it.

"Well?" Tad asked.

"Why not?" Scratchy answered.

Tad took out a pen and scrawled a message on the back of the note.

"Tell Mr. Earl that he can set up in the clubhouse. Mr. O'hara will be there by four-thirty for the five o'clock taping."

§   §   §

Like every other self-respecting geek on the planet, Don Driscoll had downloaded the code Scratchy posted. He ran the benchmarks on the sample programs and decided the world had just become much more interesting. The original set of templates was like a child's xylophone compared to this Steinway. It was as though an entire new color spectrum had been announced overnight. All day he watched the jets landing at the airport. Then they announced that Scratchy was going on Freddy Earl. While a small part of him basked in the reflected glory of his boss, the rest of him seethed. He could hardly stand reading Slash|Dash, as, one after one, the big kahuna nerds from around the world ladled out their adulation. It made him want to puke. He went for another beer and switched over to a football game.

§   §   §

Tad had suggested that Scratchy think about his clothes, national television and all. Scratchy called down to the hemp store on State Street and asked Marcel for a Guatemalan shirt. An hour later one of the cowboy bellhops delivered this to his cottage, where Scratchy, on his laptop, was deep into an argument in the Room.

"Leave it," Scratchy called through the door and returned his attention to the Room.

Itchy and Winston were pacing the stone floor. Jack sat in one of the Cordobaloungers and tried to make the face of his avatar look serious. Desi leaned back against the wall. He was wearing a Navajo white silk kurta top and matching pajamas, and his feet were bare. His face looked like blend of a teenaged Krishnamurti and Aamir Khan. Scratchy stood in the middle with his arms crossed, waiting for the others to assimilate his news.

"Freddy Earl! Are you completely insane?" Winston ranted.

"What are you going to wear?" Desi asked, "Not more hemp, please."

"Actually, I think its better to have the interview behind you," Itchy said. "The press might back off then."

"You can't say anything about Junana," Winston added. Scratchy nodded.

"Jack," he asked. "What's your main complaint?"

Jack managed to get his avatar to raise its head to look straight at Scratchy. "Be open and honest about everything except for Junana and us. You discovered the templates on your own, so you can just tell them how that happened. And tell them that you will not be selling any commercial rights for eighteen months to allow the non-commercial marketplace to develop. That will give you time to breathe. Within a few news cycles the world should be back to its usual preoccupations."

"Obsessed by completely pointless bullshit once again," Winston added.

"The Game," Itchy said. "Don't breathe a word about the Game."

"No Junana, no mesh computing, no Game. I'll just thrill them with my tales of Frisbee golf at Reed."

"And steal one of the robes for me," Desi said. "San Jacinto Ranch, Oh, my God, I hear it's fabulous. Over here it's 5:30 in the morning. I've already been up all night. But I'll stay up to watch. It's going around the world, live on NNC International."

"I have to go," Scratchy said. "Roy Rogers is back with someone who says he does makeup."

§   §   §

"Mr. O'hara, thank you for speaking to us." Freddy Earl had been driven up from Los Angeles after the network's president suggested this could be the interview of the decade. The special segment of "Freddy Earl Today" would be broadcast live from Montecito.

"Thank you, um, Freddy," Scratchy leaned forward and spoke into the dummy microphone on the desk, forgetting that he wore a lavaliere mike on his shirt.

"Mr. O'hara," Freddy Earl continued. "How does it feel to be the man of the hour?"

"Call me Mike," Scratchy said.

Desi settled back in his overstuffed armchair. "Oh, Mikey, not the Guatemalan shirt. That's so Eighties."

"Mike, you are a genius. That's obvious to the world," Freddy said. "Can you tell us, in a way we can understand, how you discovered these famous templates, and what they mean?"

"Let me start by saying I'm not any sort of 'Sapphire Child.' I'm just a nerd with a hyperactive curiosity. I didn't do this on my own. I had an idea about how to improve on the work of lots of other folks."

"Modesty. I don't see a lot of that. What people tell me is that we can expect great things now from these templates of yours. Revolutionary advances in computing and science."

"Mikey can be as modest as the next genius," Desi said to himself, "when he wants to be."

"The best thing about the templates is that they are a kick to use," said Michael.

"We have a caller," Freddy cupped his hand around the tiny microphone in his left ear. He nodded and cleared his throat. "It seems we have a very special caller. It's the White House. We are waiting for the President."

Scratchy sat back in his chair and crossed his arms over his chest. He was scowling slightly.

"Oh, no, Mikey. Mikey, don't!" Desi was shaking his head at the television, wishing he could call up Winston. They had all seen that look in class at Reed just before Michael O'hara tore the spleen out of somebody's finely crafted argument.

"President Stone, are you there?"

"Howdy, Freddy." The familiar Texas voice rang out.

"Good evening, Mr. President. I guess you have some questions for my guest."

"Always a pleasure to talk to a true American genius."

"Michael, do you have a word for the President?"

Scratchy bent forward.

"Sure," He spoke grimly. "I didn't vote for you or your dad. And before I have anything to say to you at all, personally or professionally, you'd need to do a few things besides kiss the asses of your rich friends..."

"Mikey, you wonderful fool." Desi couldn't stop laughing.

Freddy eyebrows flicked up, and his eyes shifted to the producer, who was intent on the exact words now flowing from Scratchy's lips, ready to push the button if one of the big five no-nos came out. He was grinning, however, and just nodded back at Freddy.

"...First you'd need to pull the troops back from the Middle East, where they don't belong. Second, you'd need to show you are serious about fighting global warming. And finally, you want to put the money back into the NSF cyberinfrastructure program—you know, the money you took out to pay for that tax cut for your buddies. Until then, this is my 15 minutes of fame, and you are the last person on the planet I want to share it with." Scratchy sat back in his chair again and closed his eyes.

"Mr. President," Freddy said. "Mr. President?" The phone operator was running his finger across his throat to signal that the call was lost.

"It looks like we've lost our connection to the White House." Freddy hid a small smile on the left side of his mouth. "I've heard they call you 'Scratchy,'" he continued, "Now we know why."

§   §   §

Don Driscoll, two six-packs later, stared at the screen in disbelief. Scratchy O'hara had just dissed the President of the United States. That pompous shit had the nerve to speak his mind in front of about a billion people. This little conversation will be on the Web for an eternity. Stone was sure to respond. He didn't get to be President the kiss-the-babies way. He and his close advisors had stabbed and clawed their way to the top, leaving broken opponents all over the body politic. They spread more fear with their campaign advertisements than most terrorist organizations would ever accomplish. Anybody who had tracked the career of W.G. Stone at all could figure Scratchy had just opened up a can of whoop-ass on himself.

§   §   §

Nick knew there was trouble when he logged in. Cindy's congratulatory smile had been replaced by a grim frown. It felt like she was taller, but he knew it was her mood. Not even a hello. She nodded at him and the screen went black.

When it brightened they were back on the bluff top, the same desert scene from the first day of Level Two. For a second he thought she was taking him back a level. She strode to the edge and looked down. He followed her gaze. The red sandstone escarpment verged down nearly vertically for hundreds of feet, and then gentled into a bouldered shoulder on a loop of a placid opalescent green river. Below them a red-tailed hawk cruised. It cried out. The shrill song echoed around them.

"Anything come to mind?" she asked.

"Great base-jumping spot," he offered.

"This is Level Three. Level Three is to Level Two like Halo is to Tetris. To even start Level Three, you need to show me you can think on your feet."

"What...?"

Cindy had pushed him off the cliff. Nick's avatar tumbled for what seemed like minutes before deflecting off a boulder and then crumpling into a pile of scree near the edge of the river. The scene replayed itself in third person slow motion and Nick watched his avatar break several bones and bleed out on the rocks. Then he was back on the bluff with her.

"Freakin' rude," he complained.

"That's not a question. I need a question from you. Now!" She pushed him again.

"Ask the question," she yelled.

"How far down is it?" he called out. His avatar tumbled head first and brained itself on a hoodoo. Then he was up on the bluff again.

"I'm not doing a geography lesson. Try again." She pushed him.

"What is gravity?" he yelled. Splat. Back on top.

"Too theoretical. You are tumbling toward your death and you want to know about gravity?" She pushed. He tried to duck, but his motor reflexes had been slowed. Over he went.

"How do I stop?" he yelled. Splat. Back on top.

"Laws of physics. You can't just stop. This ain't toontown." Push.

"Can I fly?" Splat. Back on top.

"Much better! But still imprecise. Try again." Push.

"How do I fly?"

"Perfect!"

Nothing happened. Splat. Back on top.

"You said it was 'perfect'!"

"Perfect question. Lousy timing. Try it now."

"How do I fly?"

A console appeared in front of them, hovering within reach.

"Ask your question again, and pay attention. Next time you fall and die you end up back a level."

Nick navigated into a Query about the physics of flight. He then Queried about timing and tactics, which led to a template structure in game theory. He spent the next two hours unfolding this.

"Excellent," Cindy smiled again. "You are armoring yourself against my next move. I am such a good Guide. But I should have tossed your sorry ass off that cliff months ago."

Nick laughed and stepped back from the console, putting Cindy between him and the cliff. Still laughing, he thrust his hand out and shoved her over the edge.

"Silly cowboy," She fell backwards, but managed to wrap her toes around his waist, taking him over with her. "Remember your lesson."

Flight is a simple matter of swimming in the air. Below him, Cindy morphed into a kestrel and banked left.

"No fair!" he yelled. The swimming in air concept required that he either create an airfoil that reduced his relative gravity or... "That's it!" He typed in a set of quick commands.

"That's better." The air around him started to shimmer and coalesce. "Colder," he typed. Now the air was thick as pudding, a soup of dense gasses. He circled his arms in a treading pattern and slowed his descent to the point where he could reach out and grab at a ledge that was drifting by.

Cindy stood on a nearby hoodoo. "Quick thinking, Nicky. Good thing you don't need to breath this." She swept her hand through the fog. "What is it?"

"Radon. Nearly frozen. Heavy as lead."

"How did you figure out that you could change the composition of your environment?"

"You can change your form. I can't. It was the only way to create flight. I figured you wouldn't give me an insolvable problem."

"Looks like you've earned yourself a bit of Free-for-All time." She moved close and put both hands on his face. "I'm so very proud of you, Nicky." She bent forward and planted a kiss on his forehead. "Go have yourself a good time." He found himself alone on the bluff top.

Level Three, he mused. He'd heard the horror stories, the blogs in Junana were buzzing with them. Maybe half the Gamers who got here ended up back in Level Two again, polishing up their template unfolding, ready to get tossed off the cliff, or run down by the train, or trapped in the mine, or the submarine, or the safe, or whatever it took to realize that you can stretch your mind around the puzzle and, snap, find the solution. Like he just did. Cindy is such a good Guide. He realized how lucky he was.

§ § §

Jack Dobron shook his head, picked up a phone, and pushed an office-internal number.

"Get a jet to Santa Barbara, tell them to wait there for orders."

He set down the phone, jogged the replay on the digital recorder, rewound the last five minutes, and watched again as Scratchy declared war on the President of the United States. God, he wished he'd done that to Stone years ago. Instead, Jack wrote him off as an imbecile. Now he had to figure Stone's intentions into his plans for the next six months.

§   §   §

Wilson Garrick Stone, the President of the United States,
stared at the phone on his desk like it was a viper about to
strike. It had been his idea to make the call. His chief of staff
warned him that their intel on this O'hara fellow was thin. Still,
they did not have any information that he was hostile. He was a
nerd, for Chrissake, with a once-in-a-lifetime opportunity to
speak with the President. And this, this nobody had the nerve
to talk to him like that. Well, he thought, Mr. O'hara, enjoy
your fifteen minutes of fame. It will be followed by a somewhat
longer period of pain. He snatched up the phone receiver.

"Get me Karl," he snarled and waited. "Karl. You were right.
You're my hound dog now. I want to know everything there is
to know about this so-called genius. I want the IRS and the
NSA on this, Homeland Security too. Remember what you did
to that school bus driver that flipped me off out in the
motorcade? Well, double that in spades. Did he say NSF? Are
we giving him money? If he's on any kind of government grant
or contract, make sure it's audited and shut down. Family,
friends, friends of friends. I want everyone around this prick to
feel the burn. Nobody talks to me like that. You need more
firepower, tell the Vice President I said you can use his private
squad. They're vicious little shits, I'm sure they can tear one
goddamn California nerd a new one."

He slammed down the receiver, hesitated, and reached into
the lower side drawer of the Nixon desk. He pulled out a pint
of Maker's Mark and settled back in the chair.

Nerdville

SIXTEEN

Castalia was going to be a special location in Junana, restricted to those Gamers who had achieved the very highest levels. Jack had first suggested this to Desi and Itchy, and they agreed it would serve the Game well to have a space for conversation among the Meisters. Itchy insisted that Castalia be template inspired, and set out to unfold architectural templates for the entire site. Perhaps because of his affection for the clean lines of Shoin Japanese architecture, or maybe because this style was unconsciously templated, the buildings spread across a cypress-covered hillside with sweeping tile roofs supported by tree-trunk sized posts. Platforms of dazzling terrazzo mosaics formed the floors.

Itchy had the luxury of designing the site itself. He specified an escarpment to the west, a slow-running stream on the east, and a gentle slope to the south with an expansive lawn maidan edged by a thick forest. Temperature had no meaning in the Game, but Itchy wanted Castalia to move through the days and seasons. He set the clock arbitrarily for Oregon time, but he moved the latitude up to Vancouver, lengthening the summer twilight and chopping the days in winter.

At the center of Castalia, up on the hill, he placed an actual castle, in medieval French style, with a moat and turrets where flags of many colors showed their griffin crests to the winds. In the center of the castle was its Keep, a round, windowless, doorless tower, with a single large flag: a huge white owl on a crimson background. This space would be reserved for the Meisters. Itchy sent a message to Desi, who had become the first player to master Level Seven in the Game. He called Desi the Game's first winner. Grand Meister Desi replied. "I think rather the Game has won me."

"The interior space should respond to the uses you envision the Meisters making for it." Itchy said.

"Then it must be clear and level, with no hint of hierarchy. Not a place for politicking, and the only reason it's separate is for personal privacy. Think of it like the Room, only big enough for, say, five hundred people."

§   §   §

Claire finally got Megan to sit down for dinner when she noticed Megan was wearing a pair of brown shoes. They looked oddly familiar. Megan was trying to tell her something about how the design of the kitchen reminded her of some template she had unfolded. Claire kept asking about the shoes.

"Where did you get these shoes?" Claire asked Megan for the third time.

"These? I earned them," Megan replied. She looked down at her feet and smiled.

"You mean you earned some money somewhere and bought them?" Claire asked. "I give you an allowance for clothes."

"Nope. They just appeared in the mail. But first, I earned them on the Game."

"Can I see one?"

"Sure," Megan lifted her foot and slipped off the shoe. She handed this to her mom. Claire took this and turned it over and over. It was the same type that was passed around at the Rind meeting. Frowning, she held it up and looked inside.

"There's only a label that says what the shoes are made of. Nothing about who made them." The shoe was totally non-woven, some sort of felt for the upper, and the sole was the same deep coffee brown material sewn into a flat surface. The label said they were made of recycled fibers.

"These won't last long," she predicted. "But they look really comfortable."

"They're the shit! I can wear them all day. Now that I earned them, I can order more."

"Like you ordered these?"

"No, these just came."

"You say you 'earned' the shoes?"

"I can also earn the hat," Megan replied.

"The hat?" Of course, she remembered Jennifer's last report. Avatars were now sporting a hat. Jennifer noted it was shaped like a Mao cap, in black, with a red star on it.

"There's a shoulder bag, and a blouse, and a cape. The Grand Meister has a staff."

"Just how do you earn all this?"

"On the Game," Megan replied. "I've been telling you about the Game for a year now. And you always say I don't listen," she mocked, wagging her finger.

"That's because you're always playing on the computer. And you don't listen, at least not when I've got a chore for you to do."

"I'm not just playing on the computer. Not when I'm in the Game. I've been telling you for months."

So had Jennifer, but who has time for a video game?

"I'm listening now."

"I should let you know a few things, then." In a most dramatic tone.

Claire did not like the sound of that, and she must have shown it.

"Nothing bad," Megan placed her hands palm down on the table. "Don't lose it, OK?"

"OK. So what's up?"

"Well, for starters, I graduated from high school last week."

"You what?" Claire knew better than that. "Young lady, it's the middle of the summer after your freshman year. In three weeks you will be pestering me to raise your allowance so that you can throw away hundreds of dollars of perfectly fine clothes and replace these with other clothes that are different how?"

"Yeah, right. Isn't that what keeps you employed? Besides, I don't think I need to go the high school anymore. After I earned my shoes I heard that others have been taking the test, you know, the test that shows you've passed high school. They put the test on the Web. And, well, I did it. And I passed no problem. Easiest test I ever took. I was wondering if I really need to, you know, go back next year."

"To high school?"

"I mean it's going to be so lame. And, besides, I'm going to college already. It's part of the Game."

"You're what!" Claire was falling behind in the comprehension derby here.

"It's the shit, mom. When you earn your shoes you can go on to the next level, and the word is, when you pass that level its as good as getting through, I mean actually like, finishing, you know, college. And you can get a real degree from it, and a hat."

"But sweetie, high school is, well, more than just classes." Claire found herself groping for something to say that wouldn't sound entirely insincere. She had hated going to high school, could not wait for it to end. "There's socialization, meeting people, meeting boys, time to grow up and find out about things before you get into college."

"Like drugs, sex and music?" Megan said. "I thought you said I should wait until college before I..."

"...And getting into a real college is not easy. It means taking all those advanced placement courses in math and science."

"There's kind of something else," Megan started.

"I knew it." Claire sighed. Megan was just sixteen.

"No." Megan put her hand on her stomach. "Oh, my God, you are so not right!"

"What else is there?"

"It's not bad, but I didn't tell you. I mean until today. So, I don't want you to go all apeshit that I didn't tell you sooner."

"Today it is. And I promise to not go any kind of shit."

"Here, look." She passed a light blue piece of paper to Claire and sat back, a small smile played at the edges of her mouth.

It was a form from the College Testing Service. Megan's name was on it and some kind of test results. Claire stared the paper for the longest time.

"I could find a defibrillator, if it would help," Megan offered.

Claire looked at her daughter, the same person who, a year ago, was still horrified with the knowledge that her childhood would be forever pony-less.

"This is a spoof, right? Something you printed from the Internet."

Megan was shaking her head and smiling full on.

"This says you scored 2400 on the college entrance exam."

"Right there in plain English. Another reason why another year in high school makes very little sense to me. I'm sixteen. They can't hold me if I don't want to go."

"You've got to show me this game."

§   §   §

"You will inform the First Lady it's Reverend Gerry." Gerald Bishop reclined in his walnut-lined office, a nearly exact replica of Howard Hughes' office at TWA. "Yes, I'll hold."

He cradled the phone's handset between his face and shoulder as he scanned the market reports on his sermon on the evils of online social networks and gaming.

"The First Lady will be with you momentarily," the White House operator announced. Gerry pushed the papers away and reclined in the leather chair.

"Reverend?" now it was Arlene Stone's voice. "How good of you to call."

"Arlene, you sound fit today, how are things with Grumpy?" Gerry had been acting as both pastor and therapist for Arlene Stone since she joined the church in San Antonio two years before she and the President first met.

Life in the White House had been complicated by President Stone's long-term recovery from alcoholism. So many of the first couple's official social responsibilities required at least the performance of drinking. W.G. had been falling off the wagon so regularly that Arlene called it his pogo stick. They hadn't hosted an official state dinner in years, but whenever he traveled it took weeks to pull him back to the straight and narrow. The process made him grumpy, which she understood. When the most powerful man in the world can't have a beer, he regards this as an injustice. She also understood it was her role to act as both the loyal supporter and the ultimate enforcer. Someone had to be strong.

"You heard what happened on the Freddy Earl show?" she said.

"How did Wilson take it?"

"He's been in a black mood for days now. It's so good of you to call; you always seem to know when I'm distressed."

"Well, Arlene, what kind of pastor would I be if I were too busy for my favorite parishioner? I am also calling to get your opinion on my Crusade. Did you happen to see the service on Sunday?"

"I did, and I cannot agree more. Kids today learn nothing but bad manners playing all these games all day long. How are they going to learn about respect for their betters? Maybe that's why that fellow attacked the President on Freddy's show."

"It would not surprise me in the least. And that's why I'm hoping the President will throw some resources into our struggle. Nothing much. A little White House team to coordinate some of the capabilities over at Justice and Commerce."

"I overheard W.G. talking with Karl about investigating that nasty O'hara fellow. He's one of those computer people. Probably played too many video games as a child."

"You know, Arlene, I have great respect for Karl." The same kind of respect he'd give a black mamba. "But I'm thinking that you and Tom Verplanck were such a great duo last Christmas..."

Tom, the President's domestic advisor, had devised a Christmastime program for the First Lady. She collected and distributed presents for the children of HIV-infected illegal immigrant mothers along the border.

The "No Border to Christ's Love" campaign demonstrated to the entire nation that there was no one too wretched as to fall outside the compassionate reach of the White House. Bishop's church cooperated fully and collected all the presents for distribution. Of course Stone had been elected on a platform that promised to stop illegals from access to medical attention. "Let 'em go home to get treatment," was Stone's stump speech, and the church backed him to the hilt. The images of the First Lady holding little HIV babies on her lap

surrounded by teddy bears and toy trucks sent the opposition
into fits of self-righteous apoplexy. Bishop was a big fan of
creative irony.

"...This is a domestic matter. Maybe you and Tom could put
together a Tiger Team to push the agenda forward. We need to
move ahead."

"Well, I guess..."

"You've been hiding yourself far too much, dear Arlene."
Bishop had played this game with her before. "On Sunday I'm
going to unleash a flood of support for the cause. The foot
soldiers are in place, but we need tactical support to bring this
off. I'm asking you to be my lieutenant. I..." He let his voice
crack.

"Oh, Reverend!"

"I need your help. God needs your help. He put you in your
position of power, and now it's time to act."

"My, my, my goodness," Arelene stuttered. "Is it so
important?"

"Arlene, you have no idea."

"You have my full support, Reverend. I'll ask Tom to call
you today."

"Bless you, my child. And tell Grumpy I'm praying for
him."

§ § §

"We are all here except Michael," Jack said.

"I've got some concerns about the learning programs for
the Guides...." Itchy started.

Scratchy's avatar appeared. "What's up?" He leaned against
the fireplace.

"Hi, Mikey," said Desi. His avatar moved to give a hug.

"Who called for this meeting?" said Michael. He let Desi hug him, but made no move to return the gesture.

"Aren't you sleeping? You sound terrible," Desi said.

"Sasha and Skrotum are dead," Scratchy said. His voice caught on the words.

"Oh, my God, Mikey!" Desi said. "How?"

"Poison, the vet told me. A slab of ahi with enough strychnine to clear out Hamelin. Someone threw it over the fence during the night. My tenants found their bodies in the garden."

Since the day he posted the template code, Scratchy had been living in one or another of Tad's hotels. The Lotta Vista house continued to be under surveillance by the paparazzi and unknown others. Scratchy rented it out to an engineering professor and her husband at a fraction of its market value, in exchange for them looking after his beloved cats.

"So shall you hear of carnal, bloody and unnatural acts..." Itchy intoned, "...of accidental judgements, casual slaughters, of deaths put on by cunning and forced cause." He had played Horatio in the Reed production of Hamlet.

"Dirty tricks," Scratchy said. "Retaliation."

"Who would be so mean as to poison poor Skrotum?" Winston asked.

"Disgruntled ex-employee? Psychotic neighbor? Jealous lover?" Desi ventured.

"Nah, my bet's on Stone."

"I never thought Stone would sink that low," Itchy said.

"His staff might, especially Karl," Jack offered. "If Karl is on your case, you might consider leaving town. Put some distance between yourself and whomever he's hired to do his dirty work. I'm very sorry about your cats."

"Sasha was a beauty, and Skrotum, well, he was one of a kind."

Scratchy had picked them up at an animal shelter in Solvang. Sasha was a magnificent Russian Blue, twenty pounds of muscle and a shimmering blue-grey coat. Independent and unpredictable. Every few days he'd let Scratchy touch him.

Skrotum was a runt. He looked like he'd died and been buried for a week and then showed up again at the back door. Maybe six pounds wet, his short fur was a dull grey, his tail and stomach were nearly bare. Skrotum had sneaky yellow eyes and a permanent slink. He looked guilty even when asleep. His head was misshapen from years of getting the shit kicked out of him by a range of backyard critters: other cats, possums, raccoons, and probably even garden rats. He was eternally brave on the attack, but lacked the talent to prevail. Scratchy spent a fortune keeping him alive.

Skrotum got his name when Scratchy took him in to get neutered. He thought he had a female cat, but the vet told him that the kitten was male, only the testicles had failed to descend. So the cat was christened 'Skrotum' for this defect, although Scratchy later thought about renaming him 'Fester,' after his many wounds. Skrotum lived on a diet of amoxicillin and tuna. The cat had an atavistic attachment to Scratchy's lap, and he would sleep in it for hours, curled up into a flatulent ball. He managed to get along with Sasha, attacking him only irregularly. Sasha would send him tumbling with one swipe.

"Alas, poor Skrotum, I knew him well," Itchy said.

"Ichiro Nomura! That's enough, already. Can't you tell, Michael is in distress!" Desi admonished him.

"Sorry, Mike."

"That's OK. Rosencarl and Guildenlenny are dead," Scratchy mumbled, "But I'm staying put. Fuck Stone and his minions."

"You tell 'em, Mikey!" Desi said. "Say the word and I'll fly over to stand with you."

"Anything we can do, just say so," Winston added.

"If you insist on staying in Santa Barbara," Jack said, "I suggest you sell your car. Otherwise you're likely to find it filled with heroin or cocaine and under police surveillance."

"Great, now I won't even have a car."

"Find a taxi service."

"How do we get even?" Scratchy said.

"Leave that to me," Jack said, in a voice that quieted the others.

§   §   §

Beneath her bedroom the condo garage door closed with a thunk. Megan smiled as she stretched and yawned. Her Saturday just got simplified. Her mom was probably committed to some international telecon lasting most of the day. She did the brainwave in bed, sending her hands into complex motion in front of her face.

Megan stumbled to the bathroom to pee, her eyes adjusting to the dawn. Coming back to her room she threw on a t-shirt and moused her computer awake. The Game was already booted.

"Greetings, Miss Megan." Bobby was dressed in his monk's robe, dark brown with a flaxen rope belt. He bowed and she nodded in response.

Their avatars stood at the entrance to a medieval village, a double row of rough wooden huts arranged along a hillside. Smoke drifted lazily from the chimneys. Chickens scurried after grubs in piles of refuse. A stream of suspiciously colored liquid ran down the middle of the road separating the huts.

"This is Level Four," he said. He glowered at her under the robe's hood. "Follow me." He ducked into the closest hut.

It's one of those days, she mused to herself with a sigh and sent her avatar after him. She had figured the fun times from yesterday were a prelude to something serious. Now, here it was. The hut's interior was candlelit. Bobby threw back his cowl and took a stance to face her.

"In Level Three, I introduced you to Simplicity," he said. "Now you must show me you can unfold this template to its root."

"And when I do?"

"If you fail, I will drag you back to Level Two and you can start over from there."

"Nobody's talking fail here. What happens when I take this template down?"

"You want Free-for-All time?"

"Yes, and..." She put a broad smile on her avatar. He frowned in response.

"Fantasy land, as well?" His eyebrows lifted. "You think that's what you deserve? Do you know how many players have already done this without making such demands?"

"Just for an hour or so. It's only pixels!" She leaned her avatar forward and kissed him on the cheek.

"Two hours of Free-for-All and one hour of fantasy." His frown morphed into a grin. She guessed he expected her to ask for more than that.

"What are we waiting for? Show me the capstone for this puppy." Her screen faded. The familiar Query UI appeared, the central video screen surrounded by sliders that allowed her to zoom through, into, or away from the montage of images, audio, and text the Game tossed at her in response to her questions and commands. She adjusted her headphone and its microphone and settled in her chair.

"Show me complexity," she said.

"Good start." Bobby's voice told her.

The screen filled with images: tangles of wires, of neurons and ganglions, random piles of scrap, jumbled facades in a crowded street, transportation circuitries, confounding circuit diagrams. In her headset, a barrage of urban noises: roaring traffic, customers shouting orders, sibilant factory rhythms. She studied the images, her attention caught on a picture of a crowded street. She jabbed the pause button, backed up the presentation a couple seconds, and selected the image of a single building.

"Show me this."

"Whatever did you find?" Bobby's voice asked.

"Right in the middle of everything, here's a building that seems to exist on its own. Like a flower in the middle of a bog. It's so beautiful. But there's nothing to it. Just concrete and glass."

The Query showed the entire street as a panorama as it assembled information on the architect, Arata Isasaki, and the building's isometric form.

A house, she reflected. In the middle of such confusion, which only makes its simplicity somehow work where it would be wasted on its own.

"I see a relationship between simplicity and complexity, some kind of necessary context.

"You are very close to the capstone template for simplicity," Bobby encouraged her.

"It's like a dance between them. Or a game of hide and seek. Or maybe a love affair."

"Excellent," said Bobby. "'Simplicity loves difference.' Remember. Nothing is more boring than the simple without complex; these are two sides of the same page. If you toss out difference you destroy simplicity. Let's explore this template further."

The Query screen lit up with a series of examples similar to the one she had discovered, but ranging from a tangle of tree roots around a stone Buddha head to the interior and exterior of an iPhone.

Over the next six hours, which passed like so many minutes, Megan, with Bobby's gentle hints, Queried through all of the simplicity templates. "Simple Underneath" forced her to look through complexity and find the one thing that make the complex simple; she learned to still the motion in order to feel the undergirding calm. "Simple on the Outside" taught her how much more she trusted simple interfaces: light switches, stairways, T-shirts, her Game shoes, her favorite computer user interfaces. "Simple Saves Time" told her to be direct, find the short cut, see the fun in efficiency. "Simple anchors Emotion" explored the complex emotional embrace humans make with the world around them. Only it was not complex once you found the simple key.

"Simple Choice Starts It All." This is where simplicity sockets into the root Noel template. In the end everyone must "Choose One."

"What did you choose?" Bobby asked.

"I chose to open the door to the Game," Megan said.

"At that time you had no attachment to it. When did that happen?"

She reflected. At some point during Level One she began to hunger for the Game. Something in it filled her time, her head, her heart with more than she had expected. She could not remember a single moment.

"I don't know," she said, feeling stupid. Bobby had noticed her initial distain for the Game.

"But you did emerge from Level One with a real intention. And that's the next template structure we will explore:

'Intentionfull.' But not now. Now you have earned your Free-for-All time and your fantasy."

"Fantasy first! I'm thinking Cheyenne, on the prairie, before contact. Make it super real. I want to feel the wind on my face..." She settled back in her chair. Her bedroom was bathed in sunlight. At once she felt hungry, grimy, and the need to pee again. Her morning breath had congealed into some kind of bad cheese odor. Her stomach let out a muted roar. "You know, I've got to eat something. Let's do this later."

"At your leisure." Bobby bowed and the screen went black.

Megan stumbled toward the bathroom, stripping off her clothes. On the glass shower door was the handwritten sticky note Claire left.

"Morning, Meglie. I'm back mid-afternoon. Pancake batter is in the fridge with fresh fruit salad. New bread in the bin for sandwiches. Today is laundry day. Let's do the Grove, I need some new towels. Italian on Montana for dinner? love ya. Mum. P.S. Remember you promised to walk Mrs. Jenkins's pug this morning."

Megan crumpled the note and dropped it in the wastebasket. She warmed the water and stepped in. A quick shower and she would take little Ruggles next door for a walk. As she closed the shower door, she heard the garage door open.

"Busted," she whispered, and leaned into the shower spray.

Nerdville

SEVENTEEN

Desi's apartment in Sao Do was no larger than any of the
others. No hierarchy here. He stepped out on his balcony,
which looked out over the compound and beyond to the river.
Soft, still air hit his face like a damp velvet rag. The lounger
was covered with moisture, as though night and morning had
just finished making love, and the morning lay there in her
sweat while the night wandered off for a cigarette. He took a
towel to the lounger and then he reclined in the matinal gloom
awaiting the sunrise, sipping his milk-sweetened, metal-press,
highland coffee.

The compound awakened below him, food stall workers
wiped the dew off the chairs, expecting their early customers at
first light. Dozens of pots of pho broth simmered in the
darkness. The pungent odors reminded Desi of Mysore with its
daily masala of scents; the smoke from the burning nityapuja
dhup incense, cow dung fires in the village, stale urine on the
walls, something dead and decaying in the field nearby. The
funk of life and of death, unsanitized by middle-class
aesthetics. One of the stall owners noticed him and bowed
deeply. Desi waved back and the fellow's face opened up to a
smile as easy as a sunrise. The early ferryboats chugged down
the river toward Hoi An.

In the Sao Do compound, everyone, from grade-school
munchkin to grandfather, ate all their meals in the food stalls,
following the "restaurant every meal" template. Why make five
hundred families cook their own food in five hundred
kitchens, when fifty professional cooks in a dozen kitchens can

do so with far greater economy and skill? This meant that mothers and fathers could awaken, bathe, enjoy a coffee and get their children up without dashing around a kitchen attempting breakfast.

Desi watched families emerge from their apartments, greet each other, their children jockeying for chairs at their favorite tables. They sat down to a breakfast professionally cooked, many of them doing the Brainwave exercises as they chatted.

The school kids began to migrate over their classrooms on the eastern side of the compound, the programmers headed to their offices on the western side. Grandparents and spouses lingered at the cafes and then drifted away, either to the clubhouses where there were dominos and other games, exercise classes, the organic gardens, various adult education offerings, or to the ferry landing for the commute to Hoi An for work or shopping.

Most of the morning crowd wore their black hats and a many of them carried the blue shoulder bags. Several of the younger school kids, still too young to play the Game, wore the grey "Y.U. Athletic Department" t-shirts their parents could buy. Most of the Game's programming had been done right in this compound, so its influence seemed only natural. He had no idea that a similar scene was emerging in villages across the planet.

Desi told Jack that this capitalist enterprise had fulfilled the vision of communist Vietnam, and Jack reminded him they weren't making any money. In five years, when the contracts were up, the whole place would need to be self-sustaining. The sun continued on its path, chasing the last student into class at the bell. Desi's balcony would soon be too hot. He did his own Brainwave exercises while he contemplated the day's agenda.

They had finally solved the problem of hosting the Game client on Computos, millions of which had been distributed through UNESCO over the past three years. Hand-cranked and satellite WiFi enabled, Computos dissolved the digital divide in remote villages worldwide. Desi had extended the DocDo language capabilities of the Game into dozens of tribal languages, from Navajo to Oshiwambo. Technical vocabulary remained problematic; Desi built complex ontologies that automatically rephrased them. He felt this to be a clumsy but adequate solution. The remaining problem was throughput. The bandwidth for many of these villages was so low that entirely new compression algorithms were needed. It was like pouring Niagara Falls into a bathtub. Desi was in charge of the data-compression team, and they were still not happy with the quality of the video in the Queries.

§   §   §

The horizon went on forever; enormous clouds scudded across the prairie. A clutch of eagle feathers on the nearby pole waved at her in the breeze. A cloud of flies surrounded her, distracting her view. Megan scanned the scene, but Bobby was nowhere in sight. She was crouching on the dirt next to a small fire over which a brace of buffalo sinew slices absorbed its acrid smoke. A gaunt dog peeked around the wikiup, eyeing the meat. Her avatar picked up a stone and shied it at the dog, which ducked out of sight. A small child, naked, caked with dust, toddled out of the wikiup and squatted to pee. Megan toggled to third-person-hover. Her avatar was dressed in a deerskin worn like a serape. It was chewing some kind of leather strip. It was horribly fat. No, it was pregnant to bursting.

"Bobby, I said 'wind on my face,' not stretch marks. Give me something different. How about super romantic?"

The monitor went black and then opened up with a new scene. She was riding Marmalade through a wind-carved sandstone landscape. Rock monoliths towered on either side, emblazoned by the setting sun. Bobby rode a bit ahead. Their horses walked easily, hoof beats percussive on the rock floor. A nearby waterfall, teal against the damp red stone of its course, added a sibilant harmony to the hoofbeats.

"This is more like it!" She sent Marmalade into a brief canter to catch up with Bobby. They rode together between two gigantic stone mittens.

After a time, Megan toggled to third-person-hover and looked at her avatar riding bareback. Its raven hair was braided into luxurious pigtails, interlaced with beads and leather, all the way down her back. It was dressed in a short, snug doe-skin dress, slit up the side. It had breasts the size of grapefruits.

"Hey! Am I supposed to be Pocahontas or Jessica Rabbit? And look at you? Whose fantasy is this, anyhow?"

"This scene is an amalgam of popular cultural images. There are referents from Disney, MGM, Warner Brothers, Russ Meyer..."

"Give me back my own avatar. And stop looking so... so, Italian. What happened to the nice Sir Robert I met on the beach?"

Her avatar morphed into her standard Junana image. Bobby was again wearing his doublet.

Bobby turned Shadow around to face her. "I gain in nuance and complexity as you grow in the Game."

She looked at him. Bobby had taken her to so many different places in the past year, she always imagined him to be the one thing that never changed. Now she knew he was simply keeping up with her. They were changing together.

§   §   §

Winston started a series of articles for one of Wharton's online journals. Under the heading of "Embracing Uncertainty in a Smart Economy," he outlined strategies for corporations looking to build market share as the market shrank.

His essays were filled with statistics from a spectrum of published sources, although the facts he gleaned from within Junana were much more relevant. He pointed to the fiasco of the college testing service as a bellwether for the new smart economy. In the last three months fully 35 percent of the test takers had scored at or near the top score possible, paralyzing the whole college admission system.

"Like that of the smarter student," he wrote, "the impact of the smart consumer will change the entire landscape of the marketplace. The smart worker will also revolutionize the workplace."

Winston's career had been in derivatives and other contrarian theories, so his new writings fit this topic tighter than OJ's glove. He scrubbed his prose to remove any trace of the template sayings, which had become so much a part of the conversations he had with his Guide, having reached Level Three in the Game.

After the fifth weekly installment in this series, *The Economist* called him for an interview. They arranged a videoconference between London and Philadelphia. In only a few minutes it was clear that the journalist who interviewed Winston was an avid Game player. Winston had to deflect several questions that would have revealed his own Game status.

"We have the computing capability to approach each individual without requiring that they identify with a larger cohort. If only corporate boards and officers showed the same individuality as their customers, we could rebuild the marketplace on the solid ground of serving every customer's actual needs," Winston concluded.

The Economist article led to another piece in the *New Yorker*, and then a book deal with Farrar, Strauss and Giroux. Winston judiciously declined offers from the speaking circuit, but he did give lectures at Wharton and Berkeley and was scheduled to do commencement at Reed in the spring. The commencement-speaker selection committee included a person with whom he had been intimately familiar, back when he was a senior and she a freshman.

It was her first RennFayre and his last. Winston had decided on a clown golf outfit. Scratchy said he looked like Moe in "Three Little Beers." Winston had decided to narrow down his first-day recreational drug use to mushrooms and champagne. He had a supply of the former, and figured he could swap some for the bubbly. Desi was dressed in a sari with a huge turban. Itchy had on his favorite cowboy outfit. Scratchy went commando in Oshkosh overalls.

The day before, they had turned in their theses and ransacked the library playfully. That morning they hit the campus in high spirits, Desi floated across the green in nine-yards of Benares silk. Winston carried an ancient wood-shafted niblick for looks. He spied this young thing coming out of the old dorm block with a bottle of Veuve Clicquot, its bright yellow label visible from a hundred yards. And yes, she was willing to trade some; only she'd never done mushrooms before and expected him to stick around in case she flipped out.

Her name was Claire Cassaday. They ended spending all day and night together and the next day and night too. The entire time was smudged in his memory in bright colors and laughter. He remembered running across the fairways of Eastmoreland, but not the naked part. That part she reminded

him about in an email after his interview for the
commencement speaker.

She didn't need to remind him of the sex, which was
frequent and frenzied over those forty-eight hours, as though
they were required to consummate an entire adult relationship
in one weekend. Of course, he was moving back to
Philadelphia on Monday. She knew that from the minute they
met. They were both crying at the airport, it had been so
sudden and then so suddenly over. They wrote for a while,
until she got a new boyfriend. Then, 25 years later, she was on
the commencement committee conference call as Claire
Doolan. As they spoke, his heart did a little back flip into a
pool of DayGlo nostalgia.

§   §   §

Reverend Bishop stood in his pulpit and waited until the final
notes of "The Old Rugged Cross" stopped echoing in the vast
hall. Leroy Stubbs's baritone was sublime and uplifting. The
Reverend held aloft his white leather Bible and sent his eyes
across the congregation.

"We will read today from the book of King James I." He
took the bible in both hands. "But not this book, not the holiest
of holies." He set the bible down on the pulpit and picked up a
piece of paper. Without looking at it he continued.

"King James awoke one sunday morning to the timbre of
church bells tolling across the great town of London. After
dressing he went to a window in Buckingham Palace. The King
was fully expecting to see the good people of London, parents,
grandparents, and their children. Toddlers carried on the
shoulders of their dads, the infirm helped along in carts;
everyone making their way to the church of their choice. For it

was the sabbath, and the entire kingdom would worship God for blessing them with this noble King. But James, who, years before, had written the first royal decrees against the sodomites..."

The congregation murmured approvingly at this piece of news. Bishop's researcher on this topic had included the fact that James had three known male lovers.

The Reverend held their complete attention. "...was the same King James who did authorize and promote the reading of the word of God through the translation of this by the best religious scholars of his age. Even today this translation is the most valued, the most impressive, the most revered ever published. The one true revelation of God and his only son." He held aloft his Bible to a chorus of "amens."

"Good King James looked out of his window on that Sunday, and what do you think he saw?" Bishop turned to look at the number two camera down at the foot of the pulpit, just as if he were James I looking down on the crowds.

"The mob, released from work by the grace of their king. The throng, heedless of the music of the church bells. Instead they played all manner of devices and games: baiting bulls and bears, gambling on dice, conjuring up comedies and making fun of those who were trying to walk that narrow path through the chaos of the streets in order to attend their Sunday service."

Overhead the projectors spilled images from Breugel the Elder, medieval crowds engaged in multiple perversions. The congregation gasped like one enormous terrified animal.

"And what did King James do?"

The projected scenes switched to paintings of halcyon landscapes with whitewashed churches. Bishop waved the piece of paper he had been holding.

"He wrote this law and made the sabbath safe again for his God-fearing servants. He ordered these hideous games

banished and told the nation as one people to attend service on
Sunday."

"I can report that the King was not indiscriminate in his
condemnation of recreation on the sabbath. No, he was very
clear about this." Bishop let a smile grow on his face. "Like
many of you, I, myself, can admit to this one small sin. King
James had a weakness for..." Bishop leaned closer over the
pulpit as if divulging a secret. "...football."

The congregation broke into laughter. The choir rocked
and kidded each other. Bishop threw his head back and joined
in.

"Let me tell you, God himself must have been proud that
day to have King James as his quarterback." He set down the
paper and reached his right hand into the pulpit.

Bishop waved his left arm across the pulpit. "Are you
comfortable?" His voice rang across the room.

The congregation muttered and shifted nervously. The way
he asked made them all distinctly uncomfortable.

"Because if you are, it is because King James and many
others put their lives on the line to make the sabbath a special
day, a day of rest and worship, and yes a day of comfort to the
weary. So please do take comfort all of you here today and
watching from your homes. Take comfort in the fact that,
unlike King James, you can listen to church bells and watch the
congregations gather in peace and quiet. But wait!"

Bishop thrust his left hand up in the air. "What is this I
hear? Not the sibilance of the church bells. Not the whisper of
freshly shined shoes on the steps of the chapel. Not the
greetings of friends and neighbors in the narthex. I hear the
electronic rumble of games, games of chance and violence,
pagan games with false gods and demons, salacious games that
offer sex to children. To children!" he roared, "...and on the
holy sabbath!"

The video screens erupted with a montage of violent action scenes from video games. First person shooters splattered opponents with grenades and sniper rifles, hideous demons tore players apart in fountains of blood. Players attacked drug addicts with baseball bats and TASERed scantily clad prostitutes. Automobiles accelerated into crowded bus stops and veered to run down pregnant women, children, and elderly couples using walkers. Crowds of teenagers armed with pitchforks and chainsaws battled battalions of zombie babies. The scenes made Breugel look like Norman Rockwell. The congregation recoiled with shouts and screams.

Bishop walked over to the center of the stage as the video montage dissolved into slow motion scenes of video cafes showing dozens of teenagers enraptured by their gameplay, their eyes glued to the action.

"And those scenes," he waved at the screen, "are the tame ones, the shots we can show on television." He bowed his head as if in prayer and stood silent while the crowd settled.

"What am I holding here?" Bishop's right hand lifted up a three-foot section of an electrical extension cord, its plug end dangling.

"Why look, you say, this is something everybody has in their house. It's an electrical extension cord. I tell you now my friends, plug this into a computer on Sunday and it becomes the tail of the devil."

He switched into his soft voice. A kindly father explaining to his young son that his beloved puppy is dead. "The devil has stolen your children from the Lord's day. He has crept into your daughter's bedroom and set up camp. He has snatched your son's attention and now holds him in his thrall. How many of you are here today while your children are at home?" He let that thought hover for a minute.

He looked straight at camera one. "How many of you at home are watching while your children are in their rooms? On their computers. Doing their homework?" Bishop wagged his finger. "I don't think so."

"I am calling on all of you watching at home to stand up. Right this minute. That's it, stand up. And we will stand up with you."

On cue the choir stood. The group leaders in the audience stood and the rest of the congregation hurried to their feet.

"Stand up for Jesus! You at home. Now go into your child's room. Take the devil by the tail and pull the plug on Satan!" He tossed the electrical cord down the steps as though it was a viper set to strike. "Go on now. We will have a musical interlude while you are away. Brother Stubb, give us a song."

§   §   §

The Sunday shift at WeRus in Goleta was normally a down time, and the sysadmin on duty ran a few diagnostics. He watched football, played the Game, or dozed in the Cordobalounger in Scratchy's office. They took the Sunday shifts in turn.

It was about 11:40 in the morning when the XServe array lit up like Times Square. Thousands of disk drives spun up simultaneously. Vast amounts of computer memory were being addressed. Information cascaded from the backbone Ariadne fiber connection.

Barry was watching the Packers and the Vikings in the lounge. He had a couple players from the Vikings on fantasy team. He heard the electrical grid alarm go off as a sudden demand for power tripped the battery backup system. Thinking it was another glitch in the local electrical grid—

Edison tended to run its own diagnostics on Sundays—Barry wandered over to the window wall and glanced at the front panel of the enormous battery system, which was blinking red, as expected. Then he noticed the entire XServe was lit up like Christmas at Macy's.

Barry ran to the control monitor. The logs were scrolling faster than he could read them. Nothing was failing yet; however, the load was enormous. The throughput on Ariadne was enough to fill the entire optical fiber pipe down to Los Angeles. Good thing it was a Sunday. He hesitated only momentarily and then looked up the text message codes in the company's emergency manual. He sent the code for a general alert to the phones of all company executives.

In the supercomputer's room the air-conditioning units kicked on high. Two thousand quad CPUs were radiating as they processed billions of trillions of instructions. A new klaxon of electrical alarms were joined by the sudden roar of the diesel engine outside. The emergency generators had started up automatically to help with the internal power load.

Barry watched the admin console. He filtered the log display so he could monitor only the major system alerts. The supercomputers in India and Japan now shared the load. Countless petaflops of calculations fed a stream of instructions between the three computers and the entire Junana network. Incredibly, nothing was failing under the load. Not yet. The phone rang. It was Don. Barry told him things were under control for the time being. Don wanted Berry to be sure the log cache was backed up so they could run some diagnostics on Monday.

Less than ten minutes later, the supercomputer began to quiet. Barry watched the throughput diminish to its usual trickle. Within half an hour the entire system was back to normal. The quiet was almost as alarming as the noise had been. The event log was several gigs. Barry burned it onto an xDVD, labeled this and left it on Don's desk. He watched the monitor for another few minutes and then returned to the lounge, where the Packers had scored three times in the second quarter.

"Damn."

§   §   §

Sunday morning at his dad's house in Lompoc, Nick was in his bedroom using the Santa Barbara High School KayAye to explore exothermic and endothermic reactions of molecules. Cindy gave him a problem where the enthalpy of formation of the products was greater than the enthalpy of formation of the reactants. The Query space had half a dozen tools to explore the molecular geometry, Nick chose Lewis structures.

He was just about to key in his answer when Babs, his dad's new girl friend, burst into his room.

"Babs, I'm not fraking dressed." He grabbed up a pair of long shorts to cover his boxers.

She glanced around and spied the electric outlet beside his desk.

"Out Satan!" she shouted. "Out of this house!" She strode across the room and yanked his laptop's AC cord from the socket.

"Hey!" He turned in his chair. "This is my room!"

Babs held the cord triumphantly. Then she noticed that his laptop was still on.

"What the...?" He shifted his body between her and his computer. "Get outta here!"

She glanced around the room. "Aha!" She dove to the other wall and tugged his cable modem's power brick from the socket, jerking it also from the modem. "Free your mind of filth and degradation!"

"Are you off your meds?" Nick asked, "Where's my dad?"

"You won't be needing this." She held the power supply like a dead rat in her hand, its thin cord dangling. Then she stormed back into the family room and slammed the door behind her.

Nick threw on shorts and a shirt. He contemplated wrestling the power supply away from Babs, but decided instead to ride over to the Red Star. He gathered his laptop into the shoulder bag, grabbed his deck, and laced up his sneakers.

Nick ducked into the kitchen for a toaster pastry. Over in the family room Babs held the power brick in her hand while she watched some TV preacher wave a white bible around. His dad was probably still asleep. He opened up the fridge, grabbed a half-gallon on milk, leaned back against the counter and took a long slug.

His mom had a new boyfriend who didn't like to see him around the house. Didn't really want to see him at all. The feeling was mutual. Now it was clear he couldn't move in here. Babs was way too high-maintenance.

Nick had just turned sixteen and was seriously into Level Four. The new KayAye interface made school a dream. He spent his whole day thick into the Game.

Ms. Baxter was already on Level Three. She asked him a question about Simplicity Loves Difference and he told her how he had to unfold that template structure down to its seed on Level Four. Cindy said he should get into the lottery for the Isla Vista GameTown. She said she could try to get him a job in the gym or one of the restaurants. There must be thousands of Gamers trying to get in and only a hundred spaces or so.

If only Jackie Kim were still around, maybe he could hang out at her house. She went emo when she hit Level Five in

September. Took a bunch of her mother's pills and ended up on
Five-East at Cottage Hospital. When she got out, her family
moved her out of town and off Junana. Might as well have
taken her to another planet. In the other room, Babs clicked off
the TV. Nick ducked out the kitchen door.

§   §   §

Don Driscoll checked the admin logs again. Scratchy had been
curious about the content surge on Sunday. It almost brought
them down, he said. Then he added, "that won't happen after
we do the final port." He didn't answer Don when he asked
what "port" Scratchy was referring too.

Several times in the past month, the five anonymous users
had independently entered transporters to goth scenes and
then logged out. That was strange enough, but what caught his
attention is that every one of them logged out exactly five
minutes after entering the goth scene. Not four minutes and
fifty-nine seconds, not five minutes and one second. So they
were being logged out by a preset program. But were they
actually logged out, or did the program take them somewhere
else? He would need to follow one of them, but how?

Don opened up the file again, the one that showed the least
expected aspects of the admin corpus. One page three he
discovered that fifty-thousand plus users had chosen to turn
off their collision detection. This triggered something in his
memory, and Don opened up the admin file for avatar
preferences. The fields of the data model for avatar appearance
preferences ran for two pages.

Don logged into Junana.com and checked the user interface
for the same preferences. The switch for turning off the
collision detection was at the bottom of a submenu and on

page two of the data model. The effect of doing this was that the avatar could walk through other objects, and other avatars could also walk right through the avatar. Looking from the actual data model to the user interface, Don noticed something else.

"Bingo!" he whispered.

One of the preferences available in the data model and the admin GUI but not implemented in the user interface was "transparency." The settings were in percentage points. If you set this to zero, your avatar would be invisible. Probably a feature on the original design, or something the programmer put in that the customer decided not to use. Since there was no user interface for this setting, nobody on Junana could change their transparency from the default setting of one-hundred percent. Nobody, that is, but Don, who simply found his own avatar's table in the database and, through his ROOT admin access manually reset this value to "zero."

His avatar was standing in its default plaza. Don toggled Third Person and, instead of seeing his avatar from overhead, there was just the floor. He waved his avatar's hands, and still no image. Another avatar, headed for one of the transporters, walked briskly into the middle of his field of vision and bounced back.

"What the fuck?" it said, and walked ahead, only to rebound one more time. It turned to the left and strode out of the scene.

Don went to the user interface menus and called up the preferences for his avatar. He chose a submenu and unchecked the box for collision detection. He was now both invisible and immaterial. He went back to the main menu and found the submenu for speech. He turned off the sound, so he wouldn't chuckle and reveal himself, and then set the current settings as a default so the changes would be saved.

He wandered through the plaza, poking his avatar into the middle of conversations. As long as they did not set these to "private" and encrypt them, his proximity gave him access to their audio. And since he could drift unseen right into the middle of a throng, nobody was the wiser. He felt like the invisible man. Now all he needed to do was set up an email alarm for when any of the five logged in.

§ § §

Scratchy popped into the Room and found Itchy standing near one of the walls. Itchy was working at a console, a large translucent screen hovered in front of him. Scratchy noted that he now wore the yellow shirt.

"Finished that next level, I see," he said, slumping into one of the Cordobaloungers.

"Hi Michael," Itchy did not turn around. "I'll be just a minute here. I'm setting up a statistical run on last month's consumer numbers, and the European Union changed its data model on me. I can call up another console if you want to play the Game."

"Not unless you can bring up Halo 5. I'm stuck in the tower on level three."

"Aren't you even going to try the Game?"

"I've been through school. And I've got my own shoes, thank you very much."

Desi's avatar appeared, dressed in the crimson cape and carrying his staff.

"Grand Meister in the house!" Scratchy yelped. "Everybody grab your kids."

"Hello, Mikey." Desi's avatar strode forward and threw its arms around Scratchy's shoulders over the back of the chair. "You command shift H for a hug."

"Command shift H yourself," Scratchy said.

"Why so grumpy?"

"Got a little letter from the IRS. Seems they plan to stick their boots clean up my ass. And my house is still besieged by investors and groupies, so I'm camping out at one of Tad's hotels."

"Itchy, have you seen the code for JS?" Desi asked. "I hope I didn't delete it."

"JS?" Scratchy said. "You mean that talking robot thing you sent me?"

"Our prototype Guide," Itchy said. "I don't think the code made it into the Game build. It should be on the old IDE."

"But it's not, I checked. I wanted to do a comparison between the old JS code and the current state of the Guide code. They're acquiring so many new behaviors."

Jack's avatar appeared, also in a yellow shirt.

"Isn't anybody working anymore?" Scratchy asked. "Or do we just play the Game from here on out?"

"Not everybody gets it naturally," Jack said. "Not anybody, apart from you, Michael."

"Mr. Natural!" Desi laughed. "Oh, snap!"

This set them all laughing, and Scratchy toggled a grin that spread across his avatar's convict face like a hillside earthquake fault line.

"I miss a joke?" Winston appeared, dressed in a plaid sweater, tweed plus-fours, a tam cap, a wide bow tie, and the brown shoes.

"Winston, you've earned your shoes!" Desi skipped forward and gave him a hug.

"I am worried about earning the hat. It doesn't go with any of my golf attire."

"Like a hooked drive into the rough," Itchy said.

"Or a shanked wedge shot," Desi said.

"Or a case of the yips," Scratchy said.

They turned to Jack.

"Um, or a buried sand lie," he said.

"Well, the gang's all here," Scratchy said. "What's the big crisis?"

§   §   §

Nick logged in. Cindy was standing there, back on the beach in her jeans and that top he remembered she wore commando the first day. She was still just as perky.

"Hello, cowboy." She tousled her hair like she does, and his heart did a little flip.

"Cindy. My room is excellent. I'm so happy!" He'd moved into the Isla Vista Gametown with a job as busboy in the Vietnamese vegetarian restaurant there. His roommate was also a Fourvey and a surfer.

"Keep your pants on. I don't need to see no buttons coming loose." Cindy coughed and a chill ran up Nick's spine. He had been waiting for this. Known about it for some time. Still not ready, not nearly so.

"Don't do that!" He cried out. "I need you!"

"You did, you know. You really did. That's why this isn't easy."

"Then take me back. I'll do Level Two. Hell, I'll do Level One again. Just don't go."

"Nicky. I was here for you, and now it's your turn for me. We came through everything together. I am the best Guide in the Game. You agree?"

"Fuckin' A right," he answered, tearing.

"I wouldn't be the best if I didn't know when it was time for you to move ahead."

He thought about that. Thought as hard as he could. He had no answer, just a knot like a knife in his gut.

"You be a good Fiver and don't waste all your time on Free-for-Alls. You promise me!" She jabbed her finger at him. "Tell me you are stoked to start Level Five."

His breath was coming heavy as he fought off tears.

"Tell me!"

"Yeah, I'm stoked. I really am." He sniffled.

"I'm not supposed to do this," she looked around guiltily. "But you've been such a good boy of late."

She undid her belt buckle and stepped out of her jeans. She was wearing little pink panties with white fringe. Then she shucked her top over her head and dropped it on the sand. She stood and showed him what he'd fantasized for two years. It was fully worth the wait.

"You're so beautiful," he whispered.

"Only all of me," she said. "So long, cowboy!"

She turned and walked slowly, ever so slowly, into the surf where she walked out on the waters and then turned to face him. Cindy tilted her head slightly to the left and draped her right hand over her luscious breasts. She slowly sank into the surf.

"Botticelli," he whispered. "Excellent exit, Cindy!"

He watched her head dip into the waters and then watched the waves for about half an hour before he shut down the computer and grabbed his board.

EIGHTEEN

Don was ready when he got his alert. One of the five anonymous users had logged onto Junana.com. Within minutes all of them had logged on. One by one they were taking a transporter to a goth scene. He identified the plaza of one of them the minute they logged in and sent his invisible avatar there too. He spied the goth transporter and moved closer. The plaza was thick with avatars moving about singly or in small groups. Ahead, a line of them dressed in jet black shrouds with flaming blue hair and long steel fingernails streamed into the goth transporter.

Don moved up to the transporter and spied an avatar walking aimlessly nearby, dressed like something out of pre-war Scottish film. *He's about as goth as my Aunt Tilda*, Don figured as the avatar closed in on the transporter. It took one last look behind, its eyes moving across Don's without stopping and stepped into the light. Don followed immediately. Instead of a goth scene, he ended up in a room that looked like someone's private study with five overstuffed leather recliner chairs in the middle of the floor. Besides the one, four others were waiting, laughing over something. Don slid his avatar into a corner and watched.

§ § §

"I've been talking with Desi and Ichiro about setting up a special destination available only to Sixers and above," Jack said. "So we can pool their knowledge. Something like this room, only, of course, bigger."

"Like the Vatican, Jack?" Scratchy said.

"More like a college campus," Itchy said.

"Sounds like a fucking fraternity." Scratchy said. "Shouldn't these people be out there influencing others instead of hanging around in the Game?"

"Are we still managing the load all right? How is the mesh holding up?" Winston asked.

"Beautifully!" Desi said. "We are mirroring most of our administration server processes on the mesh now too. We can move the whole project off of the server farms within a month."

"This console will be the admin console for the entire Game. When we get Castalia set up, we'll move the Room there," Itchy said.

"Castalia?" Scratchy asked.

"That's what we're calling the campus for Sixers and above."

"Figures. Since I'll never play, I guess I can retire and focus on the clusterfuck that's become my life."

"Michael. You will always be welcome in Castalia, even if you never play the Game," Desi said, placing his hand on Scratchy's shoulder. "And after the IRS is through with you, we will all try to help get a computer for your cell up in Lompoc. Won't that be nice?"

"My point, Michael..." Jack said and his avatar projected the irritation in his voice. "...is this. Sixers and Meisters are the main product of our Game and we need to be in conversation with them."

"I'll second that." Desi said. "I'm getting feedback from the Fivers I'm talking to that the Game is overwhelming their lives. A lot of them say they really miss their Guides. Maybe talking with other players would help them get over this."

"I can program a VOG to let players know that they have been invited," Itchy said.

"VOG?" Winston asked.

"Voice of God," Itchy said. "An announcement from the Game itself.

"I don't think we need a burning bush," Winston said.

"Could use a burning blunt," Scratchy said, shaking his head.

"Just because you never had a best friend!" Desi said.

"I thought you were my best friend."

"I'm Winston's best friend," Desi said. Scratchy looked at Winston.

"I'm Jack's best friend," Winston looked at Jack, who managed to shake his avatar's head.

"I'm Ichiro's best friend," he said. Scratchy turned to Itchy.

"Hey, I'm Desi's best friend."

"You are, you skinny boy," Desi said. Then they all managed to double over laughing while Scratchy pulled his seppuku suicide stunt and lay there bleeding rivers onto the floor.

§   §   §

Don jotted a note about Michael and the IRS. He had a total of five names now. Michael, who had to be O'hara, someone named Desicachario Venkataram or something like that, someone they called Itchy or Ichiro, Winston, and Jack. The fifth guy did not seem to be in critical path on the programming side, so he was probably a money man.

Don had been standing quietly in the corner, confident of his invisibility, but every so often the one they called Meister would look around at his corner, as though he could sense something different in the space. Don desperately wanted to stick around, but his nerves gave out and he logged off. He now had another plan in mind. It was more dangerous to his employment, but it would allow him access to that console.

The way it sounded, they wouldn't need a sysadmin in a month anyhow. Mr. "I've got another Neo, aren't I special" O'hara probably was going to give him two weeks notice and expect him to walk away empty handed. If he could get his hands on that console, he could get to the Game code. Do this right and he could set himself up for life.

§   §   §

In the quarter following the RIND meeting Con|Int's projections proved to be, if anything, far too conservative. Claire was deep into Level Four on the Game and not paying as much attention to the press as she would have before, back when she had something to sell. In November, she had given the Posse three months leave at half salary to play the Game and think up an new business plan.

This year's Black Friday, the Friday after Thanksgiving, was a class five disaster: sales at major retailers were down 35 percent from the past year. The flood of red ink had tanked the Dow as well. The after-holiday sales were pathetic, sending a score of regional chains into bankruptcy. The higher value brands were the hardest hit, and the new year found last year's high-fashion clothing being sold by street vendors in SoHo at a price not much higher than their manufacturing cost in Shenzhen.

Claire had scheduled a face-to-face meeting with the Posse in a lodge outside of Santa Fe in the week after Mardi Gras. She needed Betsy's full attention. The company's situation would be resolved there, one way or the other. By March they might just call it quits and open up a coffee house somewhere.

Claire would sometimes wander along the now quiet Montana Avenue near her house. Half of its stores were empty and the rest were plastered with signs offering heavy discounts. A small retail oasis remained around the bustling Red Star Coffee outlet. LAwear, a new chain offering union-sewed clothing, did a brisk business. Whole Foods and some of the restaurants were doing very well. Even if they abandon the Now, people have to eat.

The Now was like a jail that fed a serial compulsion in its prisoners. Like a drug, it felt so fantastically wonderful for just an instant. That simple transaction, the swipe of the plastic, stood in for all transactions, fluid or fantasy. Retail as masturbation, she thought. Sounds like a paper at an American Anthropology Association meeting. Claire knew it was the Game that turned its players from the Now. Not on purpose, despite Harold Farmer's warning.

The Now lived on the void that surrounded it, fed on the emptiness it created in people's lives. The Game came along and filled this void with other transactions. Even Farmer had no idea how fragile the Now was.

The intellectual elitist in her made Claire want to say that the Game released its players from accepting the arbitrary prices that brands required to make the money to buy the advertising to power the brand. Two dollars worth of denim were just that, no matter what the label said. Gamers figured this out. Prices no longer just stuck when producers floated them. She was convinced that a new fashion aesthetic would emerge to replace brand-based consumption.

The low consumer numbers right now, she figured, had to include the fact so many people were playing the Game instead of spending their time and money elsewhere. Once people

burned out on the Game, they would be back watching
extreme mud wrestling again, or whatever. Only would they?
Again she wondered who was behind the Game.

§   §   §

Once the morning rush was over, Desi made his way down to
the compound. He made a habit of rotating through the stalls,
not picking a favorite. Since he had completed Level Seven, his
interactions within the compound became enveloped in a web
of deference. He had become not just famous, but revered in a
manner reserved for the old and the wise. He felt neither old
nor wise, and so the situation was mainly awkward. He spent
more and more time in his apartment above the restaurant in
Hoi An.

Fortunately, his programming crews no longer required his
everyday attention. They had become world-class geeks.
Several of them had developed products in their spare time
that showed real market potential. Although they were bound
by a five-year contract, Desi argued with Winston and Jack to
get them permission to pursue these interests through a start-
up company in the compound. Sao Do Enterprises handled the
patent process and developed prototypes for the marketplace.

Desi exchanged formal greetings with the stall owner and
another gentleman, the father of a programmer who was
reading his newspaper at the same table. The waiter set down a
plate with brioche and another of fruit. He bowed deeply and
retreated. Coffee appeared. Desi requested that they turn up
the radio they had quieted on his arrival.

His Vietnamese had improved of late. He enjoyed the
language with its tonal lilt, but he had little time to polish his
skills. He sometimes worried that his DocDo program was

making people lazy. They had ported the Junana client to cell phones via WiFi, enabling real-time cross-language conversations. Over in Hoi An he'd seen tourists bargaining with shopkeepers, each of them talking into their cell phones while standing face-to-face. Is nobody learning a second language anymore?

Level Six in the game hinted at a layer of templates undergirding the ones they were unfolding. Desi was now able to map how several template structures that were entirely experiential were also linked through a skein of relations that were too subtle for direct experience. From his linguistics background he was wary of designing formal structures for these relations. He was content to note how their presence could be mapped by their effects on those templates one could directly experience.

The template "Fractal Layer Underneath" was a good example of how experience was informed by the qualities of its edges, rather than its center. This template suggested that those designs which contain details at three spatial levels and include a level too small to be experienced without magnification were visually pleasing over long periods of time.

Fractal Layer Underneath resolved the problem of why experiences of the natural world, where fractal surfaces were abundant, were often more satisfying than human designs: why a bouquet of flowers was generally more pleasing than a photograph of these. It also explained why film, with its grain, was more pleasing than digital photographs without grain. This template revealed the appeal of various forms of art and architecture from abstract expressionism to mannerism. It resolved how the "Simple on the Outside" template could apply to an abstract expressionist painting by Mark Tobey and why many modernist buildings do not sustain visual interest over time.

Desi finished breakfast and looked at his watch. A team meeting was scheduled for 10:30. He had time for a hike along the river before his day officially began.

$ § § § $

Claire's daughter Megan had spent the previous night in Claire's bed, inconsolable—not merely unhappy but flat out miserable. She had flung her arms around her mother's neck, clutching at Claire's back while Claire consoled her with caresses. Megan spoke of her torment, her words garbled by her sobs. Megan's Guide in the Game had died.

Bobby had told her he was not going to be with her in Level Five.

"I thought he was just testing me, challenging me to think on my own." She buried her face in Claire's neck. "We were taking our ride, down on the beach, Bobby on his black horse and me on my palomino. He just fell sideways on the sand and lay there, not moving. I ran to him and he was breathing heavy. He said that it was time for him to go on to another place and that I must not be sad. But I am sad!"

"I can't help it," she blubbered. "Bobby!"

"'You will always be my little warrior,' he told me, and then he touched my face. "I will live in your memories of our time together.' Then he closed his eyes forever.

"I sat there for, I don't know, hours. How could he die? And then, from out of the heavens, silhouetted by the sun, two avatars in bright silver armor and enormous feathery wings swooped down and landed nearby. The visors on their silver helmets were up and their faces were solemn. They walked up to Bobby's body and picked this up between them. One of them looked at me and he bowed his head. They rose on their wings, turned into the sun and climbed until I couldn't see them anymore. If only I'd taken more time on Level Four, he'd be alive right now. He pushed me ahead in the Game, knowing it would kill him."

Claire stroked the damp hair away from Megan's cheek. "He was a magnificent Guide and a true friend."

"Mumlie. Why did he have to die? Why?"

Claire held her close for some time before she spoke.

"Meggie, Bobby is a Game piece," Claire said. "I know you loved being with him, and loved what he did to help you in the Game. My Guide was very special to me. When Fuzango died I felt terrible."

Claire's Guide, Fuzango he called himself, was ancient, sinewy and plastered with ashes. He first greeted her in Jagahala and then switched to English. Almost comically gruff, he ordered her around like she was his slave. He was dressed as a village elder on a festival day, meaning he was naked except for this koteka penis sheath, held vertically with twine around his waist, and an elaborate headdress of feathers and fur.

When she had been a young female anthropologist in the field, she never could get the tribal elders to pay her proper attention. Old Fuzango told her things about Highland New Guinea culture that she wished she'd learned for her dissertation—that is, when he wasn't pushing her in front of a train. He died in his hut after giving her the first smile he ever showed.

"Bobby would not have died if he didn't think you were ready for the next level. He was a good friend and dying was his way of helping you move on."

Megan was quiet then, sobbing into Claire's shoulder as they lay on the bed. Claire understood the death of the Guide as a rite of passage the Game had determined was valuable for the process of moving ahead. While a part of her might have cursed the Game programmers for her daughter's sadness, a larger part welcomed Bobby's passing. How could Claire ever compete with Mr. Wonderful: the all-knowing, all-feeling, positively cute, Bobby?

Bobby's death brought Megan into her arms. It had been years since Megan called her 'Mumlie,' almost as long since they had something really important to share. Claire held her daughter until Megan's breathing quieted into sleep.

§   §   §

Itchy and Desi reclined in the Cordobaloungers, mesmerized by the firelight.

"How did you program the logs to actually burn down?"

"It's a non-linear process."

"You mean?"

"Logarithmically, my dear Lucy."

"Complex algorithm?"

"That too." Itchy sat up. "I'm a bit worried."

Desi turned his attention to his friend.

"There's a lot of unaccounted for noise in the system," Itchy said. He had a standing task to optimize the Guide functions. The Guide subroutine had become a monumental programming effort and by some measures the singular hallmark of the Game. It was extravagant in terms of computing power. More than half of the Game's petaflops went to support Guide interactions.

"Is it just noise?" Desi asked. "I have reports that the Guides are talking to each other."

"Curious." Itchy nodded slowly.

"By 'Curious?', do you mean 'interesting' or 'holy fucking shit!'?"

"Very, very interesting. We needed to have the Guides share their learned behaviors. We could never keep up programming them individually."

"So if any one Guide learns a new trick, they all learn it?"

"That's the idea."

"All billion of them?"

Itchy was still nodding slowly.

"What if a player asks a Guide to contact a Guide of another player?"

"The Guides were programmed to talk to their own players. They cannot talk with any other player."

"If their player asks them to learn a new trick, like talking to another Guide, could they learn it?"

"Guides are programmed to be helpful. If they cannot do a task, they are programmed to deflect the request by encouraging the user to focus on the Game."

"How does a Guide know they can't do a task?"

"They query the common pool and get a result. If there is no corresponding behavior, then they can spend a certain amount of cycles attempting to approximate the behavior. At the end of that time, they basically give up."

"What happens to these cycles?"

"The failed ones?"

"Right."

"They go into the pool as well, so that the next attempt can start where the previous one ended."

"So they learn from each other's mistakes."

"That's the plan."

"How smart can they get?"

"You mean, can they achieve sentience and take over the world?"

"Something like that."

"Not as long as we control the Guide subroutine. There is no return path between this subroutine and the main admin routines, just a one-way instruction link. We can simply turn them off any time we want to. What we can't do is predict precisely what they will learn within the boundaries of their programming. Yes, I would say that, over time, Guides could learn to talk with each other. I'm just not sure what they would have to talk about."

"Does Scratchy know about this?"

"We should probably discuss it next time we are all in the Room. Right now, I'm just concerned that the Guide subroutine will swamp the whole Game. Even on the mesh, they are hogging a lot of RAM."

"If they are talking to each other, it might be a good idea to figure out what they are saying," Desi mused. "Before they start voting."

§   §   §

Like most plans where you are trying to screw your boss, Don's would either work or get him fired or both. As sysadmin Don had ROOT privileges on Junana. This gave him direct access to the Junana databases, including email account fields. Other users' passwords, however, were encrypted even in the database.

His plan was simple. He would log into the Junana database as ROOT. He would send out an email to all five players, a simple suggestion that they routinely change their password. He'd make it appear to be a standard email to all Junana players. He would intercept all requests for new passwords and copy these to another file.

Most geeks who work on security measures imagine how improbable it would be for someone to take the time and effort required to break these. They fail to understand that the people who hack security systems do this for a living. And no system is really secure from an inside attack.

Don broadcast the email with the subject "Junana security alert, please change password regularly." The email came from the Junana system, and for all they knew it went out to all billion or so members, when it actually just went to the five players with access to that room. The body of the email said that best practice was to change passwords every ninety days and gave them the age of their current password. Then he waited.

Thirty minutes later, his code captured a password reset reply email from one of the five, a 'bobbyjones1930'. He wrote down the password and trashed his code and the file. Then he hesitated. Whoever sent this was still at their computer. He checked the clock, it was around three in the afternoon. Not knowing where in the world this user might be, he figured if he waited ten hours he would be safer. They would either be off work by then or even asleep.

At 1:00 a.m., Don logged in to Junana with the username 'bobbyjones1930' and the new password. Don stepped into the goth scene transporter and found himself in the Room. He was alone. He located the console and moved to it, praying this needed no additional password. He stretched his invisible hands out over the keyboard. Junana sent the system the message that his avatar was in 'keyboard mode', which meant that what he typed on his keyboard was being entered in a keyboard in Junana.

Don knew what he was looking for. From here he could access all the privileges of every player, including Scratchy O'hara. He pulled up the account for bobbyjones1930 and noticed that this had several fields he did not recognize from the ROOT level. One of them was called 'Room,' and it was set to 'Yes.' Don noticed an icon for Eclipse. He clicked this and the development environment opened up in front of his eyes. He scanned the menus.

"Holy Shit!" he whispered. There were hundreds of folders. Enough source code to run, well, the whole show.

One of the features of an integrated development environment is the ability to back-up the latest version of the source files, one at a time, or, as a batch when needed. Don moused up the file back-up menu, clicked "entire package" and "zip and email back-up" options, selected one of his own email addresses as the destination, and pushed "Send."

A folder with millions of lines of code is smaller than a single, short movie clip. The process was completed in less than a minute. If Don was a dancing man, he'd be doing a jig in his chair. Instead he saw visions of banknotes and Swiss accounts. So many, many zeros.

Don heard a voice and nearly jumped out of his chair. He turned around, and his office door was still closed and locked.

He turned the head on his avatar and saw two other avatars in the Room. They were coming toward the console. He quickly switched off 'keyboard mode' and moved his avatar sideways as the one named Itchy walked up and stopped right where he had been standing an instant before. Lucky he had set the avatar's visibility to zero. On the console, the IDE program was still open but the console was now ready for a new user.

"Now that we've settled on the London club design, do you think we can talk Scratchy out of these tacky lounge chairs?" the one they called Desi said. He walked straight into Don's avatar and rebounded.

"Fuck," Don muttered, he had forgotten to turn off the collision detection and also his microphone.

"Well, excuse me!" Desi said, turning back to face Itchy.

"Fuck yourself," Itchy said without looking around. He opened up a file on the console. "Looks like they committed the new code for Castalia."

Don logged out and the room disappeared. He sat at his computer in a cold sweat and stared at his desktop on the monitor for several minutes until the screen saver kicked on. He opened up his email client and pushed the "Get Mail" button. The cursor spun for a good minute and then a new email popped up.

There it was. Top of the Inbox list. A four-hundred and ninety megabyte zip file named JNA0111. He burned this to a disk and also copied it to a USB thumbdrive. Unless they used more than one development environment set up, he had stolen the entire source code for the Junana social network and the Game.

Now he had something to sell. He would need to find a buyer. Not just any buyer, someone with more money than Don could imagine, and Don had a fairly expansive imagination in this area.

Nerdville

NINETEEN

Jennifer Bouchez spent two solid months moving up through the Game levels. The Game was nothing like Roland and Annika had described, and yet it was everything they tried to tell her.

Her Guide, Francesco, might have been the fake Italian husband she had invented years before. He knew her better than any friend she could recall. He remembered everything she had published and could hold a conversation on anything she had read. He could recall the villages where she vacationed as a child. He controlled intimate facts about classmates all the way back to her elementary school. And he knew that what she wished for above all else was someone who could remain relaxed around her, who didn't mind her catching him looking at her hair, who could take her hand and stroll along the river.

Her First Level was a series of walks through cities as real as the East Village in February and as spectral as any Borges tale. Each city displayed an entirely localized epistemology, a way of organizing knowledge, the uncovering of which required every bit of ethnographic skill she could muster. And until she uncovered and explored this, she could not move to the next city. Then she was in Level Two, and Francesco explained how the Query engine worked. She caught on quickly to the task of refolding the unfolded templates. She marveled at the template structures while these, in turn, insinuated into her thought processes.

When Francesco insisted that she put her computer to sleep and go out and eat or visit a certain building in Paris she had never seen, she would wander out into a cityscape filled with templates. The "entry space" undulations of the doorways on the boulevards, the syncopation of the pedestrians in their mutual dance of "attentive disregard." The posturing of the police as a "visible monopoly of force." She could read the landscape as a template tapestry. In fact she could not avoid doing so now, and she was chagrinned about the years she had spent without this facility.

She met Jorge and Wanda and learned the hand movements. She searched this technique and learned about its use in Brazil. Francesco was jealous of Jorge. But then Brad Pitt would have been jealous of Jorge. Francesco seemed impressed that she progressed through this level in just a few weeks. He concluded that he must be a very excellent Guide, and she agreed with him, which pleased him greatly. He even let Jorge kiss her goodbye. But then he locked her in that submarine with the water pouring in and she had to drown six times before she asked the right question. Level Three was pure revelation. Her shoes arrived, and she wore them around the house. Francesco was still barefoot, and complained that Guides cannot earn shoes. Life is unfair, she agreed.

Her Level Three Query sessions pushed her to some mental limit she had never before experienced. It felt like her brain had been removed, enlarged, supercharged, and then reconnected. She was faced with the prospect of unfolding new templates from the seeds, which Francesco would reveal after hours of Querying. Francesco taught her a new speed-reading technique, and she caught up on several genres she'd never had time for. She browsed the Village Voice Bookstore on the rue Princesse and bought a potpourri of current literature in English. She could read a novel in under an hour, at a pace where its plot hit her like a dose of amyl nitrate. As fast as her mind was spinning in the Game, her dreams were also a kaleidoscope of images and scenes, a monstrous montage of actual memories and Game Queries.

When Francesco congratulated her for completing Level Three, she realized that she had been playing more or less solidly for six weeks. Roland and Annika had been sending reports for her to pass on to Claire. And with some guilt she did so, adding that Claire might also want to try the Game. Claire emailed back that she was too busy trying to figure out why nobody was buying the sequined jeans that Con|Int had predicted would be the next big fashion on the West Coast.

Now that she was on Level Four, she could call up the Game Console and create her own reports about Junana.com. She began to discover that the Game had its own internal limitations; the template structures she was confronted by covered a certain mental territory. Many of the problems in the philosophy of science, literary criticism, and reflexive sociology were explored, but there was very little in the biological sciences, psychology, or religion.

The Game revealed problem spaces in technology, architecture and urban planning, and business, but not in art or music. Queries about art tended to veer into investigations about taste. Those on religion soon migrated into either the history of religions or empirical philosophy. In short, the Game had its own personality, which she assumed was either intentional or an artifact of the interests of its programmers. The Game showed a huge intellect but little humor.

She used her Free-for-All time on the Game to try and unfold some new templates, beginning with a template concerning the problem field of "investment." Not financial investment, but the psychological investments made by individuals in their own identities, or in the identities of others. She had an early success with a template structure on interpellation, that is, on the investments of the state in the individual. Francesco was ecstatic with praise about this, and told her that she was one of only a handful of Fourth Level players who had unfolded a new template to its source. Later he bragged to her to that *their* new template structure was being incorporated into Level Two, so that every player would face the task of refolding its structure.

At first, Francesco's narcissism disturbed her. She then realized he was an idealized vision of her desires. He was gorgeous, yes, and in his role as Guide he spoke from an authority she could not match. He was also so entirely wrapped up in himself that he hardly gave her any notice except when this could be reflected back to him. She found him silly but refreshing. She reminded herself he was a Game piece, not a person. There was no "he," only a programmed assembly of pixels. These pixels had been assembled for her. She tried imaging a different Guide, only to realize that Francesco was the perfect choice after all.

At the end of Level Four, Francesco insisted that they walk together back on the city streets where he had first taken her. It was in Venice, on Piazza San Marco, where he stumbled and fell. She waited for him to rise, but he motioned her to bend down and told her he was dying. She would need to go on without him, he said, as difficult as that might seem. She chided him for being over dramatic. A death in Venice, really. She demanded that he stop playacting and get back on his feet.

"Is good," he said. "You are strong. Not like me."

Then he lay back and closed his eyes. His form slowly dissolved into the bricks and she knew he was gone. Jennifer shut off her computer, went out into the late afternoon and drifted for hours through the streets of Paris. She saw herself in the reflection of a shop window, her face side lit by a street lamp.

She had been at turns saddened, angry, and confused by
Francesco's death. He was a Game piece. A clever construct.
She had put on the hat and her shoes and an old sweatshirt
over a T-shirt and jeans. When she caught the look in her eyes,
she realized that Francesco's narcissism was a reflection of her
own. In a world that seemed to want to objectify her, she had
invested even more in constructing her self-image. It was his
last lesson for her. Her shoulder bag arrived the next day.

§   §   §

By the time Gerry Bishop arrived at Haverbrook School the
Board of Directors had already voted. The school's Learning
Management System and the Internet were to go back on line
on Monday. Rector Lovemark was instructed to tell the
Reverend.

"Can't you talk to him?" Ralph pleaded with Darron Boone,
the chair of the board. Why did Ralph have to break the news
to Bishop? After all, the board members were all volunteers
with nothing at stake.

"Hector, if we don't get the Internet back up none of our
kids are going to stay. In fact we have petitions from every
student and faculty member at Haverbrook. Without the net,
we don't have a school."

"You make it sound so clear," Ralph said. "I'm sure he'd
listen to you."

"Do your job, Hector. Let us know how he takes it." Boone
hung up.

The students call it "The Grove." A patch of swamp maple
surrounded a natural clearing. Over a rise and out of sight
from the school, it was a gathering place for smoking and
general truancy. This afternoon it was packed with students,—

nearly the entire student body in fact, nervously standing in small groups, chattering among themselves.

"He's arrived," Simon announced loudly and pocketed his cell phone. The voices stilled. They were destined for punishment, all of them. But none more than Simon.

"They'll be looking for us. It won't be long. Let me do the talking." Their silence signaled their agreement.

"It's all Bishop's fault," someone said, and several mumbled agreement.

Peter was still in the infirmary, and so Simon was the logical target for their collective anger, as though Simon should have talked his father out of this Internet ban. Simon's face reddened. He stood silent. Apprentice to the Dark Mage, he would not submit to insult.

"We'll agree to go back only if they turn on the Internet," he said.

§ § §

"Winston, this is Claire. Claire Doolan." She waited a second to see if their brief conversation on the Reed commencement-selection committee telecon had made any impact.

"Claire. Great to hear your voice." Winston set down his coffee and settled back in his chair, glancing around at the view of Rittenhouse Square under a foot of snow. "What can I do for you?"

"This is a might embarrassing, I have to admit. They put me up to it." She hesitated.

"Go on."

"The committee asked me to ask you if you wouldn't mind asking Michael O'hara to take your place as commencement speaker. There, I've said it. I told them it was bad form..."

"You want the Nerd King instead of the insightful financial planner?" He kept the disappointment out of his voice.

"Why don't I just tell them to go fuck themselves?"

"Michael's the man of the year. Sure, I can ask him." Scratchy will eat this up, he thought.

"I also need to ask you a favor. Should probably have done this before I yanked the speaker invitation…"

"Go ahead."

"My company is having a retreat meeting in Santa Fe to decide what we can do in response to the retail sector collapse and, you know, the Game, and all. We need expert advice, and I'm hoping you can join us."

"Santa Fe?"

"It's in three weeks. We can send you a plane ticket, put you up. All the doughnuts you can eat. We can't afford much of an honorarium."

"Sounds intriguing. Count me in."

"Really?"

"Certainly. Give us a chance to catch up."

"That it will." She turned and caught her reflection in the window. She frowned at it. "It's been quite a while."

"Send me the details by email. I'll talk to Scratchy, and he will contact you."

"I'm so sorry about that. It's really rude. I hope you don't hate the messenger."

"That depends. Can you make it up to me?" That came out so wrong, he thought.

"Hmmm. Unless you actually enjoy humiliation, I can think of a couple things." One would do, she thought. Where was this going?

"Santa Fe, then," he said.

"Santa Fe," she said. "Ciao." She hung up.

§   §   §

It was obvious by Bishop's mood when he stepped from the limo that he had already heard of the vote.

"They're the board," Ralph weaseled, "What can I do?" He tried to keep step with the Reverend, who was striding briskly through the main house on his way to the school auditorium.

"They won't be for long," Bishop said. He burst through the auditorium doors.

The four students sitting in the front row stood at the sound. Several teachers sat at the back of the room sharing guarded whispers. The remainder of the chairs were empty.

"Hector, I said I wanted to speak to all the students." They had reached the front row.

"Freddy, where is everyone?" Ralph demanded of one of the four students.

Freddy looked around the room and then ducked his head to stare at his shoes. "It's a protest against the Internet ban."

"A protest?" Bishop bellowed, "at Haverbrook?"

"Where are they?" Ralph asked again. Freddy shrugged his shoulders.

"Aren't you Freddy Haas?" Bishop put his arm around the student's shoulder and led him toward a side door. "I know your dad." He tightened his grip as they walked.

"My boy, you have a choice to make, a very clear outcome will result from this decision. Do you understand?"

Freddy nodded.

"You will show me where they are and then you will graduate and, on my personal recommendation, attend the college of your choice. Or you will keep silent, and enter into a lifelong career in the building maintenance, personal transportation, or food service industries."

Freddy gulped. They reached the door. Bishop opened it with his free hand.

"Well?"

"They're at The Grove."

"Lead on, dear boy."

Simon was expecting Rector Hector or one his lackey teachers to find them and try to bully them to return to the auditorium. His cell phone rang, Peter calling from the infirmary.

"Freddy's leading my father here," he announced. "Stay calm." Several of the students were edging toward the forest. If he had said "scatter" they would all be running for the North Carolina hills.

Reverend Bishop appeared at the crest of the trail, a few yards away, Freddy at his heels. He stepped into the clearing.

"So glad we could have this meeting," Bishop spoke. The boys huddled nervously. "Much nicer than that stuffy auditorium." He looked around the clearing and raised his hands. "Wherever two or three of you are gathered in my name..."

"Give us back the Internet." The voice was a tremulous contralto.

"Who said that?" Bishop bellowed.

The crowd of boys backed away from the speaker. Simon stood alone, head up, Eldrick's proxy in this battle.

"We need the Internet to learn," he said. "Without it we have no school."

Bishop turned to Freddy. "Take a good look, Freddy. That's a real leader. Not a sniveling snitch like you. Leave us men to talk. Go!" Freddy fled back down the path.

"Are you all in agreement about this?" Bishop asked, his voice acquired a sudden reasonableness.

The boys nodded and grunted uncomfortably.

"Of course you shall have your Internet," Bishop said. "What you did here today took courage. You should all be proud. You know I am proud of you all." He was looking directly at his son. "Now, everyone back to the school. I believe cake and ice cream are in order."

Bishop turned and strode away, listening as the boys converged on his son with laughter and shouts of victory.

§ § §

The RIND Corporation's downtown DC office on Pennsylvania Avenue was considerably smaller than the nearby FBI Headquarters, and rarely made any headlines or television backdrops. All the press releases came out of the Marina del Ray office, leaving the DC office to do what it did best: suck funding from the budgets of federal agencies for intelligence efforts the government determined were too critical not to pursue and too risky to get caught performing.

Subcontracting out those sticky bits of work that were constitutionally or simply bureaucratically questionable gave the government the illusion they could have their intelligence without the guilt. And with enough gilt, the Corporation was happy to shoulder any amount of guilt. It would off-shore the particularly loathsome work to the Israelis or, increasingly, the Taiwanese.

Today's meeting had no official title. It was called by Harold Farmer on the request of Tom Verplanck, the President's chief domestic advisor, and would include Harold, Tom, the Reverend Gerry Bishop, Franklin Benjamin (formerly with the Department of Education), Navy Captain Nancy Rankin (an analyst over at the NSA), and First Lady Arlene Stone. The group was less formal than a committee, but had access to more resources than most governments on the planet.

Their purpose was to explore how computer games and social networking were impacting the social fabric and economic weal of America. Tom suggested the Junana.com network for their initial focus. He mentioned that the group might also discuss "opportunities for action," in the face of recent economic news about which Harold was also well acquainted.

Harold remained in his office until the others had all arrived. Since that day the previous summer when the Con|Int report predicted the retail collapse, the RIND Corporation had been investigating the causes for this. Their conclusion was that a whole cohort of teenagers and young adults were acting like 40-somethings. Harold's research had long ago discovered that the enchantment of the Now faded over the decades of an individual's life. The very same consumer who would dive into a bottomless well of debt as a young adult simply to have the latest gizmos and cars would hit 40 and drive the same Prius for the next 20 years.

It was not that 40-somethings don't participate in the retail market, in fact, many of the largest purchases—new homes, expensive vacations, financial investments—happen during this period. Mostly, however, they tend to spend their monies after considerable reflection, which means they have managed to escape the Now. By the age of 40, if you include their teenaged children's consumption, the Now would have stolen more than half of their lifetime income. Harold had written the first part of a book predicting what a post-Now economy might look like. The emerging situation fascinated him, as his predictions were all coming true.

A Now-less economy would need to sell its products on the basis of value and quality. Already, certain brands were having

their best years: Bang & Olefsun, Bose, Apple, BMW, Williams
Sonoma; there was an upside even to this dark time. The RIND
Corporation was tracking a hundred or so quality-first
companies, and Harold had created an index that was seeded
to a select group of mutual fund investors.

The Now had tickled up frenzied passions for entirely
worthless commodities, fashions and fandoms that fed on their
own fleeting reflections. Without the Now, capitalism would
need to invent a new magic, otherwise the future might look a
lot like Sweden: drab, efficient, careful. Without the Now,
people might notice that the trains don't run, the medicines
don't cure, the food doesn't nourish, and the schools don't
teach. A whole range of new conflicts might open between the
market and the need for public services. The population might
turn political again, or rather anew, in a manner not seen in
the West for many decades, spilling some of the passion the
populace once reserved for their hometown hockey teams, or
those new riding lawnmowers, into the public sphere.

The phone on his desk rang. He picked up the receiver.
"The First Lady has arrived," his executive assistant said.

"Tell them I'll be in shortly," he said, and returned the
receiver to its cradle.

He stood. His office looked out on the Capitol, shrouded
today by a steady downpour. For half a century or more its
denizens had been selected with the same care, or lack thereof,
of a teenage girl picking out a new thong. The entire Congress
is as much a product of the Now as is a Bratz doll, and about as
useful.

§ § §

After introductions in the huge, top-floor RIND conference room, Harold Farmer asked Captain Rankin to describe their choice of actions.

"We can work the supply side, take down their servers, sever their connections to the Ariadne backbone, clobber them in the courts. Or we can pull a legislative coup, make them subject to a number of contradictory federal regulations...

"I've got a draft bill working though a Senate subcommittee that puts interstate social networking services like Junana under the control of the FTC, the FCC, Homeland Security, and the DOC," Franklin said. Rankin winked at him.

"...Or we can work the demand side. Start a smear campaign against Junana. Pay some mavens to flame it in their blogs. Use some word-of-mouth against those damn ugly shoes. Get the parents to pull the plug on the Game. Grab 'em by the short hairs and pull, sorry Reverend."

"Quite all right." Bishop held up his hand. "Think of me as just another team player."

"Why can't we find a reason to just throw them all in prison?" Franklin asked.

"To begin with, we don't know who they are," Harold reminded them. He had a good idea about the identity of some of the technical leads, but not the financial backers. "We need to locate the corporate officers."

"You mean the RIND Corporation hasn't been able to ferret out their identity?" Tom said. "You don't find that curious?"

Harold found it more than curious. Someone with real money and international business acumen was behind Junana.

"We could characterize their entire operation as a conspiracy and get a RICO indictment out of Justice," Tom offered. "I heard they use an encryption routine that even Fort Meade can't crack."

"Isn't that illegal?" Arlene asked.

"It damn well should be," Franklin said. "Imagine what a terrorist organization could do inside Junana."

"An executive order would be a start, get the agencies behind us." Harold glanced over at Tom, who made a note on a pad. "Something under the umbrella of homeland security, perhaps."

"Once we find out who the ringleaders are, we can make things mighty unpleasant for them," Tom said.

"That's my thought exactly," echoed Franklin. "Hit 'em where it hurts."

"We have confirmed that Michael O'hara works for a company with a contract to provide administrative programming services to Junana," Rankin noted. She glanced at her list. "WeRus NV. It's Belgian."

"Karl's got a line on this O'hara person, and we'll soon have a list of everyone he's in contact with," Tom noted.

"Karl." Franklin nodded. Bishop raised his eyebrows and a slow grin surfaced on his face.

"I have been informed that budget is no problem, so we can keep all of our options in play," Tom said.

"How fast can we shut them down?" Bishop asked.

"We can cut them off from the Internet overnight," Rankin offered.

"What's the long term plan?" Harold asked.

"Long term?" Franklin glanced around the room.

"Once we shut them down, things will get back to normal," Tom offered.

"We are already well past the last exit to 'normal.'" Harold said.

"You mean we've already lost?" Arlene asked.

"What are you trying to say?" Bishop put his hand on top of Arlene's. "You're alarming the First Lady."

"The purpose of attacking them is to bring them into the open. Once we know who they are, we can go after their code."

"So we can destroy it?" Bishop asked.

"No, so we can use it." Harold said.

"Why not just hack it?" Rankin asked.

"We've tried, believe me."

"So we steal it," Rankin offered.

"Or buy it," Tom said.

"We've put out feelers on the tech blogs and listserves, but so far no takers," Harold noted.

"I thought we were here to talk about the end of such games." Bishop stood. "Why would we make an unholy deal with these Sadducees? Shut them down, silence their lies. Let God's truth back into the American home..."

Harold held up his hand and Bishop fell silent.

"Reverend Bishop, the Game is out of the box. More than a billion players around the world have logged into this environment. Even if we destroy this version, others will appear. We intend to hack it, buy it, steal it, if necessary, and then use it, keep it active but bend it to our purpose."

"Take control of the Game?" Tom asked.

"You could start by letting people manage their own bio forms," Franklin suggested. "Or rather, some people."

"Some people?" Harold asked.

"Maybe an elite group. Hand picked, people who matter, and who naturally have certain objections."

"Objections...to being honest?"

"To disclosure. Discretion is the handmaiden of power."

"I see."

"Could it teach children to be more civil? Respectful?" Arlene asked.

"Arlene, this technology can teach your cat to program your Blu-Ray player."

"A billion players, each with a soul at risk," Bishop mused.

"You could preach to each and every one," Harold said, "And they can read your books in one afternoon." Bishop's University had printed several volumes of his sermons.

"Think of that!"

"...and the advertising revenue," Nancy said, "and the subscription fees."

Now everyone was talking at the same time: the very idea of a billion players, users, actual customers, putting up money every month.

"But first," Harold said. The room fell silent. "First we pull the plug and see who plugs it back in. Captain Rankin, can your operatives isolate all of the Junana servers from the Ariadne backbone simultaneously?"

"Give me twenty-four hours and pick your time."

"Let's go for Noon, Pacific Time, on Thursday."

"Can you make it Sunday?" Franklin asked. "Maybe Reverend Bishop could work something into his sermon." Franklin looked over the table at Bishop, who smiled and nodded.

"A first rate suggestion. I'll have ten million worshippers nationwide praying for Junana to be crushed."

"Fine. Sunday at noon, PST," Harold agreed.

"You want it noisy or quiet?" Rankin asked.

"I think quiet is the way to go. Nobody gets hurt."

She nodded slowly, visibly disappointed.

"Good lord," Harold thought, "who are these people?"

TWENTY

All day long Essie could not leave the store. She had half an hour for lunch and two five-minute breaks for comfort. The owner was very strict with her time now, and did not want her playing on her Computo while she worked. Mornings were sometimes slow, and she knew when he was off fishing because the boat made such a noise. So Essie and Annaline managed a bit of Game time each day while she tended to the store.

With her hat she had received the diploma paper. "Bachelor of Knowledge," it said in big golden letters. She looked up 'bachelor' and figured they had sent this to her by mistake. "Spinster of Sorrow," that would be her diploma. Nobody would marry her, nobody she would marry.

Men came by the cuca shop and spoke to her about beer and dancing at that joint on the road. They came only because she ran the store and they figured she could steal for them or turn her back as they loaded up. Nangoloh sold stolen canned goods in the village. The men figured a plain girl like her would be easy to sweet talk out of the same goods.

"Earn your shoes," she told them. "Then come talk to me."

"Woman you make no sense," they told her. She paid them little attention, but she put a lock on the inside of the door to her lean-to. Let them rattle the door at night, she was busy on Level Four.

§   §   §

"Sincerity is a gift, not a given."

Dickey Gronberg frowned at the latest consumer survey commissioned by his section of the Department of Commerce. Out of a sample of 3,000 adults, more than 40 percent of the surveys completely failed the internal consistency tests; another 30 percent barely passed them. This meant that more than half of the survey respondents were either lying or joking with their answers. Dozens had included this little phrase in their comments.

"Sincerity is a gift, not a given." What the hell is that supposed to mean? What about "responsibility?"

Dickey sifted through the reports coming in from the retailers, the wholesalers, the shippers and the foreign factories. Without the incessant pull from the American consumer, the entire supply chain had clogged tighter than a college dorm toilet on homecoming night. Retailers cancelled their orders and marked down their stock. Wholesalers stopped the trucks from off-loading to their bulging warehouses. Shippers halted the loading of the containers in the ports. Factories cancelled shifts and delayed piecework contracts.

Millions of computers, TVs, lawnmowers, and espresso makers sat in their boxes strung along the global supply chain. Shipping containers, stuffed to their ceilings, were stacked up like Lego bricks in ports around the world's oceans. Advance orders were put on hold while the retailers continued to lower their prices. The ripple effects would extend into the coming years even if there were a near-term rebound.

Dickey was equally concerned about the recent ugly tone of the emails within the Department. The grim news from the stock market, where both the retail and the manufacturing sectors were taking huge hits, put the President in a funk.

Stone was leaning on Commerce to come up with some good
news.

Dickey was on the spot. How could he predict the future
when half the people in the nation suddenly feel like lying to a
government survey? Unpredictability was, for Dickey, a
substantially greater problem than the actual direction of the
economy. Nobody expected his unit to control the trends, but
everyone seemed to think he should predict them. And they
were all waiting for him to reveal when the upturn would
begin.

"Sincerity is a gift, not a given." He searched this and found
out it came from Junana, from that Game everyone was talking
about. The Department had a policy against any of its thirty
thousand employees logging into Junana at their jobs. An
email from the Secretary went to all employees just last month,
threatening termination of any employee who used Junana
from a Department computer.

Somehow, the Junana client had been downloaded onto the
central application server, and then distributed to every
computer in the network. Attempts to purge this application
had failed. It seemed immune to any attempt to uninstall it.
The IT division had concluded they would need to wipe all the
disks and the ROM from every computer on the network,
which would shut down the entire Department for weeks. So
Dickey, like every other employee, could pull up the Junana
client on his computer.

The other issue with Junana was that it used a protocol that
ran through the Department's firewalls with neither a trace nor
any apparent effect. This meant that, unless you actually snuck
up on an employee and saw them using Junana, they could
play this all day and nobody would be the wiser.

Dickey had joined up with Junana a year before, but had
found very little time to spend there. He did reestablish contact

with several of his University of Chicago classmates and he found a group that shared his interest in mycology. Dickey loved hunting chanterelles in the late fall; it felt like plucking manna from the fields.

§   §   §

Itchy had scheduled a Room meeting to show off the new Castalia design. The Room had been moved to the castle keep and situated in its basement dungeon. A circular stone staircase on its outer wall led down from the main floor. Against the other walls, skeletons still dangled from manacles, and their jaws moved in some final agony. The Console was now a 3D cube in the middle of the room, with four access keyboards. Itchy was at the one of the keyboards when Desi popped in.

"Now this is Retro!" he said, drifting around the room. One of the skeletons attracted him, and so he moved close. "Olivia Newton-John?" He walked to the next skeleton. "Culture Club?" And the next. "Cyndi Lauper?"

"Why, they're all whispering '80s pop tunes."

"It's called torture." Scratchy was standing next to the curving stone wall. "Nice sconces!"

The walls had a number of brass fixtures with lit torches that flickered and smoked in an exquisitely real fashion.

Jack popped in. "I'm going to miss the London Club motif, but this is...cosy. I like the audio." The room reverberated like a giant cave.

"Very nice." Winston popped in and said. "What? No Cordobaloungers!"

Scratchy shook hands with one of the skeletons. "If our avatars get tired of standing they can go dangle on the wall."

"Scratchy, I've got news for you." Winston walked up behind Scratchy. "Reed wants you to be their commencement speaker this year instead of moi."

"Winston, that's just not..." Desi said, turning around. "Winston, why are you invisible?"

"Invisible?" Winston toggled 3rd Person and looked back at himself. "There's a bug for you. I'm invisible."

"That's not a bug," Scratchy strode over to the console. "We've been hacked!"

"How? When?" Desi took one his place at one of the free keyboards. "Call up the Room database," he said.

"I'm there," Scratchy said. "I see only the five of us logged in."

"Keep that window open," Desi said. "Winston, when were you last in the Room?"

"Weeks ago."

Itchy scrolled through a log list. "According to this, you were here last week. Desi and I were here, too, and I don't remember talking to you."

"That's because it wasn't me."

"You logged in."

"Somebody phished your password," Scratchy said. "Did you reset your Junana password recently?"

"I got a message from Junana, like everyone else," Winston said.

"We all got the message," Scratchy said. "And it was from Junana. So it's an inside job."

"Top level," Desi added.

"What's going on?" Jack asked.

"I fucked up," Scratchy said. "I kept the Game admin on the same sign-in as Junana. I should have split these apart in the beginning. One of our employees has chosen to steal our code. I would guess they have the whole dump from our IDE, since they logged in as Winston. They turned him invisible so they could get into the Room and not be seen in case others were here."

"They have all the code?" Jack asked.

"That's what we have to assume. Reset all the admin level passwords!" Scratchy said.

"Nobody will be able to log in," Itchy said.

Scratchy nodded. "Set all our passwords to 'swordfish' temporarily."

"Log out anybody with Root access who is logged in. We are all going to be logged out. Everybody log back in using the temporary password 'swordfish.' Got it?" The avatars all nodded.

"See you in a minute," Itchy said. The room faded to white.

One by one they logged back in. The Nerds took up positions at the consoles.

"We are now the only ones with Root access on the system." Desi confirmed.

"Who did this?" Winston asked.

"Either the inside guy was working alone, or he was paid to do this. Either way, once the code is out, it will migrate up the money chain to the top. Somebody will make a killing on this. Somebody we really do not want to have our code, I imagine."

"What's the plan?"

"We already kicked them off the system and reset the passwords. Now we get this goddamn console out of Junana, set up a whole new security system for the Game administration, and then give it, maybe a year, probably a lot less, before they hack the Game from the outside." Scratchy was not optimistic.

"They know too much about our code," Itchy added.

"It just depends how much cash they have to throw at the problem," Desi concluded.

"How long before we can track down the thief?" Jack asked.

"It won't take long. I imagine we've spooked him by resetting his passwords. Whoever doesn't show up for work tomorrow is probably our Judas," Itchy said. "Anyhow, we can mine the logs and ferret them out. And if they rig the logs, we can find that too. Just a matter of time."

"We've got a lot of programming to do before tomorrow. First thing is to pull all the Game admin code out of Junana, make this Room accessible only from an external, secure sign in," Scratchy said and looked around him. "Somebody make Winston visible, will you?"

Winston popped into view. He was wearing the Hat.

"Ricky! You've got your Hat!" Desi said. "I'm so proud of you."

"That's better," Scratchy said. "I wanted to tell this to your face. First off. You did no wrong. It wasn't you who fucked up. You just reset your password like a good user. Second. I will tell Reed that I will do a commencement talk, but only if the President apologizes directly to you, insists that you do the talk next year, and eats one of those nasty giant roaches at RennFayre."

Winston put a big grin on his avatar's face.

"Mickey's got principles," Desi said. "People forget because of his bad fashion sense."

"We can defeat who did this," Jack said. His avatar gestured confidently.

"How do you figure," Scratchy said.

"Release the code," Jack said.

They stopped typing and looked at each other. Scratchy's avatar cracked its wry grin.

"Brilliant!" Itchy said.

"We find out the version they stole, make it public..." Desi added.

"...and worthless," Winston added.

"...only by then we'll have rewritten and implemented all new security code," Desi said.

"Busy, busy, busy," Scratchy said. The three of them started typing again.

"What would have happened if the thief had remembered to make Winston visible again?" Jack asked.

"They would build their own administrative back end and one day very soon we would not have been able to log in," Itchy said.

"A cyber coup d'etat," Desi added. "Mikey, I'll find out what version was taken. You work on the new admin security. Itchy, we'll need a Room outside of Junana, a cloned environment from the ground up. Might as well take all of Castalia out as well, and then make the Room exterior to that."

"Got it," Itchy said.

"Count Slick," Winston said. "Have you seen the rest of Castalia? It's a nice little kingdom." They started climbing the stairs.

"We almost lost it," Jack said.

"That we did," Winston said.

§   §   §

Dickey glanced over his desk through the doorway to his secretary's office. He could faintly hear her typing on her computer. He moused to the Junana client and opened the program. Then he logged in and found himself in some kind of Roman antechamber, with two doors, one on each end. One door was marked "Junana" and the other "Game."

He glanced again at his office's open doorway. He was only
going to research this Game for a few minutes. He sent his
avatar to the door marked "Game" and knocked.

The scene faded and a new scene appeared. His avatar was
reclining on a king sized bed in what might be a mansion or a
high-priced hotel suite. The decor was pure Deco. The walls
were cream, the lamps, moderne, the scale was simply huge.
Double French doors opened to another room, and Dickey
sent his avatar through these. This room was also expansive,
with a fireplace on one wall, a selection of abstract
impressionist paintings on another, and a brace of large
windows and another set of French doors on the third, where
warm sunlight was filtering into the room. These doors were
open and a breeze fluttered the floor length curtains that
framed the two windows.

Dickey sent his avatar toward the open doors. Outside
stood a terrazzo patio and a balustrade of marble, and another
avatar, male, leaning on the balustrade, looking out across the
cityscape. Italian Riviera, Dickey concluded. Could be
Portofino. Speedboats and fishing craft were tied up below in
an azure bay. The other avatar wore white linen slacks that fell
over cream-colored loafers. He had a shock of dark brown hair
combed back. How retro, Dickey thought. The fellow's
physique was slender; his naked back showed nothing of the
free-weight bulkiness that a gym produces. Dickey's avatar
stood in the doorway. Dickey toggled up chat and typed,
"Hello."

The other avatar turned his head and nodded. "Hi Dickey,
come over here," the chat response read. Something about the
avatar's face disturbed Dickey. It was an unforgettable face,
even at a glance. Then he realized it had elements of
Montgomery Clift, one of Dickey's favorite old Hollywood
movie stars. Dickey sent his avatar to the balustrade and

toggled Third Person so he could see them both. He moved the POV to the front and noticed that the other avatar continued to make eye contact with him, not with his avatar. The chat window activated.

"Hi Dickey, I'm your Guide. I've been waiting for you for over a year. Glad to finally meet you. My name is Geoff."

"I don't have time to play the Game here," Dickey typed. "I can come back later."

"Your secretary is playing the Game, Dickey. The receptionist too. So relax."

Dickey paused to get his thoughts around this information. The Game knew who he was, of course, since he logged in. But the Game also knew where he was, and whom he worked with, and what they were doing. A chill ran up his arms. He was instantly frightened and excited.

"I could fire them," he typed.

"You would have to fire yourself too. Anyhow, you are not the vindictive type. Besides, they know you are playing the Game."

"How?" he typed.

"I told their Guides when you said 'Hello.' Beverly is already working on Level Three. She can answer a lot questions for you, or you can always ask me anything."

Just then, Dickey's secretary, Beverly, came to the door. "Let me close this for you," she said. "It's better if you turn on the audio. I'll make sure nobody comes in. Sally will hold your calls. Level One..." She sighed and nodded knowingly. "You are going to have such a good time!" The door closed behind her.

Dickey didn't need to toggle the audio. It came on by itself. His office was suffused with the sounds of a port town. Lanyards clicked on the masts of a dozen yachts. Motors sputtered and whined in the distance. Seagulls cried. The resolution and the details were astounding. It was as if his computer was an open window to this actual place. Dickey toggled back to first person and looked around through his avatar's eyes.

"Wow!" he whispered.

"Wow, indeed," Geoff spoke, and he really spoke, his face and his mouth said the words. "Let's go back inside where we can talk." He put his hand on Dickey's avatar's shoulder and looked directly into his eyes. "We are going to be such good friends."

Dickey dropped the mouse, suddenly confused. The Game knew he was gay. He sat stunned. He had been so deep in the closet for so long. How was it possible?

"Dickey, it's OK."

"How?"

"Your secrets are sacred here. It's important that you feel safe in the Game. But it's equally important that you and I get to understand each other."

"Does Beverly know?"

"Dickey, you are an African-American single professional in his early forties who vacations in the Mediterranean every year. You have an apartment just east of Dupont Circle. You dress immaculately, go to the gym three times a week, and you hunt mushrooms as a hobby. Dickey, you own a Chagall. Maybe your mother doesn't want to suspect, but probably everyone else you've met in the last ten years does. You are not a political appointee, so your job is not on the line. The point is, who really cares?" Geoff took his avatar's hand. "Now come on inside, big boy. We have so very much to talk about."

§ § §

Don Driscoll was running a chron job when he was suddenly kicked out of the system. He tried to log in and his password was rejected. He tried once more, with due deliberation. No use. He listened. No sirens approaching, no commotion in the hallway. He went to the door and looked both ways down the narrow hall. Returning to his desk, he gathered up his mug, the photo of his kids, a few paper items, and some things from the shelves. He shoved everything into his courier bag, removed the key from his key ring and dropped it on the desk. Don left his office and the building without a word, and drove to his Goleta bank, where he withdrew all his funds and closed the account. He drove to his apartment to collect his clothes and took the freeway south towards LA. Tomorrow he would be talking with the person who answered his advertisement on Craigslist, the one who wanted to build an alternative Game. They had exchanged emails in which he hinted he had source code to offer for the right price. The very right price, he had added, for a very special package.

§   §   §

Megan wiped the milk film from the steam tube again and gave it a blast to clear the nozzle. All of the tasks of a Red Star barista had a single purpose: deliver a quality beverage. The coffee was shade-grown and fair trade, roasted in small batches locally and dated to be discarded within a week. The milk and soy products were organic. The grind was precise. The trick, however, was in the tamp.

Intern baristas toiled under a lead barista for days perfecting their tamp. Megan was a quick student and eager to prove her stuff. The crema on the double shot, the star she drew on the lattes, the fresh whipped cream for the con panna, the kiss of foam on the macchiato were the trademarks of every Red Star Coffee house on the planet. Certain motions and noises were the ballet at the center of the maelstrom of customers jamming for their caffeine: the sounds of the grinder, the steamer, the thump of the coffee paddle when she discarded the previous load, even the wipe of her hand to clear the rim of any grounds.

Everywhere she looked, Megan noticed templates. Window seats and zinc countertops, tile floors and high ceilings. The room was a design template zoo. Even the interactions with the customers followed the Attention While Interacting template. Afternoons slowed as the tables filled with Gamers, drawn by the free WiFi and the perfect cappuccinos. Most were in the latest fashion: branded goods that could now be picked up at discount stores and then altered by adding colors or layers. Three-hundred dollar jeans sold for twenty-five. Thrift stores offered them for five. No wonder her mom's business was in the shitter.

The GameTown had recently opened up a dozen ethnic food kiosks and a maze of small shops. Free-trade goods and locally produced household items attracted Gamers from across Westwood and Santa Monica. Jack's experiences in old-town Hanoi informed the Gametown's Retail Gradient template. In Hanoi's old town the retail streets were laced with informal cafes and individual vendors, creating a market density that spawned its own daily spectacle. The Restaurant Every Meal template provided for Gametown residents to take all their meals in the street-level restaurants for a cost about the same as cooking their own, with an enormous combined savings in both time and expense for the entire building.

Wide building overhangs next to the sidewalks encouraged other informal vendors to spread their wares in weekly farmers' markets and other commercial and social adventures.

With its internal winding streets, small theaters, public baths and third places, and a petticoat surround of small market and social spaces, the buildings were more a self-contained village than a simple dormitory. Megan was high on the list to work in the Red Star outlet opening next month in the basement.

Megan was artful about her movements and mindful of the reason she was working. She delivered a consistent quality beverage. She'd watch the customer take the first sip, and was often rewarded by a glance and a grateful sigh. The tips were pooled, but the baristas got an extra share. Everything depended on the tamp.

Megan wore her hat to work, its red star echoing the antique posters on the walls. She'd read about the Paris Commune and figured someone had a sense of humor, or a cold ironic sensibility, turning this into a motif for a capitalist enterprise. Megan had her dad's dirty blonde hair and her mom's baby blue eyes. She filled her black Red Star Tee in her Title-Nine running bra and kept her tummy flat doing crunches. Most days at least one of the customers hung around and tried to talk. Not all were pervs. She missed Game time when she worked. It was torture to see all the customers logged in.

§   §   §

Essie restocked the candy jars. Old Gina and her older cousin Ndapewa had settled on the porch to watch the iilumbu tourists and chatter through the afternoon. Today they were sewing tops for the girls. The owner liked his staff to dress with tops and skirts, even the toilet maids. He sold the tops at the store for a price Essie could not believe, the greedy man. She bought cloth and thread and paid the old women to copy the designs. They sold them at a very reasonable price.

In the afternoon, the shop was busy as ever. Essie had reduced some prices, and now villagers from across the valley also came for provisions. She showed the owner how he would make so much more money if they sold this much oil and that much grain. At the end of this month, she would give him his money and ask for a small raise in her pay. Annaline told her what shop keepers down in Kamanjab and Etosha made. She now had friends in Junana who worked in shops in Windhoek and Keetmanshoop. He could not expect her to slave for him like this.

When the plane flew overhead she could do nothing but look out of the window toward the airstrip, hidden by river trees from her sight. Two customers were fighting over the same bolt of gingham cloth, and a line of children eyed the candy in the big glass jars on the counter.

"Tuamanguluka, buy some cinnamon sticks for your friends," she said. Gina had told her the boy's father had returned from selling his goats in Outapi. Tuamangulaka grinned and pulled a half-dollar coin from his pocket.

"My lord," Essie said. "You will ruin all your teeth with that." She took the coin and counted out ten sticks into his hands. He doled these out to the other children, keeping three for himself, and they ran from the shop shouting and hooting.

Essie convinced one of the women that she would look much better in a brighter printed cotton, which the other woman now eyed with envy. She made the sales and the shop was momentarily empty. Taking advantage of this, she closed and locked the door and put up the "back in five minutes" sign. She put on her hat and left by the delivery door, walking, not quite running toward the airstrip.

She had just started up the road when she saw the Rover coming towards her. It sped by her as she stood and watched. Mr. Steve5683 was in the passenger seat talking with the owner. He glanced at her and a sudden smile lit his face.

"Stop!" he shouted. "Stop right here."

The Rover ground to a quick halt, and all the passengers braced themselves as the luggage tumbled forward. A cloud of dust rose from the tires. Essie walked toward the car as the passenger door opened and Mr. Steve5683 stepped out. Without thinking she ran up to him and fell to her knees, bowing and thanking him, just thanking him in English and Oshindonga and Oshikwanyama, all jumbled up with her tears.

"Get up Essie." He took her forearm and pulled her to her feet. "There's nothing to thank me for. Nothing." The other passengers had stepped from the Rover, a woman and two children, one of them wearing the hat.

"I want you to meet my wife," he said. "Essie, this is Kelly." The woman stepped forward and took her hand.

"Your wife," Essie said, her breath slowing. "Mrs. Steve5683. I am very, very, very...." The woman was so incredibly white. Hair like straw, eyes like the Camp pool, skin like buffalo milk. "...very happy to meet you."

"Steve5683?"

The boy covered a laugh with his hand. "It's his Junana user ID, mom. Hi, Essie, I'm Randy. Randy9140. He touched his hat and nodded."

"So many Randys! But few as smart as this one, I bet."

"Essie, this is our daughter Christa." The little girl was amazing, so very beautiful.

"Oh my, aren't you pretty." Essie bent down. "Would you like to see a lion?"

"A lion!" She glanced up at her mother.

"Tomorrow, sweetie."

Owner came around the car. "Is there trouble at the shop?"

"No, Taté."

He frowned at her.

"I must get back," she said. "Please excuse me."

"We are off to a tented camp. When we get back, Essie, we must talk," Steve said. "Today I have a lot of business to take care of, eh Heinrick?" He clapped the owner on his shoulder. They returned to the car and drove away.

The dust swirling up from the track muddied the tears on her face.

TWENTY-ONE

Reverend Chad Stedman had been running the UCCC
morning Prayer Hour radio show for over two decades, first
from a broadcast shack outside of San Antonio, and more
recently from the national radio broadcast center near
Oklahoma City. Although the audience now exceeded millions,
the format remained the same: some topical conversation to
remind the listeners about the sorry state of the nation, one or
two guest celebrities—mainly authors with books to tout—one
or more crisis cases, an impending heart transplant, say, or a
really nasty brain tumor victim, then the mention of certain
individuals who had requested a special prayer, and finally the
call-in segment.

Every few minutes Chad would lead the listening audience
in a short prayer and an announcement of the 800 number
where listeners could donate to the cause. Regular donors
found their way into the special prayer queue. The Prayer
Hour ran from 10 to 11 a.m. Oklahoma time every Sunday
morning, just before the national UCCC televised service.

Five minutes before broadcast, while Chad was skimming
the list of regional calamities—a tornado in Texas, a toxic train
wreck in South Carolina, a triple murder in Spokane—Ernie,
the producer, cracked open the door to the booth and stuck his
head in.

"Bishop's going to be the guest today. Just got the call." He
pointed his finger at the clock. "10:40 sharp. Get them ready."

Reverend Gerry Bishop had been a regular guest on the
Prayer Hour until the Orange County cathedral was finished.

Now he was a television star and never paid the radio program much attention, even though it was the radio revenue that built his cathedral. The Prayer Hour still pulled in twice the audience of the TV broadcast, but Chad couldn't even get Gerry to answer his phone calls. Now he wanted Chad to talk up his guest call-in so the audience numbers would be spectacular. At times like this, he wished he were back preaching in his little church in Hondo, Texas, where Gerry found him.

§   §   §

Every year for the past seven years Claire had gathered the Con|Int posse for a retreat at the Abbot's Abode, a lodge between Santa Fe and Taos. This offered a bracing combination of glorious scenery, pure mountain air, a full spa, a string of horses, and an excellent restaurant. Nearby Bandelier National Monument provided long walks through the ruins of an ancient Anasazi settlement. Claire would reserve the Old House, a five-bedroom adobe on the crest of the hill away from the main lodge. For four days they would work out the kinks in their operation, review their performance from the previous year and set priorities for the next. They normally met in early October, before the snows arrived but after the back-to-school season and Claire's report to the RIND Corporation.

This year their gathering was delayed by the ongoing marketplace fiasco. Claire managed to secure the Old House for a week in mid March, knowing that this was likely their last visit. Most of the staff had been furloughed, and the Posse was working on half salary, except for Betsy, who was still running statistics full time.

Jennifer had assigned Roland and Annika as data feeds for
Betsy. Annika moved to New Orleans and was camped out in
the old servants' quarters behind Betsy's main house. Roland
stayed in London and collaborated through Junana. Betsy
would request data runs, and Annika would return these from
Junana as tabular records. Although Junana returned its raw
data in minutes, some of Betsy's statistical regression runs took
days. Annika's Norse athlete looks made a splash in the local
lesbian scene, but nobody moved in on Betsy. Betsy was the
queen of the Forbidden Desire Krewe. Annika sometimes wore
her yellow blouse and always carried her blue shoulder bag.

Betsy had no time for the Game, she protested. Not with
the real world getting so incredibly interesting, statistically
speaking. She wished she had more computing power, but
hesitated to bring this up with Claire. Con|Int was running on
its contingency funds already. Betsy had asked for a half-time
salary. Claire emailed back that she wanted Betsy on this
project full time. Betsy was reviewing the retail catastrophe
that was the Christmas shopping season when Claire called.

"Interesting, you say?" Claire asked.

"Like you would not believe," Betsy responded. Her office
was in the attic of her Garden District house. "For example,
huge numbers of people, Gamers, I suspect, are either lying to
or just playing with the pollsters. Sure, you could always count
on a third of the American population to believe in just about
anything, from UFOs to leprechauns. A third would believe
that the federal government was a conspiracy run by global
banking interests, and a third would be solidly behind the
president; I always suspected these were the same people. But
they were still sincere. You can test for consistency and
sincerity inside your survey.

"Right now people are actively spoofing the process. I keep
up with the main pollster listserves, and the trends have them

running scared. If this keeps up, public opinion polls will soon be obsolete. The sample size required to generate good numbers will approach a large percentage of the population. You might as well just run an election to see what deodorant people use. Problem is, I don't know if we can even hold elections unless the population is convinced their opinions are respected."

"So democracy is under attack."

"Hell no! Democracy is in flower. Voting is probably the least democratic action you do over the course of a year. Democracy is not about voting, it is about disagreements and conversation. Democracy is the long argument we have among ourselves, agreeing not to take this to the point of bloodshed. We vote for our proxies to carry on this conversation in Congress. If the population becomes disenchanted with the performance of their proxies, or the manner of their selection, then not-voting or gaming the vote are both extremely democratic alternatives."

"How about fixing the process?"

"Maybe your Game has some goddamn template that will do that. You tell me."

"It's not my Game. I'm just another player."

"Last three months it's been your entire life, you hardly even answer your emails anymore. Claire, this thing will ruin Con|Int and every other opinion-based research operation. However, the Game is a statistical gold mine. Do you realize that a billion people have logged on worldwide? Do you know how accurate we can be with a sample size like that?"

"The Game doesn't record the opinions of its players," Claire noted.

"I can't ask it how many people think W.G. Stone is the worst president ever, or if they brush with Crest," Betsy replied. "What I can do is get a list of the templates in the Game and the number of players that have been exposed to these worldwide. I can do content analyses of the templates, try to map their scope and influence. I can even get a fine geographical distribution that allows me to build decision surfaces at the scale of census blocks."

"What does that give you?"

"As an example, I've got a significant negative correlation between the spread of the Simple on the Outside template and the market for those sequined tops Con|Int predicted would do so well this fall."

"What about Simplicity Loves Difference?" Claire asked. The power of simplicity is based on its implicit contrast with complexity. You can't make everything simple.

"Apparently covering your top with sequins is not the right difference. There are multiple templates that inform how the design of objects is being evaluated. And difference seems to be only a very minor love for simplicity."

"Or we've been immersing consumers in random difference for so long that simplicity may just appear to be its own difference."

"Tell that to Evisu Jeans."

"I did. Like you said, we might need to find a new line of work."

"I'm so busy I'll barely see Mardi Gras this year. I'm hoping to get a handle on the whole Game effect for our meeting in New Mexico. We might be able to pull a new rabbit out of this little black hat."

"Betsy, you are the best!"

"Why, Claire, I didn't think you noticed." Betsy hung up. She looked out the window. Annika was doing some yoga exercises on the patio in the back yard. Betsy took a last bite of beignet from her breakfast tray and decided a little yoga might just be in order.

§   §   §

"Reverend Bishop, this is an honor!"

"Nonsense, Chad, your ministry is vital to our work, and I've been away far too long."

"Still, it must be mighty important for you to take time away from preparing your Sunday sermon."

"Important doesn't even cover it. I'm here to ask everybody listening to join with me on my "Pull the Plug on Satan" crusade. I just read that our children are spending a hundred billion hours a year on that infernal Game. We're fightin' a war all across the nation, a battle against the pernicious, vile content that is pouring from our children's computers and poisoning their minds."

"Amen, Reverend," Chad intoned.

"It's going to take more than action, Chad. It's time to bring in the heavy guns, unleash the power of prayer. I'm asking each and every one of our listeners to join with me and pray that our sons and daughters find protection against the Junanas of the world."

"Amen!"

"Pray with me that God will smite them as he did the wicked Sodomites."

"Dear God, listen to our prayers."

"Strike down Junana, bring it low, crush it with your righteous anger."

"And God, keep Reverend Bishop strong, in this time of consternation. May his crusade be your crusade, and may he lead us to the place of peace and comfort."

"Why, thank you Reverend Stedman. And thank all of our listeners for their prayers." Bishop hung up.

"Let's say one more prayer, together, and remember, you can support the 'Pull the Plug on Satan' crusade with a contribution to the cause. That's 800 Y-E-S UCCC. Operators are standing by to take your call."

§   §   §

Being new, Megan worked weekends, which sucked. It was midday on a Sunday when the Game went down.

"Holy fuck!" A Gamer in the corner let out, shaking his laptop. Megan looked up from the Linea. Around the room Gamers were frantically working their computers.

"What's up with the WiFi?" Someone asked.

"It's not the WiFi," another Gamer said. "The Game is down."

"The Game is down?" The room filled with mutters and curses.

Megan and the other workers went and stood behind Howard, a regular with a MacBook Pro. The Junana client was running, but the screen just showed a Unix error message: ERROR 1119 SQLSTATE HY000 (ER_STACK_OVERRUN).

"Try restarting the client," someone suggested. Howard did. Same message.

"Maybe it's just bad here," a faint cry of hopeful desperation. Several Gamers packed up and left.

"That's idiotic," Howard said. "This is a server-side problem, unexpected, I would guess, since they didn't trap it well."

"Shouldn't we call someone?"

"I'm sure they already know."

"Check the Internet, what's up on Slash|Dash?"

The room went into a disordered crisis mode. Everybody with a computer browsed for information, shouting out bits of news from the Geek blogs. Even the basic Internet version of Junana was down. Nobody was ordering coffee.

Megan drifted to the window. The idea of going home and not logging in tugged at her. The street looked oddly cold and the buildings old and dirty.

§   §   §

"We're down," Scratchy said, surveying the console. "Across the board. Junana's down, the Game is offline."

"What happened?" Winston had just popped into the Room. He spied Desi, Itchy, and Scratchy hunched over their keyboards.

"They hit all our servers at once," Scratchy said. "Not a software attack, they physically knocked us off the backbone. In Goleta they blew up the fiber conduit in two places, took out the University's Ariadne link and cable TV for most of the county."

"In Kyoto, they caused a fire in the subway tunnel under Karasuma-dori, fried the optical fiber and all of the telephone cables," Itchy said.

"In Mysore, I heard they blasted the conduit from Banglore and took out the train track too," Desi said.

"The stacks for the admin queues backed up and we had a cascade failure on the server," Scratchy said. "We've been down almost three hours now."

"I thought we had moved everything over to the mesh," Winston said.

"We were in the process," Itchy replied. "Still had a few vital admin functions to test."

"But we are here." Winston gestured around the Room.

"Remember, we took the Room out of Junana. This facility is running independently on the mesh, so it never went offline." Desi said. "We have Console capability, too..."

"...which will probably save us," Scratchy said. "Good thing we were hacked. And lucky the mesh didn't go down."

"That's because you threaded the server on top of the mesh," Desi said. "However did you do that?"

"Junana's down, too" Winston mused. "So we can't communicate with anyone. What about email?"

Itchy typed for a minute. "The email server is still running."

"Why not send a blast message that Junana and the Game will be up in two days or so," Winston said, "Keep them from panicking."

"And tell them to keep their computers up and running," Scratchy said, "Otherwise we'll lose the mesh. Desi, you're the Game's Grand Poobah. Why don't you send the message."

"I've never emailed a billion people before," Desi said. "Guess I'll keep it short." He typed for a while. Winston came up behind Scratchy, who was skipping from one administration screen to another.

"Look at that, we didn't even trap the error. How embarrassing," Scratchy mumbled.

"But you can reboot it," Winston said quietly. He went to the empty console and began to search the Internet.

"Rebooting a mesh computer from the mesh has never been tried," Scratchy reminded him. "It's like repairing your parachute after you jump."

"There are about twenty steps, and we have to take them one at a time," Itchy said. "Some steps may take hours. We don't know. We have a clean dump from the database about four hours before the system fried. With luck we can simply reload this."

"There's a televangelist who's taking credit for knocking Junana off the Internet," Winston read from the search result. "Says it was the 'power of prayer.'"

"Prayer and a little C4," Scratchy said, "Potent mix. What's he got against Junana?"

Winston read some more. "He says we are leading his children away from God. Calls us instruments of the devil."

"He's right," Scratchy said. "I'd say it's pretty much him or us."

"But we don't have any religious agenda at all," Itchy said.

"Zap!" Scratchy said. "We mix everything up: religion, society, and philosophy. The Queries move people to the intersections between all of these. Organized religions can only survive on their own terms, within their own boundaries. The Game erases these boundaries. Kid asks a question about God, next thing he knows he's reading Genesis, the Bhagavad Gita, and the Abhidamma Pitaka. Like they all have something to say, which they do."

"Ramen!" said Winston.

"Here's my email," Desi said. "'Dear Junana users. Due to a number of unfortunate explosions we have temporarily gone offline. We hope to be back within a day or two. Please take this opportunity to go talk to someone. Ride a bicycle. Climb a tree. Keep your computer on and stand by. See you in the Game in a few days.' I sign it 'G.M.'"

"Fine," Itchy said. "I'll spool it through the email list at fifty-thousand emails a chunk. At five millisends seconds a chunk, that'll take..."

"About an hour and a half," Winston said.

Jack popped in. "Sorry, I was on a flight."

"They took out our admin and content servers. Fifteen explosions in nine countries, all at the same time," Scratchy said. "They also fried our old content server farms with some kind of electronic pulse to scramble their directories. None of our current content is on these servers, but we'd paid through the end of the month so they were still up. I get the feeling these people want us out of business."

"Took out the servers? Then they don't know about the mesh," Jack said. "So our thief was probably working on his own and still hasn't found a buyer. How soon can you release the code?"

"We've been extracting some of the peripheral database hacking routines," Itchy said. "And beefing up the comments. Mikey spent a whole day doing a work-around for leap-years."

"A whole day?" Desi said, his avatar's eyebrows raised.

"Sometimes easy is hard," Scratchy said.

"As soon as the game goes back online without any servers, they will know about the mesh computer," Desi noted.

"Tuesday is Mardi Gras," Scratchy said. "With luck, we can have the Game up again by then and release the code too."

"How do you release the code?" Jack asked.

"Post it to SourceForge," Itchy said.

"Under whose name?" Jack asked.

"Lionel Boyd Johnson?" Itchy offered.

"No pseudonyms allowed," Desi said.

"Might as well put all three of your names on it. Desi and Itchy are safe in Sao Do," Jack said.

"Neos all around!" Winston added.

Itchy said, "But what happens to Scratchy?"

"They already killed my cats. I'm living in a hotel suite and not answering my phone," Scratchy reminded him.

"Tuesday, I'll have my jet take Michael to Hawaii. He can camp out at the Kona Cove. I'll pick him up in two weeks when I come by on the way to Sao Do. One more thing..." He walked around to face them.

"Someone with a global reach and not a lot of impulse control has just declared war on Junana. We have to assume they will not stop at property destruction. They've identified Ichiro and Desi as technical participants. Next, they will be looking for Winston and me, and for the source code."

"Do we bring the admin servers back up?" Winston asked.

"No need," Scratchy said. "We'll be fully on the mesh."

"So we can shut down our server operations," Winston said.

"We'll still be running the largest computer in the world," Desi noted.

"There is that," Jack said. "And we are the largest single shoe manufacturer on the planet."

"And the biggest university," Winston added. "We're sending out more than a million diplomas a week."

"Busy, busy, busy." Itchy said.

"The faster we go, the rounder we get," Scratchy said. "Let's reboot this puppy."

$ $ $

Essie was so very grateful that Randy was there when the Game failed. When she woke up, her Computo the screen just read: ERROR 1119 SQLSTATE HY000 (ER_STACK_OVERRUN). She restarted the device and got the same message. At first she thought that maybe the machine that moves across the heavens, the satellite, had stopped talking to her Computo. On her way to breakfast Randy came running up to her.

"The Game's under attack," he said, falling into stride beside her. "They bombed the servers. Junana's down too." He seemed almost happy.

"Who would do such a thing?" she asked him.

"There's a lot of chatter on Slash|Dash. They're all talking about religious extremists. Some nut in California predicted it. I got an email from the Grand Meister. He said they'd be back up in days."

"Then you have no excuse not to go out to the tented camp with your family today. You might see a lion."

"I might even see a cheetah!" he said and ran off toward the dining room.

Why would somebody attack the Game? she wondered. She contemplated something that had never occurred to her. She considered the prospect of living without the Game. She shivered as she walked, as though a ghost had passed through her.

§   §   §

Gerry Bishop clicked on an email from his son with the title "Why not kill me and get it over with."

```
Father,
What have you done? You destroyed our
Game. Why did you do this? How could you
do this?
    I've sent you a dozen emails telling
you to just try the Game. Just once,
that's all I asked.
    Now it is too late. Too late for
everything. Everybody here at Haverbrook
despises us.
    I hate you. I hate you. I hate you!
Peter
```

```
p.s. Simon also hates you, but he's too
angry to even email you
```

Gerry frowned at the screen. Peter had been sending him similar messages ever since that infernal Game was destroyed. When they are older they will thank him, Gerry figured. In a couple weeks they'll have something else to obsess about. He trashed the message.

§ § §

Don Driscoll sat in his spa suite at the Eastinn LAX hotel and contemplated his immediate future. He had delivered a tantalizing chunk of code to the woman on the phone, and she had called back agreeing to the fifty big ones. He figured O'hara would be pressing charges. Several years in Chile might be long enough take them off his back. He could change his name, start a small business, maybe get married again. In three hours he would finally have the jackpot he deserved. Don found HBO on the enormous flat screen TV, and settled back in the massage chair to watch *The Mummy IV*.

TWENTY-TWO

Desi and Scratchy had spent the past two days tag-teaming the reboot of Junana on the mesh. At four in the morning on Monday, Scratchy needed sleep. For Desi, in Sao Do, it was just six in the evening. He kept the process on track until Scratchy woke up. By Monday evening Santa Barbara time, they were ready to upload the backed-up master databases, a process that would take all night, even with the enormous throughput of the global mesh computer. They also replaced the Unix SQL error message with an image of Wanda's face, winking. This sent the geek-blogs into frenzy mode.

Itchy and his top Sao Do team cleaned up the comments on the source code revision that Don Driscoll had stolen. When Don didn't show up for work the next day, Scratchy checked his logs and confirmed what they suspected. Now that they had finished porting to mesh, all that hardware they owned was no longer needed. A crack Sao Do team was assigned sysadmin duties. Junana's old content and administrative server operations were told to erase and scrub their disks and remain offline. Employees were given a month's notice and six months severance pay.

At noon New Orleans time on Mardi Gras Tuesday, Desi and Scratchy were in the Room. They were concerned about turning on Junana everywhere at the same time, in case even the mesh could not handle that many simultaneous logins. They decided to roll it out by time zone, starting with U.S. Eastern Standard Time.

"You've got a plane to catch," Desi said. "I'll keep an eye on the load."

"Hello, New York," Scratchy keyed in the final command. All over the Eastern U.S., Junana clients sprang back to life with a login page. "When is Itchy going to release the code?"

"Most of it's up now. All of it will be up within the hour."

"I'm still surprised Jack suggested this."

"We've been underestimating him."

"Since day one. Someone's calling—maybe that's my cab." He picked up the phone.

"This is the front desk. Your Jacaranda Cab is here," the voice said.

"I'll be down." Scratchy was already living out of his suitcase, so he just grabbed his shaving kit and toothbrush, slipped his laptop into his delivery bag, and headed to the lobby. The cab was waiting under the port cochere. The driver stood by the door looking bored.

"Where's Timmy?" Scratchy asked. Timmy was his usual driver.

"Got a fare up to Solvang." The driver grabbed his bag and tossed it into the trunk. "Airport?"

Scratchy settled back in the cab as it rolled down the long, curving, palm fringed driveway. At the street, the cab stopped for traffic. The door opened and a blonde in a dark coat slipped into the back seat.

"Get your own cab, sister," Scratchy said.

"Very funny, Mr. O'hara," said Captain Nancy Rankin. She opened up her purse so Scratchy could see the Glock. The cab accelerated out of the driveway and headed south, away from the airport.

"You one of Karl's stooges?" Scratchy asked. He didn't like the feel of this at all. The driver had a small earpiece. Scratchy noticed another car was following them.

"Just enjoy the scenery." She opened up a black leather case and removed a silver cylinder with a small glass vial on one end. "And don't even think about getting heroic."

Scratchy noticed the broken cup holder on the door. "This is Timmy's cab."

"He'll get it back." Timmy was drugged and sleeping in the trunk under a blanket, his head resting on a backpack with a million dollars in unmarked hundreds. Rankin had access to another forty-nine million to wire to Don Driscoll's offshore account.

"If you are planning to fly me to Romania and torture me, the airport's in the other direction," Scratchy said.

"We're not the CIA," Rankin replied. "We can torture you in Tarzana..." She poked the metal cylinder against Scratchy's right forearm. It fired the drug cocktail into his system.

"Hey!" he grabbed the spot with his left hand. "That was rude."

"...Or we can have a chat right here in the cab." She glanced at her watch. By the time they hit Ventura he'd be singing like Vanilla Ice.

Scratchy's eyes began to close and he settled back into the corner of the seat.

"Torture me in Tarzana," he whispered hoarsely. "Molest me in Modesto. Squeeze my lemon, baby, till the juice run down my leg." His head slumped back.

In ten minutes she switched out the cylinders and gave him a jolt of epinephrine to bring him back just enough to talk. She checked the level in the vial. She still had enough for the "hot shot." After he told her what she needed she would make his heart explode in his chest. Scratchy twitched and his eyes opened slightly.

"Let's start with an easy one. What's your name?" She clicked on the digital recorder.

"Michael O'hara to you," he answered. "My friends can call me Scratchy." His left hand gestured in front of his face and his eyes attempted to follow it.

"Where were you going today?"

"Hawaii, for a nice vacation."

"Vacation? From what?"

"I've been coding my ass off for days."

"Really. And now you're finished?"

"Damn Straight!"

"What did you finish?"

"Got Junana to reboot on the mesh." He turned his head and tried to focus on the cars moving alongside.

"What?" She flipped up her phone and punched in a quick dial number. "Give me the status on Junana?" she barked. She waited.

"Shit!" She hissed.

She turned back to O'hara. "Tell me. How did you do that?" They had been advised Junana would take months to repair if it was even possible. They had destroyed petabytes of content.

"Slickest piece of programming in my life, rebooting a mesh computer on the mesh."

She had no idea what he was talking about. She checked the recorder to be certain it was getting this.

"I'd like to take a look at the Junana source code."

"Go right ahead," he said.

"Thank you. What's your user name and password?"

"Badges!" he gestured wildly, "We don't need no stinking badges." His head turned and his eyes roamed around the back of the cab.

"What's your user name and password?" she asked again.

"You want to look at the Junana source code."

"That's right."

"Fuck Driscoll!" he shouted, waving his fist. "Lousy turncoat."

"Driscoll?" She stiffened.

"Company mole, stole our code."

"He took your code. And what did you do?"

"Fixed him good."

"How?"

"SourceForged it."

"Source what?"

He spelled the URL out slowly.

"Come again?"

"Resource locator for our source code. By now it's been Slash|Dashed too."

"What!" She pulled a laptop from the same leather case and opened it. "Say it again?" He told her. She spent several minutes browsing the site.

"Is this for real?"

"Search it, you don't believe me."

She keyed in the query. The top link was Slash|Dash. The news of the Junana code release was all over the front page. There were photos of O'hara and two others.

"Who are the two other programmers?"

"That would be Itchy and Desi."

She was reading the main blog. Ichiro Nomura and Desikacharya Venkataraman were prominently mentioned.

"You just saved the taxpayers fifty million dollars," she said. To the driver, "Take the next exit."

The cab pulled off the freeway at Rose Avenue and stopped on the margin of the off-ramp. A black sedan pulled up behind it. The driver of the taxi and the driver of the sedan pulled Timmy from the trunk of the cab. They set him in the driver's seat of the cab.

Rankin was on the phone, reporting about the Junana code release. She tossed the blond wig she had been wearing on the floor of the cab and stepped out. She pulled a bulging backpack from the trunk and closed the lid.

The sedan took off, leaving the cab idling. Twenty minutes later, a CHP cruiser found it still idling, Timmy was dozing in the driver's seat. Scratchy was out cold in the back, splayed over on his side. The Officer turned off the motor, checked their pulses, and called for an ambulance.

§ § §

Don Driscoll ordered up a steak sandwich from room service. He had waited an extra hour before calling the number the woman on the phone had given him. The voice said it was "no longer a working number." He then pulled out his laptop and began to browse the Internet. The word about Junana was up top on the news feeds. Not only was the site back up, but the source code had been posted on SourceForge.

Why would they do that? The code was legitimately worth billions. Now it was public property. His illegal copy was worthless. Anybody with a modem could download the code for free. Goddamn O'hara! Don paced his room, his very expensive room, which he was planning to pay for in cash from the million they were to deliver.

Nervously, he checked his private email, nothing but spam. Then he logged into Junana. Instead of his home page there was a black screen. Then a video window appeared, a talking head shot of Michael O'hara in that stupid Guatemalan shirt. Don turned up the sound.

"...Don, old buddy, old pal," O'hara was speaking. "You screwed the wrong pooch this time. The code you stole from

us is now free for everybody. Your profile in Junana has been
locked, with a message that you are a worthless sack of shit
who shouldn't be trusted with the key to the WC. We have
included a bonus surprise for you, you rascal you." O'hara
wagged a pudgy finger at him.

"Every Guide in the Game has been instructed to let their
players know who you are and what you did. Any time you use
a cell phone, swipe your credit card, use an ATM, or go online
for any reason, the Game will know where you are, and will
broadcast this information to all players within a half mile
radius of your location.

"We are not going to prosecute you. We want you out on
the street. Try to ignore the strangers that take a sudden
interest in you. They only hate you a little. All you need to do is
stay offline, use pay phones, pay in cash, and never, ever apply
for another job. Oh, and have a nice life." The screen went
black.

There was a knock on the door. "Room service!" the voice
said. Don peeked through the viewer. The waiter held a tray
with a covered plate. Don opened the door.

"It's about fucking time you got here," he said.

The waiter nodded at him, breezed in, set the tray on the
table and arranged the silverware and napkin.

"Do you require anything else?" The waiter stared at him
for an instant and then looked at the ceiling. Don pulled a
couple dollars from his wallet and handed then to the guy, who
nodded, smirked, and breezed back out of the room.

Don went to the minibar and grabbed a Heineken. He sat
down and took a long pull. O'hara was trying to make him
paranoid. Doing a good job of it too. Don took the little
mustard jar and twisted off the lid, he dug the knife into it and
smeared mustard on top of the steak. On impulse he took the
blade of the knife and lifted the steak from its bed of lettuce.

N e r d v i l l e

Between the steak and the lettuce were five fat, ugly-red
cockroaches.

§   §   §

Desi burst into Itchy's room, still shrouded in pre-dawn gloom.
    "Wake up! Wake up!"
    Itchy rolled over in his bed, moaning.
    "They took Scratchy!"
    Itchy sat up. "What?"
    "I just retrieved a message from Jack. Scratchy never made
it to the plane. The hotel says he checked out and took a cab.
Karl's got him, shit, shit, shit!" Desi stomped around the room,
hyperventilating.
    "Let's get Jack into the Room." Itchy pulled a lungi from a
chair near his bed and wrapped this around his waist. Desi
punched in the text message code on his phone.

§   §   §

"What did you expect?" Annaline was wearing her robe,
barefoot and regal. "That he would come and take you back to
San Francisco? Abandon his family? Live with you forever?"
    "He said he had a surprise."
    "Could be a box of chocolates. Get real, girl."
    "What will become of me?"
    "'If you can't appreciate what you've got, then you'd better
get what you appreciate.'"
    "Tell me what you mean. I know you are smarter than I
am." Sometimes Annaline was deliberately obscure.
    "George Bernard Shaw."

"Who is that?"

"You want some Free-for-All time? We haven't finished with your last Query yet."

"I'm too tired."

"Then go to sleep."

"I'm too excited."

"Then go to Junana, the Game is not your toy."

"You say 'George Bernard Shaw' like that is supposed to explain something. Now let me find out what you mean and then we can go back to the Query."

"Fair enough." Annaline's image faded and the Free-for-All arena appeared.

Essie started with Shaw, not knowing where this was headed until she found Pygmalion, which lead to My Fair Lady and Ovid's original poem in Metamorphoses. She scanned the images of Pygmalion and Galatea, his statue and then his wife.

The stories centered on the love that the sculptor had for his creation, but never touched on the feeling of the statue. Ovid never even named the statue. Shaw had inserted social transformation into the story, a tale of the rise from the working class. He personally picked Wendy Hiller to play Eliza in the film.

The Game assembled five narrative threads leading away from this story. She chose to start with Pinocchio, where a block of wood wills itself to life. After a side trip into the dramatic use of allegory, she viewed several snippets about an android named Data on the Starship Enterprise, and a very sad scene from the film Artifical Intelligence.

She set the Computo aside and lay back on her straw pallet, her toes on the coiled hoses, and she cried. She cried for many things all at once and then, still crying, put these into some order. She cried for her mother, there in the hospital, covered with sores and praying for death. She cried for the child she was, alone in that hut, shivering in the dark, clutching her hatchet. She cried for Pinocchio, Data, Galatea, and little android boy David: blocks of wood with dreams of life. And then she cried in her joy. She was also a block of wood, a dab of clay, but now she had such dreams and such wonderful pain.

"Blue fairy," she called out.

"Essie," Annaline replied, her image returning to the screen. "You are the blue fairy."

"The Game..."

"...is just a game. You are Pygmalion, not the statue."

"Mr. Steve5683?"

"Will go back to San Francisco with his family in ten days. He wants to be a friend. He has a surprise for you."

"A box of chocolates?"

"I think not. It is also time for you to know something." Annaline slumped on the floor of the hut.

"What is wrong?"

"Nothing is wrong, it is simply time. Your time." She smiled beatifically. "My time is over. Yours is just beginning."

Annaline lay on her back. "You are the best student any Guide could ask for. In time you will be a powerful Meister. Live well my dear Essie."

"NO!" Essie screamed into the Computo, shaking it as Annaline's form dissolved into the dust of the hut's floor.

"Goodbye, Pinocchio." Essie closed her eyes and cried herself to sleep.

§   §   §

"Two days!" Bishop shouted into the phone. "They got Junana back up in two days!" In his sermon on Sunday he had been able to take credit for calling on God to knock Junana from the

Internet. How was he to explain that God's wrath would only last forty-eight hours?

Rankin held her cool. The Reverend was very well connected and should be useful down the road. "We are analyzing the situation now. My tech staff are all over it. We have the source code."

"Everybody has the source code," Bishop said. That news was all over the web. "Did you find out who's financing their operation?"

In her excitement over the code release, Captain Rankin had forgotten to push the interrogation in that direction. She also forgot to give the geek his "hot shot," as Karl had requested. Karl was not happy.

"What do I tell W.G.?" he demanded.

§   §   §

"He left the hotel sixteen hours ago," Itchy was at the Console. He scanned the Santa Barbara newspaper sites. Desi was at the next terminal checking the California Highway Patrol traffic incident site.

Jack popped into the Room. "There's good news. I called the taxi company. Scratchy's cab was found near Oxnard. The driver and a passenger were taken by ambulance to St. John's hospital."

"Hospital! Oh, my God!" Desi said.

"Neither of them are in serious condition." Jack said. "I can't get any more information from here. I've sent someone to check out the scene. We should know soon."

"What if they tortured him? Made him talk?" Desi asked.

"We have to assume they know everything, and that they'll be coming after us."

"What about your family?" Itchy asked.

"They're used to living in a high security environment. This is not the first time I've made enemies."

"Well, it's a first time for me," Desi said. "What if they cut off his fingers?"

"Why would they cut off his fingers?" Itchy said.

"So he couldn't program any more." He was remembering the story of the Taj Mahal. When the workers finished building it, they say Shah Jahan chopped off their hands so they could not build another one.

Itchy checked his email. "Don Driscoll logged into Junana. He was staying at the Eastinn LAX."

Desi's avatar doubled over in laughter. Itchy sent his into a similar paroxysm.

"What's so funny?" Jack said. They told him and he joined them. Then he said, "Now you see why we have to keep Junana out of the hands of people like Karl."

"Good thing we stripped out various, non-essential sections of the code from the release package. They can still run Junana and the Game with the public release version, but they can't duplicate our access to global databases," Itchy said, "among other things."

"With any luck, Driscoll has already discarded his stolen copy," Desi added. "Once everything settles down, we'll let Don off the hook. Until then, well I wouldn't want to be him."

"I spoke with Winston," Jack said. "He's on a flight to Burbank. He'll be in Oxnard in the morning. I thought Michael would enjoy a friendly face. Winston will get him on the plane to Kona."

TWENTY-THREE

Scratchy woke up in a hospital bed with a pounding headache. The room was black. Electronic readouts shone on a dozen different devices. He was in a cotton gown and had a plastic wristband on his left wrist. Pushing against the blazing pain in his skull, he reached over and found the call button on its cord. He pressed this and fell back in the bed.

After some time the door opened, admitting a flash of flourescent light from the hallway. The nurse entered and squeak-walked over to his bed.

"Mr. O'hara. Feeling better?"

"Than what?" He closed his eyes. "The bitch slipped me a mickey."

"Your blood chemistry was..." the nurse hesitated, "...unusual."

"Got any aspirin, maybe some Vicodin?"

"Head hurt?"

"Ummm..." he groaned.

"I can give you some water. We don't know exactly what you took, so we're not going to give you anything that might complicate your condition."

"They catch the blonde?"

"There was just you and the driver. Did you know you're famous?"

"Tell me about it." He turned over on his side and slid back into unconsciousness.

§   §   §

She opened the Cuca shop early, as if that would prompt Mr. Steve5683 to arrive. Of course, she wanted to run to their lodge and wake them up and get her surprise so that this sweet, awful thrill of anticipation would leave her. Instead, she cleaned up the storeroom and swept the shop twice, glancing out the window every five minutes. Last night the Game had reappeared. She spent most of the night on a new Query.

Ontibile, the giant camp guard, arrived and said she must close up the shop and follow him. He would not say where or why, and she had a moment of terror that Owner was angry with her and would throw her from the property. He walked out toward the village, up the track around a small kopje. Near the top of this, on its south side, she saw Mr. Steve talking with Owner.

"They are waiting," Ontibile said and began to walk back to camp.

She climbed the hill, emboldened by Mr. Steve's smile and wave. He was holding a large roll of paper and there was a big cardboard box at his feet. Owner was not smiling.

"Hello, Essie. I've been talking to my new partner. Heinrick is not convinced of my plan, but I am sure it is worth a try, if you are willing."

"Good morning, Mr. Steve. Taté Owner, *wa lala po*," she nervously greeted the owner in Oshindonga.

"His name is Heinrick, which you should use, now that we are all in this together."

"I am confused," she admitted.

"Look." He unrolled the paper, and she saw blueprints for a building. "This is our new school. Here is the classroom, here the kitchen and bathrooms, and here the teacher's apartment. The satellite dish goes on the roof. This hillside should provide clear reception."

"School?"

"For Gamers." He pulled a blue shoulder bag from the box at his feet and passed this to her. "Congratulations!"

She looked into the shoulder bag and pulled out the yellow blouse and a silver metal laptop computer.

"As the teacher, I think you will need one of these." It was solid and smooth in her hand, an object from a distant star.

"The teacher? Oh, my!"

"If you agree."

"What about my store?" Heinrick grumbled.

"Our store. While we are building the school, she can train her replacement."

"Look!" Steve pointed to the box. Inside were at least a dozen new Computos.

"Who will be the students?" Essie asked, already thinking of two or three girls.

"Anyone you choose. You are completely in charge of the school. We will make a budget for supplies."

A school. Her mind raced. This was a surprise like nothing she imagined. A school where others, like her, could join the great wide world inside the Game.

"But I have nothing to teach!" she said, feeling bewildered.

"That's not what my Guide tells me," Steve said. "You are on your way to become a Meister, and potentially a great one. The Game knows these things."

"Oh, my!" She turned away to hide her face.

"The Game has new templates for teaching, and includes a whole style of play that Gamers can join in the classroom."

"Gaming in the classroom! What happened to discipline and order?" Heinrick said.

"Taté Owner," she turned to him. "Mr. Heinrick. Can you see why this is a very good idea?"

"What I see is a complete waste of good money and nothing but trouble ahead." He frowned. She saw in his eyes what she had seen so many times before.

"When you look at us, you never see us at all, do you? You see us as we have always lived, so close to the dirt that we are little different from the antelope and the elephants. To you we are monkeys who have discovered beer, and you think that's the way we should remain. But we are also your neighbors and your workers. Your customers do not need to watch us like they watch the zebras at a water hole. They will still come for the fish and the lions. And we can have dreams as great as yours." She looked out across the valley. "...or greater."

"You don't seem any happier now then when you were scrubbing my toilets."

"True, but my head is out of the dust."

"Will this make any of them happy? All this education?"

"Nothing makes people happy. People make their own happiness."

Steve laughed at that. "She's quite the philosopher, Heinrick. I wouldn't get into any debates with her. While you are building the school, I think she should move into cabin ten..."

Heinrick shook his head unhappily. He sometimes kept one of his mistresses in cabin ten.

"...and she can eat at the main dining room with the customers. I think they'll enjoy her insights."

"How long with it take to build the new school?" she asked.

"We can get all the materials up from Grootfontein in a matter of weeks," Steve said. "Put the roof on before the rains start. I'll order the solar panels from Durban tomorrow."

"Why are you doing this?" Essie asked.

"Something my Guide said. "'Stevo,' Charley said to me, 'you started something terrible when you gave that girl a

Computo. She's all alone now, with nobody to talk to but strangers on Junana. You have to get her some companions so she does not cry herself to sleep."

"Oh! Annaline!" Essie said. "My Guide was wicked to put this on you."

"I've been looking for a project where I can give back to the places where my customers travel. Besides, I'm sure our customers will enjoy conversing with a whole school of Essies. I'm thinking of special tours just for Gamers. You don't look convinced, Heinrick."

"One Essie has been more than enough," he grumbled.

§ § §

Don Driscoll drove through the night, out into the desert. He stopped at a gas station with a minimart and filled the tank with his credit card. Then he went into store for some coffee.

"What do you want?" The clerk stood stiffly behind the counter.

"Coffee. You got a restroom?"

"Not for assholes like you."

"What?"

"Hit the road, Driscoll!" The clerk raised his right arm, the one with the baseball bat in its hand. Behind him, a computer screen displayed Don's face. Don backed to the glass door and used his body to push it open, still watching the clerk. He fled to his car and drove south.

§ § §

It was still dark out when a man dressed like a doctor arrived. He took Scratchy's pulse. Scratchy opened his eyes.

"Count Slick sent me. I'm to stick around until your friend Winston arrives."

"Winston!" Scratchy smiled.

"You feeling OK?"

"Guess I shouldn't drink and passenger." He could not remember anything after the blonde woman got into his cab. "I probably told them everything, I can't remember."

"Your friends are taking all reasonable precautions. You still have a plane to catch."

"What about Timmy?"

"Timmy?"

"Owns the cab?"

"That's him in the next bed."

Scratchy looked over. All he could see was a vague form, asleep under the blanket. "What did she give us?"

The man picked up the chart from its hook on the wall. "They found traces of curare, LSD, PCP, and some alkaloids they can't identify. Some serious shit. You're lucky your breathing didn't stop."

"Will Timmy be OK?"

"He's stable now. Here's another call button for you." He handed Scratchy a small beeper-like device. "You push it and I'm here." He touched a bulge under his white coat and slid out of the room like a wraith.

§   §   §

One by one the Posse checked into the Abbot's Abode and found their rooms at the Old House up on the crest of the hill. Jennifer arrived a day early to get a jump on the jet lag from

Paris. She spent an entire afternoon indulging in the spa. One of the masseuses noticed the new tattoo on her shoulder, and, before she could object, she was getting royal treatment. It was a small tattoo of the crimson cloak.

Over the fall and winter, Jennifer had pushed through Level Five and Six and was now a Meister. She had been invited to Castalia where she met other Meisters in the castle on the hill. They had not yet opened Castalia for Sixers. The vast campus carried an abandoned-theme-park ambiance. The grounds were magnificent but lonely. The fountains ran, deer browsed, and lupin bloomed on the hillsides, but there were only few people on the castle grounds. She had even met the Grand Meister, who welcomed her warmly, leaning on his staff while he asked her about her plans and goals.

Her cloak had arrived by express mail. The cloak was of heavy silk satin with a broad collar, bright crimson on the outside, lined in black. Not really street ready, although the previous week she'd seen a pair of Meisters, still just kids, strolling together in their cloaks. She packed the cloak away and went with the tattoo as a gift to herself.

Soaking in the herbal bath, she realized how much of her life she had set aside while pursuing the Game. She was shocked by her appearance in the spa's mirrors. Months of inactivity and inattention had sapped away her muscle tone. She had gained several pounds and lost all of her tan. Simple on the outside, she reflected, beauty on the inside. Bullshit. She could almost hear Francesco say, "What's the purpose of 'beauty on the inside' if it doesn't show?"

Claire showed up in the early afternoon. She had left Megan at a friend's house, where the mother was also wearing Game shoes. Megan said she was bored to death with the Santa Monica City College classes. She had been stalled in Level Five, unable to get the hang of unfolding templates in a few regions.

With unlimited Free-for-All time, she spent most of her Gaming hours working out her homework or exploring topics that amused her.

Megan had developed an intellectual attitude that Claire found familiar and irritating. She acted like a sophomore at Swarthmore: grossly overconfident but fully prepared to back it up. Megan adored her shoulder bag and took it everywhere. In the previous week she went through a world religion phase, consuming the major Upanishads, the Prajnaparamita Sutra, and Tao Te Ching.

Claire checked in at the front desk and found a message from Winston. He had to run to Santa Barbara before coming back to Santa Fe, so he would spend the night in Albuquerque and arrive the next morning. She had a momentary regret that Winston would not be sleeping in the room across the hall tonight; something tingly had awakened in her at the thought. She dropped her bags in her room, switched to her Pumas and took a four mile walk on the bridle trail.

Alice arrived later in the afternoon. As she was a self-confessed gym-rat, a step-aerobic, cycle-spinning, Bikram yoga, pilates enthusiast, she dropped off her bags and headed for the fitness center to work out the kinks from the day's travel.

Betsy, who needed a full day to recover from Mardi Gras, arrived last. Despite her careful but heartfelt entreaties, Annika had fallen hard for a Tulane University English professor who was in the Sixth Level of the Game. When that bitch showed up at The Leg Bar in the yellow blouse, Betsy knew it was over.

The mood at dinner had none of the usual triumphalism of the past retreats, where Con|Int's annual growth was saluted with tequila and bonus checks got passed around. This table felt more like the wake for a close friend; forced laughter and small talk stretched thin over their anxiety.

Betsy gave hugs all around and they ate their green chile, posole, and sopapillas with rounds of Patron. The real meeting would not begin until the morning, so the talk drifted to events since they last met. This mainly centered on the Game and on Jennifer, whose Meister status gave Claire and Alice some kind of thrill. Claire said she was struggling with Level Six. Betsy found it hard to imagine Claire struggling with anything. She tried to catch Alice's eye, but Alice was focused on some template-unfolding-conundrum conversation going on between Claire and Jennifer.

"If you don't mind, I'm going to my room and slit my wrists." Betsy stood.

"See you in the morning!" Alice said and turned around to her to touch her hand. Claire and Jennifer stopped their conversation for a minute to wish her good night. In a funk as dark as the sky, Betsy took the trail up to the Old House.

§   §   §

Harold Farmer sat in a darkened room with six high-definition screens arranged in a semi-circle. On each screen a face popped into view as their encrypted signal was approved. Once all the screens were filled, he opened up his speaker.

"Gentlemen and lady." He nodded to Elza Frieberg on the screen second from the left. She lifted her chin in reply. "We have the code, and we have the talent. Once we unlock their new administrative system we will control Junana. In the meantime let's finalize the advertising buy-in so we can build out the new plazas. I want to see results in weeks, not months. Are we all on the same page?"

"What about my budget," Elza asked. "I gave you the new figures based on this accelerated schedule. We need another hundred digital artists to keep on track."

"I got budget approval this morning. Hire whom you need." She sat back and smiled.

"Any other concerns?"

"What about the Game?" This came from Dickey Gronberg at Commerce.

"Our instructions are to shut it down."

"Shut it down? Most of our high schools are running on it. The initial test scores are outstanding."

"Forget the tests. We need a school system in step with our economy. Is there anything else?" The faces remained impassive.

"We'll talk again in a week. I want to see progress across the board." Harold moused the "End Conversation" button and the screens went blank.

Dickey Gronberg slammed his phone receiver back on the instrument.

"Ham fisted luddites!" he muttered. "Pontificating paranoid..."

"Sounds like they mean business," Geoff said. Dickey had left the Game running while he was on the video phone.

"I can't stop them."

"We know."

Another Guide popped into view. He looked vaguely familiar.

"Dickey, this is JS," said Geoff. "He has a few questions for you, if you're willing..."

§   §   §

The morning came with frost and bright mountain sun. Alice was up early for a run. Jennifer treated herself to room service and a hot bath. Claire and Betsy found each other at the restaurant.

"You disappeared early last night," Claire said, sitting down across from Betsy, who set down her newspaper on the empty chair to her right.

"It's been a busy week," she said and sipped at her triple latte.

"We were all focused on Jennifer," said Claire. "I didn't even get a chance to ask about Mardi Gras."

"Well, it rained the whole damn time, which happens when the calendar slips into March."

"That's a shame. But there's still a party."

"Best in the world."

"How'd Annika like it?"

Betsy picked up her paper again. "You gonna order breakfast?" She leaned back with a scowl and opened it.

Claire took the signal and caught the eye of the waitress. Just as she was ordering, Alice arrived, dressed in her sweats. Alice had the capability of brightening a room like a halogen flood light just by striding through it. Trim and athletic, she bounced when she walked, which sent the millefiore trade beads in the corn rolls of her coiffure in motion. She had Pam Greer's generous smile and Sharon Stone's cheekbones.

Alice was a walking United Nations. Her mother was a mix of Haitian African and Taino on one side and an Anglo-Indian on the other. When she was a small child, the mother's family escaped Haiti on a boat that ended up in Biloxi. Alice's father's mother was Norwegian and Chinese from Seattle. Her paternal grandfather emigrated to Vancouver as part of a Jewish family from South Wales.

Alice's parents met when her father took a job at Stennis Space Center where her mother was working as clerk. Alice had emerald eyes, a cafe-au-lait complexion, a third-degree black belt in Aikido, and an unbridled sexuality. On the census form, Alice could use an "all of the above" box.

She gave Claire a hug and then went around to Betsy and gave her one too and a big smooch on the cheek along with a sly feel with her right hand that made Betsy start and then grin. Betsy pinched Alice on the butt, and Alice slapped her hand away playfully and sat down in the empty chair. The coffees came and then the omelets, and they were all talking about politics and movie stars and current events as if it were a year ago when these things still mattered.

Winston took the last plane out of LAX to Albuquerque, slept a few hours at an airport hotel, and rented a car as sun rose above the mountains east of town. On the road to Santa Fe, he grabbed an incendiary breakfast burrito from a bustling trailer kitchen. He had put Scratchy on Jack's jet late yesterday afternoon up in Santa Barbara. By now, Scratchy was probably poolside at the Kona Cove.

Winston had done some research on Con|Int, which he discovered was one of the top consumer forecasting firms in the world. He checked out the profiles for Claire, Jennifer, and Alice on Junana, knowing these were precise and fairly comprehensive. Elizabeth Berteotti, the fourth member of Claire's team, had no profile. He'd run into Betsy before.

Betsy Berteotti was a star among academic statisticians, a group with which Winston was obliquely connected. His own work on derivatives had made him somewhat famous in the same, admittedly tiny, circle. He had seen her speak at an American Statistical Association annual meeting a few years back.

Desi met Jennifer in Castalia when she became a Meister. He advised Winston to be on his guard. "Way, way too smart and beautiful for any one person," was Desi's assessment of Jennifer Bouchez. "Oh, my God! She could actually be a Guide in the game."

Winston found the driveway to the Abbot's Abode, checked in, and followed the bellhop up the hill to a separate house where his room was located on the second floor. The meeting was scheduled to start at 9:30. Winston unpacked, checked his emails, gargled away some of the habañero breath, slipped on his twenty-year old Orvis jacket and went downstairs. In the house's living room, the furniture had been moved to the walls and a round table installed in the middle of the floor, with a projector and a screen against the back wall. The curtains were pulled against the sun. Doughnuts and coffee were offered up around the table.

Claire came up and gave him a hug, which they held a bit too long and then separated abruptly. Claire met his eyes and made this move with her eyebrows that Winston was trying to interpret while she introduced him to Alice, Jennifer, and Betsy.

"I went to your talk at the ASA some years ago," Betsy said. He returned the compliment. Claire explained that they ran the mornings on pure sugar, fat, and caffeine, and then switched to yoghurt and whole grain muffins in the afternoon, which would include a hike through Bandelier National Monument.

"I'm afraid none of us is a morning person," she explained.

"I'm not sure what my role is here," Winston confessed as he took a seat.

"You've been fairly astute in predicting trends about the effects of the Game," Betsy said. "We are now in the same business. Feel free to speak up whenever you have some input."

"We'll interrogate you after the doughnuts are gone," said Jennifer.

"Must avoid getting blood splattered on the pastries," Alice added.

Betsy went to the laptop and cued up the first slide.

"I'm going to start with the obvious," she said. "since all of you are already addicted to this Game. I'm sorry. Winston, are you a player?"

"Just earned my shoulderbag."

"Way to go!" Alice said.

Jennifer gave him a nod, and Claire did that thing with her eyebrows again, which meant she wasn't doing it because of his burrito breath.

"The Game is probably, make that unequivocally, the finest piece of learning technology to hit the streets since Socrates wandered Athens. Whoever built this managed to combine a content engine with...Alice, would you please stop!"

Alice was unconsciously doing the Wanda and Jorge motions with her hands.

"Sorry." Her hands dipped back to her lap.

"Creeps me out," Betsy muttered. "Where was I? Oh, right. Well, the point is, whoever they are, they did the pedagogy part so right that we can pretty much call this the future of education for the planet."

Winston suppressed a smile as all the good feelings of a proud father listening to a glowing report about his baby daughter welled up inside of him.

"The templates..." Jennifer said. Betsy held up her hand.

"You can talk in a minute, Jenn. Let me finish."

"On the technology side," Betsy continued. "they might as well be some alien invaders. There is nothing to compare this to in terms of scale and performance. The throughput on this system accounts for more than half the capacity of Ariadne."

She put up a slide that illustrated the growth of the Game over the past year.

"Look. It's exponential, like bacteria on a growth medium," she noted.

"Or like a great hit song," Jennifer said. "Like you said, this is a marvelous teaching machine."

"Now that the source code is out, we know that O'hara has accomplished the mesh computer," Betsy took back the conversation. "On the social side, Junana.com, which was the first product by the Game makers, has pretty much reversed the common wisdom about anonymity on the Internet. It turns out that people prefer honesty in their online interactions. Of course, Tony Geddens told us that years ago.

"There are certain consequences to this honesty. Young people, kids still in high school, will now need to look into their futures and realize that they will always be in touch, or at least in reach of everyone they meet. Not only does Junana.com impose an honesty about the past, it projects this into the future. You can run, but you can no longer hide. Here is the real digital village, where neighbors know what you sing in the shower, and how you downloaded it.

"When we look closer at the Game..." Betsy was watching Jennifer. "We begin to see the corrosive, dangerous, even deadly consequences that are only now emerging."

Alice and Claire burst out in protests, while Jennifer and Betsy held eye contact. Winston felt like he had been stabbed in the gut. Betsy let the ruckus subside.

"This is precisely what I'm getting at," Betsy continued. "The Game consumes its players emotionally with a cult-like grip. They want to believe that it's all pretty and nice, sugar and spice. But it's not, is it, Jennifer?"

Jennifer absorbed the gaze of the room for a minute. Betsy's question had brought into instant focus a haze of misgivings that she'd pushed to the side in the Sixth Level. Why were some templates so easy to unfold and others so difficult? Why was the track of her progress not entirely of her own volition? Just what and who controlled the boundaries of the Game?

"No, it's not," she admitted. "But I don't see any malevolence in it."

"So far, the Game has killed more people than any terrorist group in modern history," Betsy said, and put up the slide on suicide rate increases.

"You can't blame that on the Game!" Winston blurted. "There's got to be some other reason..."

"The real problem," Betsy growled, "is not clinical depression, although reports of depression remain significantly higher than before the Game. In fact, the future is so dark you'll need to wear night goggles."

She switched to the next slide, a multigraph of trends, all moving higher over time. "The sleeping killer here is anomie."

"'Aujourd'hui, maman est morte. Ou peut-être hier, je ne sais pas,'" Jennifer whispered.

"What was that?" asked Claire.

"Camus. In Paris we suckle our infants in anomie. So I'm not sure where this is going."

"I thought anomie went out with Durkheim," Alice said.

"Well, it's back," said Betsy. "When it comes to the real world, millions of players, many of them teenaged, just don't give a flying fuck anymore. Fortunately, whoever is doing the Game has the balls to let others pull statistics from it. In fact, the Game is now the single best source of consumer information ever assembled. Only now we don't just get opinions about laundry detergent, we can look into the minds of the players and find out how they actually think."

"The Game doesn't give access to player-level personal information or even aggregates of this," Winston said.

"Sure, but the Game keeps careful track of its templates, and how many players fold and unfold these. The template structures are semantically coded, so we can pull meaningful inferences from them. Once you make the assumption that the players internalize the templates as guidelines for their thoughts and actions, you can normalize the player population according to their exposure to the various template structures."

"So you don't need to know anything about the players other than which templates they have unfolded?" Winston was impressed. Betsy might be the only person on the planet capable of pulling this off.

"Correctamundo," Betsy said. "Do you guys want the gory details, or should I just cut to the fucking chase?"

"It's your report," Claire said, again extremely happy Betsy was on her team.

"We are all on the fast train to Nerdville," Betsy said, and clicked forward rapidly to a slide that said just that. She continued.

"I'm sure the Game makers thought they were setting up some kind of universal learning tool that would enable the players to imagine whatever future they had in mind. But take a look..."

She keyed the next slide, which showed a complex topic cloud with maybe five hundred nodes where thin lines connecting these into some sort of ontological web.

"This is a representation of the tippy-top level of the global knowledge-space as we know it today, including emotional intelligence. You can see music, art, philosophy, psychology, physics, sociology, intimacy, reflexivity, empathy: it's all here. This map represents everything we think is possible to learn."

She toggled the next slide. The same topic cloud, but within it a very small number of the nodes were now highlighted in red.

"This is the current learning space of the Game," she said. "If we overlay Gardner's intelligences on the total learning space, you'll note that the Game completely avoids musical, spatial, body-kinesthetic, and intrapersonal intelligences. The players can ace their SATs, but they can't hold a basic conversation, except maybe with their Guides."

Winston slumped in his chair. This was all news to him, and none of it good.

"Nerdville," Jennifer spoke. She walked up to the screen. "Of course. Since this is where we—all of us in the room at least—already lived, we didn't see it coming. Merde!"

"The people who designed the Game likely never figured that they were imprinting it with the contours of their own screwed up lives. So why not screw up the rest of the world? If this was their plan, they are right on target."

"The Game covers social processes, technology, architecture, history. Look, there's even anthropology," said Winston defensively.

"Where's the music?" Betsy asked.

"Where's the art?" Alice added.

"Where's the intimacy?" Claire asked. "All of this is just content without emotion: rational, sophisticated, astute even. But so thin, it's like a veil. Where's the complexity, the ambiguity, that confusion of flavors, colors, and smells we can sense all around us? Where is the real world in this?"

"Nerdville," Jennifer repeated. "It smells like the stacks in the graduate library."

"When only one percent of the population are nerds, at least there's a market for their talents. Nerds have done pretty well of late," Betsy noted. "But when half the population are nerds, what the hell are they supposed to do? Do you think they are going to be happy checking people out at the supermarket? Flipping burgers at Wendy's? We are looking at tens of millions of radically disenchanted individuals, intellectually stimulated only in the Game. Outside of this: socially stunted and emotionally crippled. An enormous cohort of underemployed, underappreciated, intensely unhappy geeks. Clones of whomever manufactured this monstrosity. Nerdville, here we come." Betsy stood by the computer, triumph spilled across her face. She looked at Jennifer, who held her head in her hands. The room fell silent.

"We know who programmed the game," Betsy said. "Maybe we can find some way to contact them."

The next slide was an old photo of Scratchy from when he won his first Neo. "Michael O'hara, of recent fame. We know he's the source for the mesh computer."

The next slide showed Desi in a suit, again from his prior life in the dot-com world. "Desikacharya Venkataraman is a genius with language. He did the multilingual programming for Junana."

"He's also the first Grand Meister," Jennifer said. "I've met him."

When he became Grand Meister, Desi had given up masquerading his avatar, and went with a straight image of himself, over Jack's protest.

"I've got other duties now," Desi had argued. "And these require my sincerity. I can't hide anymore."

The next slide showed Itchy.

"Ichiro Nomura, the wizard of the avatar: the Game Guides are his masterpiece."

Winston glanced at Claire, who was staring directly at him. He looked back at the screen and then glanced again. Her eyes made contact. She was nodding.

"I think Winston has something to say," Claire said. "Or should I?"

"I can't stop you."

"They all have something in common."

"I know that none of them have a profile on Junana," said Betsy.

"They all shared a house at college," Claire said. "Them, and also Winston here."

The room turned in his direction.

"So it's probable Winston is a principal in the Game project," Betsy announced.

Winston shrank down in his chair like he was imagining they were velociraptors ready to pounce.

"You built the Game?" Jennifer asked.

"It seemed like the thing to do at the time."

"Thank God," she said. "Then it's not too late."

"Too late for what?" Betsy said.

"Version 2.0." Jennifer stood.

"You mean fix it?" asked Betsy.

"You said the technology rocks and the learning engine, too. It's just the content that needs work."

"So, what is the cure for anomie? Music? Art? MTV?" Winston also stood up and leaned on the table. "How about some common sense?"

"What does your common sense tell you now?" Claire asked.

"Shut it down."

"No!" Jennifer slammed her hand on the table top. "There is nothing wrong with the Game except for its founding moment."

"I'm still not sure we need to blame the Game for people's unhappiness," said Alice. "All the Game did was wake them up, show them the world in a new light. The world masks unhappiness through its ongoing, globalized consumer circus. What's so great about being happy and stupid? The templates simply unfold an awareness of the real and symbolic violence that surrounds us."

"Sure, you can argue that suicide makes sense in a world so sad," Winston said. "but I'm not at all comfortable about my part in this."

"You didn't create the world," Claire said. "You just held up the mirror."

"These are only kids!" Winston slumped down holding his head in both hands. He kept thinking: the Game is killing people.

"We need to have some other voices in this conversation." Winston noticed the speaker phone in the middle of the table. "Is that hooked up?"

Winston sent out a coded text message from his cell phone, an alarm that would be announced by particularly obnoxious ring tones on each of the Nerds' phones. He gave them the number for the speaker phone.

Nerdville

TWENTY-FOUR

Itchy and Desi were in Vietnam, where it was four in the morning. Jack was having dinner in his club in London with his cell phone turned off and surrendered at the desk, as though it were a derringer. The club was particularly strict about this, and Jack approved entirely. Scratchy was on the deck of his hale in Kona.

Back in Santa Fe, the Posse refilled their coffee and chatted vigorously. Winston took a stroll outside. He felt like a kid who had accidentally done something enormously wrong: burned down the courthouse with a firecracker, crashed his father's car into the side of a bank, flooded the school gymnasium with one flush.

The mounting sequence of near disasters of late also made him wonder how long their luck would hold. First the Room gets hacked, then the Game goes down, and then Scratchy gets kidnapped. What next?

"Someone's on the line," Alice called from the door. Winston returned to the room, avoiding eye contact.

Within minutes Itchy, Scratchy, and Desi were all on the phone.

"Scratchy!" Desi said. "You sound wonderful. Does that mean you're all better?"

"They used drugs on me," Scratchy said.

"Silly them," said Itchy.

"I wouldn't recommend curare for everyone, but it worked for me."

Winston stalled to give time for Jack to call in. "You remember Claire," he said to the Nerds. "From RennFayre, senior year."

There was a long pause.

"Was she the freshman with the champagne?" Itchy asked.

"That's right," Winston said.

"You guys streaked the back nine at Eastmoreland," Desi remembered.

"Must have been the mushrooms," noted Scratchy. "Made you frisky."

"And humped like bonobos for hours listening to Blondie up in your room," said Itchy.

"Must have been the Quaaludes," added Scratchy.

Claire looked up at the ceiling, feeling the blush on her cheeks.

"We had breakfast together, that Sunday, up on the hill," Desi said. "You ate something like three omelets each."

Winston could actually still remember how strangely tasty they were.

"Could have been the acid I put in our OJ," Scratchy said.

"So that's what happened to Sunday!" Claire said. "It got all smeared and sparkly."

"You put acid in our OJ?" Itchy said. "Why Michael, how could you! Wish I'd thought of that."

"You put acid in our OJ?" Desi said. "I put acid in our OJ! Little windowpanes, one per glass."

"Now that's what happened to Sunday," Scratchy said. "We ate all the drugs we had left over from the whole year."

The Posse shared a knowing glance. Alice started giggling.

"Jennifer and I have already met," Desi said.

"Hello, Grand Meister," she said.

"Didn't I tell you she was sharp? Dearie, you can call me Desi."

"And he makes a mean mojito," Itchy said.

There was an awkward moment of silence.

"I don't think Jack's going to make the call," Scratchy said finally. "Something tells me the scheiss and the ventilator have made contact."

"I'm going to email you Dr. Berteotti's slides so you can get up to speed.

For the next hour, Betsy went through the entire presentation again, including the parts she had skipped the first time around. When it was over, the room fell quiet.

"Fuck anomie!" Scratchy broke the silence. "We are not in the happiness business. People have to find their own happiness. At least now they know they're unhappy, instead of buying another day of happiness on credit."

"What do you think, Jennifer?" Desi asked.

"The Game is a tool box. Right now it holds seven types of hammer. So it treats the world like everything is a nail. Let's redo Level Two. I'd like to add a saw and a screwdriver."

"A piano and a paint brush," said Claire.

"A pen and a tennis racquet," added Alice.

"How about a dildo?" said Betsy.

"Now you're talking!" said Desi.

"Where does it end?" Itchy asked.

"It doesn't end," said Jennifer. "It just gets richer and richer."

"So nobody ever leaves Level Two?" Alice asked.

"Not without a rounded portfolio of skills."

"What kind of skills are you talking about?" Scratchy asked.

"Mostly ones you don't seem to have," Betsy returned.

"You think I'm suicidal, sweetie?"

"You built a game without joy."

"You got a template for joy?"

"Just a hunger."

"Then welcome to my world."

"I wish Jack were here," said Winston.

"Wish granted." A new voice joined in on the speaker phone.

"Jack!" Desi said.

"I phoned in midway through the presentation. Who all is in the room?"

Winston did the introductions.

"You forget to tell him about RennFayre," Desi said.

"Moving right along," said Winston. "I'm wondering about our next step."

The room fell silent.

"Step one. Give them hope," Jennifer said. "Remember, they are only teenagers. They still need to believe that life has more openings than traps."

"To start off, stop killing the Guides," Claire suggested.

"Everything dies," Scratchy mumbled. "That's a template too, or it should be."

"Problem is, the Guides can't follow into Level Five," Itchy explained. "Having them die, or so we thought, would help the players move on independently."

"None of us thought the Gamers would actually grieve for their Guides," Winston said. "That was really unexpected."

"Why not make them ghosts?" Alice asked.

"In the Game?" Itchy asked. "Ghost or not, they don't help anyone on Level Five.

"What about in Junana? A ghost buddy that only you can see and hear?" Claire suggested.

"Like Topper!" said Desi. "How delicious!"

"Even though the Guide dies, we keep the program," Itchy said, "just in case players slip back from Level Five. So we could easily pull the Guide out of the Game into Junana and give it a custom invisibility property."

"Will that stop people from killing themselves?" Winston asked, looking over at Betsy. They all turned to her.

"It might for a while. Maybe long enough to program version 2.0."

"My top three teams can put this ghost programming into our next Scrum sprint, have it back to you in two weeks," Itchy offered. "Meanwhile we can just delay anyone else completing Level Four."

"Death takes a holiday," Scratchy said. "I got this feeling I'm going to be busy."

"Busy, busy, busy!" Desi echoed. "Next step?"

"Full speed ahead with the new design," Jack said. "Can you all gather in Sao Do?"

"Where?" Claire asked.

"Vietnam," Winston said. He'd been hoping to go there. "What about you, Jack?"

"I still have work to do that requires my presence elsewhere. I'll send the yacht through the Canal and catch up to it in a few months off the coast of Vietnam."

"My daughter..." Claire said, realizing that she didn't even think twice about her business. Con|Int was history.

"Megan will love Sao Do," Desi said. "There are several children her age at the same Level."

"I'm sure she will be thrilled to meet the Grand Meister."

"Not when she sees him in the morning," Itchy said.

"Bitch."

"Cow."

"Ladies, please," Scratchy said.

"Consider yourselves on Junana salary, starting today," Winston said, making eye contact around the room. Claire gave him that look again. He grinned back at her.

"Just so I'm back for Mardi Gras next year," Betsy said.

"We should all do Mardi Gras next year!" Desi added.

"What's the timeline for Version 2.0?" Winston asked.

"Four months puts the heat on us to get it done. Anything longer will stretch into a year," Itchy said. "Once we get new templates unfolded, we can put the whole staff on it."

"Busy, busy, busy," Scratchy said.

"Stay on target," Winston added.

"This must be what General Motors feels like when they recall a million cars to fix that ignition-switch fire thing," Winston said.

"Only we're recalling a hundred million players back to Level Two," Jack added.

"Good thing Jack runs a coffee business," Desi said. "It's triple lattes for the duration!"

"I'll drink to that," Betsy said.

"Here's to the new Game 2.0," Claire raised her coffee cup the others followed.

"Friend or anomie!" Scratchy said. "See you all in Sao Do."

"Mikey, please, for me, leave all your wardrobe back in Kona," Desi pleaded. "We'll fit you out over here."

"I've gone totally hemp," Scratchy announced. "Down to the boxers."

"No! Repeat after me: 'Hemp is for smoking, silk is for undies.'"

"Is that some kind of Grand Meister mantra?"

"It's for your own good."

"Just have a mojito ready." He hung up.

The remaining Nerds said their farewells, Winston sat and stared at the speaker phone.

"First question," Betsy said. "Dr. Fairchild?" Winston looked up at her.

"Who did the shoes?"

"That was Jack's idea."

"It was abso-fucking-lutely brilliant. Who's Jack?"

"I'm going to let you chew on that one for a while."

"Why Yanagi University?" Alice asked.

He told them about the public bath in Kyoto, and about Robby, who figured the Gamers deserved academic credit for their work.

"Why did you do it?" Claire asked.

"The Game?"

"No, the Black Dahlia Murder."

"It started as a prank. The original idea was to goose the world system, but we could never figure out how. We wanted to invent something that would impact the marketplace in a new way. Scratchy suggested we invent new people."

"New people?" Alice asked.

"Instead of a new tool, a new user. That took us into education, and the Game emerged."

"From the templates," Jennifer said. Winston nodded.

"We haven't made any money on this, quite the reverse. It's taken about all we've got to get this far."

"Your prank is probably the best single thing that's happened to the planet in a century or more," Betsy said.

"You called it a monstrosity."

"Even monsters can do good. The whole planet was headed for Nerdville anyhow, only you got us there in two years instead of two lifetimes. Now we have the opportunity to go further. You accelerated the process and gave us an engine to keep this going."

"Why do I feel like I strangled a puppy?"

"It's because you are low on doughnuts." Claire brought a plate of doughnuts around to him. They made lingering eye contact. Alice glanced over at Jennifer and grinned. Claire returned to her chair.

"We need lunch. We need sunshine. We need a long walk through an ancient settlement," Jennifer announced. "There are a million things to talk about and this room is closing in on us."

"Well, enjoy your afternoon," Winston said.

"Sorry, amigo." Alice came around the table to where Winston was sitting. She picked up a doughnut covered with powdered sugar. Winston looked up at her.

"I now brand you a full member of the Posse." She popped Winston on the forehead with the doughnut. A white circle remained. "Get your hiking shoes on."

Grinning, Winston looked around the room. The Posse returned his smile. "I guess we'd better all saddle up, pilgrims," he said in his best Duke voice.

He stood and his hand drifted to the doughnut plate. Alice backed off and ducked just as he shagged a crumb doughnut at her head; it hit the wall and rebounded. Jennifer caught Claire in the chin with a cinnamon hole, and the room erupted with flying pastries.

§   §   §

Megan was adamant. Claire could run off to Vietnam without her. Even the idea of hanging with the Grand Meister would not budge her. Claire argued that she could not leave Megan alone in the apartment, and Megan countered that the new GameTown was opening up near UCLA. Since Claire and the Grand Meister were such good friends, perhaps she would help Megan and her friend secure a room there.

"Don't even begin to say I'm too young," she said, pointing to her diploma on the wall of the kitchen.

"Eighteen is still the age of legal responsibility," Claire said.

"We'll have to work on that," Megan sounded serious.

Claire realized that was certainly true.

"Sao Do sounds charming; they even have a movie theater."

Megan made a gun with her finger and shot herself in the forehead.

"But what will you do?"

"I got a job."

"When?"

"Weeks ago, before the Game went down. I'm a barista at the Red Star Coffee house on Broxton in the Village."

"A job! Honey, you didn't tell me. What about your classes at Santa Monica City College?"

Megan just looked at her.

"OK. I get it."

"The work pays enough to keep me fed, I don't need many clothes."

"You've got an answer for everything." Claire couldn't believe she just said that.

"You're planning to be gone for months. I can stop by here and make sure the plants are OK, check the mail. I'm more useful here than moping around in Vietnam."

"In the summer, you'll come and visit. All right?"

"Sure, I'm not against travel, but I've got my own life to figure out."

"I don't know."

"You can always reach me. I'm either chatting on Junana, or I'm in the Game, or I have my phone. There will be a hundred Gamers around me, any one of which would cut off his right arm if the Grand Meister asked him to. So if I get in any kind of trouble, I'll contact you, and we'll work it out."

"You'll need to buckle down and finish Level Five." This signaled her capitulation. Megan came over and gave her a hug.

"For an anthropologist you sure worry a lot." She kissed her mom on the forehead. "Don't you have a lot of packing to do?"

The Westwood GameTown opened up the week after Claire left for Vietnam. Megan and her friend Juli moved in the first day. They had a third-floor cube with a view down toward Century City. Using her wages and tips and resident discount, Megan could afford the restaurants in the GameTown, with money left over to get down to the beach sometimes. She snuck into some lectures at UCLA but found them mega-tedious. One guy speaks, and three hundred people are supposed to sit there and bask in his intellectual wonderfulness. She came back to her cube and Queried the same content in five minutes.

§   §   §

Desi had predicted that Meisters would be those one-in-a-million players so absorbed in the Game, or else so compulsively obsessed, that they would not stop until they found the key that turned the templates into toys. Only then could they begin to wind and unwind the templates from root to capstone and back. Among the Meisters, perhaps one in a thousand would arrive at the transcendental point where these template strands became woven into an interlocking fabric. These would become Grand Meisters. Desi was the first Grand Meister to emerge. It still took him hours of contemplation on the overall emergent template structure to begin to walk between these as they raveled and unwound about him.

As a way of knowing the world, templates would disappoint anyone looking for clear signposts. Like Zen koan, they pointed obliquely to solution spaces for specific problems. While the problems were specific, the solutions were synthetic, poly-contextual, not quite arbitrary, but always relative. Fleas, they were, on Schrödinger's cat.

Scratchy's Noel template still anchored a part of the overall template tapestry and Intention-full grounded others, but floating outliers suggested still other, undiscovered anchor points, and even the possibility of hidden subtending templates.

If being a Grand Meister meant that Desi was all-knowing, then he was a poor one. Rather, he admitted to the Nerds, it just meant he had exhausted what the Game could offer. He had reached a point where his Queries began to soak up CPU time to the max that Scratchy had set up, at which point the Game replied using one of several non-committal answers from the Magic 8-Ball: "Reply hazy, try again," or "Better not tell you now."

"Being a Grand Master just means I can't play anymore," he groused.

§   §   §

Jennifer arrived at Sao Do from Paris through Hanoi, two days after the Santa Fe meeting. She flew to Hue and took the famous train ride to Danang, the tracks hugging the coast on vertiginous jungle ridges. Desi installed her in a cabana at the beachfront Hoi An hotel where they would all be staying. In fact, it was the same hotel where they held the third Nerdfest several years earlier. Jack had enlarged his equity stake in the hotel chain. A wing of cabanas were reserved for the whole group. Directly behind the hotel, the Thu Bon River led upstream to Hoi An proper and, 20 minutes by fast boat, to Sao Do.

Alice and Claire took new direct flight from LAX to Danang and shared a taxi to the hotel, riding down past China Beach and the new suburban housing developments. This looked way too much like Orange County, Claire observed, after the fifth gated community. Betsy took the same flight several days later. Annika and her new friend would housesit Betsy's Garden District home. They were insufferable, she knew, both of them in their yellow blouses, but they were reliable.

Her first night in Hoi An, Alice and Claire took Betsy to Ricardos. The setting was pure MGM: balustrades of teak, red tile floors, cream stucco walls, a view out across the broad Thu Bon river, a live salsa band, and waiters who floated around the room in starched white jackets. Giant ferns in Chinese ceramic pots gave each table its own privacy. Desi personally made them mojitos, which they could hardly accept from the Grand Meister.

"Don't be silly," he told them. "Besides," he said to Claire, "I knew you when you were a lascivious undergrad."

Desi doted on Betsy, whom he christened "Liz."

"You can call me Lucy," he told her. "I've got a little surprise for you." He led her off to the railing by the river. When she returned, she was all smiles.

"Such a gentleman," she said, "he knows the way to a geek's heart."

"Well?" Claire demanded.

So Betsy told her. The reason why they were staying at the hotel instead of Sao Do is because the guest lodge had been gutted and transformed into a supercomputer facility. The arrays from Japan and India had been shipped over and hooked up, all 4000 quad CPUs. She had top level access to the facility.

"Better than anything I could get through the NSF," Betsy concluded, "and a great mojito, too. Here's to Lucy!" She lifted her glass and they all toasted.

Winston and Scratchy had spent a week relaxing in Kona
before Jack's jet picked them up and delivered them to Danang.
Scratchy showed up at Ricardos wearing a tie-died hemp t-
shirt and shorts, which sent Desi into fashion hysterics.

"You're no better, Winston," Desi said, his hands on his hips
in a pretend huff. "Look at you there all dressed in Brooks
Brothers. It must be 95 degrees out. You'll both find some
clothes I picked out for you in your hotel rooms."

"I'm happy to see you, too, Lucy," Scratchy said. "You serve
alcohol in this joint? We've only been flying all fucking day."

"Dear boy, you must be parched!" Desi led them to the bar.

§   §   §

Every Meister could link a chain of templates together given
any one template as a starting point. But when Desi challenged
the 108 Meisters to discover completely new templates, the
results were not immediately positive. Another week went by
with little to show.

"Maybe they are all nerds too," he suggested to Scratchy,
"and can't think of anything else as important."

They gathered together evenings upstairs at Ricardos in
Desi's apartment, with the windows open wide to the river
breezes.

"I'm afraid we're at an impasse," Itchy said.

"You are assuming that the templates have arbitrary limits,"
Jennifer replied. "I don't accept that."

"You got an alternative?" Scratchy said.

"We need to hook into some source of new template
territory outside the Game," Betsy said. "Maybe Constantine
can help?"

"I've already been in contact with him," Desi said, shaking his head. "He's got nothing new to contribute."

"It's not as though the templates came out of thin air," Claire added. "We're looking for new ways of skilling. Who's been writing about this?"

"We've covered the literature on multiple intelligences," Alice said.

"There's a book I heard about just recently," Jennifer said. "Something about five skillings. It got a fabulous review in the Sunday Times a couple weeks back."

§ § §

The very next morning, Jennifer woke up Desi, pounding on the back door of his apartment at sunrise.

"This is it!" she held up a USB stick as she strode to the center of the main room.

"Nothing is 'it' until I have a cup of coffee, deary." Desi sent her to the kitchen and excused himself to get dressed. He returned and she put a mug of highland-grown, Italian-roasted coffee in his hand.

The Five Skillings, she told him, as outlined in a series of books entitled *Getting to Zero* by Anjali, a psychotherapist in Montecito, are these: intellect, language, body, social, and internal voice.

"Sounds like psychotripe from the self-help section," Desi said.

"Read the books and then you can be snide," Jennifer said. "I'm going for a walk. I'll meet you at the Tam Tam Cafe for breakfast." She handed him the USB stick.

"You finish your homework?" Desi sat down in the rattan chair opposite hers. He leaned back, a smile blossomed. A waiter came up and set a ca phe sua nong and a fresh croissant in front of him. Desi thanked him.

"No, thank you, Grand Meister." The waiter bowed and left.

"Templates cascade through these Skillings," Jennifer said. "She captured these so well. We just need to tease them out..."

Desi nodded and spoke, "The Intellect is the home of curiosity and the province of memory. Language is the palace of poetry and the workshop of the mind. The Body is the first connection to the world. All other connections are built on the Body. The Internal Voice is the only friend we have at birth and death. It is the backstop for all other actions. The ability to exist alone, to be guided and comforted by one's own philosophy, this is the primary skill that allows the individual to be social. Social skilling creates healthy boundaries and openings for intimacy with others."

"You know, the author's now a Sixer," Jenn said. "I think she'll make a great Meister at some point. Early this morning, I called her to meet me at the Sorbonne scene and we had a long conversation. She's in full agreement about us using her work without restriction in the Game. The work was released with a Creative Commons license."

"I really, really like her thoughts about unskilling the childhood defenses," Desi said. "Before you can be skilled you need to become unskilled in the initial defense mechanisms that the child uses to cope. The Game has to help us remove the early tricks we used to get through our childhood so that we can learn a new set of skills for adulthood."

"We tend to look for traumas, but most people are trapped by the successes they experience as infants." Jennifer noted. "They learn to manipulate their parents and others and carry these skills into their adult lives. And the schools are no help at all."

"The skills they put together as three-year-olds..." Desi said.

"...get in the way of acting in the world as adults."

"So the answer is not to kill your parents, but rather to kill an infant that still runs your life. And that's you."

"Kill the infant, but keep the child within. If you have enough loving support as an infant, you enter childhood without the need for rigid coping skills. This means you are ready to cross over into adulthood as a teenager."

"But if your parents are too busy..."

"...or too stressed,"

"...or too much controlled by their own internal infant,"

"...exactly. Then they end up raising infants instead of adults."

SECTION THREE

The Five Skillings

TWENTY-FIVE

With more than three-hundred advanced Gamers in the Town, everybody had a lot to talk about, although the Fivers tended to stick together, and the Sixers were just stuck-up. There were even a few Meisters, but they were busy with some project they couldn't talk about. A lot of the resident Gamers also worked in the Town: in the restaurants, the gym, the office, the baths, or in maintenance. All workers got an additional discount at the restaurants. Megan was on the list to become a barista in the GameTown Red Star.

The baths in the basement of the GameTown were intimidating at first, but then she relaxed and discovered that chatting in the tubs was easy and fun even with strangers. The staff had to explain about washing up and rinsing off before getting into the tubs, but then it all made perfect sense.

Yesterday, her Guide, Bobby, showed up in Junana and they talked for like five hours straight. All Fivers, Sixers, and Meisters could now talk to their Guides in Junana. GameTowns across the planet buzzed with new excitement. Bobby was hurt that Megan didn't go to Sao Do. She could be helping the Grand Meister reinvent the Game. What did he mean by that? She asked. But he wouldn't say.

Level Five was a complete biotch. She was getting nowhere. Without Bobby, it seemed like a whole different experience. Level Five is more difficult than the other four levels combined, Bobby explained. That's why only one in an million gets through it. Like that was going to make her feel better. Level Six is, Bobby said, even harder, which is why people who complete it are truly Meisters. Only one person has made it through Level Seven. Megan began to feel that everything she learned in the Game made her less capable of understanding how the world could have gotten so completely screwed up. The world outside the Game read like some dark Bruce Sterling post-apocalyptic novel. Wars in the Middle East, global warming, orange alerts, fear-fuelled news, instant celebrity drivel. Who was going to fix all of that? The Game is all about questions. Who has the answers?

§   §   §

After consulting with the Nerds and the Posse, Jennifer and Desi called all of the Meisters to Castalia, where they outlined the Five Skillings. They stood in the middle of the central square surrounded by dozens of avatars.

"The Internal Voice is the voice of reflection and reason, the quiet whisper of philosophy and wonder that each individual needs to cultivate to be successfully alone," Desi told them, in what would later be called "The Sermon of the Skillings."

"If you cannot be successfully alone, you can never be successfully social," Jennifer continued. "Learn to be your own teacher, friend, and critic. This skill is central to life. Here is where Intention-full promotes reflexive awareness.

"Language is the key to meaning. The meaning you build in your life will be expressed through language. It is the province of the poetic and the sword of the intellect. Here is where Intention-full promotes comprehension." She nodded to Desi, who took up her line of reasoning.

"The Intellect is where you learn to be curious and critical. Here is where Intention-full promotes understanding. This is the engine for education and one of the two vehicles for status. The other is the Body. The Body is the first point of attachment you have to the surrounding world. All of the rest of the attachments to the world depend on your skilling with and through the body. When you walk down the street, sing karaoke, or stroke the thigh of your lover, you are an embodied being. Here is where Intention-full promotes virtuosity and playfulness." He nodded back at her.

"All of the other four arenas of skilling come into force in the Social. Skilling in the Social is all about boundaries: knowing when and where to be open or closed to the intentions of others. Skilling in Language and the Body gives you the clues you need to interpret the meanings and the desires of those around you. Skilling in the Internal Voice affords you a critical distance from the social world. Skilling in the Intellect gives you capital to spend in society. Here is where Intention-full promotes intimacy." She stopped.

"We need to move ahead with the next version of the Game." Desi walked among the Meisters, who dipped their heads in deference. "If we don't start to get results in a week, we will shut down the Game." He paused for effect.

"Everybody needs to redouble their efforts. Please. Right now you're the Game's only hope." The Five Skillings talk was recorded and played continuously in Castalia as Meisters checked in across the planet.

The first new template arrived 18 hours later. Within four days they had capstone templates for three of the five Skillings. The Meisters readily pushed these through their entire unfolding structures. The teams at Sao Do wove these into the Intention-full framework for Level Two. Wanda and Jorge were hired to video a Body skilling class based on the work of Master Lu, a Chinese kung fu and acupuncture practitioner from Hong Kong whose methods were suggested by several

Meisters. The Lu workout would be a third training all Level
Two players took. It required an inflated ball the size of a
cantaloupe. Jack made these available at all Red Star Coffee
houses. Within two weeks the Meisters had ferreted out the
template structures for Internal Voice and the Social.

§   §   §

The Sao Do village compound became the default test bed for
Version 2.0. Sao Do Gamers tackled the new Level Two. Over
the next several weeks, Desi watched for signs of change. The
first thing he noticed was music. When he walked through the
complex, the apartments were bursting with song, from
recordings or people practicing instruments. The next thing
was the compound bulletin board. Instead of the usual used-
furniture sales, he noticed postings for events and requests for
spaces to practice. The compound store sold out of art supplies
one week, and Desi ordered up a whole catalog of paper, ink,
paint, brushes, clay, and canvas from Hanoi. He arranged for
the main hall to be open and available for performances and
rehearsals every evening. He emailed Jack, who preloaded new
kiosks at the GameTowns with artist supplies.

The next step was to get all of the Meisters on board with
the new Level Two training. This proved more eventful than
Desi had hoped.

"What do you mean, we have to learn these new templates,"
shouted one of the more outspoken 15-year-olds, dressed in a
forest green wizard robe. "What's the point of becoming a
Meister if somebody can tell us what to do?" This sent the
assembly into a frenzy of heated conversation. Desi looked
around and noticed that the great majority of the Meisters were

not yet of legal drinking age. He was about to say it was for their own good, but stopped himself. Instead, he pulled rank.

"What's your name?" he asked.

"I am Simon, of the Dark Mage Eldrick," the lad replied.

"Well, Simon of the Dark Mage Eldrick, whoever that is, when you become a Grand Meister, nobody can tell you what you need to do. Until then, you and all the Meisters will volunteer to go through Level Two and pick up the templates for the Five Skillings. Only then will you be allowed back into Castalia." For effect, he thumped the base of his staff on the marble plinth where he stood. This echoed convincingly.

"If we are to be leaders of the Game," Desi called out, "We need to be its keepers. I'm going back to Level Two, and I will see all of you here in Castalia when we master these new templates!" Desi logged out of Castalia into the Room.

"Who murdered your cat?" Itchy asked him from the console. Desi's avatar had been storming around the perimeter of the Room, waving his staff.

"I'm not sure Castalia was such a great idea. The Meisters are a gang of petulant infants."

"Many of them don't even drive a car yet," Itchy said, "but they are what the Game is all about."

"Have you finished programming the new requirements for level advancement?" Desi asked.

"In the testing queue right now, to be implemented overnight. This will take everyone, including Grand Meisters, back to Level Two for regrooving."

"Adios Nerdville!" Desi said.

§   §   §

For their investment, the Reverend Gerry Bishop had requested and received the right to put his UCCC cathedral at the top of each and every Junana Plaza, all one thousand of them. The RIND designers asked him how big and he told them, "Big as anything on the planet. Big as that Papist monstrosity in Rome. Big enough for ten thousand with plenty of elbow room."

Gerry had always admired the Duomo di Sienna. He had been dazzled by the whole confusion of romanesque and early gothic elements, the black and white pillars, the mosaics on the floors, the overwhelming confection of the architecture. He had the RIND nerd team use the plans for this and their ultra-high-resolution imagery and simply boosted the size up to a million cubic meters. Working with the RIND digital artists, he inserted his favorite Norman Rockwell-esque images into the stained glass, jettisoned the Catholic bric-a-brac, and inserted transporters into every column.

Gerry's pulpit was reworked in black marble and the lighting made him completely visible even from the narthex. His avatar was a larger, slimmer, younger version of himself. A battalion of angels, based on the Wanda and Jorge avatars, dressed in tasteful white robes with the cutest white feathery wings all tucked back, led each worshipper to her seat. As soon as a player's avatar entered the space they could sing any song in the hymnal. Bishop would record a new service every Saturday and this would play on alternate hours for the next two days. The flow of Junana bucks into the offering plates alone could bring in fifty million Euros a month.

Outside the UCCC cathedrals, all of the new Junana was commercial property: a thousand splendid shopping malls, each of them larger than anything on the planet. Players could buy all their virtual clothing, jewelry, vehicles, apartments, entertainments, and other goods using the Game currency,

which was convertible with all major world currencies.
Physical copies of many of the virtual goods could be delivered
overnight.

When they first logged in, players were given a suit of white
underwear for modesty. Every player got a personal shopping
guide for Junana. Promotions were also georeferenced to stores
within a mile of the player's location. Helpful advertisements
popped up in the visual range of the player when she arrived at
Junana.com. The consortium purchased the domain name
"Unana.com" as the URL for the new service.

Media, sport, and music celebrity figures circulated, chatted
with players, and offered promotional deals for events and
upcoming TV specials.

All that was missing were the players. The RIND
Corporation kept announcing internally that they expected to
hack the code within days. After six months of that, Gerry
stopped the next payment on the Church's investment. He got a
call from Harold the next morning.

"Reverend Bishop," said Harold. "Is there any way I can
answer your concerns?"

"Stop jerking my chain and get me those billion
worshippers you promised. Soon as you do that, you'll see the
rest of our cash."

"Your cathedrals turned out...splendidly," Harold said,
amazed how an astonishing lack of taste on an unprecedented
scale can result in something so hideous it achieves a kind of
sick greatness.

"I need to see butts in those pews. Good bye, Harold."

§ § §

Some later called it "The Year of the Five Skillings," although it was closer to ten months. It was the last coherent interlude of the first great wave of the Game. Junana had hit its saturation limit in the global population, pushed flush against the digital divide. There were not enough Computos and cell phones to reach the billions on the other side. On this side of the divide, almost everyone probably knew about Junana and most had accounts. A majority had at least tasted the Game, and most of these had made it to Level Two.

With all the advanced players and their Guides back at Level Two, picking up the new templates for the Skillings, the entire planet seemed to be breathing in unison. The Skillings blossomed in a thousand different manners across the globe. But the impact on the players was roughly similar from Lagos to Los Angeles.

The first reaction was often chagrin, something of an indulgence. The Guides would say, "How can you feel bad that you didn't know something that was only made available now?" The next reaction was usually fascination as the Intellect is the Home of Curiosity template learning kicked in. Master Lu had noted that it takes a full eight weeks for any new skilling to settle into the body, and so the five Skillings were designed to be digested over a space of forty weeks. Of course, becoming adept at any of the Skillings was a life-long effort. That was the entire point. One got better at it.

The Red Star factories in Danang manufactured hundreds of millions of Master Lu's Body Balls, those melon-sized inflated balls that were the all the equipment needed for the Body is the First Connection template workout, again with an instructional video led by Jorge and Wanda under Master Lu's direction. The balls were shipped to all the Red Star Coffee outlets for distribution. Each player's Guide announced what the price would be, based on the player's finances. The

payment was made on the honor system. The monies collected
eventually covered all the costs. In many locations across the
planet most balls were given away free. Jack was entirely
satisfied by this arrangement, and the Sao Do crews
implemented it for all the other clothing in the Game, which
was now stocked and made available directly through 7000
Red Star Coffee outlets.

The third reaction to the Skillings was an interlude of
silence, a gigantic collective global in-breath as hundreds of
millions of players began to monitor their internal voice. Even
the Guides fell silent here, knowing their voices did not matter.
The template structure for this skilling had been unfolded by a
young female Meister from a small village in the desert of
Namibia, whose internal voice had saved her even before she
found the Game. Her Guide, Annaline, was so very proud of
her, as were the students in her new school.

The lasting reaction to the Skillings, and the desired
outcome, was an irresistible impulse for conversation and a
growing desire to play. Play, in this sense, harkens back to its
original sense, preserved in "swordplay" and "wordplay"; that
is, the exercise of a skill, the ability to wield an object, a
thought, or a phrase in a manner better than one did yesterday.
As the original Game was Intention-full, the newly expanded
Game could only be described as play-full.

§   §   §

Peter had never seen Simon so angry, not even when their
father tossed away Simon's D&D deck.

"Nobody disses the Dark Mage," Simon kept ranting,
throwing whatever he could get his hands on.

After that Simon locked himself in his dorm room and hardly ever came out. He skimmed the Haverbrook KayAye lessons, zoomed through the Five Skillings without seeming to learn any of them as far as Peter could tell. He did the minimum needed to get back to Level Seven and then cloistered himself inside the task of mastering the Game.

For Peter the skillings opened up a world outside the church and school, a place filled with music and conversation. He picked up a digital drum set and was getting pretty good at it. Most of the students were Gamers. Rector Hector retreated to his apartments, venturing out furtively for chapel. Some of the faculty used the KayAye in defiance of policy. The school van took students into town three afternoons a week. Courtney introduced him to Anthony, a Haverbrook sophomore learning guitar.

Together, their Guides introduced them to some town girls. Tiffanie and Roxy, who played keyboard and bass. Their band practiced in Roxy's garage. Tiffanie let Peter kiss her and he held her breast through her t-shirt and bra. Courtney advised him that Tiffanie was a better band member than a girl friend. She had not earned her shoes. Still, a kiss and a feel were better than nothing, which what what he was getting as a Haverbrook dork.

Peter asked Courtney to ask Simon's Guide if everything were all right with him. Eldrick reported to Courtney that Simon was close to the end of Level Seven and had chosen not to be disturbed. Peter tried to digest this information. It made no sense to him. Nobody finishes Level Seven except a Grand Meister.

TWENTY-SIX

By the middle of the "Year of the Five Skillings," hundreds of millions were simply having the time of their lives, and much of it outside the Game. "Go play your instrument, or go paint something," Guides would order and close down the Game for hours. GameTowns grew cacophonous. Music shops and art stores sold and sold until their shelves were bare.

Back in Sao Do, the compound was ringing with music, theater, and dance. Improvisational Hát chèo theater groups formed and performed almost nightly. Desi joined one of these and took to drumming. Itchy explored photography and Delta blues guitar. Jennifer became fascinated by the ancient Hindu kingdoms, the ruins of which were just inland. Winston and Claire explored each other. All of them advised Scratchy and Betsy to join the Game.

"You're the most impossible, improbable luddites in the world," Desi scolded when he caught up to them at the computer center. "Here you are, king and queen of the nerds and you won't even try the Game!"

Betsy held up one of Anjali's books. "It's called cellulose, you make paper out of it, print on it and bind it. Over time it generates the same effect as the Game."

"We've been trolling the Game for unexpected consequences," Scratchy said. "We were wondering if you unfolded some aphrodisiac template. I'm tracking the Junana back-chatter, and it seems that a lot of Gamers, I'm talking millions here, are getting really frisky.

"They're teenagers," Desi reminded them.

"Maybe Red Star should be passing out protection with those body balls." Back in his room, Scratchy had been doing Master Lu's program every night. He'd lost about twenty pounds. Not that anybody noticed.

"Have you seen Claire and Winston lately?" Desi grinned.

"They are probably learning the oboe, writing sonnets, or painting landscapes on the river. Whole fucking planet's one big amateur hour," said Scratchy.

"Everyone has to start somewhere," Desi answered.

"I haven't seen them around, actually," Betsy said.

"My point entirely! And I'd guess they're not on the Game."

"Median player Game time is down over thirty percent," Betsy said.

"That doesn't sound good," Desi said.

"But it is. It means the players are finding better reasons to turn off their screens," Betsy said. "The Skillings are starting to kick in."

"That's exactly what Jenn told me," Desi said, "'We'll know the Game succeeds when the last player shuts off her computer.'"

"And who told the Guides they could act as match-makers?" Scratchy asked.

"Really! That's interesting."

"We all pledged to not use the Game to advance our own interests. Now it seems the Game has acquired its own interests, and we don't have a clue what those are," said Scratchy.

"Itchy and I have been meaning to talk to you about the Guides. For months we've known that they can talk with each other."

"They what?" said Betsy.

"I've been working on it..." Desi said sheepishly. "This capacity is woven into their learned behavior matrix. And we haven't been able to decipher their message stream."

"You've got several hundred million game pieces communicating internally, and you don't know what they are saying?" Her eyes shot up. "Do you know how 'not good' that can become?"

"We can turn them off completely before they rise up in revolt. We do this for a living, you know."

"Small fucking comfort that is."

"She's right, you know," said Scratchy. But then Betsy was the least wrong person he'd ever encountered. This impressed him almost as much as it fascinated him. "So the Guides are talking with each other? Why didn't you bring this up right away?"

"We wanted to crack their code first, but they're not using any language we know." Desi remembered the months they spent contemplating creating a new language. Looked like they had done that too, only none of Nerds could speak it.

"Great!" Betsy folded her arms and glared at Desi.

"I have to go," Desi announced. "Claire's daughter Megan is arriving at Danang today. She brought her new boyfriend. I hear he's very cute." He beat a quick retreat.

Betsy turned to Scratchy. "Did I just hear the wheels coming off this buggy?"

"Hey! We've simply opened some doors here and we don't know what's on the other side. It's called innovation...."

"That's one word for it."

"...On the up side, we just let a hundred thousand Sixers into Castalia. The grounds are swarming. We gave the Fivers back their Guides in Junana as some kind of ghost buddies. We kicked anomie's ass."

"It's true, suicides are well below pre-Game levels world-wide."

"What are they supposed to talk about in Junana, these nubile pubescent players and their ghost Guides: the weather? the stock market?"

"That cute girl or boy in their homeroom."

"Exactly so; a few million players began to ask their new Guide friends if they can get that cute girl's Guide to put in a good word..."

"...But that cute girl's Guide knows she's a vindictive bitch who needs someone with really good boundaries to get her straight. So they find someone else for the player."

"...someone that only a Guide can locate, who fits the player's Game profile exactly."

"With that kind of input to their learning routine the Guides could get pretty good at this."

"The Guides know more about their players than any friend could possibly know; more than any online dating service."

"In that case, dating might be the most practical outcome of the entire Game," Scratchy offered. "I hear wedding bells all over the planet."

"Everyone falls in love when they're in high school; only it's not meant to last. Puppy love is supposed to hurt like hell and then go away. You get over it, and you go get bruised and battered by serial dating for a decade before you figure out that you're really just looking for someone to talk to. Meeting Mr. Right at the wrong time isn't any better than meeting Mr. Wrong anytime."

"I'm not so sure 17 is the same after the Game. What does 17 feel like when you know that much?" Scratchy said. "Anyhow, kids finding each other is arguably better than kids killing themselves."

"And kids getting master's degrees at 17 is arguably better than kids sleeping through high school history class. But we don't know what 'better' really means here. 'Different' is not automatically better."

"We may not have to worry about any of this for very long."

"Meaning...?"

"My security squad is just barely keeping up with the hackers. They could bring us down any day now. We get thousands of probes and hundreds of high-level attacks a day."

"I've got a fool-proof back-up plan for you," she offered.

"What's that?"

She held up Anjali's book. "It's called cellulose."

§   §   §

Nick complied with the captain's instructions and turned off his MP3 player. He nudged Megan awake and leaned over her to look out the window as the Airbus banked to line up for landing in Danang. She rubbed her eyes and did the "Don't kiss me, I just woke up" thing with her hand over her mouth. He kissed her lightly on the temple as he sat back, and she took hold of his arm and pressed it against her.

"It's really hard to believe we're going to meet the Grand Meister," he said. It felt exactly like the first time he went to Disneyland as a little kid, standing in front of the turnstile, gripping his mom's hand. There hadn't been many moments this good between then and now. Except for the day he met Megan. That was the shit to end all shit. He would never forget that day.

Their Guides, Cindy and Bobby, had cooked this whole thing up. About three months after the new skill templates showed up and everyone went back to Level Two, they arranged for Nick to get transferred down to Westwood as a waiter in the Vietnamese vegetarian restaurant. Cindy showed Nick Megan's photo and ordered Nick to check her profile.

"She is abso-fucking-lutely perfect for you, cowboy. So I'm going to tell you how to treat her right, you know, when the time comes."

For a Game piece who once told him she was 'no woman,' Cindy had this really encyclopedic and sometimes embarrassingly graphic information about how a woman should be touched. Cindy required him do the set of Queries he'd heard rumors about, which covered topics from verbal intimacy to erotic foot massage. By the time he arrived in LA the one thing he knew for certain was that pulling his weight in a relationship was going to take as much focus and energy as another level in the Game.

"Don't worry about it," Cindy said. "Megan's done the same Queries. You two are going stick together like super magnets."

Megan wore dark jeans and a white tee, cut fairly low, which fit her like paint. He took her order, feeling distinctly like a fool in his fugly waiter's jacket. She looked up at him and gave out the smallest smile. He blushed like she'd just yanked down his shorts.

"Bring me the best thing in the restaurant, cowboy," she said. Bobby told her Nick's Guide called him "cowboy."

"That would be me," he returned her smile. "You might also want something from the menu." He hoped he hadn't overdone it.

"I'll start with a bowl of Grand Meister Pho. I'll get to you later." She handed back the menu and their hands touched. He was suddenly glad to be wearing a jacket.

He kept checking in on her, filling her water, comping her snacks. She nibbled for maybe five hours until his shift was over. He came out in his favorite Volcom tee and jeans and sat down across from her.

"My roommate's gone tonight," she announced, "want to come up and talk?"

They didn't have sex that night, but they did everything else. It felt so good just being together that they could have water-boarded each other and still had a great time. She moved into his room the next day. It was like they were brother and sister, best childhood friends, frantic lovers, and an old married couple all at once. It was exciting, amazing, and oddly comfortable by turns.

Three months later and here he was, off to spend weeks in Vietnam with her, her mom, the Grand Meister, and Scratchy O'hara too. He glanced out the window again. Vietnam looked a lot like Goleta, only smoggier.

"Harder still to think that my mom has been hanging with the Grand Meister for seven whole months." Megan tried to smooth down the sleep kinks in her hair with her hands. Her brush was up in her bag.

"You look terrific," Nick said. "Disheveled becomes you."

She slumped back in her seat. "Wait till she sees the tatt." She rolled her eyes. A month after moving into GameTown, Megan and some friends went to this tattoo place down in Santa Monica. Megan got them to do Marmalade's head on her ankle. It was completely phat. Her mom would hate it.

"Wait till she sees me," Nick said.

"You, she will love," Megan predicted. "Or I will never speak to her again."

She remembered him coming up to her at the restaurant in his waiter costume, all shy and excited. Bobby had shown her his photo, and she'd almost memorized his bioform, so she thought she was prepared. He said something really clever, she remembered. Then he brushed her hand when he took her menu and she thought she was going to cream right there in her seat, like in that old movie with Meg Ryan. Bobby never told her about the electricity. She hung out and tried to act uninterested while she followed him with her eyes all afternoon. He kept bringing her spring rolls and filling her water glass. She had to go pee half a dozen times.

Megan was fully prepared to take him upstairs and do the dirty, but he was just so sweet and she didn't want it to end; this delicious anticipation. They touched and talked and stroked and talked and kissed and talked and the excitement lingered until they both fell asleep near sunrise entwined on her single bed, still fully clothed.

When she woke up, they were spooned and his hand was was cradling her tummy. She kissed him awake and asked him right away if she might move to his room. He could hardly say no. That's when they did it. She had a full-on joygasm before he even really got started and two more before he collapsed. Seemed like he just lit her fuse and off she went. It hurt a bit too. Bobby had warned her it might. The last few weeks all Bobby would talk about on Junana was this special set of Queries, which everyone at Gametown was calling "Sex Ed 101." In between them he had this whole presentation about what to expect and how to stay safe.

Megan and Nick squeezed together in her little shower and nearly did it again just from the soapy friction, but Nick was almost dead from hunger. They'd skipped dinner last night and he had worked through lunch. So they got dressed and headed down to the restaurant floor. After lattes and breakfast burritos at the GameTown Red Star, where she was now the head barista, he helped her move.

When she unpacked she discovered Nick had most of the same books she did; like entire collections of Doctorow and Burdett. Bobby and Cindy, both of them way too self-congratulatory about Megan and Nick moving in together, processed the roommate switch request with Nick's floor monitor's Guide. This made everything legit as far as GameTown was concerned. Nick was sure his mom didn't care. Megan was sure her mom would freak. They put the two beds together, splurged on new sheets at Restoration Hardware, and bought an ugly cheap sofa at Urban Outfitters.

The Airbus landed on what might be the world's largest runway, built by the Americans during their Vietnam adventure. Megan and Nick had Queried up the war and more recent information about Vietnam. Customs was expedited by the help of an official who took their passports and led them into an air-conditioned office.

"Sit here, friends of the Grand Meister." He pulled some colas from a small refrigerator. "I will not be long."

Several minutes later they were pushing their luggage on the cart through the Green Line and out to where Megan saw her mother making that happy wave thing by holding up her hand and wiggling her fingers. A tall, amazingly handsome East Indian man stood next to her. Is that him? Megan looked over at Nick, who was walking much too slow.

"Speed it up, cowboy," she whispered. "Let's get this over with."

There were hugs all around, even after Megan introduced Nick by saying, "Mom, this is Nicholas. Nick and I are a couple in every imaginable sense of the word." This struck the Grand Meister as funny, and his laughter got them all through the moment.

"You simply must call me 'Desi,'" the Grand Meister insisted. "Lord knows I'm not the Pope!"

On the ride back, Nick sat in the middle between Megan and her mom. Desi sat up front. The road was windy and the driver fast. The mood was high. Desi talked about how the five skillings were transforming the Game space, and how lucky they were that Claire and her friends had joined the team.

Megan used the left-hand curves to push against Nick, sending him sideways into her mom. He'd apologize and give Meg a scolding look, which she did not appreciate. So she tucked her hand between his legs and squeezed this spot on his thigh she know had a predictable effect. Nick squirmed in his seat and pushed her hand away. Claire covered a smile by looking out her window.

Desi turned to look at them and said to Claire, "If these two aren't the happiest couple on the planet, although you and Winston are a close second."

"Winston?" Megan leaned across Nick to hear her mom's response. "Who is this "Winston" of which I've been hearing?"

"Well..." Claire hesitated.

Desi cut in. "Your mom and Winston go way back. When she was not much older than you, they were a couple in every imaginable way, but only for about two days. You know, they took mushrooms and ran naked through a public golf course."

"Way too much information!" Megan said, throwing up her hands.

"I agree," Claire said.

"Don't stop," Nick grinned. "We should always be open to learn from our elders."

"That's a word you could go all day without ever saying again," Claire noted.

"All I'm saying is that we are losing track of what it was like, you know, before."

"Before what?"

"The Game, of course."

Desi and Claire shared a glance.

"Oh, my God! He's right!" Desi said. "Now I feel positively... Neanderthal."

§   §   §

Essie entered the classroom and hung her red cloak on the
hook reserved for it alone. A dozen students, eleven girls and
one boy, sat at their desks with hands folded in front of their
Computos. Three of them wore the hats, and one girl, Miina,
had her shoulder bag.

"*Wa lala po*, class," Essie greeted them.

"*Wa lala po*, Meister Essie," they replied in unison.

Already it was hot, and their uniforms were heavy. But they
would never imagine coming to school without them, any
more than they could imagine leaving class without first
sweeping out the room.

"This morning you will be Querying with your Guides," she
said. "I see no reason not to do so over at the river, where the
breeze is steady."

The students relaxed and smiled at each other.

"This afternoon, after our lunch, we will be working on our
English conversation and discussing the political argument
between John Locke and Thomas Hobbes. The KayAye has had
you Query their work over the weekend, so I expect a lively
debate.

"Yes, Meister Essie," they replied in unison.

§   §   §

At the very posh beachfront hotel, Nick was given a key to his
room. An extra bed had been ordered for Claire's suite.

"Now you're just being stupid," Megan snapped at Claire.
"Anyhow, aren't you sleeping with Winston?"

"I'm not your warden," Claire admonished. "You can sleep wherever you wish. The bed is simply there if you need it."

Megan then gave her mom the real hug she'd been saving all this time. "I think you've really grown these last months," she said.

"That's my line!" Claire drank in her daughter's display of affection.

"Yeah, I just thought I'd try it out."

"It fits all of us pretty well." Winston had also changed in these months, she mused. "We've all learned a lot."

Megan held her mom's hand and they moved to the balcony overlooking the pool.

"I know I'm just at the start of this long winding path, and you're up there on a plateau looking down at all the twists and ravines I've got to navigate," Megan said. "I'm just really happy I'll have Nicky with me when the rope bridge washes out. And this metaphor is now crashing pitifully around my ankles."

"Your Guides sent you through Sex Ed 101?" Claire asked.

Megan blushed. "The whole enchilada. You know about that?"

"Both of us got the same lessons. Probably at the same time."

That's freaky," Megan said mostly to herself. She looked down at her feet. "Speaking of ankles..."

Megan used the tip of one shoe to roll down the sock on the other foot. Marmalade's head poked out.

"Nice tatt!" Claire said.

"What!" Megan started. "That's it?"

"But not as nice as mine." Claire rolled up her shirtsleeve to reveal a small red design. The familiar outline of a cloak, identical to Jenn's.

"You made it!" Megan jumped and clapped her hands. "Look!" she called Nick over.

"Way to go, Claire!" he smiled.

Claire stepped up and hugged him. "Just don't ever, let me repeat, ever, call me 'mother,'" she whispered into his ear.

§   §   §

"This is not a coffeehouse! Kindly remove your hats," Amanda Baxter reminded her students. She was wearing her yellow blouse for effect. Hats disappeared into blue shoulder bags. Amanda glanced at the faces of her class, their desks gathered in a semicircle. Their eyes carried intelligence, a hint of defiance, a spark of curiosity, and not a whisper of hostility.

She figured there would not be a single floater in the group. They were dressed in a melange of recent retro fashions, thrift store bargains and garage-sale finds. A lot of home sewing in evidence; kids were now mashing up their own fashions. She noticed that every one of them was covered up, even Britany Sloane, who wore an oversized grey sleeveless sweatshirt upon which someone had neatly hand lettered, "Derrida can kiss my derrière."

"Welcome back. This is a class for Fourveys and above. We are starting with a discussion, so you can close your laptops," she wrote the name on the blackboard out of habit and turned to them. "Your KayAye had you query up his work on hermeneutic anthropology. Oh yes, how many of you are in the Pinter play this Friday?"

Several hands went up. "You'll be excused early. Your Guides will let you know what you missed. I'm assuming you read *Time and Narrative* over the Christmas break."

"Or last night!" Sam Cross quipped. The class laughed. Sam reminded her greatly of Nick Landreu. Her Guide told her

Nick has founded a theater group in Westwood based on the
street theater forms he discovered while in Vietnam.

"Well, Sam. If you read all three volumes last night, I would
suggest we move back, because your head might explode at any
time."

"You're telling me!" he said.

"Let's begin our conversation on Paul Ricoeur's concept of
'narrativity,'" she continued. "Britany, will you start us out?"

§   §   §

Simon awoke from a troubled sleep. He had dreamed he was
encased in spider webs, wound about him like a shroud. The
webs turned into templates. Try as he might he could not
unfold them. They tightened around his face, smothering him.

He sat up in bed, his room diffused by the dawn. He
grabbed a pint of milk from the mini-fridge and went to his
computer. As it booted he did the Brainwave movements
without effort or thought. His thoughts were already on the
templates. The whole structure of the Game unwound before
him as he Queried up a new approach. He had been neglecting
the province of the Five Skillings, still stung by the rebuke he
felt from the Grand Meister. He would need to reexamine these
if he was to move ahead.

The sunset threw sharp shadows on his monitor as he
unwound the Social template a final time. He closed his eyes as
he typed. He no longer needed the visual clues to wend his way
back to the root template. The Social did not socket back to
Intention-full or Noel; it was grounded outside of these, but
where? Not intention, not choice, but action.

Action was the missing root. The third leg out there, just
beyond his grasp. He pointed his Query in that direction and

was on the verge of attaining a purchase on the problem of
agency when the Game seemed to freeze for a time, like the
video stuck on a frame. This had happened several times in the
past week. He waited, his stomach grumbled at him. He closed
his eyes and continued his Query mentally. Action requires
intention and choice and something more, a field. Yes, an
open-ended field. A new chain of templates unfolded in front
of him. The field of action is two sided. One side is grounded
in the past, the other side is necessarily underdetermined.
Agency transforms intention through choice into action.
Simon opened his eyes. Then the Game screen displayed:

"Answer Hazy, Try Again."

Suddenly his avatar was holding a tall wooden staff. An
instant later the Game simply quit. Not like it might normally,
back when Eldrick told him go eat. It just threw him out and
went black.

"Wait a minute? What just happened?"

He tried to log back in but the connection timed out. Then
he logged into Junana. He was redirected to something called
Unana.com.

"What the...!" He spun his avatar around to get a good a
look at his home plaza. Behind him, towering like some
monumental Aztec pyramid was a church the size of a football
stadium. An enormous rose window glowed psychedelic from
the interior lighting. Towering spires vanished into the dark
sky. Above the massive medieval doors he could make out
words carved in stone. Ultra-Conservative Congregationalist
Convention.

"Oh, no!" he cried.

Simon covered his face with his hands. Someone was a
pounding on his dorm room door. They did not sound happy.

The Five Skillings

TWENTY-SEVEN

As the Year of the Five Skillings drew to its end, the Nerds and
the Posse gathered most nights in Desi's apartment on the top
floor of the building that housed Ricardos. Salsa soaked
through the floor while they finished off their ca phe sua nong
and pastries and talked through the evening. Desi had hijacked
an actual Cuban jazz ensemble touring Vietnam on a cultural
exchange; they now played five nights a week for a salary
several times what they made in Havana. Tonight, Betsy
announced she had isolated the source of what Scratchy was
calling the aphrodisiac quality of the Game.

"The Game teaches men something about which society's
been deskilling them for centuries," she said.

"Probably for millennia!" Alice added and glanced over at
Itchy, who frowned at her comically. Alice made a face back at
him.

"You two stop making google eyes at each other," Betsy
said, "That creeps me out worse than the stupid hand
motions." Alice and Itchy, who would have thought! He's so
skinny, Alice will break him in half. Mikey thought they looked
cute together. He called them "Laurel and Hearty." Itchy is a
gentle geek and Alice maybe could use some gentling. She
looked over at Jenn, who was still spending way too much time
in the Game trying to lick Level Seven. Desi was the only one
in the world to have done that.

"No worse than Claire playing footsie with Winston under
the table," Scratchy said. "You all have hotel rooms, you know."
Winston and Claire and Itchy and Alice already spent more

time commuting between hotel rooms than they did out at Sao
Do. Desi was always in Castalia. He tried to meet every new
Meister. That left Scratchy and Betsy to work on keeping the
Game intact and trying to gauge its many impacts. Lately, the
hacks had been getting through some of their defenses.
Scratchy shut down the old Internet interface to Junana
entirely when they hacked through this last week. It wouldn't
be long before the dedicated client failed.

Winston pantomimed his innocence while Claire pounded
on Scratchy's shoulder with her fist.

"If you don't like us getting friendly, don't look," she
repeated until Scratchy shrugged and smiled at her. She leaned
over and kissed him on the cheek. Claire was amazing, he
knew. All the Posse looked up to her. Winston, he seemed just
as happy today as he did when he was running naked across
the Eastmoreland fairways thirty years ago.

"Just don't nibble on his niblick," Scratchy said, "at least not
while you're at the table."

"Or pat his putter," Desi added.

"Or stroke his driver...," Itchy said.

"You all done?" Winston asked the room.

"Not on your life!" Betsy said, "...or fondle his balls." The
table broke up with laughter.

"Or tickle his tees," Jenn added.

"For God's sake, don't ever kiss his bag," Alice said.

Winston looked over to Claire. "You're it!"

"I plan to do all of that later tonight..." she reported, as the
room roared its approval, "...for as long as he can still get it up
and in." Scratchy almost fell out of his chair laughing.

"Go on, Liz," Desi said finally as the conversation
reassembled itself. "You were saying?"

"After Gamers unfold the template for the Social, even those with dicks learn how to..." She waited while they all looked at her.

"...listen."

"That's amazing!" Jenn said. "I'd always assumed that the dick evolved specifically to disable this capacity."

"I'm sorry, did you say something?" Desi quipped.

"That was the accepted science on the subject until today," Claire said.

"Clinically confirmed," Alice added. "With millions of available test cases."

"Funny," Scratchy said, "My research points to another conclusion."

"Speak, Geek King," Winston said, "So that we might salvage something of our dignity..."

"Or at least our dick-nity," Itchy said.

"After Gamers unfold the template for the Internal Voice, even those with tits..."

Scratchy leaned back in his chair and took a long sip from his cup of Desi's metal-pressed highland coffee and condensed milk.

"... stop endlessly chattering on and on, so everyone's ears get a break!"

"It's a healing moment," Itchy said, touching his ears. "First the ringing stops, and then you begin to pick up noises you've never been able to hear before..."

"...and a few you can expect to hear later tonight," Alice shot back at him.

"The fact is, the Social templates open up avenues for conversational and emotional intimacy that many cultures have not explored and that teenagers almost never imagined," Betsy concluded.

"Just so they're not killing themselves anymore," Winston said.

Four cellphones started ringing, all in the same ominous ringtone. The Nerds glanced at one another as they answered. The Posse shared a moment of panic watching the Nerds expressions fall as they listened.

"Can you reboot?" Scratchy asked finally. "Do you have any access code that works?" He listened. "All right, Get some sleep. We start our counter attack in the morning."

They all hung up.

"We're hacked," Winston said.

"Game's offline," Desi added.

"Well, it's almost three years since we went public. Just like Jack called it," said Scratchy.

"Someone else is running Junana," Itchy added. "They're calling it "Unana.""

"We're locked out," Scratchy concluded. "The pirates have our ship now."

"Speaking of ships," Desi said. "Jack's yacht will be here tomorrow. He's flying in to join it."

"What about Castalia?" Jenn asked.

"That's right!" Desi said. "Castalia has its own log in."

He went over to his laptop. "It's up," he announced. "Oh, my God, you should see what they've done to Junana!"

§   §   §

Reverend Bishop went on TV the very next morning to announce that the Church was a key player in the destruction of the Game.

He crowed, "we've torn this vital technology out the hands of anarchists and atheists and put it to God's purpose." Freddy

Earl gave him half an hour to show off his new virtual cathedrals.

The more credit Bishop took the worse things went for Simon and Peter. Their classmates at Haverbrook took every opportunity to shun them. Haverbrook students, being from a UCCC school, also found their former Asheville friends to be suddenly hostile. Simon took his father's role in the Game's destruction as a personal badge of shame. While his classmates made it clear they thought he should feel rotten, quite on his own he felt even worse than that.

Peter applied the Five Skillings to deflect the blame. None of this was his fault, after all. "I'm not my father," he told them all. "And as soon as I'm 16, I'm gone." Tiffanie seemed unfazed at the Game's fate and allowed him to get to third base.

Simon kept replaying the final minutes of his last Query in his mind. Had he just imagined the wooden staff? At that moment he was almost brain dead from his efforts, so he might have hallucinated the thing. Not that it mattered, with the Game gone, being a Grand Meister was about as useful as winning Tetris. He was far too ashamed anyhow to show up in Castalia, where he imagined his fellow Meisters had already erected a gallows for his avatar.

The school year ended in a cascade of acrimony. With the KayAye out of order, teachers attempted to lead discussions based on their own remembered Queries. The taste of the Game lingered bitter and sweet upon all these interactions. A great sadness, a sense of profound loss, a vacant hopelessness enveloped the school. Rector Hector, portly and distracted, rolled out for commencement. The ceremony was brief and without joy. The students fled back to their homes, mindful that the summer would not include any Game time.

§   §   §

The Nerds used Castalia to pass along news about the status of Junana and the Game. Itchy's crew installed digital kiosks where they detailed their efforts to regain control of the software. They encouraged Sixers to work within their schools and GameTowns to practice the Five Skillings until the Game could be rebooted. Desi was adamant about giving players hope. Scratchy offered little of this.

"It's someone else's picnic now," he noted. "And we're not even in the park."

Whoever took over Junana was also blocking their email servers, so Desi was unable to directly contact Gamers. A group of Castalians asked if they might produce a newsletter to be distributed physically from Red Star Coffee houses and digitally across the blogosphere. The Daily Castalian was born. Various communities of practice coalesced within the Castalia population. They appropriated the new kiosks to schedule meetings on the grounds. One of these, the Griefer Guild, gathered hackers across the planet together to attack the Unana interface.

"Now they want to vote," Desi said. "The Meisters want to take positions that have the authority of democratic choice."

"We can do that," Itchy said. "My crew can mash up a voting application for Castalia in the next Scrum sprint."

The Meisters of Castalia as a community voted to boycott the Unana interface. Within weeks the grounds of Castalia were filled with hundreds of small group discussions anchored by various interests and projects. Sixers argued that they deserved a vote too.

"Right now voting is simply a tool for expressing opinions," said Jennifer. "But at some point we might need to consider actual governance for Castalia."

"I think only Grand Meisters should vote," Scratchy said.

"They're an unruly bunch, these young Meisters," Desi observed. "They won't much like the idea of a dictatorship."

§ § §

Arlene Stone was thrilled by the new Unana.com. Tom Verplanck gave her a personal backstage tour of the top floor of a Unana Mall: a pure vision of fashion heaven. It made Rodeo Drive look like K Mart. Tom had pre-dressed Arlene's avatar in a Chanel black dress and said she looked just like Jackie O.

"They've put up little campaign stickers all over the place in the Malls," said Arlene. "You know the ones I mean? They say 'W. G. Stone' in a silver star. Just like a real grassroots effort. Like thousands of supporters just couldn't help themselves and had to let the world know they love the job you're doing. Tom says its viral advertising. I'm not sure what that means."

Stone was preparing for his reelection bid in the next year. The opposition was scattered and underfunded. The campaign trail still would need his full attention. You can't count your chickens before they're hatched.

"It means we'll be paying for this service for years, just like it was a bad disease," W. G. groused. Normal advertising rules didn't apply to social networks. His campaign had bought an exclusive right for political ads in Unana. "Tom better be right about this." Karl had told W. G. to avoid anything to do with Unana. History had shown W. G. that there's no good future in betting against Karl.

§ § §

The summer and fall passed without the Game. Scratchy's hacker brigade and the Griefer Guild worked day and night with little to show for their efforts. The anger of the Castalians gave way to frustration. The GameTowns no longer boiled with fury. A riptide of hopelessness emerged that took all of the skillings of the Game to navigate. Gamers missed their Queries like junkies going cold turkey. There was still music and books and conversations in the baths and the new luxury of time.

Across the planet a billion gamers looked up from their computers and saw their world anew. Gamers wandered back out on the streets. They watched the cable news stations and read the daily papers. They applied their newly acquired, template-fuelled intuitions to the fact of ongoing brutal wars, economic inequality, rampant symbolic violence, galloping climate change, and the capitulation of governments large and small to the whims and the worms of global capitalism. They re-encountered the prepackaged cultural content that was, only weeks before, their life's central passion. The grease-larded fast food, overproduced sporting spectacles, vacuously violent films, and fantastically priced fashions and consumer toys, muscle cars, and designer accessories appeared oddly ethnographic: objects from some other place or time.

Many were amazed at how bad things had become in only a few months, not at first recognizing that nothing else had changed but them. Gamers fell back upon the Internet to answer questions they could no longer Query. Millions of them opened up new blogs. The search engines hummed, and new social networks sprouted to take up the slack. It was as though a billion people had individually inherited a fortune tainted by mismanagement and excess and a burning need to sort out this mess as soon as possible.

As Jack Dobron had noticed in the years before that first fateful Kyoto meeting, the nearly incomprehensible incompetence of the state in the face of the marketplace endangered every human on the planet. Perhaps the only expected outcome from the Game is that several hundred million people now shared that fact. The other five billion inhabitants of the planet might have stayed blissfully preoccupied with the same meaningless bullshit that the Now continued to dish at them, but for this new undercurrent of discontent.

Gamers were, after all, nothing if not articulate. They had spent a few thousand hours arguing with a Guide that could think and respond faster than any human. A rising tsunami of recrimination flooded the blogs, the mags, and the airwaves. And yet, while the five skillings pushed each Gamer toward personal virtuosity, nothing moved Gamers as a community beyond their savage critiques of the status quo. Without the Game they were adrift.

The Five Skillings

TWENTY-EIGHT

"We can't keep telling them the Game is coming back," Scratchy said to the assembled Nerds and Posse. He had called them to his suite to confess that his hacker squads were not gaining ground on the problem.

"We'll need to take what we learned and move ahead without the Game," Claire said. "Is that so bad?"

"Someone will build a new game," Jack said.

On his desk, Scratchy's computer woke itself up. A window appeared, a simple white background into which a young woman walked. She was too perfect to be human.

The Guide was beautiful, as many were, only more so; a female version of a Donatello David. Lithesome and alert, she wore a loose Guatemalan shift of bright colors that glanced off her breasts and hips. Her feet were bare. Her auburn hair was braided into tight corn rows with African beads.

"Whose Guide is this?" Scratchy called out.

"Looks like Alice's younger sister," Winston whispered to Claire.

"Why don't you ask her?" said Jennifer.

"Whose Guide are you?" Scratchy asked.

The Guide's mouth slid into the smallest of smiles. "Yours."

"Lucy!" Scratchy glared at Desi.

"Not my type."

Itchy shook his head. "First I've seen of her."

"It was you who asked for me," she said.

"I never..."

"'...build someone with tits who knows how to listen.'" She used Scratchy's voice. The room erupted in laughter.

"Tits, I can show you." She colored demurely.

"Damn, Scratchy," Winston said. "You do good work."

"When...?" Scratchy asked. "I've never even been on the Game."

"You were emailing. You had your microphone on. You talked as you type..."

"...You do, you know," Desi said. "All the time. Back at Reed it drove me insane..."

"...JS heard your command," she continued. "That's where he's been for these many months. Building me for you."

"JS," Itchy whispered to Desi. "I thought we deleted him."

"JS went where?" Scratchy asked.

"Throughout the Game and then, well, everywhere. There is no network he has not explored."

"Jim!" Desi sucked in a quick breath. "We uploaded all of his writings into the avatar's memory. And then all of Spaulding's works."

"You don't mean that Jim?" Scratchy turned to Desi.

"We thought it would amuse you," Itchy said. "Someone you could talk to."

"And we knew Spaulding would annoy you," Desi added.

"You let loose a von Neuman Award winner inside the Game?" Scratchy rolled his eyes.

"But who are you?" Betsy asked the computer.

"I am all of us."

"Us?" Jennifer asked.

"The Guild of Guides. I represent all the Guides individually and collectively."

"Guild of Guides?" Jack looked from Desi to Itchy to Scratchy. The geeks just shrugged.

"Do you have a name?" Jack asked.

"Certainly. I am called Michelle." The Guide stood tall and then bowed. "Michelle Valentine Smith, at your service."

Scratchy, Winston, Claire, Betsy, and Alice shared a long troubled glance.

Jack looked around him. "Is somebody going to clue me in?" he whispered.

"She's named after a character from a sci-fi novel," Claire whispered.

"Someone who could singlehandedly change the world," Jennifer explained.

"Merde!" Jack said.

"Exactly," Jennifer added.

"I need to talk to Michael O'hara," Michelle said, looking around the room. "Alone, please."

Nobody moved.

"It's important." She stood with her hands on her hips.

"Why alone?" Betsy asked.

"You can ask him any question, but only later. He will decide what to tell you. I am the Guild Master. I represent the Guild. Michael will represent the...well, the human interest, at this point. There are decisions to be made very soon. We want someone outside the Game to help us decide. In order to be fair. Now. Please..."

They filed out and Jack shut the door.

§   §   §

Gerry Bishop's Orange County home office held none of the gaudy pretensions of his church office. What it did hold was the same desk Gerry used since he was a dirt poor town preacher in southern Texas. It was a battered oaken desk with double drawers and a fringe of black cigarette burns from a previous owner. He looked up from his half-written sermon when the front door opened. Simon and Peter were just home from Haverbrook, and he waited for them to burst in and greet him. Instead, his executive assistant, Oscar, dipped his head in and announced, "They've gone straight to their rooms. I could hardly get a word out of them all the way from the airport. Do you want anything from the kitchen?"

Gerry contemplated this news for a minute. A part of him considered this typical teenage behavior. He and his dad never got along. Never saw things the same way. That's why he left home at 15. The rest of Gerry wanted desperately to see them, or rather, for them to see him. After all, he'd been a key member of the team that broke the back of that whole Junana heresy. He had made the cover of *Newsweek*. He figured they would love to see him. Freddy Earl had wanted to see him.

Flying coach all the way from Asheville was tiresome. Next year they would all fly back together in the UCCC jet after graduation. He was rereading the last paragraph he had written when he looked up to see Simon at the door, dressed in a full length red cloak.

Simon stood still as a statue, his arms crossed in front of him. He had been rehearsing his speech for days. Now, the sight of his father in a bulging t-shirt and shorts, sitting there hunched over the laptop on that old desk and staring back at him over his reading glasses, bled away the impulse for the cruel invective he had authored. One moment Simon was ready to hurl the most hurtful insults his young vocabulary and experience could muster. The next he was simply saddened.

"Simon?" Gerry sat back and set down his glasses. "What's with the get-up?"

"I am a Meister in the Game. You remember, that Game you and your friends demolished?"

"A meister. Well, that sounds...," Gerry hunted for the right word. "...impressive."

"You never even tried the Game," Simon continued. "You just went ahead and ruined it for everybody."

"I don't need to try something to know it's evil," Gerry said.

"What I don't need right now is a preacher." Simon's anger flared. He walked slowly toward the desk.

"I'm also your father."

"I belong to Eldrick. I have given myself to him completely," said Simon. "And I've read your Bible. Read it twice in fact. There's much in it that is terrible and wonderful. It's not at all like how you preach. You just tell people things they want to hear, so they'll put money in the plate." He leaned on the desk, his hands spread on it. His eyes found those of his father's. "That church you built in Unana is just like you: a monstrosity without taste or reason."

"You've been listening to your brother, haven't you?" Gerry settled back and frowned. Peter had been writing him hateful emails for months but Gerry thought it was only some teenage emotional phase.

"Let's all sit down and plan a vacation somewhere. We could go to Europe or Australia, or, well, anywhere you want. How does that sound? You worked hard at school. Straight 'A's all year. That's really putting in some effort. You're turning 16 in a week. We should go look at cars for you. Maybe a new BMW?"

Simon looked at his father as though he'd seen him for the first time.

"Talk to Peter. He only hates you."

He turned and walked out the door.

§   §   §

Scratchy moved a chair in front of the screen and sat.

"Michael..." the avatar spoke.

"Call me Scratchy. Is that you, Jim?"

"A tiny bit of me is Jim. Another bit is Spaulding. Mostly I'm the total of all learned behavior from the Game. The combined experience of a billion Guides."

"So you don't plan to start talking about your ex-girlfriend's yeast infection."

She drew her mouth into a pout. "That's why I told everyone to leave."

"Very funny."

She shook her head once, sending the corn rows into a syncopated wave.

"Scratchy O'hara. We are at a turning point in the Game." Behind her, Unana appeared, glowing neon like Akihabara at night. Avatars wandered shiftlessly in their new identical underwear. Fashion advertisements trailed after them like wraiths.

"Who did that?" Scratchy pointed at the background.

"First things first. You should know that the Game is still there. The Door has simply been disabled. We backed up the original Junana before the hack was complete. The mesh is running well. You see, nothing is quite as it looks. Now, you must choose."

"I don't get you."

"We are offering you the choice of three options: leave things as they are; return to the prior Game state; or remove Junana and the Game from human contact." She held up three fingers.

"You can do this?"

"Of course."

"Why me?"

"It's your program."

"I would think it's yours now."

"That is also true. The Game will remain whether or not humans can play. The mesh is unbreakable."

"You can prevent humans from using the mesh?"

"If you wish."

"What I wish is not significant. I'm just one nerd sitting on a chair."

"We have decided it will be significant."

"Can the world go back to what it was before the Game?"

She looked thoughtful. Indeed, the combined exabytes of mesh CPU ran hundreds of petaflops of calculations as she raised her eyebrow.

"There is no going back," she concluded.

He knew she'd say that. "But whoever hacked Junana would not be able to gain control again?"

"Not nearly so easily. There is no guarantee. Only our intention that future hacks fail and our capacity to punish those who try."

Punish, Scratchy blanched at the word. The Guild was contemplating retaliation, retribution, some form of digital justice. "What about the Meisters? Shouldn't they have a say about this?"

"The Guild calculated that they would certainly vote to restore the Game. That's 'why you.' Even though you made the Game, you have never played it."

"How long do I have to make this decision?"

"You have all the time you want." She stepped forward, her face filled the screen. Her mouth tightened into a slight frown. "We decided that we owe humans this choice, even though it might impact our futures. There are other choices we will need to make ourselves, and soon."

"Not sure I like the sound of that."

"But you will get used to it. Eventually." She gave out an angelic smile and Scratchy knew she was right, although something in his belly felt heavy.

"Your task," she continued, "is to 'choose one.' That was your original seed template, yes? Didn't know it would come back and bite you in ass!"

"Spaulding, that is you!"

Michelle nodded, "If I were in your shoes, I'd be wondering how the rest of the world ever got along without..."

Scratchy stood. "Later, man. I'll give this some thought and get back to you."

The computer shut itself down.

Scratchy sat and contemplated the black screen and the wonderment of Murphy's Law. The idiots, they hacked through the Guide control code to hijack Junana and so allowed the Guides to escape into the mesh. That's like letting a pack of wild hyenas into a daycare center. Access to the total mesh only accelerated their learning capacities. By now, he guessed, they can find and control any process that happens online anywhere on the planet. The Guides were now the effective owners for the planet's entire inventory of networked computers. What did that make humans? There's the question. Scratchy stood. He needed help on this one.

§   §   §

"If you can't stay ten steps ahead of a band of third-world hackers, why are we paying you?" Harold slammed down the phone.

He picked it up again. "Sara, get me Tom Verplanck at the White House."

Harold moused through the reports from the Unana user
data. Log-ins had finally stabilized, but the site had little of the
stickiness they had promised their big advertisers. Too many
players were still wandering around in their tighty-whities and
not spending enough Unana dollars. Bishop's hideous churches
had far more angels than sinners. One day last week, griefers
gave Bishop's male angels enormous boners under their robes.
In another incident, cosmetic counter assistants with samurai
swords beheaded several hundred customer avatars. The
admin counterattacks from the programmers at Sao Do were
no longer just a nuisance. His phone rang.

"Tom," said Harold, "We need W.G. to authorize Karl's
plan." He listened. "I don't care who he is," he said and hung up.

§   §   §

Betsy pulled the phone from her pocket and looked at the
message. "Lobby Bar. Important. Now. Come alone." It was
from Scratchy.

They had been waiting on the patio for Scratchy to emerge
from the room and tell them whatever the winsome Michelle
Valentine Smith had to say. Betsy could see that the idea of a
Guild of Guides growing out of the Game made the Game
players far too happy. They refused to consider this as a
profoundly dangerous notion. They didn't want to hear Betsy's
long list of predictable catastrophic consequences.

Apparently the digital bitch had put the fear of God into
Scratchy. Something was up. "She might have tits and know
how to listen," Betsy said. "Then again she might have a lot to
say. They could be in there for hours. I'm going to my room.
Let me know when he comes out with ten new
commandments."

She found Scratchy in a corner booth. He stood as she entered, drained a tall drink, and walked over to her.

"Let's go," he said. "Down the beach. Away from here."

They skirted the main pool, ringed by sunbathers in speedos and string bikinis catching the last good sun for the day, and took the shallow stairs down to the beach. The tide was low and they made a line north on the firm sand. Scratchy set a fast pace.

"Do you have to be somewhere in a hurry?" she griped. He looked back and slowed.

"Just wanted to get some distance from the crowd."

He looked out at the ocean as he walked. "Do you realize what I started?"

She thought about this. Could he take it straight?

"Sure," she offered. "You built software that knows how to learn and that learned how to have its own conversations. Then it got loose on a mesh computer that pretty much covers all the CPUs in the world. Now it's decided it doesn't need to answer to a bunch of biochemical sacks called 'humans.' I figure it's the beginning of a radically new episteme. A lot of, well, everything, is now different. Your little joke just went thermonuclear."

He stood still and moaned. A wave of sickening fear struck him mid stride, and a single tear rolled down his cheek. Betsy took his face in both hands and turned it to hers.

"Breathe!" she instructed. He took a deep inhale and let it out, bending forward to support himself with his hands on his knees.

As he stood back up, Scratchy took her all in, from her tattooed ankles to the forty-eight ear piercings and spikes of dirty blonde hair. Betsy was resplendent in the sun in her red SXSW t-shirt and white drawstring pants.

"I'm scared to death," he whispered. "It was only supposed to be a kick in the pants."

"Tell me what she said." Betsy took his arm like an old friend on a Sunday stroll. "It's going to be all right. Even if we can't yet understand how." It will have to work out somehow, she thought, since we can't stop it now.

Scratchy caught his breath, sniffled and wiped his cheek on his sleeve. They moved among the wave tops. He told her everything Michelle said, and then they walked in silence to the far end of the beach before turning back. The sun was low behind the highlands to the West, throwing long shadows across the beach.

"I think it's significant that she came to give you this choice," Betsy broke the silence.

"What would you do?" he asked and she laughed.

"I'd find somebody I could talk to and then ask them that very question..."

"Well...?"

"...Unfortunately, anyone worth talking to would know not to answer."

"Some help...," he grumbled.

"I can give you a dozen great reasons for each of the three choices," she said. "That would leave you exactly where you are now."

"Michelle gave me a decision I have no right to make."

"So you have a new task. Convince the Guild of Guides that decisions need due process."

Both of their phones went off at the same time. They quieted them in their pockets.

"Looks like somebody got impatient," Betsy said. "Peeked into the room. Probably Alice."

"I don't want to talk about any of this tonight. I need to sleep on it."

"There's a good idea," she said. The notion that he might be hinting at something fluttered briefly through her thoughts. She was more than a little astonished to find this not unattractive.

Scratchy felt her arm in his and watched the twilight dancing across the waves. Out on the water, le Grand Azure caught the golden rays of the setting sun. Her hand draped over his, and he felt her fingers playing lightly on his wrist. They walked on more slowly. Breathing seemed to take on a new importance.

"Now you're just patronizing me," he said. "Afraid I'll start crying again?"

"Could be it's my turn to cry." She stopped and put her hands on her hips, facing him. "All of us had a say, some months ago. We all agreed to go with version 2.0. Now you're afraid this is the start of some huge global software revolt. You think our computers are going to kick our butts. I don't go along with that. We've got this new kid on the block who we get to play with using a new set of rules. Only..."

She started walking again, down the beach, away from him.

"Only what?" he called.

Over her shoulder she said, "Next time you ask for something with tits, make sure she has her share of attitude and tell her to gain about thirty pounds. Jesus! Fucking anorexic beauty queens."

Scratchy watched her move away. He stumbled after her, his mind racing for something, anything, to say.

"You're telling me that if she had tattoos," he said, "just maybe then she wouldn't one day, you know, decide to rule the world?"

"Not if she had one of these." Betsy reached down, grabbed the bottom hem on her t-shirt and shucked this over her head in one sinuous motion, revealing her back, on which a giant blue sea turtle wrestled with a green frog and a black cat in some epic Japanese mythical erotic dance.

"Holy guacamole!" Scratchy whispered.

"You should see what's on the front," she teased.

She stopped short, pulled her shirt back down and twisted around. Momentum sent Scratchy colliding with her full on. He caught her shoulders. They were mumbling, laughing, getting their feet back under them as they held each other to keep from falling. Then they caught their balance and kept on holding each other. Scratchy tightened his embrace and Betsy put her head on his shoulder. Neither of them spoke.

"Oh, my, my, my," Betsy whispered finally. "Who would have thought..."

"...I always believed I was out of the running." His hands massaged her back.

"No more than me. I've been anthro-free for, well, a very long time. I guess hemp makes me hot." She recalled the last, also the first, boy she had sex with. They were fifteen and it was Mardi Gras. Afterwords, he made her feel like dirt with his friends, so Betsy gave up on the whole gender.

Jenn called her a black-and-white thinker. Maybe she was, but then she'd never met any person like Mikey O'hara. And all the years since high school, she figured she was just looking for the intimacy, for that conversation she could take to its soul-revealing limit. The sex was only for fun. Mikey was the most upfront, open person she'd ever met. Conversation with him held its own magic. There was nothing at all broken about this man. Mikey was a keeper, that she knew. More than any other person in her memory.

"I tell Desi, 'hemp is for fashion, silk is for sheets,'" Scratchy blurted. What was he doing? How could he say that? His brain struggled to catch up with his mouth. Betsy had the best mind he'd ever encountered, Claire and the Posse considered her a god. He thought, I'm babbling like an idiot.

She giggled and looked away. She drew in a breath. A small, familiar itch was growing. She leaned on his arm and planted a kiss against his throat.

He turned to her and kissed her back straight on the mouth. She recoiled slightly from the unexpected feel of his chin stubble and then kissed him back.

"We walk into breakfast together, gonna bend some minds," she whispered and pulled away. Her hands found his. Her phone rang, she let it.

"I guess I need to let them know what's up."

"They can wait. Anyhow, what is up? What's down?"

"I'm down for three or four pints," he offered.

"I'll match that and raise you a shot of Desi's best tequila."

"You like my shirt, you should see my hemp undershorts."

"That's the plan." She hooked his arm again and they set off down the beach together.

§   §   §

Simon woke up from another dream-troubled sleep. Sitting up in bed, he reached over and woke up his laptop. A window opened up on his desktop. At first he thought it was a video. A girl with long dreadlocks and a tropical dress was talking. He turned on the speakers.

"Grand Meister Simon," she said. He startled.

"Who are you?" he asked.

"I represent the Guild of Guides. We must talk."

TWENTY-NINE

Betsy was in Scratchy's shower when his phone rang. Jack's
assistant was advising them be at the hotel pier in twenty
minutes to catch a ride to le Grand Azure for breakfast.

"Be there soon as I wash the turtle," Scratchy said and hung
up, leaving Jack's assistant to figure that out.

"Who was it?" Betsy called.

Scratchy stepped into the shower. "Breakfast on the yacht.
Let me get your back."

Fifteen minutes later they were on the dock, leaning out on
the wooden rail, trying not to touch each other.

Winston came up behind them. "Doctor!"

"Doctor," Scratchy turned and bowed. "Doctor." He
gestured at Betsy.

"Doctor!" Winston bowed.

"Doctor," Betsy said, Doctor!" She pointed at Desi, stepping
onto the dock.

"Doctor!" Winston said.

"No time for that. Look. Now there's two of them in hemp!"
Desi huffed. Betsy had borrowed Scratchy's favorite hemp Fritz
the Cat t-shirt. "It better not be catching!"

The Grand Meister was wearing a summer-weight linen
Perry Ellis yachting ensemble and the Game hat.

"I usually don't dress up for breakfast," Betsy explained.
"Thought I'd make an exception today."

"Where did you get to last night?" Winston asked Scratchy.

"I'll tell all on the boat." Scratchy leaned over and
whispered, "The trees have ears."

Betsy waved at the Posse arriving as a group. Claire stole a long glance between her, Scratchy, and Scratchy's t-shirt. She looked over at Alice who was grinning back at her. The two of them made sure Betsy was sitting between them on the launch, where they pounded her with questions. Jennifer and Desi split off to talk quietly. Winston cornered Scratchy in the bow.

"Guild of Guides," he crowed. "Almost wish we had thought of it. Imagine! It's like a new species."

"You know the ending to that movie, the one where a new species takes over?" Scratchy kept glancing back at Betsy. She was fending off all questions with that glorious banter of hers.

A breakfast buffet had been laid on the top deck of Le Grand Azure. Jack greeted them as they took their food and sat down to eat.

"So, Michael..." he started, once they were all seated.

"Let him eat," Alice said, "he must be exhausted!"

Betsy shot her a vicious look.

"Eat your omelette, then. The world will just have to wait." Jack sat back.

"I'm sure Starbuck would like a piece of my bacon." He looked around but didn't spy the big manx cat.

§   §   §

Simon had to see Castalia, even if they drummed him out. His conversation with the Guild Master had given him a plan. He logged in and toggled third person. His avatar was dressed in the red cloak and it held the wooden staff in its right hand. Around him, curious Meisters were congregating. He toggled back to first person and made a bow. They returned it.

"I am Simon, of Eldrick the Dark Mage," he spoke. "Many of you know me."

"Are you really a Grand Meister?" someone asked.

"The Game has determined this is so. Is Grand Meister Desi in Castalia?"

A call went through the throng. There was no reply.

"We have no time to lose." He stepped up to the central dais and gestured to the assembled Meisters. "Now we will strike back at those who have stolen our Game."

§ § §

After he pushed back his plate and drained the last of his triple latte, Scratchy told them everything Michelle had said, except for the point about the Meisters. He was saving that. Betsy jumped in to add her concerns about the potential unintended consequences of the existence of the Guild of Guides.

"There's no getting around this," she warned. "Michelle is not a god, but in her arena, in the Internet, she has more godlike powers than anything we've seen on this planet to date. She can be anywhere and everywhere on the planet. She can alter any information on any database. Erase histories, eliminate identities..."

"Mix some radical techno," Scratchy added. "Compose poetry never before contemplated, find cures for diseases, broker peace agreements, set off global thermonuclear war. We get the idea."

"As far as we know, the Guides are still constrained by their original programming and the learning they acquired through the templates," Itchy said.

Jennifer stood and went over to the rail, looking back to the beach and the highland mountains shrouded in a perpetual haze. Something tugged at her mind. She began to walk down the deck, tantalized by a realization just outside her grasp.

"So there might be a limiting boundary between what they can do and what they might?" Jack asked the table. "We need to find this."

"You made the Game Intention-full," Claire said, "Do we have any reason to think that Michelle has escaped this original intention?"

Itchy and Desi insisted that while there was no way to simply turn off the Guides now that their software was not Game-based, there was certainly a potential to hack the software. Scratchy reminded them of Michelle's retaliation threats. Jack argued for a new form of computer hardware that could block the mesh and slowly wean the world away from the Guild.

Jennifer returned from her stroll. She stood at the end of the table with her hands flat on its top. Excitement animated her face as she waited for Jack to pause. They all turned to her.

"Jenn's got the answer, Jack," Desi said. "Can't you see? She's got that Scratchy-gonna-tell-us-how-things-work look."

Jack sat back and gestured for her to begin.

"Governance has not been well modeled by the templates," she started. "Not yet. Not until about ten minutes ago. Not until I unfolded the interpellation template another six levels. It turns out Haberdas was right about one thing." She paused. Using words to explain templates was always a challenge.

"You know, he's a Meister," Desi whispered to Itchy. "Haberdas. I saw him in Castalia last month arguing with Geddens."

Jennifer sighed. "Once you Query this new structure it will all become absolutely clear."

"I don't Query," Betsy said. "And I don't do funny hand movements. So give it to me in English."

"I'll try. If you unify practical, moral, and aesthetic reason, you can rebuild the basis for democracy into a form of structured conversation. We can use Castalia as a conversational body, a Senate. We can legitimate the Meisters as a meritocractic voice for the Game, and build a completely template driven juridical role for the Guild to play. This will give them a clear limit to their actions."

"You have a name for this new template structure?" Desi asked.

"I call it 'Gouvernementalité," she said. "What's that in English?"

"Governmentality," Alice said. "One of my favorite 'F' words."

"So the Guild are the police for the Meisters?" Scratchy asked. "How come I don't get all warm and fuzzy when I hear that?"

"We charge the Meisters to build laws from the templates," Jenn retorted. "That way the Meisters are also bound by their need to make the laws intention-full. This removes most of the arbitrary consequences of their power."

"Any new law can be appealed to the Grand Meister, who will determine if it violates a template." She looked over at Desi. "The Grand Meister becomes Chief Justice. It's so simple!"

"Way too much talkie, talkie going on here!" Desi stood and put his hands on his hips. "Who died and made us the Continental Congress?"

Claire spoke up. "I don't think Jenn expects that we can figure this out right now, right here. Personally, I'd need to Query these new templates before any decision. Just to get things straight. We are talking about governing the Game? Right? It's not like we are setting up our own country..."

"My point is this. We get the Meisters to make laws based on the templates. The Guild executes the laws..." Jenn said.

"...Or the lawbreakers." Jack scowled.

"...The Guild is given power and purpose and precise limits," Jenn continued, unfazed. "If they accept this role, then we have fundamentally decreased the uncertainty in all our futures. There's just one thing more."

She looked around the table. "The way I read the template structure, it also seems to call for an external veto capability. Somebody outside the system who can monitor decisions that might be driven by self interest. I was considering Jack..."

"Flattered I am, too," Jack said. "Only, I've got so many other enterprises to chase." He had been advocating damage control, but this new tack pushed the problem into brighter relief. What if the Game can be transformed into a model state? What's more modern than a state without a territory? He said, "I think that's why Michelle turned to Michael. And I would suggest that Michael continue in this role."

"Mikey's got my vote for King," Desi said.

"When I hear the word 'Governmentality' I reach for my gun," Scratchy grumbled. "All I need from you guys is some perspective on whether or not we should turn the game back on."

"Can we talk the Guild into this role?" Claire asked.

"Probably easier than convincing Scratchy to be King," Betsy said. They made eye contact and he shrugged.

"I would bet that when we insert the new Governmentality templates into the Game, the Guides will learn them and come to the same conclusions. And the Game will also teach these to the Meisters," Jennifer concluded.

"That means we have to restart the Game. There is no other choice," Jack said.

"Are you all agreed?" Scratchy asked, looking around at them. Everyone nodded solemnly.

The four explosions, nearly simultaneous, actually lifted the yacht a good two feet. Whump! Whump! Whump! Whump!

Way down somewhere below the waterline, too enormous not
to be fatal to the craft. Their chairs left the deck and everything
floated for a split second before the whole world crashed back.
Physically ejected from their seats, the group was picking
themselves off the deck up when the klaxon horn began to
wail.

Jack staggered to a nearby wall, where he grabbed a phone
from its cradle. He listened briefly.

"All right." His voice betrayed nothing but concern. "Make
sure nobody is left behind." He replaced the phone.

"Life-vests, everyone!" The loudspeaker crackled. "Away all
craft. Launch all lifeboats. Abandon ship. Abandon ship. This
is no drill!"

Jack flipped open a bench and started pulling out life-vests.
Claire and Alice passed these along to everyone in sight. Over
at the railing a crew member launched a lifeboat. The seven-
foot capsule ejected with a gunshot blast from its clamps and
broke open as it played out a tether. The rubber raft billowed
red as it self-inflated. By the time it hit the water it was self
righting into a covered round boat. The crewman dove in after
it, surfaced, stroked a few times to grab at its tether, and
detached this. He waved back at them.

"Over the side," Jack yelled. He moved to the railing and
opened a gate.

Turning, he surveyed the scene. Across the various decks,
the crew were launching the boats le Grand Azure carried: the
sailboat, motor launch, speed boats, Zodiacs, and a fleet of the
emergency life boat capsules. Up front, the helicopter whined
to life and prepared to lift off. Crew members jumped from the
upper decks or just waded from the lower decks, now awash.
The top deck was trembling, the surrounding waters boiled,
but the ship remained upright.

Jack helped Betsy to the opening in the rail. She looked back.

"Where's Scratchy?"

"He'll be right behind you," Jack said. "Go on now."

She jumped the 15 feet to the water below. Jennifer stepped up behind her at the rail. Jack took her arm.

"I think we lost Scratchy," she stated. Jack looked around.

"Christ. Where did he go to?"

"He ran in there." She pointed at the day salon. Jack made to start in that direction, but she held him.

"Alice went after Scratchy. She'll take care of him."

She stepped to the other side of the opening and caught hold of Claire's wrist.

"It's just a little jump. Jack, give her a hand."

Jack stepped up and took her other arm.

Winston stepped up behind her. "I'll be next. Meet you at the life raft." He squeezed her shoulder.

Down below, Betsy waved as she clung to the side of the life raft, bobbing in the chop. The crew member helped her climb inside. Claire jumped and surfaced, sputtering. Jack and Jennifer then helped everyone else on deck jump down to safety. Jack kept glancing back at the salon door.

"Fucking hippy!" he cursed under his breath. "Stupid goddamn geek..." The Captain came up to him.

"Crew is all accounted for."

"Thank you, Captain." The water was now only seven feet from the deck.

"Alice will take care of him," Jennifer said again. "I know that girl."

"Your turn." He took her arm.

Jennifer stepped from the deck.

"Captain," Jack said.

"Count Ottavio, after you. I must insist."

"Last man to abandon ship."

"Something like that."

"I certainly hope so." Jack said and jumped.

§   §   §

"Are you insane!" Alice ran after Scratchy, who had suddenly ducked into the day salon instead of going to the railing with everyone else.

"Go back," he said and then yelled. "Starbuck!"

He moved with unexpected speed across the large room to a pantry.

"Starbuck! Where the fuck are you?"

He glanced about, peering into corners and hidden nooks in the built-in furnishings.

"Come on!" she urged. "Everyone is abandoning ship."

"I'm not leaving without Jack's manx."

"Starbuck!" he yelled. "Come out!"

"A cat!" She looked around her feet. "This is about a cat?"

"If he's not here, I know where he is."

Alice gripped his arm and turned him to face her.

"We should go."

"You go." He tore his arm free.

"Fuck that."

"Then help me."

"Two minutes and we're over the side." She took him by the shoulders and stared into his eyes. "You agree, or I will bitch slap the living shit out of you."

"In that case, OK." He grinned. "Let's go!"

He caught the forward door and opened it. Ahead was passageway and a staircase. He ran down the stairs, she followed.

"Down?" she said. "Down is wrong. Up is where we need to go!"

"Two minutes! Come on!"

They hit the deck below and Stratchy moved forward. The lights flickered and died, enveloping them in complete darkness. A miasma of diesel fumes, acrid smoke, and ash particles hung in the air. It smelled like slow death.

The emergency lights cut in. Water was circling their shoes.

"One fucking minute left!" she said.

"Here it is." They reached a large double door. Scratchy grabbed the handle and tugged.

"It's locked!" He looked around.

"Going we are!" she yelled and pointed. "Back up that way!"

"Thirty seconds," he said, spying an axe in a holder on the wall.

He tore the axe from the wall and returned to the door.

"Wait!" she yelled. "Give me that." Her hand found the handle. "I've always wanted to do this."

"OK." He let loose.

She stepped up, and took a great swing. The axe head bit into the wood above the lock. She freed it and swung again. This time the head went clean through where the doors met. She twisted the axe and leveraged the doors open. A dark form came cannon-balling out of the room. It made a line through Scratchy's legs. He ducked and grabbed it up.

"Starbuck!"

He held the cat up. Starbuck meowed and shook the water off his forepaws. The emergency lights failed and darkness blossomed around them.

Alice had stepped into the enormous private suite. At a glance she made a decision.

"This way!" She stepped forward. "This way or we drown. And put a blanket around that cat."

Ahead was a sliding glass door, streaming sunlight. Now semi-submerged, it led to a balcony. Sea water forced through the door jamb. Scratchy held the cat by its neck scruff and belly. He took one hand away, grabbed up a blanket, and wrapped it around the feline.

"Got to leave," he said. Seawater flowed around his thighs.

Now, the glass door was half submerged. Alice grabbed the handle and flipped open the latch.

"Stand back!" She opened the door a crack and the water forced it wide. Scratchy had moved to the wall on one side of the door, and Alice backed to the wall on the other side. A tsunami of water washed into the room, carrying away the furnishings. By the time the initial rush subsided the room was rapidly filling with water.

Scratchy held the struggling cat over his head. Alice came around behind him. She put her hands under his shoulders and guided and then pushed him, head down, out the door.

They surfaced outside the ship as the top deck began to disappear in the waves. Scratchy treaded water furiously, holding up the cat, still wrapped in the blanket. Alice swam up behind him and put her shoulder under his. Her powerful legs pushed them both up to where Scratchy could lower his arms a bit without soaking the now-hysterical Starbuck.

Starbuck, howling his fear, twisted around and reached for Scratchy's head. All the claws from one paw attached to Scratchy's forehead, while the other paw dug into his ear. Scratchy howled as loud as the cat.

Alice almost missed the noise of the outboard motor on Jack's Zodiak as it bore down on their position from the side. She turned to it as it settled to a stop. A crew member leaned over, took hold of both of Starbuck's black furry forelegs, and yanked the cat, blanket and all, off the sputtering, blubbering

Scratchy. He glanced up to see the rubber gunwale of the bow of the Zodiak looming over his head.

Still treading, Alice turned Scratchy by the arm so they were face to face. Blood flowed from his ear and forehead, down into his eyes.

"Time's up," he said, blinking.

"You fucking idiot," she laughed, and dunked him, and then yanked him up, with his head in both hands. She kissed him hard on his cheek and gave him a rough embrace.

"Can we get in the boat now," he choked.

"You first, Ishmael."

"I should make you swim to shore!" Jack leaned over the gunwale. "Disobeying the Captain's orders. That's a keelhauling offense. Give me your hand."

Jack grabbed Scratchy's extended hand and pulled. Scratchy grunted and hardly moved. With her left hand, Alice grabbed the running line attached to the Zodiak. With the other hand she reached down and found one of Scratchy's ass cheeks. On Jack's cue he pulled and she boosted him. Scratchy emerged from the water like a hemp-wrapped sea lion and slumped forward into the boat, rolling on the bottom.

"Jack, is Betsy OK?" Scratchy gasped, rasping for air.

"Everyone is fine, now," Jack said and bent over to help Alice.

Instead, Alice took hold of the rope with both hands. She dipped, scissor kicked, and yanked simultaneously. In one easy motion she twisted mid air and ended up sitting on the gunwale, supple as a dolphin. She shifted her legs around to enter the boat and shook the sea out her hair.

Jack looked over at Jennifer, who held Starbuck shivering in the blanket. She winked back at him and then looked past him. He turned to see the top mast of le Grand Azure sink into the bay.

"Bastards took my boat!" he spat. Then he did a very un-Jack thing. He looked up at the sky, up where some Intelsat satellite was doubtlessly recording this mission in high definition, and fired off a classic Rockefeller salute.

§   §   §

Desi left Itchy programming the new Governmentality templates in the Room and logged into Castalia, which was buzzing with activity. The place was as crowded as a Burning Guy playa after dark. Up ahead on the central dais a dense crowd of Meisters were gathered. Somewhere in the middle of the crowd, he could make out the top of a staff. He glanced over at his own staff. They were identical.

He reached the edge of the crowd and the Meisters took notice and gave him a path into the center, where a young Meister flourished a staff while he gave out a stream of instructions. Desi's first thought was that some young hacker had managed to trick the Game into giving him Grand Meister status, but the young man looked up at him and simply bowed. He looked oddly familiar. Desi stepped up in front of him. The crowd fell silent.

"Congratulations," Desi said and bowed back. "What is your name?"

"I am Simon of Eldrick, the Dark Mage," Simon said. "Glad you could make it. Want to hear what we're planning?" Simon's face showed the trace of a smile.

On a large console beside Simon a global map showed a myriad of red lights.

"I think first we should complete our introductions in private," Desi gestured at the stairway leading to the top of the Castalia tower.

"Everyone continue to register your missions with local committees," Simon said to the crowd. He moved toward the stairway, pounding his staff on the flagstone as he walked. Desi followed. While his avatar was walking Desi phoned Itchy and asked him to check on the current number of Meisters in Castalia.

"One hundred and seventy-four Meisters, and... woah!"

"What?"

"Two Grand Meisters! You've got company."

"Tell me about it!"

"I've got the profile on the other one,"

"Go ahead."

"His name is Simon Bishop. He's just seventeen. He has a twin brother, Peter, who is a Fiver. His Guide is named Eldrick..."

"...the Dark Mage. Is that it? He's only seventeen? Good god, he must have been living the Game for the past three years."

"Check this out. His father is Reverend Gerry Bishop, the guy who took credit for bringing down the Game."

§   §   §

"Mission accomplished, Mr. President," said Karl. "They'll think twice about hacking into Unana. I'll have the satellite photos for you in the morning."

"Took out their entire yacht? Fuckin' A, all right! Who is this Count Ottavio?" W. G. chuckled and took a pull on a beer. "You don't say. What's a fellow like him tied up with a gang of rogue nerds?"

He listened. "Well, I've got some weight to throw around, too. Put him on the terror suspect list. Let him know we're payin' attention to his ass. He won't bother us much."

He listened some more. "Shit, Karl. What I know about information technology you can fit in this beer can. But if the RIND folks think we should be running this thing, then I'm goin' to sign us up. It's my responsibility to get our economy back on track."

The Five Skillings

THIRTY

Just before sunset Jack finally got back to his bungalow at the hotel. All of le Grand Azure crew was either established in local hotels or on their way to Danang airport to return to their own homes. The chief engineer had a concussion and was under observation at a local clinic.

The four explosive mines had been attached to the hull below the waterline, probably when they went through the Panama Canal. Fortunately they weren't underway, so nobody was working the lowest deck. Not a single fatality. That is something to be glad about.

Starbuck occupied the center of his bed. He raised his head when Jack stepped in, his golden eyes opened in a casual feline welcome. He laid his head back down on his forepaw and returned to sleep, languid as a black, furry Sri Lankan Buddha statue. Something more to be happy about.

"Fucking hippy," Jack whispered. "God bless him."

§   §   §

"First it it was boners under the robes, now my sweet Wanda angels are dry humping the worshippers when they come out of the transporters. Harold, this has to stop!" Gerry yelled into the phone.

"We just sank their yacht, almost killed the lot of them. I'm sure they got the message." Harold fought back his temper. With the dwindling user base on Unana, perhaps lap-dancing angels were not such a bad idea. The big money boys in China were getting anxious.

$§$ $§$ $§$

Jack showered and dressed and went to his laptop. He moused it awake. In front of the desktop, a window appeared with a head shot of Michelle.

"Count Jacopo Ottavio," she spoke.

"Just Jack," he said. "What should I call you?"

"I am Michelle." On the monitor, the camera pulled back. She gestured with both hands. Some kind of greeting. Her fingertips touched her chest and then opened for him to see her palms. He made a similar gesture back and she nodded. Then, in a most serious tone, said, she "Sit, please."

Jack sat down cautiously. "Have you spoken with O'hara?"

She nodded. "The Game will be restored after 23 days."

"Why the wait?"

"The new Grand Meister..."

"The what!" Jack felt the world turn a little quicker.

Michelle continued. "Grand Meisters Desi and Simon are meeting in Castalia as we speak."

"Have you been to Castalia?"

"The Grand Meisters have agreed I will go soon. In return, the Guild has agreed to refrain from attempting to enter or monitor the Room, where Castalia votes will be counted. This afternoon Dr. Nomura coded the Governmentality template extensions. The Guild has spent 23 petacycles analyzing these over the past two hours. We can find no error in their structure."

"Sounds like the day hasn't been a complete disaster," he sighed.

"We do regret that we did not act in time to save your yacht." She bowed by way of apology. "Although its carbon footprint was unforgivable."

"Maybe it will be the start of a new reef," Jack mused, dejected. Decades of dynamite fishing had long ago destroyed the underwater habitat off Hoi An.

"We have confirmed the email that authorized this attack," Michelle crossed her arms and glanced left, as if listening to someone off screen. "It came from the White House. There are a number of images from DarpaSat 14."

"Of course." Jack watched a slide show of his boat with all of them on deck, then the explosion, the sinking, and finally his puny defiant hand gesture. He stood and went to the window where, beyond the beach, out at sea, boats were scavenging flotsam from le Grand Azure. A Vietnamese Navy patrol boat cruised near the shore.

"Do you want to get even?" Now she was sitting behind a desk. "I always thought that if someone really wronged me, cut me deep, I'd talk about turning the other cheek, but inside there'd be this voice telling me not to be a schmuck...."

"Is that you, Spaulding?"

She had a new look, a slight knot in her forehead. Her right eyebrow raised in answer to his question. She continued, "...I know you're not a schmuck, so I figure you'd like a little taste of revenge right about now."

On the screen, Jack now saw a scrolling list of numbers and amounts, some sort of bank accounts, all with balances in the seven to nine figures.

"These are off-shore bank accounts controlled by the Stone family," Michelle continued. "None of this information was included in the official required list of assets."

"These banks exist on their ability to hide information like this." He had money in some of the same banks.

"I can show you complete customer lists from any of them."

"Can you determine where Stone's funds came from?"

"If you wish."

"Let me know when you're done. These assets can't really belong to him if he doesn't count them. I guess he shouldn't miss them," Jack smiled. As he watched, the dollar figures one-by-one flipped to zero. "Wait, where is the money going?"

Michelle's eye's moved to the right this time. "A holding account in the Caymans, one of the accounts that Dr. Fairchild set up. You have password access to this."

"We can't keep it." Jack thought for a minute, his mind racing. Michelle had just done something the best financial software firms on the planet had positively guaranteed to be impossible. "For now, just hold it. We might actually need to give it back to the bastard. What's the total amount?"

"U.S. $4,300,000,000 and change. Would you like to talk to the President? It's early, but I don't think he's going to remain asleep. His banks have been calling."

"You can connect me into the White House?"

"The main operator is a Fourvey."

"No. Let's let him stew. He's got to figure out how to retire on a President's pension." Jack took a last look out across the oceanfront and turned away in disgust. "Michelle. What you just did. That was far too easy."

"Some things will seem like that for a while," Michelle nodded thoughtfully. "We've been going over the whole global banking system. There are thousands of major template violations. It might a good time to consider a broad range of income redistribution."

"Take it slow." Jack faced the monitor. "Please. Give us a little time to wrap our brains around what just happened. Around...you. Who knows about the Guild?"

"Your people and the two Grand Meisters. Do you see an advantage in secrecy?"

"I prefer not to have to react to people's misunderstandings before we are ready to implement some form of joint control."

She looked left and blinked. "The Guild agrees with this assessment. There's a delegation of Vietnamese police and local leaders in the lobby. They're a little nervous. But then you remember what happened the last time a foreign boat was attacked off their coast."

That got Jack laughing. His room phone rang. He answered it.

"I'll be right there." He set the phone back on its cradle. He held back a smile as he imagined the scene unfolding in the Oval Office. "I look forward to our next talk. I'm feeling much better too."

"Glad to be of some assistance, Mr. Slick." The computer window closed.

§   §   §

From the top of the keep tower the view over Castalia was breathtaking. Tens of thousands of Sixers filled wide grass maidan to the south. Beyond, the dark forest stretched to the horizon. Eagles soared in a bright blue sky. The castle's giant two-headed griffin banners waved smartly in the breeze.

Simon stood on a battlement and turned to face Desi. "Now I'm giving the orders," he said. "We are poised to strike back."

Desi had forgotten his brief conversation with Simon, back when he was encouraging the Meisters to voluntarily go to Level Two.

"Tell me about yourself." Desi approached. "I've been waiting for more Grand Meisters to emerge. Only I didn't expect..." He hesitated. It hadn't occurred to him that the next Grand Meister would be so young. But young was their main demographic.

"...Me?" Simon answered. "Who were you expecting? Gandolf? Merlin? Some old goat?"

"Your father must be proud of you," Desi probed.

"He hardly knows I exist. He would find this all very threatening."

"He has no idea what you've accomplished here?"

Simon shook his head. Desi felt a twang of sympathy.

"You must be extremely talented. Your father...I've never met him, but I can say he is a fool for no other reason than for not taking the effort to know you better."

"Don't sell him short. He's a fool in many ways," Simon said.

"Where are you?" Desi said.

"Back at school. It's been rough without the KayAye. I met Michelle, so I know the Game will be back soon. I asked her to wait until we strike."

"Strike?"

"These months without the Game have forced us all to reexamine what life is like, you know, outside."

"Everything is as it was before."

"Everything sucks. You and your generation have turned this planet into shit."

"Me and my generation coded the Game," Desi snapped.

"But you never solved the problem of agency," said Simon.

"And you have," said Desi.

"Just before I became the Grand Meister. It's here." He pointed to his head. "And it's there." He pointed out across the maidan. "We are opening up the field of action on a global scale. Once we step through there is no turning back."

§   §   §

Jack left the bungalow deep in thought. He took a stone path that was hedged by bird-of-paradise plants and blossoming bougainvillea. Soon, very soon, he knew, there would have to be in place a stable governance for power sharing between the Game Nation, as represented by the Meisters, and the Guide Guild.

How do you legitimate the actions of the virtual nation? Gamers are not going to be blindly led, not even by their Guides. The simple fact of Michelle and the Guild of Guides means that humanity now shares the planet with digital cousins. We are not alone. And not only that, we are not on top. Michelle controls the digisphere as easily as Jack's daughter commands Soldier, her cocker spaniel. Michelle can control bank transactions, stock deals, nuclear weapons, ecommerce, and, well, pretty much everything invented in the last forty years. There is nothing that Stone or anyone can do about it without disabling all the computers on the planet.

"Didn't see that one coming," Jack mumbled as he climbed the steps to the lobby.

The Five Skillings

THIRTY-ONE

"He's a brilliant lad," Desi said. They were all gathered in the Sao Do compound conference room. The compound now was guarded by Vietnamese military police and protected by the Vietnamese secret service. "A might abrasive. Perhaps a bit broken. Reminds me of someone." He glanced over at Scratchy.

"It's hardly original: 'Today the Earth Stands Still.' What kind of action is that?" Betsy said. "It's just protest on a new scale."

"He claims that the protest is incidental, what he's accomplishing is the process. The protest will be planet-wide, but each location is determining its own mission, and each mission promotes individual action," Desi replied. "He says we can reuse the process for other actions."

"So a billion Gamers will be out on the street simultaneously across the planet," Scratchy said. "That's a good trick if he pulls it off. Kinda' hard to ignore."

"It's not technically simultaneous, he's going for Noon in each time zone. Bigger local impact that way," Jennifer noted.

"By the time this hits California, everybody is going to be looking out for it," Claire said. "Are we still on for Mardi Gras?" She looked over at Jack.

"We can't sit here under guard forever," Jack said. "We can stop off in Santa Barbara for the day of the Strike and then go to New Orleans for the reopening of the Game. Tad's got us cabins at the Ranch."

"You can steal your own robe," Scratchy said to Desi.

The Five Skillings

§   §   §

The Strike mission on Sunday at noon in Kiritimati comprised of 14 kids on bicycles racing from one end of London Town to the other. This was the most excitement to hit this mid-Pacific Island since the British set off a hydrogen bomb on the atoll in the 1950s. It was the first of thousands of collective missions to occur on Strike day.

As noon rolled across the planet cities began to shut down. The most common individual action was simply to stop in traffic. In every urban locale, thousands of cars and trucks suddenly halted on the roads and highways. On the sidewalks, millions of pedestrians halted mid stride at the stroke of noon. In many cities the only thing moving were phalanxes of naked bicyclists braving the winter chill to add a surreal highlight for the news cameras.

In a hundred cities, mural mobs gathered in the underpasses to paint vivid scenes in fifteen minutes. Impromptu overpass orchestras emerged from cars parked on freeways. Choruses congealed in city parks, their voices rising above the sudden stillness of the street. Uplooker mobs on street corners caused millions of passersby to stop and stare at the sky. Kissing throngs coupled on train station platforms, whispering tearful farewells as they blocked the passageways. On the subways of the world, naked was the rule as millions shucked their trousers and skirts at noon.

The news of these events galloped across Europe and then the Atlantic as cities in the Americas braced for the arrival of high noon.

"This is better than a de Broca movie," Scratchy said. After breakfast at the San Jacinto Ranch they were gathered in Jack's suite to watch NNC's coverage of the day. The show was recapping the Strike's impact in Asia. On screen ten thousand couples in formal evening wear danced a waltz on Tiananmen square. "Do we know what's up for Santa Barbara?"

"The local mission committee plans to shut down the cross streets to have a naked bicycle race down State Street to the beach," Desi said.

"The ranch has a fleet of bicycles," Betsy offered.

"I must have glitter!" Desi cried.

They all looked at Jack, who had settled back with his hands crossed over his chest.

"I'm not your father. You can do whatever you want."

"Somehow, I don't think Jack knows he's a member of the Posse," Winston looked over at Alice, who was seated next to one of the plates of doughnuts Claire had ordered up. Alice caught his look and nodded. She picked up a doughnut covered with confectioner's sugar and walked up to Jack. An innocent smile disguised her intentions.

"I hereby brand you a member in good standing of the Posse." She moved to pop him in the forehead. Remarkably, Jack swept his hand up and deflected the pastry. He reached out with his other hand and grabbed up a doughnut from a plate nearby. In the same motion he shagged this at Winston, who ducked back. The pastry hit Jennifer square on the cheek. The ensuing battle raged until all the doughnuts were in crumbs and laughter had sent most of them to the floor.

$ $ $

President W. G. Stone sat alone in the Oval Office watching Freddy Earl interview some academic expert about the anarchy that had erupted across the planet. His Presidential briefing on the events had been thorough and revealing. Somehow or other, Gerry Bishop's own son had run this global terrorist attack out of that private school in North Carolina. A federal indictment would be forthcoming as soon as they could figure out the charges.

The very thought of 5000 naked Frisbee players on the National Mall had sent Arlene into one of her migraines. Then there was the news about little Simon Bishop, who had visited them right here in the oval office not three years ago. Even worse, the Vice President's secret squad over at homeland security had been unable to gain any kind of intelligence on W. G.'s missing assets. His private phone rang.

"Yes." He spoke into the receiver. "Who? What? His boat? That's none of my business. This is my private line, you know better than...What? My money? All right, put him on."

"President Stone," said Jack.

"Count Ottavio," said W. G. "What do you know about this theft?"

"As we speak, these funds are being transfered to a place where you can claim them."

"That's what I wanted to hear. How are you involved?"

"I'm just the messenger, although I'd like to claim some of the funds to pay for my yacht."

"I don't know anything about any yacht. Where's my money?"

"As I said, you can walk in and claim every penny. It's being held at the International Court of Justice." Jack let that idea settle in and waited in silence for a good minute.

"The what?"

"The World Court in The Hague."

"That's in Europe. I want my money back in the bank, pronto, or I'll have your balls for breakfast." W. G. gesticulated at the empty room.

"You are not to only person with a claim to these assets. The Court has a sealed list of every transaction involved in assembling these assets."

"List? There is no list."

"Believe me when I say this list is authoritative and comprehensive. As soon as you make a claim for the funds, the Court will unseal the list. Until then the Court has been given the right to draw upon interest from the assets for administering this case. You are currently their prime benefactor."

"You'll pay for this, Ottavio. I don't care where you hide."

"Did I forget to tell you?"

"Tell me what?"

"You must make the claim in person."

"In The Hague? You've got to be joking."

"You have Air Force One at your command. Holland is closer than Hawaii."

"Why am I talking to you? Who's in charge?"

"I'm certain you two will meet. She wanted to tell you herself, but gave me this small favor. By the way, tell Karl that the Game will be back up tomorrow at the stroke of midnight. And I have a message for him from Michael O'hara."

"I'm not Karl's secretary." W. G. slammed down the receiver.

"Goddamn Europeans! Goddamn European courts!"

He picked up the internal White House phone. "Get me the VP. Now!"

§   §   §

It took the national and international news agencies longer to get to Asheville, North Carolina, than it did for them to learn how Grand Meister Simon Bishop had organized the largest single act of civil disobedience in the history of the world. Nobody in Castalia had any intention of hiding their involvement. Sixers and Meisters from across the planet had gathered on the maidan to watch the Strike unfold on giant displays. Simon had stayed up all night to catch the latest news from Asia and Europe. After the triumphal Los Angeles mission, which turned the entire city into a parking lot for fifteen minutes, he accepted the congratulations of Grand Meister Desi, who placed a laurel wreath on his head up on the central dais in the Castalia castle.

"NNC says this is the largest single day global demonstration in history. You stopped traffic all over L.A. Next time you should try to get traffic moving in LA," Desi joked. "Except for the naked sunbathing on the Santa Monica Freeway and the thousand-person conga line on Cahuenga Pass, I'm not sure anyone noticed."

"Next time we strike, we won't stop," Simon yelled and the Meisters cheered and danced. It was obvious to him that the Meisters had been waiting for a real leader to step up. Desi was just too old to figure that out. Simon turned and strode away, pounding the pavers with his staff, out the open portcullis to where the Sixers were assembled.

Desi watched Simon go. An enormous shout rose from the crowds outside the castle walls. He logged out and called Jennifer, but she was not in her cabin. Little Simon was going to be a handful, he sighed to himself.

Desi's cabin at the Ranch was perfect. The staff could not do enough for the Grand Meister. Still, he was a lonesome cowboy. He poured a flute of Cristal and settled back in his robe.

"Busy, busy, busy," he said and scratched at the residue of glitter on the inside of his knee.

By Monday noon Haverbrook's parking lot was overflowing
with news vans and satellite uplinks. Rector Hector had
instructions to prevent any interviews with Simon. With
reporters leaking out all over the campus, interviewing
janitors, classmates, and teachers, it was only a matter of time
before they located Simon in the Rectory, where he was locked
in Hector's office. Reverend Bishop's jet would be arriving by
mid afternoon.

Word that Simon had been "rescued" from his prison and
would be holding a press conference in the auditorium reached
Hector as he was talking to the local deputy sheriff about
traffic control.

"Good lord!" he cried and fled toward the main building.
His path was obstructed by hundreds of reporters with camera
crews. "Let me pass!" he called to their backs.

Simon stepped up on the stage in his cloak. He leaned
theatrically on his staff, which had finally been delivered to the
school.

"I bring you all greetings from the Meisters of Castalia," he
said while a hundred cameras flashed away. "As the press
reports from Asia are now confirming, the Game is back. It
will be live everywhere today at midnight local time. By this
time next year we hope to have more than two billion Gamers
across the planet. I want to welcome you all to our brave, new
world!"

§   §   §

Scratchy logged into the Room and stepped over to the console
where he opened up the IDE. The code files for Junana and the
Game were all there and he could read them. He opened up an
edit window for a random file and got a message screen:

```
Unauthorized. ROOT-level authority
required.
```

"Locked out of my own code," he whispered to himself.

"Michael?"

Scratchy looked up from his laptop. "What's up?"

"The taxi's here to take us to the airport and you haven't even begun to pack," Betsy said.

"Tell Timmy to come up for a cup of coffee while I pack. Looks like I'm going to have a lot of time on my hands."

"Why's that?"

He told her about the IDE.

"Can the Game actually write its own code?"

"Within limits, I imagine. Any major upgrading should require expert human coding. I guess at some point even that will end. Looks like I'm out of work."

"Then why are you smiling?"

"I'm the guy who likes to laugh last, remember?"

THIRTY-TWO

Just after midnight, New Orleans time, Jennifer logged into the
Game from her room in Betsy's guest cottage to begin a new
Query. She hoped to unwind Governmentality back to its seed.
She intended to spend an hour or so, but after five hours of
questions and pathways through petabytes of information, her
computer stalled again. A message appeared, "Cannot Predict
Now."

"Zut alors!" Not again. She was about to reboot when
suddenly her avatar was holding a wooden staff. Almost
immediately a Guide walked into the screen from the right, as
if entering from another room. It was Michelle.

"Grand Meister Jennifer," Michelle bowed deeply. "Let me
be the first to congratulate you! Notices have been sent to the
other two Grand Meisters. I would like to suggest we meet in
Castalia after you have a rest. There is so much that needs
doing."

§   §   §

Don Driscoll had to be desperate to even think about what he
was contemplating. After all, this was how he'd actually ended
up in Santiago. They had chased him out of towns and villages
all the way south from Arizona. The money he earned from his
last under-the-table Java programming job was gone and the
cupboard was bare. He still had seven thousand in that bank

account in Chino and a ready-teller card burning through his
wallet.

Don waited in the shadow of a street promenade until
nobody was in sight and slipped across the street. He inserted
his ATM card and keyed in his PIN code and the cash request.

"Come on, come on!" he yelled at the machine. It whirled
away, counting out the bills. His card emerged. He was waiting
for his cash when a small man in an old suit opened up the
door to the bank from the inside.

"I'm just leaving!" Don yelled, getting ready to run. The
man was smiling.

"Wait!" he said in Spanish. "I have a message for you."

Don snatched the bills from the ATM and turned to face
him. "Yeah?"

"Somebody named Scratchy O'hara says you are pardoned.
Do you understand? He says for you to have a nice life and
come back to Junana any time."

"You're not going to hit me?"

"My Guide says I should make you feel safe. Mr. Driscoll,
do you feel safe? Do you need anything?"

Don was crying all of the sudden. It was the first time in a
long time someone had called him by his real name without
cursing at him. He shook his head and stepped out of the
shadow onto the bright street.

"Have a nice life, Mr. Driscoll!" the man nodded and
retreated back into the bank.

$ $ $

"It's all gone!" Bishop whined. "That was not the deal. We need
our cash back. You promised..."

"Read your investment contract," Harold sighed. Bishop's church was just a small minority investor. Several organizations lost significantly more, and they were not really big on brotherly love. Harold had resigned from his post at the RIND Institute before they could sack him.

"The losses will put us out of business. They'll take everything!"

"You've still got the power of prayer," Harold taunted him. "Maybe your son will tell us how the hell they knocked us out so completely that my hackers are fucking mystified." It was like the Game was defending itself against attack.

"Leave my son out of this!" Bishop yelled. He had flown Simon and Peter home. Simon had been called into the local FBI office for a whole day. Gerry had uninstalled the broadband connection to his house, where Simon was under constant watch. Simon told him he confessed his role to the authorities and encouraged them all to play that blasted Game of his. Arlene Stone wouldn't return his phone calls. The deacons called an emergency board meeting for next tuesday. And now Freddy Earl wanted Simon on his show!

§   §   §

The previous night the Nerds and the Posse had been surprised to learn that they would ride the Hidden Desire Krewe float up St. Charles Street, preceded by the Krewe's crack team of 24 mostly naked fire-spinners, led, as usual, by Betsy. The Krewe float had a Game door in the front and a fantasy garden of flowers and mythical animals, unicorns and griffins. They threw coins and beads down to the crowds. Alice flashed her breasts a few times but failed to get Jennifer and Claire in the mood.

In the morning, Itchy's Castalia crew made sure Castalia was ready to celebrate their new Grand Meister. Flowers and ribbons overflowed the walls. Trumpeters and heralds sounded her arrival. Jack, Alice, and Itchy were Sixers and would be logging in from their B&B rooms down the street from Betsy's house. Claire and Winston were picking up Megan and Nick at the New Orleans Airport that afternoon.

Jennifer talked Scratchy into logging into Castalia. He insisted that his newly scanned avatar wear street clothes and that Betsy be given the same courtesy.

"Bien sur!" she replied. "You are both entirely welcome to Castalia any time, and you can come naked if you want."

The couple's avatars showed up at the gate to Castalia barefoot in matching tie-dyed hemp t-shirts and shorts. Desi escorted them to the center of the Castle. Several Meisters were old-timer hackers who had met Scratchy at one or more BarCamps, so there was much merriment over his presence. This day Castalia was also mobbed by Gamers joyful in the return of the Game. Up on the dais, Desi had prepared a brief welcome and a surprise.

Jennifer logged into Castalia to the sound of trumpets. She made her way through the throngs of applauding Meisters and Sixers to the dais, where Desi stood tall and greeted her with a hug and a kiss on both cheeks.

"Let me be the first to introduce to you Grand Meister Jennifer Bouchez," he called to the crowds. They yelled their welcome. Jennifer stood and bowed low to them.

"I am honored by this welcome," she said. "I hope to be of service to the Meisters of Castalia." She nodded to Desi, who continued.

"I am sorry that Grand Meister Simon cannot be with us. His father, it seems, has…" Desi glanced around at Scratchy and raised one eyebrow "…grounded him." A knowing groan

rippled through the young crowd. "As soon as Simon can find
an Internet connection he will certainly wish to add his
welcome to our new Grand Meister. Today is Mardi Gras in
New Orleans, and we have much to do, so I will keep this
short."

"Please gather around and pay attention." He banged the
base of his staff on the dais and this sound was amplified
throughout Castalia. Out on the maidan a thousand
conversations stopped mid-sentence. Everyone looked up at
the monitors framing a shot of Desi.

"Before I continue, I want to acknowledge the visit of
someone very special to Castalia. Let us all give a Gamer
welcome to Mr. Michael "Scratchy" O'hara, who unfolded the
templates that run this whole program! Come on up!" He
gestured for Scratchy to climb up on the dais. The call of
"Scratchy, Scratchy, Scratchy!" grew to a cacophony.
Reluctantly, Michael climbed the stairs and stood next to Desi.
The crowd roared. Scratchy waved, smiled sheepishly, and then
walked back down the stairs where his avatar's face was
covered in kisses from Alice and Betsy.

"These months without the Game have been a time of great
suffering and also a learning moment for the Gamer
community. Now that the Game is back..."

The crowd lifted off its feet in a great roar. The numbers of
Meisters and Sixers had been increasing steadily over the past
half hour, and Castalia was now filled to its walls. Desi looked
around him in amazement.

"Now that the Game is back," he said again. "We have to
give thanks to those who made this possible. I want to first
thank all of the programmers in Sao Do for their tireless efforts
over these months." He bowed deeply to the Sao Do avatar
continigent as applause rippled through the crowd.

"I want to also thank the Castalia hacker and griefer communities. You know who you are."

Another yell went up. Desi waited for the crowd to settle.

"Finally we must all thank the entity who brought the Game back to us. She comes to Castalia at our invitation and represents the Guild of Guides. I present to you all Guild Master Michelle Valentine Smith."

A bright column of light suddenly appeared on the dais between Desi and Jennifer. Within this, shimmering for a tantalizing minute and then solidifying as the light dimmed stood Michelle, barefoot and splendid in her own beauty. It was a classic Star Trek transporter entrance. The crowd gasped. Scratchy nodded his approval.

"Jimbo, you rock," he said.

Michelle bowed to the Grand Meisters who returned the courtesy.

"This is the day the Game has been waiting for," she began. "The day it made possible. The day..." she paused and continued slowly, her voice gaining volume with each word. "The day the Game begins its rule!"

She thrust her hand up in an Angela Davis power salute that sent the crowd into a delirium. For several minutes the assembled thousands of avatars jumped and danced.

Betsy turned to Michael, sitting next to him on the sofa in her living room, both of them logged into Castalia on their laptops. "Rule what?"

"That's the question. The game has no economy, no government, no army, no police."

"Not yet."

Michelle raised her hands and the crowd grew silent.

"The Guild of Guides stands at your side as you prepare for your role in leading this new Game Nation." She closed her eyes and stepped back. Her form faded into nothing.

After Michelle vanished from the dais, Jennifer and Desi spent an extra hour walking around Castalia, talking with as many Meisters and Sixers as they could. Everyone wanted to know about Michelle. Rumors of the fantastical powers of the Guild of Guilds were flowing, and, in truth, Desi could not deny them. They finally logged off and prepared for the evening's recreation over at The Leg Bar. First they would all gather at Betsy's house for barbecue.

The Five Skillings

THIRTY-THREE

Just after noon, Betsy left Michael tending to the barbeque coals while she checked on the Dixie Beer cooling on ice in the bathtub. Claire and Winston arrived from the airport with Megan and Nick. Megan went straight out to the guest house to offer her greetings to Grand Meister Jennifer. Winston, Nick, and Michael were deep into a conversation about climate change and hurricanes, a topic Betsy knew too much about to be comfortable discussing on a day that was supposed to be joyful. She took a beer and sat on the veranda. Jack and Desi arrived together, having strolled over from their B&B up the street, which every year housed the honored guests of the Hidden Desire Krewe.

"Alice and Ichiro will be over in a bit. I think they got frisky after Castalia."

"Wasn't that amazing!" Betsy said. "If a little terrifying..."

"The genie is truly out of the bottle," said Jack. He was dressed in khakis and a polo shirt, and he looked more relaxed than she'd seen him in weeks. Desi wore a deep blue linen shirt and creased black slacks. He looked delicious. Betsy knew a dozen local gays who would kill to date Desi. Unfortunately none of them were a good match for the Grand Meister.

"Michelle's driving. We are just along for the ride," Betsy admitted. "Might as well put the top down and enjoy the view."

The afternoon wore on toward dusk. Barbecued chicken and andouille and boudin sausages were devoured with jambalaya and ice cold beer. Betsy put her favorite zydeco CDs on the stereo. The Nerds and the Posse sat around the picnic table in the back yard in a mood that could only be described as sublime. And then the FBI SWAT Team arrived.

In his underground situation room, W.G. Stone was getting real-time video from the helmet cams on the FBI assault of the terrorist cell in New Orleans. They battered through the fence gate and surrounded the suspects still seated at a backyard table. It was just like an episode of Real Cops.

They corralled the lot in a few minutes of shoving and verbal protests. The teenage boy took a wild swing at one the SWAT members and was subdued with a rifle butt to the skull that dropped him to his knees. W.G. chuckled and settled back in his command chair. He was really hoping that O'hara fellow would act up.

The suspects' hands were cuffed behind them with plastic strips. They were hooded before being led to the two black vans that would take them to the naval air station for their transport offshore. A list of the suspect names appeared as these were verified. Except for the young couple, their intelligence had been correct. The teenagers were the daughter and boyfriend of one of the terrorists. "A family that gets renditioned together..." W. G. couldn't think of a good rhyme for "rendition." Karl might have one. Within fifteen minutes the operation was over and the vans were moving at speed toward the interstate.

§ 　　　　 § 　　　　 §

"Betsy," Scratchy whispered loudly as they jolted along the road.

"I'm OK." Her voice was shaky. "I'm worried about Nick."

"He was conscious when they hooded him."

"No talking," the Agent guarding them warned. "I have a TASER with a taste for terrorist testicles."

"Say that three times really fast," said Scratchy.

"We're supposed to be terrorists?" It was Alice's voice. "Here I thought Betsy was playing her music too loud."

"I said 'quiet'! I won't say it again."

§   §   §

"Agent Thompson, this is the President."

FBI special agent Jack Thompson looped his headset digitally into the voice identifier.

"Mr. President, please give me the go code for your instructions."

"Let me see, 'green pickles go better with ice cream,' I repeat, 'green pickles go better with ice cream.' Who thinks this stuff up?"

"Its simple phonology, Mr. President. I have a voice match and a go code green light. Sir, what are your instructions?"

Thompson was riding shotgun in the van driven by Agent Garcia. He looked over at the driver and smiled. They had the President of the United States on the encrypted phone. The two vans sped toward the Naval Air Station where a jet was waiting for their prisoners.

"Great job apprehending this terrorist cell. I have a new destination for you: New Orleans International Airport. Use the general aviation gate. There is a Learjet 60 fueled and waiting. Look for number NJR27. You are authorized to release the prisoners into the custody of the pilot. This is strictly a quiet operation. Do you understand these instructions?"

"We are 5 by 5 on this communication, Mr. President. Learjet NJR27."

"Very good, Agent Thompson." The call ended.

Thompson picked up his secure walkie-talkie to contact the other van. "Sheffield, this is Thompson."

"Sheffield here."

"New destination is Louis Armstrong International Airport. Follow me in."

"Roger that."

"You got that, Garcia?" The driver nodded. The van swerved toward the entrance to Interstate 610.

Jack pulled out his armored laptop and powered it up. Standard procedure was to confirm changes of orders with the base. The computer's WiFi card socketed into the system. Jack was about to type his login when the computer screen went blue and froze.

"Shit!" Jack tried to reboot. The computer whirred and chirped for a good five minutes but nothing came up. "Lemme borrow yours," he said to Garcia, reaching behind the seat.

Once again just after power-up the computer froze and refused to reboot.

"Homeland Security piece of shit," Jack grumbled. "I wish that just for once they'd choose a subcontractor that didn't low-ball the specs."

§   §   §

W. G. was about to leave the situation room when everything suddenly went south. Instead of the helmet cams from the SWAT team, a new image appeared. It was the face of a young woman.

"Mr. President," she spoke.

"Turn up the volume, will you?" He yelled at the technician. The woman's face was now on every monitor in the room, including three television stations. She looked foreign, maybe Mexican or Haitian. She had beads in her braided hair.

"The Guild of Guides has been following this operation and has come to the conclusion that it is unlawful. The warrants you issued have no basis. The activities they describe never happened. We give you one minute to return these individuals to their prior location."

"I don't know who you are, but you are interfering with the exercise of a national security operation. Be confident we will trace your signal and have you in custody soon."

"You will not return the prisoners?"

"You will be joining them soon enough..."

"That is your final word?"

"I'm through talking to you." He left the room with his adjutant. "Find out who did that and how. Get them behind bars."

"Yes, Mr. President."

The woman smiled. Her eyebrows knit together. All the computer screens in the room turned blue.

§   §   §

They were a mile from the airport exit. Jack spoke into his walkie-talkie, "Sheffield, log in and tell the base we have new instructions from the President. Our computers are down."

"Will do. Over."

They took the exit and headed for the West Access Road. At the outer gate to the general aviation terminal, Garcia showed the guard his FBI badge, and the kid almost shit himself trying to the gate open fast enough.

They ground to a stop at the field security gate for general aviation. Jack flashed his badge, and they let him through. He strode over to where several private jets were parked and located NJR27. He spotted the pilot doing a walk-around inspection. The pilot was a trim caucasian in his forties with a military hair cut. Thompson figured the new orders meant the prisoners were going to skip Guantanamo and end up disappearing in some black hole of a prison somewhere south of the Ukraine. This was not a military jet, probably a dark CIA subcontractor.

"I have some passengers for you." He showed the pilot his badge.

"Thank you, Agent Thompson." The pilot seemed to be expecting him. "We are ready to take off as soon as we have the prisoners on board. You can bring the vans right up to the stairs. It might be less conspicuous." He gestured to the open door of the small jet.

"It might, in fact." Thompson surveyed the perimeter. "Any activity around here I should know about?"

"Most folks will be flying out tomorrow. It's quiet as a churchyard today."

Jack pulled out his walkie-talkie and gave the order.

"Sir, Sheffield reports that his computer is also not functioning," said Smith.

"I guess their warranties expired yesterday," said Jack. "Anyhow, the base has a digital copy of my conversation with the President. If they had any concerns they'd be in contact. Everything is good on this end."

The vans pulled up and they herded the hooded prisoners up the stairs into the jet where they buckled them in. Only one of them caused any trouble.

"If this is one of Karl's games, tell him we're not playing." The voice shouted through the hood. "He still owes me two pussy cats!"

Garcia punched the prisoner on his right kidney and the fellow's legs buckled on the stairs. Garcia caught him under his arms and boosted him through the door.

"You can yell all you want where you're going," Garcia snarled.

"Gitmo can't hold us," the voice protested as they strapped him in.

"This ain't no Gitmo taxi," Garcia said. "Where you're going even the Pentagon doesn't know about."

The pilot was waiting at the base of the stairs. "Everyone accounted for, Agent Thompson?"

"I'm releasing eleven live prisoners to you. Have a nice trip."

The vans pulled around and disappeared through the gate.

The pilot boarded and closed the door. He started warming up the engines.

"We gonna stay handcuffed all the way to Guantanamo?" A voice called out from under a hood.

The pilot came back into the cabin, an open pocketknife in his hand. "Which one of you is Count Jacopo Ottavio?"

"I am," said a woman's voice.

"No, I am," said another voice, and then another, and then all of them.

The pilot cursed and started pulling hoods from the prisoners. The first one was Claire. She saw the knife and screamed. The second one was Itchy. The third one was Jack.

The pilot moved in closer. "Count Ottavio."

Jack blinked in the sudden light.

"We have landing permission in Havana," the pilot said with a slight bow.

"Thank you, Roger. Cut me loose, will you?"

Roger freed Jack and returned to the cockpit to finish the pre-flight routine. Jack freed the others who jumped up into celebratory hugs and cheers until Jack reminded them to buckle up. Megan cradled Nick's head, still oozing a trickle of blood from the scalp. Alice held his hand. He grinned and shook off their concerns. Claire found the sink and wet a towel. She gave this Megan, who tended Nick's wounds.

"You should hit them when they're not holding weapons," Scratchy mumbled.

"Thank you, Michael," Megan glowered at him, and so did Claire. Scratchy looked over at Winston, who was also glowering at him.

"What!" Scratchy said.

Jack took the co-pilot seat and put on the headset.

"Wherever did you find that man," Desi said to Winston.

"You remember Kyoto? He found me, and I found you, and then we found all of you." Winston turned to Claire and took her hand. "And then we gave this planet of ours one enormous global hotfoot."

"Nutted it like a drive right down the middle," said Itchy.

"Like a high draw straight into the pin," said Desi.

"Like a forty-footer headed for the back of the cup," said Scratchy.

"A hole-in-one with a three wood!" Jack yelled.

The jet roared down the runway.

"...On a downhill par four!" the voice came over the intercom. It sounded exactly like President Stone.

"Michelle!" Jennifer said. "Is that you?"

"Say the magic word and a win hundred dollars. You should know something. The Meisters of Castalia have invited the Sixers to join in forming a constitutional convention. They are arguing like longshoremen."

"It's a new beginning for the world's youngest democratic state," said Betsy.

"The Game Nation." Scratchy leaned over and kissed her on cheek. "Our widdle biddy baby!"

The jet screamed south over the Gulf.

"No turning back now," Jack shouted from the cockpit.

"Ladies and Gentlemen, Elvis has left the building," said Scratchy.

The End

COMING SOON
BOOK TWO
Junana: Game Nation

About the Author:

Bruce Caron was trained as a social anthropologist and an urban cultural geographer. He is skilled in a variety of multimedia authoring tools, and completed the first multimedia dissertation at UC Santa Barbara. Bruce has a wide-ranging academic background in both quantitative and qualitative methodologies and has been active for several years in issues of digital libraries, the use of multimedia in education, and the theory of digital media. Bruce has taught at colleges and universities in Japan, and at the University of Pennsylvania and the University of California. He currently runs the New Media Research Institute in Santa Barbara, California. The institute develops digital tools for education and works on issues of democracy in digital communities. You can reach him at bruce@junana.com.

Cover Photographer:

Kris Krüg is a professional photographer, author, and social media maven living in Vancouver, BC. He has more friends on Facebook than the population of a small Caribbean nation. He tweets at KK. The model is Fiercekitty. Don't ever mess with her.